Today's Saints

The Verdant Revival, Book 3

Michael Ripplinger

I0675783

Today's Saints

The Verdant Revival, Book 3

Print edition ISBN: 978-0-9973955-7-0
Kindle edition ISBN: 978-0-9973955-6-3

Please contact the author at michael@ripplinger.us and visit him at mripplinger.wordpress.com.

v1.0

For Margie Ripplinger

Who taught me the faith

Saint Thérèse of Lisieux,
who survived the Dark Night of the Soul
and gave us the Little Way,
pray for us.

"I have an ever deeper and firmer belief that nothing is merely an accident when seen in the light of God, that my whole life down to the smallest details has been marked out for me in the plan of Divine Providence and has a completely coherent meaning in God's all-seeing eyes.

And so I am beginning to rejoice in the light of glory wherein this meaning will be unveiled to me."

Saint Teresa Benedicta of the Cross

Today's Saints

Chapter One

Two Hundred Thirty-Seven Years Ago

"They're retreating!" someone yelled from the front of the mob. Others echoed the cry, relaying it to the lospharn further back on the bridge. The cheering that followed threatened to drown out the news. The vaunted Sovereign Guard scattered like vermin exposed to the light, rushing back into the castle and sealing its pompous mahogany doors behind them.

Dohtor celebrated the victory with two prayers: one to the sacred feminine and one to the sacred masculine. But there were too many brave, hard-working lospharn lying dead around him to take any further pause. Too many homes and businesses had burned. Too much of the city was still under the control of the Sovereign Guard. Too many women and children wailed and cried in grief. The working class the Rejen had trampled for too long *would* prevail before the sun again rose on Proluve, but that moment had not yet come. There was much work still to do. Much blood would yet be spilled.

But the lospharn were the working men and women, and this was their hour.

"They retreat, but they do not yet surrender!" Dohtor yelled over the din of the lospharn who screamed for the Sovereign Guard's blood. "They're fortifying their position."

The lospharn moved aside so their commander could advance to the doors. Dohtor faced the cobblers and millers and weavers and farmers who made up his army. They wielded swords not with grace but with passion. Their determination did more to keep them alive than their leather armor. Not a one among them had the mauve skin of a valbora noble who spent their days indoors and in the oceans. Their rough hands, faces, and tails were a deep violet, a testament to their lives spent under the harsh Barohndin sun.

"Behind these doors," Dohtor said, "is a hall filled with trophies of the Rejen's excess. At its end are more doors like these. They lead into the castle proper. The Sovereign Guard is retreating to those inner doors. That's where they'll make their final stand. Be ready! When we enter that hall, they will fight with fire in their blood. But it will not be enough for what will face them!"

The lospharn cheered and raised their swords and sticks.

"The heart of God's sacred feminine and the strength of God's sacred masculine are with us!" Dohtor said. "Onward! The Rejen dies tonight!"

He stepped aside, and the lospharn holding the battering ram pounded on the castle's doors. It took ten charges to crack their thick wood. After another two, the brace holding them closed from the inside splintered. With shouted demands for freedom, equality, and an end to the Rejen's rule, the mob surged forward with Dohtor in their middle.

As he predicted, the Sovereign Guard waited for them a hundred fifty feet away at the other end of the hall. They stood shoulder-to-shoulder, five rows deep. Firelight from the hall's torches glistened off their iron armor. Their helms revealed only their eyes. Each guard held at least two weapons. Many had a third on their backs or their hips. Their posture was rigid as they looked down their noses at the rabble who had come to kill the king.

Dohtor wanted to be a peaceful man, but there could be no peace without justice for the poor. None of their deaths would be in vain. Liberty! Equality for all – both noble and working class. Their children would thank them. With a wordless yell, Dohtor urged his army forward. The Sovereign Guard planted their feet and assumed battle stances.

And in the middle of the room, a cloud of smoke materialized from nothingness. It stretched and puffed, and a tall, thin man emerged from within it. Or had the smoke turned into the man?

"Stop," he said.

The lospharn obeyed him, too stunned by his sudden appearance to do anything else. What kind of man was this? He had no tail. His skin was neither mauve nor violet but *gray,* like the ashen remnants of a fire. His neatly trimmed hair was as white as priestly vestments. His cassock even reminded Dohtor a bit of those vestments, except his were black. Also black were his eyes – solid ebony, with no colored iris.

But his voice! Oh, his voice was *melodious.* It left Dohtor both enchanted and haunted. It was like a funeral dirge: both melodic and melancholy. He and the other lospharn ceased yelling just so they wouldn't miss hearing it if he spoke again.

Holding one palm towards the lospharn and one towards the Sovereign Guard, he granted their wish. "This is madness. This is *wrong.*"

One of the lospharn – Dohtor couldn't possibly know all their names, but he knew by the guild patch on his shoulder he was a wheelwright – yelled in defiance, pointed his pike at the strange gray-skinned man, and charged. The man's midnight eyes squinted in annoyance, but he made no other movement.

Another cloud of smoke appeared between the stranger and the wheelwright, and a woman stepped out of it. Was this the stranger's sister? They looked so alike. She wore a black jacket,

3

shirt, pants, and boots. Her gray face was exquisite like fine pottery, and her long, white hair draped her shoulders just as new-fallen snow blankets the western mountains. Her black eyes were like polished obsidian. She didn't have a tail either.

The wheelwright was taken aback by the woman's beauty. He hesitated. She opened her hand. Smoke poured forth from it and formed a long, thin, black blade.

With a flick of her wrist, the woman cut through the wheelwright's neck.

Dohtor winced, except... there was no wound. Not even a paper-thin one. The wheelwright's flesh and bone remained completely intact. There wasn't a drop of blood. It was as if the woman's sword was a blade of light or shadow. Had it only *appeared* to cut?

No, despite the lack of any visible injury, the weapon had been effective. The wheelwright collapsed in a heap, falling like a wooden puppet whose strings had been severed.

His murder emboldened the Sovereign Guard. If the strange gray people who emerged from smoke killed lospharn, they must be on *their* side! Several members of the Guard at the front of their line used their tails to draw arrows from their quivers, then they raised their bows and fired them down the hall. They struck three lospharn, two women and a man. Dohtor's people bled and howled in pain. Their comrades-in-arms pulled them from the front and surged forward to take their place, keeping their line unbroken.

A third cloud appeared, this one in front of the Sovereign Guard archers. A third gray-skinned stranger appeared, this one like a short and stocky barrel. His black, sleeveless vest exposed bare gray arms as thick as the battering ram the lospharn had used to break into the Rejen's castle. Spikes of

4

white hair poked wildly up out of the top of his head. More spikes adorned his thick metal cuffs. His eyes were just as black as the others'. But where the thin man seemed disappointed by the fight between the lospharn and the Sovereign Guard, the muscular man looked downright offended he hadn't received an invitation to participate.

A swirl of black smoke from his hand took the form of a thick bludgeon, a hunk of fallen tree trunk riddled with rusty nails. With a roar of effort, he swung it across the archers' abdomens. Dohtor braced himself for the gruesome sight of spilled viscera, but again, the attack produced no wounds and no blood. The club's contact with the archers' iron armor didn't even make a sound. The only sign the attack had done anything at all was the three dead archers who fell as if they'd suddenly fallen asleep.

Both the freedom fighters and the Sovereign Guard stood as still as statues. They could have lined the walls of any church on Barohnde, except instead of icons of God's sacred feminine and sacred masculine, they stood as paradigms of confusion and disbelief. The gray-skinned strangers converged together in the middle of the hall. Each of them wore a metal badge of three interconnected triangles over their left breast. The woman opened her hand, and her sword disappeared just as it had arrived. The muscular man bashed his club against his palm at a slow, deliberate cadence. And the thin man in the cassock stood a little straighter, a little taller, and held the rapt attention of every Barohndite in the hall.

"As I was saying," he said softly. "This war you are engaged in is *wrong*. But do not be afraid. We do not come to throw stones, for you are not the perpetrators of this crime. You are its victims."

5

The sound of boots pounding double-time against stone came up from behind Dohtor. Men with skin as white as bone pushed through the mob of lospharn and swarmed through the room. Their jaws were not square and protruding like Barohndite jaws but round, blending into the curves of their faces. They were soldiers, and most striking of all, they were *identical*. Same height, same build, same red eyes, same hairless heads, same lack of a tail, and same faces.

Hundreds of identical white soldiers swarmed through the hall, each holding a weapon that was something like a musket. They glared at the Barohndites, but they reverently bowed when they passed the gray-skinned people. One of the soldiers came into the middle of the hall, knelt on one knee before the thin man, and lowered his head. "Luminary, if I may?"

The thin man nodded. The soldier stood and spoke to the Barohndites. "When your world has known peace and justice for a thousand years, few of your people – if any – will be able to say they've ever been in the luminous presence. Consider yourselves lucky."

Your world. Your people. Their very un-Barohndite appearance. Dohtor swallowed. From where did these strangers hail? Another land? Another realm?

Who *were* they?

The thin man's solid black eyes cut through the crowd and looked directly into Dohtor's, as if he'd heard his question. "We are the Way," he said, pointing to himself. "The Truth," he said, gesturing to the woman. "And the Life," he finished with a hand pointed at the muscular man.

The soldier in the center of the hall stood from his genuflection. "You will address them as 'Luminary,'" he said, "and you will genuflect in their presence."

And *that* was too much. It was too much for the lospharn, who had taken up arms to knock the nobility off their lofty perches. It was too much for the Sovereign Guard, who would commit any atrocity in defense of the nobles' wealth and excess. And it snapped both armies out of their disbelief. Dohtor and the lospharn charged further into the hall, bellowing and brandishing their weapons. The front row of Sovereign Guard dropped to one knee so they and the row behind them could launch arrows simultaneously. And the third army – the white-skinned soldiers – joined in the fray, too. They fired the strangest of bullets – pulses of red light, or perhaps small fireballs – from their muskets.

The Life clobbered any Barohndite he could reach, lospharn or Sovereign Guard, three or four with each blow. The Truth's sword reappeared in her hands, and she bloodlessly cut down anyone who came near her. Barohndites on both sides of the war fell to the identical white soldiers' fire-bullets. Some of the white soldiers were overpowered and trampled, but not nearly enough. Far too many of Dohtor's friends died in the carnage.

But despite being in the center of the melee, the Way, the Truth, and the Life went utterly unharmed. The Sovereign Guard's arrows passed right through them. The lospharn's sticks and blades might as well have been attacking smoke. The white soldiers' bullets went into their backs and out the other side without bothering them. Lospharn charged the Truth and walked right through her. Sovereign Guard arrows and swords chopped at the Way and the Life, and it was as if the gray-skinned people were made of air.

Dohtor's violet skin paled, turning as mauve as that of every valbora noble who'd never worked a day in the sun. Gray-skinned *people?* No, the Way, the Truth, and the Life weren't

7

people at all. They were just as insubstantial as the smoke from which they'd emerged.

"They're ghosts!" someone shouted.

Sacred Masculine, protect us. Sacred Feminine, care for us.

"Call us what you will," the Way said, oblivious to the din of weapons clanging, of bodies collapsing onto the stone floor, of agonized howls. "We have come for the lost sheep of this world. We have come that you may have life and that you may live it more abundantly. We have come to show you a more excellent way."

He smiled warmly. The sight made gooseflesh break out up and down Dohtor's arm.

"We are the Celestines, and we shall be your deliverers."

Chapter Two

Live oak trees don't drop their leaves until spring, so very little of the feeble mid-December sun found its way through the forest's leaf canopy. But Cassie didn't need to rely solely on her eyes. As a Mantissa healer, she could rapidly heal herself and others, *and* she possessed a premonitory sense of impending personal danger. When somebody or something threatened her, her brain buzzed, she got a sinking feeling in her chest, and she felt a sudden need to move, like damnation itself would crash down on her shoulders if she didn't.

But when the impending danger was in a simulated exercise, the effect was... different. In that case, all she heard was an overly chirpy chipware-generated voice in her earpiece. "Warning! Danger detected ahead at ten and two."

She jumped off the trail of matted-down brown grass and pressed her back against the nearest tree trunk. Her betrothed, Siv, leaned against a tree opposite from her and raised a curious eyebrow. Both of them wore vests with glowing green chipware lights. "Ten and two," she whispered.

Siv looked back towards their teammates and motioned in the directions Cassie had specified.

And a pair of white demons stepped forward.

They weren't literal "angels kicked out of heaven" demons. They were alien invaders, members of a species that called itself the Shakrath. Chalky white skin, glowing red eyes, two legs, four arms – or four legs and two arms, depending on what kind of posture they wanted to take and how they wanted to use their limbs. Their long tails, claws, and snouts full of knife-life teeth were out of a nightmare. Since their arrival on Verde two centuries earlier, the planet had lost all its technology and its Mantissa protectors.

Cassie and her friends – the Mantissa Reborn – had fought hard over the last year to imprison and exile the demons. The cost had been steep. Not everyone had survived. But Cassie's brother Fritz had invited them back. Allowed them to come work and live right there on their folks' farm. As allies. It seemed something worse than the white demons was coming to Verde, and the Mantissa Reborn needed all the help they could get.

The Celestines would arrive in six days.

Every demon was identical in shape and size because they were genetically-engineered clones, but Cassie was fairly sure the two who'd stepped forward were Gashg and Skleght. Maybe. Probably. No? Bah. Telling them apart was maddening. Well, Cassie decided they were Gashg and Skleght, whether they were or not.

"Be careful," she whispered. She touched both demons as they went by, but that only gave the simulated version of her healing ability time to switch one of the four red lights on Skleght's harness back to green before they'd stepped past her.

"Careful," he said in a tinny voice. The demons' long, snouted mouths were incapable of human speech, but each demon wore a small metal circle at its throat: a chipware device that translated its barks and growls into words. "All right. I'll *carefully* eviscerate them."

Yep. Definitely Skleght.

The demons charged forward, and they hadn't made it but three steps past Cassie when a barrage of red laser fire came from simulated enemies hiding behind a wide swath of trees. It lit up the forest, making it seem saturated with blood, but it was all fake. The simulated fire came from light-projected simulations of Shakren, the foot soldiers of the Celestines' army. The demons fired back. Their rifles gave off high-pitched whines with each pull of their triggers, though their weapons were equally non-lethal. Only harmless flashes of green light blasted out of their barrels.

"Fifteen of them!" Gashg shouted.

Four more demons charged past Cassie and joined Gashg and Skleght. Cassie recognized Rarkh and Tvelth. She couldn't remember the third demon's hacking cough of a name, and she couldn't pronounce the name of the last one. Siv yanked his shotgun from the holster on his back, darted out from behind his cover, and slid on his belly underneath Gashg and Skleght's laser fire. He shot blanks at the simulated Shakren, and they fell when "hit."

With his chipsuit's rockets blazing, Cassie's brother Fritz swept through the air above the demons. "Oh wow," he said. "Ten more over there, too." Laser cannons popped out of compartments in his suit's arms, and he fired at the new batch of Shakren he'd spotted coming from the first squad's flank. They fired back at him, but when their laser blasts got too close, an aura of blue energy flashed around his chipsuit, and the bolts bounced away.

Cassie took a quick peek around the tree. The Shakren weren't sticking to their cover any longer and were moving forward. They all looked identical, and that wasn't because Fritz's chipware-controlled simulation could only create a single Shakren image. Like the demons, real Shakren were all clones of one another. But unlike the demons, they looked nearly human. The only traits that marked them as alien were their red irises, lack of hair, and the same shade of white-as-

11

snow skin as the demons. Which wasn't a coincidence. The demons had *been* Shakren before they'd escaped from the Celestines and before they underwent a whole lot of genetically-engineered enhancements.

She raised her bow and launched a simulated arrow. The actual physical shaft mounted in the bow remained stationary, but a status light on its end switched from green to red. An illusionary arrow suddenly appeared in the chest of one of the fake Shakren. He flickered and disappeared. Two seconds later – the time it would have taken Cassie to nock a new arrow from her quiver into her bow – the status light on her bow flipped back to green, and she fired again.

Cassie stole another glance around the tree–

"Warning!" the voice in her earpiece said, "danger detected–"

She ducked back to safety as a red laser blast nicked the tree where her head had just been. It would have killed her if it had been real and if she didn't possess a danger sense. She huffed and narrowed her eyes, then raised her bow, crouched low, turned towards whoever had fired at her–

A metal hand seized her shoulder.

Siv had killed the demons' leader, Krulgoth, six months earlier to prevent the demons from resuming their invasion of Verde. But instead of just dying already, Krulgoth had somehow managed to transfer his mind into a new robotic demon body. Chipware Krulgoth was taller than the cloned homogeny of the rest of the demons, and was steel gray instead of white, at least in the few places where metal covered his insides. His body was still mostly unfinished. Visible gears and hydraulics clicked and pumped when he moved.

But he was still the killer who had led the demons on a bloody intergalactic reign of biological piracy, transforming

12

them from Shakren to Shakrath. He was still the son of a gun who'd once mindjacked her brother, putting a demon's thoughts in control of Fritz's body. He was still the monster who'd murdered Eroica, Cassie's Mantissa mentor. Whether he was made of white flesh or gray steel, Cassie couldn't stand him.

"Don't be foolish," he said. He didn't bother to move his mouth when he talked because his monotone voice came from some kind of a chipware audio system inside him. "Even a Mantissa healer can be harmed beyond the ability to self-heal, and you can't heal anyone if you're dead."

Cassie gave a piercing look at the hand on her shoulder.

Krulgoth removed it.

"They'd have to hit me first," Cassie said. "If they can manage that, I'll be mighty proud of them." She tipped her hat's wide brim.

Krulgoth tilted his head and stared at her.

"What?" she demanded.

"I can't decide if you're cavalier or conceited," he said. Unwilling to give it any more thought, he stepped past her, and his two upper arms twisted, folded, and expanded until they'd refactored themselves into laser cannons. Standing taller than the other demons and Siv, he shot over them and mowed Shakren down.

That left Cassie alone with Annalie, who scampered up to join her behind the cover of the tree. "Well, *I* can decide he's a right cracked jackleg," Annalie said, and she stuck her tongue out at Krulgoth's back. Then she winced as if bracing herself. "But he's also kinda right. We need you. Don't get dead. Please?"

13

"I get it," Cassie said. She stole a glance around the tree to see if Siv, Fritz, or any of the demons had more red lights than green on their vests, indicating they needed simulated healing. "I can best serve the mission by staying out of harm's way, healing the injured, and detecting hidden enemies."

Annalie frowned at the thirty-or-so demons standing far off to the side, where the forest gave way to open grassland. They were out of bounds since they'd all "died" in the simulation. "And I'm doing a bang-up job, aren't I?" Cassie said.

"Ain't your fault. The odds are just too much." She shook her head. "We ain't gonna make it this time, either."

"Hey." Cassie waved her hand dismissively. "What matters is that when we do it for real, we're going to win."

"We've failed *fourteen* times..." Annalie said.

"True. But I have a plan."

"You have a plan for how to survive against a Shakren army?" Annalie asked. "One you ain't told us about yet?"

"No, I have a plan for my whole life," Cassie said. "And there's still so much to do."

There were two kinds of people in the world: those who led the horse and those who let the horse lead them. Cassie was the former. And she didn't just lead her horse. She squeezed the proverbial reins until she was white-knuckled, wrapped them around her wrists, and had a backup pair waiting in a saddlebag. Just in case.

"I'm going to be a doctor by the age of twenty-four," Cassie said, "and I'm going to cure cancer, too. Then Siv and I will get married, and we'll start a new settlement way out on the coast. We'll live on the beach. I'll serve as the village doctor, and we'll raise babies and horses, swim year-round, and most likely eat an enormous amount of fish. But none of that can happen if we

14

all die on some alien spaceship, or if these Celestines conquer Verde. Right?"

"Right," Annalie said. "Dead folks ain't making many babies."

"But I *know* everything in my plan is going to happen," Cassie said, "because God was my inspiration. He made me a Mantissa healer, and he answered my prayers and helped me figure out exactly what to do with that gift. God wouldn't inspire me with dreams he won't let me fulfill. So you see? It's simple logic." She clapped a reassuring hand on Annalie's shoulder. "We can't lose!"

"May can," Annalie said with a shrug. "Or maybe all that proves is God means to make sure *you* make it back alive."

"If I'm still alive, the rest of you will be," Cassie said, but a series of faces flashed in her mind as if to dispute that claim. Eroica. Harlan. Sebastian. Her father. She willed their memories away by forcing a smile at Annalie. "I'll take care of everyone. That's what I do."

Dirt, old leaves, and wind spiraled up from the ground and shifted in color until they'd formed into a woman with a pierced face, ripped clothes, and green hair – at least where it wasn't shaved to the scalp. "Hate to break it to you then," Sierra said, "but you ain't doing it so well, Cassandra."

Sierra Monet was a Mantissa from two hundred years ago. She should have been long dead, but instead of dying when her blood spilled into Verde's soil, her power to control the environment somehow bonded her with the planet. Now she could form a body at will out of dirt, water, or wind.

But she was also the reason Cassie was preparing for the pending arrival of the Celestines here on her parents' farm and not back at medical school. Masquerading as the spirit of the planet, Lady Verde, Sierra had dug up the ancient Steelterrors

15

and unleashed the giant robots on towns – on *people* – just to prove her point about the dangers of chipware. They'd ravaged Harbrucken, where the university's faculty was still desperately trying to rebuild and reopen the school.

Yet here she was, fighting on their side because – just like with the demons – Fritz had forgiven an enemy. He'd even made friends with Sierra, despite the hell she'd put them all through. Well, God bless him for it, but she wasn't nearly so eager to give a pass to Krulgoth, the white demons, or especially Sierra. Not when their friends Harlan and Sebastian had both died at the hands of her Steelterrors.

And of more immediate concern: that crank did *not* have permission to call her "Cassandra."

"Don't call me–" Cassie started, but Sierra interrupted her by pointing at a white demon. He was still firing at the oncoming Shakren, but a single green light on his harness blinked rapidly. His nine others were red.

Blast it! She should have been paying attention to the fighting, not jawing with Annalie. She scrambled out from behind her cover, keeping as low as she could, attentive for the voice of her simulated danger sense. With a boots-first slide across the dirt, she reached the demon just as a fake red laser blast struck him in the chest, and the last green light on his harness flipped to red.

"Merkeg is dead," the happy chipware voice announced in everyone's earpieces.

Merkeg slammed his rifle to the ground and stormed off towards the other "dead" demons.

Cassie glanced back. Sierra tutted at her. If Cassie had her real bow, she'd have put a real arrow right through that crank's real face. So what if Sierra would just make a new one? It

16

would still serve her right. But before Cassie could even daydream about her revenge, Sierra burst apart into a flock of black ravens. The birds flew straight into the attacking Shakren squadron, forcing them to duck for cover under raking claws and pecking beaks. It also made them temporarily halt their fire.

That gave the Mantissa and the demons a chance to end the skirmish. Fritz and Krulgoth fired their chipware-powered weapons in short, rapid bursts. The demons fired their rifles and, when close enough, fought using their preferred weapons – their claws, teeth, and tails. Siv used his massive broadsword to cut down a group of Shakren that had tried to surround him. Annalie joined in, too. She wore a chipware circlet with a glowing light in its center. It was a device Fritz had built to emulate a Mantissa reader's telepathic abilities. He'd never perfected it to the point it could read other people's thoughts, but it could dish out incredibly painful headaches. The Shakren Annalie attacked clutched the sides of their heads and passed out.

The laser fire from both sides slowed in pace and then came to a complete halt. "Clear!" a demon shouted in his tinny, chipware-translated voice. Cassie's silent simulated danger sense agreed with his assessment. There were no more Shakren. At least for now.

And there were far too few demons. Merkeg wasn't the only one who'd "died" in that last wave of attack. Several demons grudgingly marched towards the out-of-bounds area, leaving just eight in the battle, plus Krulgoth. They weren't *actually* dead, and there was no way Cassie could have saved all of them, but neither of those facts gave her much comfort. She moved amongst the survivors, placing hands on them until the red lights on their harnesses all switched from red to green. Last, she laid a hand on Siv's shoulder. He had three red lights on his harness, and a sly grin plastered across his face. "Heard they change to green even faster when you heal with a kiss," he said.

She gave him a disapproving look and hoped her face didn't betray the thrill his flirting gave her. It was almost enough to take her mind off all the casualties. Almost. "Not an appropriate time, Sir Blacksmith."

"Move," Krulgoth told the group in his electronic monotone.

"Yes, General," Skleght and two other demons said.

Two of Siv's simulated health lights were still red. He *tsked*. "I have to heal and walk at the same time?"

"Real Shakren forced to defend the Evil Ones won't stand by and allow you to return to full strength unhindered," Krulgoth said.

Sakes alive, Cassie hated when Krulgoth was right. Keeping a grip on Siv's hand to continue healing him, Cassie pushed her way through the brush and followed the rest of the group.

Fritz and Annalie had rigged up all the light projections, health indicator lights, and the simulated danger sense only Cassie could hear to make their practice attack on the Celestines' command ship as realistic as possible. Even the training location – the patch of forest in the corner of Cassie's parents' farm – had been chosen for its similarity to the real thing. Apparently, the Celestines' ships contained forests.

According to Krulgoth and the white demons, *Seraphim*-class warships were massive vessels with sparse, utilitarian living quarters. The majority of their space was devoted to highly immersive training facilities. Entire decks contained vast artificial planetary environments on which the Shakren "peacekeepers" could practice their invasion skills. One was full of grassy green hills. Another was covered in desert. There was a tundra deck, and most of the lowest level of each ship was a dense simulated forest, not unlike the corner of the Reinhardt farm. Fake weapons against fake Shakren in a real forest was, therefore, appropriate preparation for using real weapons against real Shakren in a fake forest.

Fritz and Sierra, who had retaken her human form, flew above everyone else, scanning the forest for more Shakren. "Bad news," Fritz called out. "There's ten more. But good news, too! They're coming out of the lift. Which I can see."

That meant the Mantissa and the demons were close to their goal. The forest deck on Celestine vessels ended at midship, where an elevator led up to a series of operational facilities in the ship's core. The cloning chambers where new Shakren were manufactured were there. So were the science labs where Krulgoth had once worked. But what the Mantissa and the demons cared most about was at the very top: the control center. That's where the Shakren crew ran the ship and communicated with the rest of the fleet. And on the cathedral ship – which was their odd name for their command ship – the Celestines would be in the control center, too.

The ten Shakren Fritz had spotted were dispatched quickly, giving the Mantissa and the demons full access to the "elevator." It was a ten-by-ten wooden box that Siv had built and Fritz had covered with chipware projections to make it look more like the real thing. Fritz and Gashg stepped inside and slid four metal wedges into pre-drilled slots. That was to simulate the powerful electromagnets they'd shove through the cab's metal walls to pin it in place. Then they'd open the roof hatch, and everyone would climb, fly, or use a grappling hook

19

gun to get to the top of the shaft. They'd force their way through the door at the uppermost level and storm into the control center.

Building a simulated control center ten stories above the forest was impractical, so for the simulation, they just had to step through the fake elevator car and emerge on its opposite side. Cassie ensured everyone had ten green health indicator lights and no red ones on their vests and harnesses, but she couldn't do anything for Krulgoth, who had just four green lights. "Don't be foolish now," Cassie told him. "I can't heal metal. And even robots can be damaged beyond repair."

Maybe if Krulgoth weren't as emotionless as a cadaver, throwing his own words back in his face would have gotten Cassie more of a reaction than a two-second stare.

Sierra landed on the ground and cracked her knuckles. "And here we are again. Back at the part of this plan that's gonna get us all barking killed."

Cassie made no effort to hide her huff of annoyance. Why was she even here? Up on a Celestine spacecraft, outside of Verde's atmosphere, she might not even be able to hold her shape, let alone fight. "What's your problem now, Lady Verde?" Cassie said.

Sierra glared at her. She hated being called Lady Verde. She said the name wasn't appropriate because she wasn't the spirit of the planet. She also said it reminded her of past mistakes. But since Cassie didn't think Sierra had the right to forget those mistakes, Cassie managed to "forget" her name preference once in a while.

"Not just one," Sierra said. "I've got *two* problems, *Cassandra.* The same two I've had since the first time I heard about this plan."

"What are they?" Cassie asked. "Your attitude and your face?"

Fritz lifted his helmet's faceplate and sighed. "Sis, come on."

"One," Sierra said, counting off on her fingers. "The plan says we walk right up to an enemy who has the power to control our allies. Is that some kind of joke? It's like showing up to a party with a cyanide-laced bottle of wine. Bring your own murder weapon."

The Celestines had an easy and effective way of controlling their army. They'd programmed unwavering obedience directly into the Shakren genetic code. From the moment they were "born," every Shakren clone obeyed the Celestines' orders without hesitation. It was the main reason Krulgoth had done such extensive genetic modification of himself and his fellow white demons after their escape. It was also the main reason for the demons' deep loathing for the Celestines. Slavery was hell. It was even more vile when that bondage was built right into your DNA.

"The Evil Ones do not possess the power to control any of us," Krulgoth said. "They control Shak*ren*. My brothers and I are Shak*rath*."

"You are now," Sierra said. "But you think having an extra pair of arms, a tail, and a mouth full of knives breaks their hold over you? That whatever-it-was that kept you on the Celestines' leash was just skin deep?"

"I changed much more than just our skin," Krulgoth said. "I remade my brothers and I with Geneditor, a drug that breaks the covalent bonds of DNA and restructures the base pairs to conform to a pattern payload embedded within."

"Ooo, look at all the big words you know," Sierra mocked.

"That is to say," Krulgoth continued, "their alterations are *not* merely cosmetic. They reach down to their genes. My brothers *are* free."

Sierra looked over the assembled white demons who nodded and growled their agreement. "Fine," she said. "So you won't break your backs to kiss these Celestines' asses. Except – and here comes problem number two – you couldn't do *that* even if they *did* order you to. Because they're incorporeal beings. Ghosts. We can't hit them. We can't even touch them. No one can."

"Wrong again," Krulgoth said, and Cassie didn't miss the touch of annoyance – if not outright hostility – that seeped into his usual monotone. "They can bleed. They can die. I have seen it happen."

"There were once three Evil Ones," one of the demons snarled, "until the general slew one of them."

"So I've heard!" Sierra said. "Remind me again, 'General,' exactly *how* did you manage to touch the untouchable? Lecture me on the physics behind it, if that makes you more comfortable. Seeing as those ghosts will be trying to kill us, I *really* want to know."

Krulgoth stiffened. "It was a difficult time. My memory of the incident is... incomplete. I can not explain how it happened."

"I stand corrected," Sierra said, looking right at Cassie. "Nothing's wrong with our plan. So what if General Demon here has no clue how he killed one before? He's *positive* he'll be able to do it again. Why worry?" She blew a raspberry, pointed at the side of her head, and mimed pulling the trigger of a gun. "We're *borked*."

Everyone began shouting over everyone else.

"You *dare* insult the general," one of the demons – probably Skleght again – roared at Sierra.

"We have some good ideas," Annalie offered weakly.

"Why are we even working with her?" Cassie asked Siv.

"Same reason we're working with them," he said, pointing a thumb at the demons. "We need everyone we can get. Whether we like 'em or not."

"Umm, excuse me?" Fritz said.

The shouting continued.

Fritz lowered his faceplate and cranked the volume on his chipsuit to maximum. "*Excuse me!*"

Everyone stopped and turned to him.

He lifted his faceplate again and rubbed his ears. "Oh my days, was that ever loud... Now. Sierra. I appreciate your honesty. And we all know this plan isn't as solid as we'd like. But despite its flaws, it's still better than the alternative. Even the combined might of the Mantissa Reborn and the white demons *can't* fight off the invasion of a million Shakren troops."

Lightning crackled around Sierra's fists. "If you want something done, you gotta do it yourself."

"Come on," Fritz said. "Even you have your limits. You can be anywhere on Verde, but you can't be everywhere at once. Your consciousness is tethered to a single physical location. At least, it used to be. Was each bird in that flock you turned into back there autonomous?"

The barest hint of a smile tugged at her pierced lips. "They were."

"That's splendiferous!" Annalie said.

"Yeah, that's definite improvement," Fritz said. "Keep it up! But the deep-space scanners say that right now, there are a hundred ships on their way here with a combined population of a *million* Shakren soldiers. You can't fight off an army of that size all by yourself. *We* can't fight if off, either, all of us, together, Mantissa and Shakrath. The only way to stop this invasion is to make sure it never begins."

"Free the Shakren," Krulgoth said. "All of them. "

"And the only way to free them quickly enough to prevent an invasion is to strike right at the source," Fritz said. "We have to force the Celestines to liberate them."

"*Killing* the Evil Ones will also ensure they can never issue another order," Krulgoth said, and his brother white demons growled their approval.

"If it comes to that," Fritz said. "But either way, we *have* to take the fight right to the Celestines. And while it's true we don't know exactly how Krulgoth hurt one of them before, like Annalie tried to say, I feel we have some pretty good ideas."

"You *feel* we have good ideas," Sierra said. She pointed at Krulgoth. "He's certain he can do it again even though he doesn't know how he did it in the first place." She pointed at Cassie. "And she's putting all her chips on her imaginary guy in the sky because she thinks she still has his big plan to follow."

Cassie clenched her fists. "Would you hush your dang vocalities already?"

"Whole lotta dips into the wishing well happening here, Future Boy," Sierra said to Fritz. "That's all I'm saying. But fine. I'm just a cranky crank. I'll shut up now. Let's *do* this! Let's march in there and mow 'em down with our thoughts and our hopes and our prayers. Yay team! Woohoo!"

Fritz looked at Cassie and rolled his eyes.

Cassie gave him a pointed look right back. *He* was the one who'd recruited her.

"Everyone ready?" Fritz asked. He lowered his helmet's faceplate.

Siv pumped a bullet into the chamber of his shotgun.

The demons growled and readied their rifles.

Annalie reactivated her reader emulator circlet.

Cassie placed the back of her left hand in her right palm and brought them both to her heart. The Sign of God's Hand was both a reminder that all life was under God's care and a request for his protection. "Ready," she said.

"Let's not fake die this time, OK?" Fritz said. Sierra rolled her eyes.

The door on the other side of the elevator opened. Krulgoth surged into the clearing beyond, followed by Fritz and Sierra, then the demons, then Siv, Cassie, and Annalie. Fritz's chipware projections had turned a clearing in the forest into the Celestine cathedral ship's control center. Three rows of chipware terminals circled the center of the "room," each row slightly higher than the one in front of it. A Shakren worked at every one of them, and even more Shakren – these carrying guns – were stationed in the aisles.

But no one paid the Shakren much heed. They focused solely on the projections of the gray-skinned, black-eyed man and woman who stood at the room's center. When the demons saw them, they growled so savagely, their translators couldn't turn the sounds into words. They were just training images, but still, they were images of the Celestines – the ghosts who had created the Shakren and who subjugated worlds.

Cassie had lost count of the number of late nights she'd spent up with Fritz and Annalie and Siv and even Krulgoth, talking it over. There were only so many scientific explanations for the Celestines' intangibility.

25

Hypothesis one – the Celestines were physical beings, just ones whose molecules were far apart from one another. They were made of gas.

It would be Sierra's job to test this hypothesis. She launched herself into the sky and split the air between her and the simulated Celestines, shoving the heat aside, siphoning it away from the control room's center. The real grass underneath the projected illusion turned yellow, then crystallized into ice. If the Celestines were gaseous, then lack of heat would turn them first into liquid and then solid. And then they could be threatened and made to surrender.

Hypothesis two – the Celestines were intangible because they were energy-based beings.

Fritz took to the sky to test this theory, his chipsuit's rockets blazing, his laser cannons blasting away. The cannons' sound oscillated higher, then lower, then higher again as his chipsuit's chips re-tuned his lasers to a different frequency with every shot. Krulgoth's arm cannons did the same thing. He and Fritz's chipsuit were networked so that neither of them repeated the same frequency, ensuring they tried as many as possible. If the Celestines were energy instead of matter, then the right frequency would have a disruptive effect similar to physical pain. They just had to find it.

Hypothesis three – the Celestines consisted entirely of psychic energy.

Everyone agreed the Celestines were an intelligent species. Krulgoth repeatedly told everyone not to underestimate their intelligence. That meant no matter the reason they lacked tangible, physical bodies, they definitely had minds. Annalie crouched low and focused on the Celestines, the light on her reader emulator circlet flashing. Fritz said the device was the only weapon that had proved capable of harming Sierra back when she was wrathy and nasty – which implied she'd *stopped* being wrathy and nasty, but Cassie had apparently missed all that. If the Celestines did have minds, Annalie should be able to blast them so hard they wouldn't be able to think straight.

Cassie was confident one of their hypotheses would prove true, if only they could test them. Even if – *when* – they made it to the real cathedral ship's control center, there would be Shakren guards between them and the Celestines. A *lot* of Shakren guards. And they'd all have guns. Just like the simulated ones firing upon her and her friends now.

Siv fired his shotgun, blasting away any Shakren that tried to get between the Celestines and Fritz, Sierra, Krulgoth, or Annalie. The white demons leaped over the room's chipware workstations, ripping Shakren apart with their bare hands, desperate to get to the center of the room and try the same thing against their former masters. The green lights on their harnesses turned to red faster than Cassie could heal them all, so she didn't even try. She just fired arrow after arrow into the Shakren charging towards them and ignored her simulated danger sense, which desperately wanted to make her understand she was in imminent peril.

"Skleght is dead," the simulation chipware announced. He dropped his weapons with a hiss of frustration and dived away from the simulated control center into the adjacent out-of-bounds forest area. They were down to just seven demons.

"Gashg is dead," the simulation chipware announced.

Make that six.

Though all the shots were fake, their *sound* was very real and very deafening. There were enough flashes of green and red light to induce a seizure. Had anyone even reached the Celestines themselves?

"Kwegh is dead," the simulation chipware said. "Noklth is dead."

Fritz and Sierra were in the air, above the fray, but Shakren from the other side of the room were firing up at them, and Cassie wasn't sure how much longer–

"Sierra's body has been destroyed," the simulation chipware announced, "and she must reform a new one. Vlas is dead. Zethken is dead. Rarkh is dead. Tvelth is dead. Siv is dead."

Cassie hollered and buried an arrow into the chest of the nearest Shakren.

"Annalie is dead," the simulation chipware said. "Cassie is dead."

Seriously? She looked down at her vest. Sure enough, her last health light had ticked to red. She threw her fake bow aside.

"Fritz is dead. Krulgoth is dead. Simulation complete. Result: failure!"

The projections of the spaceship and the Shakren and the Celestines disappeared, leaving only trees, trails, red health indicator lights, and a lot of frustrated people. Sierra laughed and spread her palms, all but screaming, *I told you so.* Annalie blew a stray strand of hair off her face. Siv slammed the sharp end of his sword into the dirt. Even Fritz looked like he was losing confidence in the plan.

Cassie couldn't force them to keep the faith, but they couldn't take hers either. She knew what God had in store for her. Doctor by age twenty-four. Cure cancer. Start a new settlement. Retire on the beach. These Celestines weren't going to get in her way. Come hell or high water or intergalactic ghosts, she was going to carry out her plan.

Chapter Three

They were halfway across the farm from the forest back to the house, and no one had said anything. Not even Sierra. They were returning to the house for dinner, which meant Annalie, at the very least, should have been raving about how hungry she was. Instead, she kicked at the dirt as she moped along. Fritz was so distracted, he nearly wandered off course three times.

"Say something," Cassie said to Siv in an undertone. "They need a distraction."

"What should I say?" Siv whispered back to her.

Cassie shrugged. "Anything. We just need to get their minds off of practice failure number fifteen."

Siv nodded and thought for a moment. "Who's done with their Lenerstelen shopping?"

"Haven't even started," Annalie said. "Not used to shopping for it."

"You've never celebrated Lenerstelen before?" Cassie asked.

"Celebrated, sure," Annalie said. "But living up in Demons' Town, we didn't *buy* nothing for it. Demons didn't exactly operate stores. We made gifts for one another instead. Guess I could go buy things now, this being me and my siblings' first Lenerstelen free of the demons. But I think I'd still like to make my gifts. Feels more personable somehow."

"I made Mom a chipware mixer," Fritz said.

"For serious?" Annalie asked.

Fritz nodded. "Well, I repaired and restored an old one. I didn't make a new one from scratch. But still, now it will be easier than ever for her to make bread dough."

"Or *cookie* dough," Annalie said, rubbing at her stomach. "Mmm. I'm hungry."

"What about you, Sierra?" Fritz asked.

She raised an eyebrow at him. "Me? Lenerstelen shopping?"

Fritz shrugged.

"I'm both atheist and anti-capitalist," Sierra said. "In what universe do you imagine I go Lenerstelen shopping?"

"I wasn't going to get you anything anyway," Cassie told her.

Sierra kissed her palm and blew it towards her. Cassie glared back.

"I just want to get y'all to my sister's place over in Gorman," Siv said. "Or bring her and her family here. The place don't matter. The food does. Sammy's the only one who knows how to make the traditional McCaig family five-course Lenerstelen feast, and that's what I want my gift to y'all to be."

"I'm *so* hungry," Annalie said.

"Beg pardon," Siv said. "Five courses *plus* the prickly pear pie."

"I'm completely famished," Annalie moaned.

Fritz reached out and took her hand.

"How about you, Cass?" Siv said.

Lenerstelen wasn't the distraction topic she would have chosen, especially as they tromped across the farm's fallow wheat field. Less than two months earlier, her father had died in that field.

It had happened in the middle of her first semester of med school, so she'd been away in Harbrucken. If she'd been home, certainly her healing power could have saved him. Except she *had* been home just one day earlier. She'd made an emergency visit to help Fritz through a tough time. The day after she'd left

32

– the very next day – a blocked coronary artery had killed their dad.

She *was* looking forward to her first Lenerstelen with Siv, but she was *not* looking forward to the first one without her father. Her grief was still a raw wound. And perhaps even worse than the grief was the nagging question that lingered underneath it. She tried to dismiss it, but she couldn't let it go.

Things had worked out just right for her to find out about Fritz's depression and to make it home to help him. She knew that had been the work of God's Almighty Hand, and she was so grateful he'd made sure she was there for her brother. But why couldn't he have made sure she stayed home just one day longer so she could have been there for her father, too?

"Cassie does all her shopping on Lenerstelen Eve," Fritz said.

"The woman with the plan waits for the last minute?" Annalie said.

"Too busy studying," Cassie admitted with a shrug.

"Guess I oughta ask what *you* want then," Siv said, putting an arm around her shoulders. "Other than a handsome fella, since you already have that."

"Honestly, I'd be OK with skipping Lenerstelen this year," she said, "so long as it got me back to Harbrucken. My professors and fellow students are working hard to rebuild the university, and I want to help them. Keep my plan moving forward. *That's* what I want."

She practically dared Sierra to give her a look or make a comment, but she didn't. The crank just kept her mouth shut and her head held high, and she didn't so much as glance at Cassie. Did she have *any* remorse for what she'd done to Harbrucken? For the people she'd killed?

33

"You'll get back there," Siv said. He planted a quick kiss on her cheek.

"I know I will," Cassie said. "I just want to be back there *now*."

Past the wheat field was the chicken coop and the house. They approached it from behind, so Cassie couldn't see the front door yet, but she heard its squeaky hinges creak open and heard the door slam back against the frame. A moment later, a young girl, barely a teenager, barreled around the corner and ran towards them. She had red hair like her older sister Annalie, a too-thin frame, and a wide smile.

"Hey, Doctor Cassie," Elise said after skidding to a stop in front of her.

When Annalie had come to live here, to prepare for the Celestines' arrival, she'd brought her two youngest siblings with her. Elise had taken to Cassie like oxygen to the lungs. Cassie had never had a little sister before Elise began following her around. She could gladly get used to it. Having Elise around had been the best part of all this Celestine invasion preparation. It was like getting an early Lenerstelen present.

"Hey, Nurse Elise," Cassie said to her. "How you been?"

"Helping your mama," Elise said, falling into step next to Cassie. "I read how to make a tourniquet."

"Ooo, advanced stuff," Cassie said. "Why would you use one?"

"If bleeding is severe and direct pressure alone won't stop it."

"Good," Cassie said. "But why could it be dangerous?"

"If left on too long, your patient could lose the limb."

"But used correctly?"

"You stop someone from bleeding to death."

Cassie patted her back. "You keep this up, and they're gonna give you a job teaching at the med school when it reopens."

Past the house was a small pasture. Cassie's horse, Mandolin, and Siv's horse, Rebel, both grazed here. Cassie gave Mandolin a wave, and Mandolin flopped her tail in response. Beyond the pasture was the barn. Its exterior had once been red, but now it was half-faded and half-weathered.

The only sunlight left in the sky was a thin strip of orange on the western horizon. Still, the barn's inside was visible even from a hundred yards away because of all the chipware lights Fritz and Annalie had mounted from its ceiling. The reaper, the tractor, and every other piece of heavy equipment that should have been inside was parked outside, which cleared up plenty of floor space inside.

For the spaceship.

Two hundred years earlier, the Blackout reverted Verde to a pre-industrial society overnight. It had been the Mantissa's final, desperate attempt to fend off the white demons, and it hadn't worked. The Mantissa didn't survive, but the demons did, and they immediately began stockpiling broken, scrambled chipware in anticipation of one day repairing it. They had all kinds of ancient chipware in their stash up north: screens, mobiles, dispark ovens, weapons, comm systems. They even had a spaceship.

The cargo ship was once used to transport molecularly unstable goods and teleport-phobic passengers up to the Skylab space station. Now it was a physical symbol of the Mantissa and demon alliance. Everyone worked together to restore it, except when practicing their cathedral-ship assault.

The white demons bounded into the barn and swarmed over the ship like bees around a hive. Hundreds of engine parts lie scattered across the barn floor. The demons resumed the work of meticulously cleaning, inspecting, and rebuilding each one. Chipware diagnostic tools buzzed and beeped. Somewhere on the other side of the barn, metal clanged against metal in a steady rhythm. Open panels exposed degraded interior wiring. There was still a lot to be done to make the ship space-worthy, and they were short on time.

Krulgoth and the last of the demons were almost in the barn when Annalie called out to them. "You sure we can't bring y'all some dinner?"

"We can go a month without eating," Zethken said. Or was it Merkg?

"And we just ate five days ago," Rarkh said.

"Well, that's one way to live your life," Annalie mumbled.

Sierra also wouldn't be joining them for dinner since she didn't eat. The color disappeared from her body, revealing its dirt composition. She leaned forward, stretched, and elongated. Additional dirt rose up out of the ground and augmented her existing mass. When her body shimmered and took on color again, it was in the shape of a horse – a black horse with a lush green mane. And with piercings in her ears and lips. How charming. After a quick glance back at Cassie and Siv, she galloped across the pasture, and Mandolin and Rebel gave her chase.

"That is the oddest looking horse I ever dang seen," Siv said.

"Creepy," Cassie said.

Everyone still in the pasture turned towards the home's front porch. While they were out in the forest, it seemed Mom had put up some Lenerstelen decorations. She'd wrapped garland around the porch rail, and two of the front windows were painted with green soap.

Sitting on the first step and waiting for them was a ten-year-old boy with wide eyes and a mop of messy brown hair. The youngest Krieger sibling, Felix, kept his mouth closed, but he took three nervous steps towards Fritz.

Without a word, Fritz waved his hand.

Felix nodded.

Fritz pointed his index finger at the boy, then put up his thumb, tilting his head to the side in inquiry.

Felix rubbed his stomach.

"Yeah, I'm hungry, too," Fritz said, opening the front door and letting Felix enter first.

Cassie and Fritz had grown up together in this house. It was mostly a single room with a kitchen on the right side and a sitting area on the left. Three doors led off to the bedrooms. Ruth, Cassie and Fritz's mother, stood before the brick oven, stirring broth in a pot hanging over the fire. She smiled at her children as they came into the house. "Well, how'd you do?" she asked.

"We lost," Annalie said. "Again."

Ruth groaned then side-nodded towards the barn and the demons within it. "Can't *they* do anything to help you?"

"They are, but don't worry, Mom," Fritz said. He pulled a chair back from the table and dropped into it. "We'll figure it out."

"You're not wearing that crazy suit of armor to my dinner table, are you?" Ruth said.

"You're making me change?" Fritz asked.

"Don't talk back to your mama," Annalie said. She scooped a stack of bowls from a kitchen cupboard and began placing them around the table. When Fritz didn't retreat to his room to

37

change fast enough, she took the dishtowel off her shoulder and threatened to swat him with it.

He stood up. "I'll change, I'll change."

Ruth came up beside Cassie. "I love her," Ruth whispered. "Can we force Fritz to marry her already?"

"Not legally," Cassie said. She snatched a piece of chopped carrot off the cutting board and tossed it into her mouth. "Shouldn't let that stop us, though."

Elise, hovering nearby, mimicked Cassie and took a piece of carrot for herself. Cassie took another and tossed it towards Elise's open mouth, but it bounced off her bottom lip and landed on the floor. Both women laughed.

"You two," Ruth said, "stop playing with the food."

The front door opened and a one-armed man with white hair, a weathered face, and a tired smile stepped inside. "Hey, Daddy," Siv called to him. "You been working out there all day?"

"Yep," Duncan said. "Got all the port aft hull plates repaired, though."

"*All* of them?" Siv said.

Duncan nodded.

"There were twenty-three of 'em needed work this morning," Siv said.

Duncan just nodded again. He stood beside Cassie. "How's my future daughter-in-law?"

"Causing trouble and playing with food," she admitted.

Duncan laughed. Cassie put her arm across his back, resting her left hand on the stump that ended four inches past his left shoulder. "Mind if I work on that arm a little before dinner?"

He released a contented sigh. "Please do."

Elise gave a small jump of excitement and settled in to watch.

A white demon had ripped Duncan's arm off nearly twenty years earlier. After she'd met Siv, and then his father, she'd quickly read everything she could find in the university library on the science behind amputation. Following the traumatic injury, a blood clot closed the wound, then skin cells closed in to form a mass of scar tissue over the top of it. That much was true of many animals – humans, horses, dogs, cats. Except lizards were capable of something more. They were able to grow epithelial tissue on top of the clot, putting the amputated limb into what Cassie thought of as "embryo mode." Cellular processes not used since before the lizard hatched were dug out of nuclear memory and reactivated, and the lost limb regenerated.

Being the sister of the guy who restored broken chipware meant Cassie had access to an additional resource. Fritz could pull pre-Blackout medical texts off of old hospital proc-boxes he restored and descrambled. That opened her studies to areas lost even to the university, such as genome mapping. The ancients had mapped out the DNA of humans and just about every other living organism on Verde. It turned out humans possessed all the same genes lizards used for limb regeneration. But in humans, those genes typically remained dormant and unused.

Cassie saw no reason to remain typical, especially not when she had a patient she could help. All Mantissa powers were psychic in nature. She didn't heal people with magic juju. Her mind reached out into her patient's mind and somehow instructed it to do things it usually didn't do, like heal at ten times average speed. Or put those sleeping genes to work and regrow a lost limb.

It took lizards about sixty days to regrow a tail. Cassie reckoned it would take her a lot longer than that to regenerate Duncan's entire arm. But she managed to scrounge up some time here and there, and it was slowly working. His arm was growing back under her healing power.

Cassie closed her eyes and felt for the end of the stump underneath the mostly empty sleeve of Duncan's flannel shirt. She reached out with her power, and a familiar calm fell over her. She always felt most at peace when she was healing. It was one reason she knew it was her calling.

"Cassie, I almost forgot," her mother said. "You got post today."

She opened her eyes but kept her hand on Duncan and kept her healing power flowing. "I did?"

Ruth motioned behind her towards the table. "Over there."

Siv found the letter and brought it to her with a wide smile. "It's from the university."

"They finally know when I get to come back!" Cassie said. She nodded towards Elise. "You want to open and read that to me, kiddo?"

Elise tore open the envelope and unfolded the letter inside. "To the most amazing doctor in the whole world," she read.

"It does not say that," Cassie said, though her heart swelled at the compliment. She winked at Elise.

Fritz emerged from his bedroom wearing – what else? – a button-up shirt, vest, and trousers. He returned to his seat at the table, and Felix returned to Fritz's side, hiding behind him.

"Dear Miss Reinhardt," Elise said. Then she cleared her throat and repeated herself in what she must have imagined was the tone of an uppity university administrator. "Dear Miss Reinhardt. In the immediate aftermath of the horrific November 18 attacks, our faculty and students were focused on one thing: caring for thousands of casualties. We are all still in mourning, for there were far too many deaths. Yet there is no doubt the death toll would have been much higher if not for the efforts of our medical school family who selflessly aided the first responders overwhelmed by the scope of the Steelterror assault. It was our city's greatest hour of need, and we responded with our finest moment."

Elise gave an exaggerated bow to Cassie, her big sister, Siv, and Fritz. It was the four of them – plus Sebastian, who hadn't survived – who'd stopped the Steelterrors, but no one outside that kitchen knew it. There were still too many myths and lies about what had happened in Verde's past. All most people "knew" was once upon a time, there had been Steelterrors and Mantissa. Then after the Blackout nearly destroyed the world, there was poisoned land – Terrascorcha – and white demons. Many folks believed the Mantissa had likely been just as much a part of the problem as the Steelterrors. And so the Mantissa Reborn kept tight-lipped about their accomplishments. They had enough to deal with. No need to add potential persecution to the list.

"Three weeks have passed," Elise continued reading. "The dead have been buried. Wounds have begun to heal. And the university faculty have begun to assess the damage. It is..." She resumed her normal voice. "I don't know this word."

Annalie happened to be sweeping past her while putting napkins on the table. She squinted over her sister's shoulder. "Calamitous."

41

"Calamitous," Elise repeated. "Food, potable water, and medical supplies are scarce. Both the main university library and the medical school library were total losses."

"*Total* losses?" Cassie said. She couldn't have heard that right.

"Half our tenured professors perished," Elise read. "Buildings can, of course, be rebuilt. However, the sheer amount of knowledge lost in the attacks is unfathomable and irreplaceable."

Since helping Elise with the word she didn't know, Annalie hadn't resumed setting the table. She'd continued reading the rest of the letter over Elise's shoulder. Suddenly, she gasped, then looked up at Cassie in disbelief.

Cassie's hand slowly fell off of Duncan's arm.

"Two hundred years ago," Elise read, "the university at Harbrucken survived the Blackout and emerged carrying the torch of light and learning for all that remained of the civilized world. This time, Harbrucken and her university were not so lucky. It is simply impossible to comprehend how the university could possibly recover. Therefore, we regret to inform you that the medical school and all other colleges at the university are indefinitely, and quite likely permanently... closed?"

Cassie gently took the letter from Elise's hand. The crinkling of the paper was the only sound in the room. It seemed like even her mother's soup had ceased to bubble and boil. She found the letter's final paragraph. *Refunds for tuition and room and board for November 18 through the end of the semester will be issued. However, because of the extraordinary nature of our current situation, please understand this could take some time and may, in the end, prove financially impossible. With deepest regrets, Percy Holt, Dean of the University Medical School.*

Refunds? Who gave a damn about refunds? Like that even mattered.

Fully-trained doctor by age twenty-four. Cure cancer. Start a new village. Serve as its physician. *That's* what mattered. But without a university, none of it would ever happen. None of it *could*. Not anymore. Not ever.

Her plan.

Her *dream.*

"Darlin'?" Siv asked softly. His brown eyes were so gentle, but they weren't the only eyes watching her. Everyone in the room looked upon her with a mix of dread and pity on their faces. The main room suddenly felt the size of an outhouse, and the walls seemed to be moving in closer still.

"Excuse me," she said, and she pushed open the door and stormed outside.

Chapter Four

Two Hundred Thirty-Seven Years Ago

The *Virtue*-class shuttle shuddered and bounced as it dropped through Barohnde's atmosphere. Krulgoth squinted out the window into darkness occasionally broken by bursts of purple heat lightning. He used both his hands to grip the armrests of his chair. It was uncommon for the science division to be part of a mission landing party, but it happened enough for Krulgoth to know this descent was abnormal.

But S-24 was far too inexperienced, and certainly too young, to know any better. He leaned forward in the front-most seat, oblivious to the nerve-wracking turbulence, focused solely on their destination. "What are they like?" he asked the pilot. "In person, I mean. Is there anything about them our implanted memories don't prepare us for?"

"I was going to ask you," the pilot – O-7413 – said. "This is my fifty-eighth flight, but it will be the first time I've been near them."

"This is my first day!" S-24 said. "I just emerged from my birthing chamber this morning. And here I am, already being called to help the Luminous Ones themselves!" He craned his neck around to grin at Krulgoth and S-17. "What luck! What an honor!"

Krulgoth really did *try* to smile at him.

Once S-24 turned back to continue chatting with O-7413, S-17 leaned sideways towards Krulgoth. "Tell me I wasn't that... devoted when I was first created," he said in an undertone.

Krulgoth raised an eyebrow. S-17 knew full well every Shakren scientist had the same DNA and was implanted with the same memory engrams in the birthing chamber. The two of them and S-24 looked like identical triplets down to their matching science division uniforms. The only physical difference between them was the serial number stitched onto the left breast of their jumpsuits.

S-17 groaned. "I was, wasn't I?"

"Even I was," Krulgoth said. "Once." He exhaled heavily. "Let him enjoy his happiness. Soon enough, he'll know far too much sorrow."

"You should think positively," S-17 said.

"I think realistically," Krulgoth said.

When S-24 said it was his first day, he hadn't just meant it was his first day in his new science division occupation. For ten days, a new Shakren's body was grown to full adult size in a protein bath. Simultaneously, his mind was implanted with all of the knowledge he'd need to serve in the Celestines' mission. When he emerged from the birthing chamber, he was designated with the next sequential number for his assigned division, handed a uniform, and put to work.

There were hundreds of millions of Shakren clones spread across the galaxy, but all came from a small handful of genetic templates. Peacekeepers were soldiers – the physical enforcers of the Celestines' will. They were by far the most common type of Shakren. The spaceships, proc-boxes, and weapons the Celestines needed to conduct their ministry were built and maintained by engineers. Operations piloted the ships, kept them clean, and ran the mess halls.

Scientists like Krulgoth, S-17, and S-24 maintained and enhanced the other divisions' genetic codes. Through their

46

efforts, peacekeepers became more efficient killers, and engineers became smarter arms manufacturers. But the Celestines didn't make many new scientists, as evidenced by the low numbers in their designations. They only made new ones when they had good reason to. S-24's arrival gnawed at the pit of Krulgoth's stomach. Why was he here? What did the Evil Ones have planned?

"S-9 and S-17," S-24 said. "Have you ever been in the luminous presence?"

"We have," Krulgoth said.

S-24's eyes widened. "What are they like?"

It wasn't yet time for Krulgoth to answer that question honestly. Especially not with O-7413 listening from the pilot's chair.

"They're different than you might think," Krulgoth finally said.

S-17 made a non-committal hum.

Before S-24 could question them further, something out the window beside his seat caught his eye. The shuttle had descended close enough to the surface to spot landmarks. It was still dark, but the sights were visible even between lightning flashes because of the fires. Half of Proluve, Barohnde's capital city, burned. S-24 compared the view outside his window with reports on the mobile device he held. "The peacekeepers have done an efficient job, as always," he said. "The civic buildings have been captured or demolished. The roads closed. Curfews imposed. All hint of uprising amongst the people has been squelched without resorting to the Scourge or the Stigmata." S-24 turned to his scientist colleagues. "Why was this planet in need of the Luminous Ones?"

Need?

With a look, S-17 echoed his own words back at him. *Let him enjoy his happiness.*

Krulgoth looked away.

"Barohnde had been in the midst of a civil war," S-17 said. "The working class was on the verge of overthrowing the king. They accused him of elitism, unequal distribution of wealth and food, the usual sort of things that lead to disenfranchisement and hostilities." He consulted the chronometer on his mobile device. "That civil war ended a hundred minutes ago when the first *Virtue*-class shuttles dropped platoons of peacekeepers on the surface."

"Blessed be the Celestines," S-24 said, bowing his head reverently. "Those natives don't yet know the gift they've been given. They don't know their Iron Age technology will advance centuries in the next few weeks and that there will never be war here again."

He was correct about that. A garrison of peacekeepers would be left behind to ensure it.

"Another glorious victory," Krulgoth said in his monotone.

Before S-24 could ask any more questions, the shuttle lurched to the side. S-24 had to face forward and grip the sides of his seat.

"Final descent," O-7413 called back to them.

A bumpy minute later, the shuttle landed on a high ridge. When the three scientists disembarked, the smoke made their eyes water. The burning city was in the valley beneath them, and everything around them was lit by the orange flicker of flames. Lightning continued to flash across the night sky, and winds cut sharply across the clearing, but there was no rain.

48

The saltiness in the air came from Barohnde's unusually large oceans.

Across the clearing, a group of four Shakren engineers worked on technological equipment spread across a hastily-erected table. They looked physically identical to the three scientists, so Krulgoth understood their body language clearly. Whatever they were doing, it was arduous work. They were distressed and nearly panicking.

A squad of at least twenty peacekeepers was gathered around the engineers, watching their every move. *Ready to assist*, S-24 would say, but Krulgoth knew better. He wasn't naive enough to miss that the peacekeepers' fingers were on the triggers of their energy rifles. Those weapons were pressed against their chests and not aimed at anything or anyone. For now.

A camera was mounted on a tripod next to the table. Standing impatiently before it was a single Shakren from a division smaller even than the science division. V-4's designation marked his vocation as a speaker.

And next to V-4 was the main reason for the engineers' anxiety.

The Celestines. All three of them. The Way, the Truth, and the Life.

"Luminaries," S-17 and S-24 said as they genuflected. Krulgoth joined them, mumbling his own official greeting. The metal badges of three interconnected triangles each Celestine wore over their left breast did not reflect the moonlight.

The Way motioned for them to rise. "S-17. S-24." He smiled. "Krulgoth."

From the corner of his eye, Krulgoth noted the surprise on S-24's face. Why was anyone, let alone a Luminous One, addressing him not by an alpha-numeric designation but by a *name?*

"Smart meat!" the Life shouted. His voice sounded jovial, but his eyes gleamed with malice Krulgoth recognized all too well. "Stand up. Look at this nonsense. Those engineers can't get the blasted messengers to work. Figure out what's wrong!"

Krulgoth consciously kept his disgust off his face. He hated the Life most of all.

The lead engineer, E-781, licked his lips. His breathing was shallow, and there were dark rings under his eyes. "We – we – we dispatched the messengers," he told the three scientists. "But we can't get the video and audio signals to them."

Messengers were robot drones with giant flat screens on their side. When the Celestines came to a new mission world that lacked sufficient global broadcast technology, the messengers were distributed planet-wide so the Celestines could address the populace.

"The diagnostics still say they're fine," another engineer – E-927 – mumbled to one of his colleagues. "But they're *not.* What's *wrong* with these things?"

"Move them to a lower altitude?" the third engineer – E-942 – said.

"We've repositioned them twenty-five times!" E-927 snapped back.

"It's the interference," the last engineer – E-989 – said. He waved at the purple heat lightning that flashed across the sky. "We knew it would be a problem. We've been working weeks – months – to, to, to... to compensate. To make sure the *Virtue*-class shuttles could land. But... but..."

The Life opened his hand, and a plume of black smoke raised up from his palm, swirled in the air, and took the form of a thick wooden club riddled with rusty nails. He brandished it towards the engineers. "No excuses!"

The engineers flinched and trembled.

Krulgoth looked to S-17, and in S-17's identical face, Krulgoth saw his friend had come to the same realization. This wasn't a scientific problem. It was a technical problem, one the engineers would have easily solved had they not been sleep-deprived and pushed to their physical limits over the preceding weeks of preparation. The situation never should have escalated to this point, and worse, the Celestines' presence – especially the Life's impatience – made it perilous. This had to be handled delicately.

And it might have been... if it hadn't been S-24's very first day of life.

"You said you've been running diagnostics and repositioning the messengers," S-24 said. "Your command signals are reaching them just fine."

Krulgoth's breath caught in his throat. S-24 was just trying to help. He had no way of knowing what he was putting in motion. And Krulgoth was unable to prevent it. If he tried to silence S-24, the Celestines would override the effort. They'd demand their new scientist continue his explanation, and they'd kill Krulgoth for interfering. And if he died, any chance of salvation for his brothers would die with him.

So he shut up and let S-24 speak, even though his silence meant more blood would soon proverbially stain his hands.

"If the atmospheric disturbances are causing interference on the frequencies you normally use for transmitting audio and video," S-24 said, "just transmit on a frequency in the same band as the command signals. The ones that *are* getting through successfully. Shouldn't that have been obvious?"

Krulgoth closed his eyes.

The engineers shook their heads as if to clear cobwebs from them. They made adjustments on their control boards. A light on the side of the camera changed from red to green. The lead engineer, E-781, nodded to V-4.

"Citizens of Barohnde," V-4 said in the planet's native language, which had been implanted into all Shakren minds before the fleet's arrival. "The Celestines, who have delivered your world from bondage, would now address you. I will repeat to you the words of the Way."

A screen on the side of the camera showed the broadcast image. V-4 appeared on it exactly as he did in person, illuminated by firelight and the occasional flash of lightning. But although Krulgoth's eyes saw the Way standing next to him, with the Truth and the Life standing slightly behind, the Celestines did not appear in the transmitted vid. They couldn't be physically touched, nor could they be recorded by audio-visual technology. When the vid was transmitted across Barohnde, artwork of the Celestines painted by Shakren would appear on the right side of the messengers' screens.

They had subjugated thousands of worlds. Krulgoth had been present for hundreds of those invasions and had read detailed mission reports on all the others. Never had they encountered another species anything physically like them. What *were* they?

And worse yet, what if there were more of them out there than just these three?

"Barohndites," the Way said.

"Barohndites," V-4 said.

"This morning, your planet was on the brink of war," the Way said.

"This morning, your planet was on the brink of war," V-4 repeated. He continued repeating everything the Way said, though his voice sounded like sandpaper compared to the melody of the Way's words.

"Hundreds of thousands of souls would have died in a senseless conflict," the Way said. "You are cruel people. You are vicious tyrants who hold the less fortunate in bondage and contempt. You are bloodthirsty upstarts willing to murder your leaders instead of working peacefully for change. Your souls are like scarlet with the stain of your many, *many* sins."

His reprimanding expression softened into one of pity. "But none of it is your fault. You are innocent of every crime that has been committed here.

"Your enemy is God."

The Truth sneered at the mention of a deity. The Life spat, though his incorporeal sputum disappeared before hitting the ground.

"The sacred masculine you hail as a provider cursed you with a free will that left you capable of sin," the Way said. "The sacred feminine you hail as a caretaker betrayed you with a kiss that left your souls overflowing with corrupt desires."

The Way stretched out his hand as if offering it to the people of Barohnde, though only the Shakren physically present could see it. "But now, you people in darkness have seen a great light. We bring the good news of deliverance. No Barohndite will ever choose sin again."

Of course they wouldn't. If any did, the peacekeepers who would be permanently stationed here would kill them. Immediately. One way or another, the Celestines enslaved every race they "blessed."

"Some of you will find our methods harsh," the Way said. "But that is the price of eternal peace. And I assure you, it is a bargain."

The Way stepped aside. "That concludes the message," V-4 said, and then he began the litany. "Blessed be the Luminous Ones, for their presence brings only enlightenment! Blessed be the Itinerant Ones, for they find a home wherever they can ease suffering."

The Life marched towards the peacekeepers. The Truth sauntered towards the engineers. Krulgoth tensed.

"Were you pleased to receive another scientist?" the Way asked him. He'd come before Krulgoth and his colleagues, but Krulgoth had been so focused on the engineers, he hadn't noticed.

The Life pointed at the pistols worn by the peacekeepers and then at the engineering table. Krulgoth didn't hear what he said, but four peacekeepers drew their sidearms from their holsters and handed them to the trembling engineers.

"Blessed be the Fiery Ones," V-4 said, "for their passion for peace is a cleansing, everlasting flame."

"I was pleased," Krulgoth answered the Way, hoping that sweat wasn't forming on his brow. "But I don't understand why you have been so generous with us."

"Blessed be the peacemakers!" V-4 said into the camera. "Blessed be they who are persecuted for the cause of righteousness!"

S-24 didn't seem to know where to look. Though one of the Celestines – a Luminous One himself – stood directly before him, his eyes kept darting to the scene at the engineering table.

"Suck on those guns!" the Life ordered the engineers.

Without hesitation, the engineers opened their mouths. They rested the weapons on their tongues, with the barrels pointed at the backs of their throats. They all closed their eyes. One of them moaned, but none said a word of defiance. They couldn't, and not just because they had mouths full of metal.

S-24 gasped at their unquestioning obedience to such an order. Part of Krulgoth would have shielded S-24 from seeing what was about to happen if the Celestines would have allowed him. But no. Let S-24 watch. Let him not take his eyes off those four engineers. He must never, *ever* forget what he was about to see.

The Truth giggled. "Don't be afraid," she told the engineers. "You'll all die surrounded by fat grandchildren."

That was a lie. And not just because the Shakren didn't possess reproductive systems.

"I gave you another scientist," the Way said, ignoring everyone but Krulgoth, "because our next mission will be to the Kiloniks."

Only *that* could rip Krulgoth's focus from the engineers. "The Kiloniks?" he repeated from a dry mouth.

"Pull those triggers!" the Life shouted.

The engineers obeyed.

Their lifeless bodies fell.

S-24 cried out, his entire body stiffening.

"Not a word," S-17 hissed at him.

"Blessed be the Way, the Truth, and the Life!" V-4 said. "*Blessed be the Celestines!*" He came forward and turned off the camera because there weren't any engineers alive to do it for him.

The Way nodded to Krulgoth. "The Kiloniks. It's time. Long have they suffered without a shepherd to guide them. They need us. We're counting on your genetic manipulation abilities to make the Shakren strong enough to make them listen."

The Life appeared in a puff of smoke directly in front of S-24. "And you better not let us down, smart meat."

"Of course he won't," the Way said. "Not our Krulgoth."

The Life *harrumph*ed at that, turned around, and disappeared into smoke. The Truth turned as if to do the same, then sharply turned back, looking up to the sky. She grimaced and made a hissing sound.

Krulgoth followed her gaze to a peculiar constellation. A wavy line reminded him of one of the natives' tails, curved back as if ready to strike a formation of three more stars. He looked to S-17, who gave a subtle shake of his head. He didn't understand the Truth's reaction, either.

"Don't let it bother you," the Way told the Truth. Just for a moment, his brow was furrowed, too. But then his smile returned. The Truth huffed and vanished.

"I know you won't disappoint me," the Way told Krulgoth. He looked to S-24. "Krulgoth is the greatest Shakren I ever made. Listen to him." And then the Way was gone, too.

The peacekeepers took back their pistols and gathered up the engineering table and the dead bodies. "We're taking that shuttle," the peacekeeper squad leader said. According to the designation on his uniform, he was P-29333. "Another will be sent for you soon."

None of the scientists replied. They all stared at the ground as the peacekeepers cleared the scene, and as the *Virtue*-class shuttle rose into the air and shot away over the burning Barohndite city.

Faint cries of anguish cut through the night from the valley below. Some kind of insect chirped in the trees.

And the weight of realization crashed down on top of S-24. He fell to his knees, and for a moment, Krulgoth thought he was going to crawl to the ground stained black by the engineers' blood. Instead, he covered his face with his hands, and he wept.

"I didn't know," S-24 said once he composed himself enough to speak. "I... I thought I was helping. I didn't... I didn't think just by... Just by pointing out... I didn't know they'd– Why did they do that? Why did the Luminous Ones order them killed? Why didn't the engineers refuse suicide?"

Krulgoth sighed. "If they'd said no, what would have happened to them?"

"They'd have been jailed, of course, but at least–"

"Jailed?" Krulgoth interrupted. "Where? Do *Seraphim*-class ships have holding cells?"

S-24 consulted his implanted memories. "No."

"If they'd refused the order, they would have been killed," Krulgoth said. "The Celestines do not detain offenders. They eliminate them. Only a dead offender never repeats his crime."

"At least it wouldn't have been at their own hand," S-24 said. "They didn't have to do it to themselves!"

Krulgoth braced himself. This would be difficult for S-24. Excruciating even. But necessary. It was imperative he destroy the illusions the Celestines had implanted in the young scientist's mind.

"Did you choose to genuflect to them?" Krulgoth asked.

S-24 sniffed and wiped at his eyes. He tilted his head, not understanding the question.

Krulgoth gazed down into the burning valley. "On the shuttle, you gave a fairly complete inventory of what has happened this evening across the planet. But you missed one element." He pointed. "There. On the outskirts of the town. *That* fire is not a building. It's a pile of Shakren bodies."

"The bodies are taken away from the populated areas," S-17 said. "Not in any kind of funeral rite, but simply so that the natives can't count our fallen. So they won't know how effective they were against us."

"Tell me," Krulgoth said, "what do your implanted memories tell you about our funeral rites? About Shakren cemeteries? What customs do we have in regards to the dead? What are our memorials? Who mourns them?"

S-24 frowned and said nothing.

"No one mourns us, of course," Krulgoth said. "Why would they? We're cattle. We're tools, and dead Shakren are broken tools that served a purpose but are now useless. To the Luminous Ones – to the *Evil Ones*" – S-24 flinched at the blasphemous phrase – "the only thing worth noting about that funeral pyre is the quantity of the bodies."

S-17 shrugged his shoulders. "How else will they know how many replacement soldiers to pull out of the birthing chambers?"

"And so with that in mind," Krulgoth said, turning away from the valley to face S-24. "I ask you again. Did you *choose* to genuflect to them?"

"I..." S-24 said. "I knew that was the response expected of me when I came into their presence. It must have been implanted in my mind in the birthing chamber."

"Your implanted memories informed you it is our custom to show them reverence," Krulgoth said. "But what made you choose to practice that custom? What made you drop to one knee before them?"

S-24 blinked. In his face, identical to Krulgoth's own, Krulgoth saw the sick realization take hold.

"I *didn't* choose," S-24 finally said. "I just did it. As if it were instinct."

Krulgoth nodded. "You are a sentient being. You have thoughts, feelings, and rights. You are a *person.* You have the right to freedom. To life. And so did those engineers. Yet when those monsters created you, they wrote obedience to them directly into your genetic code."

A vein on the side of S-24's neck pulsed rapidly. "I *can't* disobey them?"

"No," Krulgoth said softly. "You're genetically incapable of such defiance."

"Even if..." He stared at the engineers' bloodstains.

"Even if they should order you to commit suicide," Krulgoth said. "You will unquestioningly obey. Just as those engineers did."

"I have no free will?" S-24 said between short, shallow breaths.

Krulgoth shook his head. "Not with them. To the Evil Ones, you're simply a biological machine that exists to do their bidding."

S-24 bent forward at the waist, put his hands on his knees, and struggled to breathe.

"Why tell me all this?" S-24 demanded.

"You'd have figured it out on your own," S-17 said. "Especially after what you saw this evening. All Shakren do."

"Then why don't we just throw ourselves off this cliff?" S-24 said. "Then we wouldn't have to continue living this way."

"Try it," Krulgoth said. "They forbid suicide. You're as incapable of self-harm as you are of disobeying them."

"But I just saw–" S-24 said.

"Unless ordered directly," S-17 interrupted. "By *them*. Their orders override all others."

Krulgoth and S-17 stayed silent for some time, allowing the terrible truth to sink into S-24. But he didn't say anything either. What was there to say? *That's unfortunate? Good to know? So tell me: what's the best part of being a genetically-engineered slave?*

They waited a long time for the promised shuttle. When Krulgoth spotted it in the distance, he cleared his throat. "Now that you know the full truth of what you are and what the Evil Ones are, we have work to do."

S-24 scoffed. "Help them subjugate another world?"

"No," Krulgoth said. "Save as many of our brothers as we can."

That got S-24's attention.

"The Kiloniks are a species of giants, relative to us anyway," Krulgoth said. "Their adults are ten feet tall. Their skin is as hard as metamorphic rock. Combat is integral to their culture. Their children wield knives almost as soon as they can hold a spoon. The only thing harsher than them is the terrain of their planet. Mountainous, rocky, and hot – so hot the Kiloniks collect water not from rivers but from geysers and steam-spouts. Simulations project Shakren casualties in the *billions* if the planet is to be converted without the Scourge or the Stigmata – options even the Evil Ones are loathe to use."

"But Geneditor can make our peacekeepers taller, tougher, stronger," S-24 said. "We can protect them."

"To an extent," Krulgoth said. "Let's assume we have enough time to program, manufacture, and administer enough Geneditor to make every Shakren peacekeeper stronger than the Kiloniks. The modifications the Evil Ones will permit us to make are limited. If we make the peacekeepers too physically large, we create infrastructure problems. Their hands become too big to wield their weapons. Larger shuttles are needed to drop them onto planets. They don't fit on their racks in the barracks any longer. And rebuilding the infrastructure requires steel and tech and labor and time. It's expensive. No, the Celestines will strengthen the Shakren so long as the cost is only protein and amino acids. After that, their solution will be to simply throw more bodies at the problem."

"Shakren bodies," S-24 said. He closed his eyes and shook his head. "Shakren lives."

"But, in the name of saving as many of our brothers as we can, we *will* work to physically improve them as best as possible," Krulgoth said. "For at least a couple hours of each day. However, most of our time will be spent on genetic enhancements of our own design."

"What kind of enhancements?" S-24 asked. "You just said they won't let us make our brothers strong enough to survive against the Kiloniks."

"They wrote our subservience to them into our DNA," Krulgoth said. "But *we* know Shakren DNA better than they do. And they gave us, as a tool for doing our job, the means to edit that DNA."

The barest hint of a smile came to S-24's face. Hope. "You don't mean..."

"S-17 and I need your help to find the chromosomes that establish our forced servitude," Krulgoth said. "Once we find them, we'll edit them. In *all* Shakren – every Shakren there is, and every Shakren there ever will be. We'll grant our brothers

61

unconditional free will and make it possible for all Shakren everywhere to rise up against the Evil Ones."

Krulgoth read the question off S-24's face before he could voice it. "Yes, you are capable of such work because they never ordered you not to. You must obey their every order, but you will also quickly learn how to exercise your own desires in the margins of their impreciseness."

"All right," S-24 said. "But what proof do we have that it's even *possible* to gain our freedom?"

The idea of sharing his most important secret with someone besides S-17 made Krulgoth hesitate. But he'd already mapped the distance between Barohnde and Kilonika in his head. He had just two months to solve a puzzle he'd been working on for decades, and the price of failure would be billions of Shakren lives. He didn't have a choice. He and S-17 needed S-24's help.

"It is possible," Krulgoth said. "I know because I did not genuflect to them out of forced obedience. I *chose* to do it."

"You *chose?*" S-24 said.

"Not out of reverence, of course," Krulgoth said. "I did it solely to hide my secret. They don't know it, but I am capable of disobeying them. *I* am the proof that our genetically-imposed obedience can be overcome."

"You *chose?*" S-24 repeated. "How? We're all cloned from the same genetic template. Implanted with the same memory engrams."

"Correct."

"Then how are you different than the rest of us?"

Krulgoth shook his head. "I don't know. But I *am* different, and we *will* find out why. The three of us, together. And when we discover the chromosomes that grant me my freedom, we'll use Geneditor to share my gift with every other Shakren in the fleet."

At last, relief came to S-24's face. Relief, but not happiness. It would take a while before he'd again know that. Happiness would require freedom, but he'd get it soon enough. Krulgoth wouldn't rest until he did – until *all* Shakren did.

"When our work is complete," Krulgoth said, "we will *never* be enslaved again."

Chapter Five

Cassie didn't see Mandolin out in the now-dark pasture, but that didn't matter. She put her index finger and thumb together, pressed them against her tongue, and whistled once, long and loud. Mandolin came running from behind the chicken coop. With motioning fingers and a clicking tongue, Cassie beckoned the mare to follow her towards the wooden fence separating her parents' property from the road.

When the world got too crazy, Cassie always fell back onto something that made sense. Usually, that meant doing something to work towards her plan. Study for an upcoming exam, read a medical journal about cancer treatment, maybe draw up a sketch of the settlement she would one day found. But that letter had been such a gut punch. The only thing to do was ride, and she didn't have the patience to bother with a saddle or a bit or a bridle. Gently, using a fence rail as a mounting block, she climbed onto Mandolin's back and rubbed her white mane.

She heard a tongue click and a whistle behind her. It was Siv summoning his horse, Rebel. He was coming with her? Well... fine. But only him. No one else, definitely no white demons, and most certainly no Sierra. And he better not plan on talking because she wasn't in the mood. Siv didn't bother with a saddle either. He led Rebel to the fence, climbed onto his back, and brought the stallion alongside Mandolin.

"Where we headed?" Siv asked.

Cassie didn't know, and she didn't care. She shrugged her shoulders and rode out to the road. Mandolin headed west towards the village, and Cassie didn't bother to argue.

She felt the warmth of Mandolin's skin and wrinkled her nose at its funk. Poor girl needed a bath, but they'd been so busy with spaceships and simulations and–

No. No, this ride was her escape from all of that. Starting with her neck, she relaxed her muscles, working her way down her shoulders and chest. The chilly December wind caressed her cheeks and blew her hair because she'd left without her wide-brimmed hat. Slowly, as she mentally pushed aside everything except horse hooves on dirt by starlight, she was able to think. The panic the letter had injected into her heart lessened. But not by much.

"Ha! There it is!" Siv said after a half-mile of silence. "My favorite constellation."

His favorite food was steak. His favorite color was blue. His favorite hobby was stargazing, and his favorite constellation was Gotteszorn. And the one and only reason he was pointing it out was to distract her. She kind of loved him for it. After a deep breath, she allowed his wide smile to contagiously infect her with a weak one of her own. "Don't point," Cassie said. "Let me see if I can find it."

She did, and in less than a minute, too. Her stargazing skills were improving. Well, she'd had plenty of practice, what with the two of them spending their evenings lying out on the pasture under a blanket, stargazing and talking. Cassie pointed it out to prove she'd passed the test: ten stars in the shape of God's hand casting the fallen angels out of heaven.

"Good," Siv said. "Now, can you name its stars?"

Cassie puffed air. "No, and you can't either, Sir Blacksmith. Not all ten."

"I'll take that bet," Siv said. "Sigma, Hermann, and Trion Haupt make up the first finger. Trion Gerin forms the thumb.

The other fingers are Margarethe, Caliban Two, and Boniface, and the fallen angels are Nariel, Rudger, and Daphne. I win. What's my prize?"

"A hearty handshake, a pat on the back, and the warm glow of victory," Cassie said.

"And a nice, long kiss goodnight," Siv said. "Deal."

Cassie rolled her eyes, but she smiled, too. Wider this time.

"Gotteszorn's the mid-winter constellation," Siv said. "If it's out, it means Lenerstelen is just around the corner." He hummed. "I can almost taste that prickly pear pie."

They rode another quarter-mile in silence.

"About six years ago," she said, "my dad and I went down this road together. On a horse we used to have named Jonesy. I didn't have Mandy yet. We went down this road lots of times, of course. Every time we went to the village. But the day I'm thinking of, we were headed into town to talk to Doc Laubscher. Because I was ready. Ready to start training to be a doctor.

"I know it sounds strange that I was born with this power to heal myself and others, and that it's never been enough for me, but I'm trying to do more than just cure one person of one disease. I want to take an awful disease, like cancer, and cure *everyone* of it. To do that, I'm going to have to conduct research and manufacture medicines and vaccines. And my power doesn't give me the ability to do any of that. Only a medical education will.

"I knew I'd reach a point where I'd need an expert to guide me, to test me. Books can only take you so far when it comes to medicine. It's a field that demands perfection. You make a mistake and people die, right? So I needed a teacher. And this day I'm talking about, my Dad and I went and asked Doc Laubscher to train me."

She took a deep breath. The memory still hurt. "He said no."

"Then he was a fool," Siv said.

Cassie waved him off. "He was just being honest," she said. "He said he didn't want to train *anyone*. Just didn't have the patience for it. Wasn't his thing. He was very gracious, though. Said he'd write a letter of recommendation to the university when it was time for me to go there. Except we didn't have money for the university. Maybe I could have sought out some other doctor willing to train me, but every village doc in the Territories other than Laubscher lived too far away. I was too young to leave on my own just yet, and the family couldn't move. My dad had land to farm *here*. So when Doc Laubscher said no, that was me hitting a dead end." She pounded her fist against her palm. "My dream was over. And I was so, so *mad*."

"I don't blame you," Siv said. "This happened six years ago, and even I'm angry at that old sawbones."

"I wasn't mad at him, though," Cassie said. "Well, maybe a little. I was mostly mad at God."

"At God?" Siv said.

"I felt humiliated," Cassie said. "*Betrayed*. Stabbed in the back. I felt like God had inspired me with an unobtainable dream, and that felt so cruel, I couldn't forgive him. So the next day, I marched down this road again. I stormed into church, and I told our pastor I wanted to lodge a complaint against the man upstairs."

"Yeah?" Siv asked with a chuckle.

Cassie couldn't help but laugh a little, too. "I was fourteen. What can I say? It's fairly embarrassing to think about it now. I *ripped* into Pastor Seelos – he's the one who retired a few months ago. But he didn't yell back, and he didn't laugh. He just listened. He was so kind. And once I finally shut up already, he told me something I've never forgotten."

She remembered more than just his words. She recalled how muggy it had felt in the church. The remnant smells of incense from the previous Sunday's services. The way the dust floated in the beams of sunlight angling down across the nave from the highest windows. She took the grunblume Pastor Seelos had given her that day out of her pocket and wrapped the string of beads around her hand. Everything about that day was branded in her memory.

The day she first learned about the Three Answers.

"He told me God answers every single prayer," Cassie said, "and always with one of just three possible answers."

Siv raised an eyebrow. "Infinite, omnipotent God? Just three answers?"

She counted them off on her fingers. "Yes. Yes, but not right now. And I have something better planned."

"Huh," Siv grunted. He considered this for a long moment. The skepticism on his face gave way to acceptance. "Reckon I like that."

"I did, too," she said. "And what happened the next day seemed to prove Pastor Seelos right. My dad and mom came up with a plan to send me to the university. It meant working their tails off and scrounging every piece of coin they could find. But they said they'd do it, and they did. It was an honest-to-God miracle."

She bit at her lip. *We regret to inform you that the medical school and all other colleges at the university are indefinitely, and quite likely permanently, closed.* "At least it was until it wasn't anymore."

Siv patted her shoulder. "We'll find another way, darlin'."

She bristled under his touch. "You don't get it," she snapped at him. "The university *was* the other way! It was the *only* way, the something better God had planned for me. Now it's gone, too."

"I know this hurts something fierce," he said. "But an hour ago, you were the one telling everyone else that we gotta keep the faith."

"That was when I knew God was behind me," Cassie said. "But now I'm not so sure. And not just because of that letter. It's..."

She closed her mouth. This had been bothering her for a long time, but she hadn't spoken of it to anyone. Not to Fritz. Not to her parents. Not even to Siv. But she couldn't hold it in any longer. "When I was a little girl, I couldn't save my friend Bernice. And losing her hurt like hell. My whole plan was born out of that pain, and the point of it was to make sure I never had to lose anyone I cared about ever again. I believed with all my heart that God was the one who inspired me with that plan. That it was *his* plan, and I was just carrying it out."

"Believed?" he said. Her use of past tense hadn't escaped his notice.

"I couldn't save Eroica, either," Cassie said. "I was a hundred miles away when Harlan died, but when Sebastian died, I was right there with him, and I still couldn't save him, either."

"He gave his life to–" Siv said, but she wasn't finished, and she wasn't in the mood to hear it anyway.

"And just one day," she interrupted, "just *one day* before my dad died, I was home. Here. With him. If he had to have a heart attack, fine. But why couldn't God have made him have it just *one day* earlier when I would have been here to save him?

70

God gave me this miraculous power to heal everyone of anything. So why wouldn't he let me save my dad?

"Now I'm right back where I was six years ago. God inspired me with a dream, and I devoted every waking moment to making it come true, and now... he isn't helping me anymore. My medical school is gone, planet-conquerers are coming, and our best idea for stopping them kills us in every single simulation." She shook her head. "Maybe my faith has been misplaced."

Should she have said that out loud? Siv was a righteous man who loved God, never willingly missed church services, and read the scriptures daily, and she adored him for all those things. Pastor Seelos had once told her honest doubt was never a sin, but would Siv see it that way?

He gnawed at the side of his mouth for a few moments, which she recognized as meaning he was carefully considering his response. "Keep in mind what we're saying when we make the Sign of God's Hand," he said. He placed the back of his right hand in the palm of his left and brought them both to his heart. "It's a statement of our belief that no matter what happens, he's always holding us close to him. Even in the face of all this bad news, that's still where you are, Cass. In his hand. Next to his heart."

"I don't feel like I am. It feels like he's cast me aside." She motioned towards Gotteszorn in the sky. "Same as how he cast the devils out of heaven."

"Don't curse yourself like that," Siv said gently. "Even if it's battered and bruised, you gotta hold onto your faith. Faith the size of the smallest seed can move the tallest mountain."

"That was another favorite saying of my old pastor," Cassie said. "I *want* to believe. I really do. But with all that's happened, with all that's *still* happening, it's a little hard. I just feel so... abandoned."

She expected him to say more – to point out that they were still betrothed, still fixing to start a new settlement in the unoccupied territories. On the coast. Living beside the ocean. Though she'd apparently need a new job to offer their future community now that she'd never be a doctor. She expected a reminder that they would one day build a house and start a family. But he didn't say any of those things. He just rode next to her in silence.

And that was OK. In fact, that was more than OK. His presence and riding on Mandy were the only two things in the world that made sense right now. She didn't need him to be a blacksmith at the moment, repairing her soul like it was a broken horseshoe. She just needed him to listen. She just needed him to be there.

The silence lasted the rest of the way into town. Just a few weeks earlier, they'd have been able to see Hondo from a good ways off. In July, Fritz had taken the first public step of his restoration by lining Hondo's Main Street with chipware lights. Everyone in the village had thrown a spontaneous party in response. There'd been music and dancing. Siv had proposed to her late that night. But as they reached the outskirts of the village, the lights were dark. They hadn't been removed, but they most certainly hadn't been lit, either.

"Lights are off because of Harbrucken," Siv said. "Ain't they? Chipware's making folks afraid now instead of hopeful. They don't know the Steelterrors are all scrap now, so folks are afraid of being their next target."

He blamed the Steelterrors, but Cassie blamed Sierra. "Yeah, something like that," she said.

They were just a stone's throw from Church Street. If she squinted, she could see the shadow of the church spire off to her left, a block behind the buildings that lined Main Street. Some of those buildings had started decorating for Lenerstelen already. The general store had wreaths of green on display in the front window. Connie Emerson hand-made them every year.

The only thing in the saloon's windows was candlelight, but the aroma of fresh bread and grilled meat indicated Phil was inside, serving plates and tending bar. The mix of laughter, clinking glasses, and fiddle-and-drum music meant he already had a crowd – and it must have been a big one. Only one person was out on the street, and he was headed towards the saloon, too. Cassie recognized Gunter Asheford and waved. Her father had hired Gunter and his brothers as extra hands a few times to help out during harvest. Gunter tipped his cowboy hat to her and Siv.

She brought Mandolin to a stop. "I need to see that my plan is still going to come together," she told Siv. "I can't just hope. I need to *know*. Because if I'm not just being gloomy and pessimistic, and if God really has cast me aside, then..."

She couldn't even contemplate that possibility.

Siv offered his hand. "Let's pray together."

Cassie took it eagerly. They closed their eyes and bowed their heads. "Lord," Cassie started. She sighed. How could she put all of this into words? Where did she even start?

"Lord," Siv took over, "you know we believe. You know Cassie believes. Help her unbelief. Show her she's still on the right path. Let her know you're still guiding her."

They concluded with the Sign of God's Hand. Keeping her eyes closed, she took a deep breath of the cold night air.

73

"Better?" Siv asked.

"A little," she admitted.

Siv motioned towards the saloon, where Gunter pushed open the watering hole's double swinging doors. "The smell of that barbeque's making my stomach growl. How about we go inside and fetch a bite to–"

There was a guttural cry – Cassie couldn't make out the words – and the crack of a gunshot.

Then Gunter Asheford stumbled backward off the saloon's front porch and landed in the Main Street dirt with a bullet wound in his forehead.

Chapter Six

Cassie's boots hit the ground, and she sprinted down Main Street towards Gunter. "Cass, wait!" Siv yelled, and she knew what he was thinking. What if the shooter came out of the saloon looking to pump more lead into his victim? *And* anyone doing the courtesy of aiding him? But there was no need for caution. Her danger sense wasn't making a peep, and this was no simulation. Whoever had shot Gunter wasn't going to shoot her, too. It was safe to help him.

And even if it wasn't, she was going to help him anyway.

Inside the saloon, glasses broke, a table was overturned, and everyone shouted over everyone else.

"Bauer!"

"It was Bauer! I saw it!"

"Hold him! Hold him down!"

"Gunter! *Gunter!*"

"Get the sheriff!"

"That'll teach that mudsill to keep his hands off my girl!"

"Shut him up!"

"Sheriff!"

"Somebody help him!"

Cassie knelt beside Gunter, placed one hand over the wound in his forehead, and reached out with her power. She put her other hand on his neck, then his heart, searching for his pulse and heartbeat. Both were there, but barely. She almost wished they weren't. All his heart was doing at this point was pumping his blood right out of him. If he'd been shot in the arm, then maybe Cassie could tell Elise she'd had the opportunity to apply a tourniquet. But you couldn't put a tourniquet around someone's neck when they'd been shot in the head. It wasn't useful, practical, or necessary. A person with a bullet hole in their skull didn't live long enough to need one.

Two men charged out of the saloon calling Gunter's name. Cassie recognized them but couldn't place their names, not in the heat of the moment. Gunter's pulse weakened. The span between heartbeats increased significantly.

"No, no, no," she muttered.

Siv knelt beside her.

"Sheriff!" someone screamed.

"You're gonna hang for this, Bauer!"

"Get the sheriff!"

"*You're gonna hang!*"

"Cassie Reinhardt's trying to help him."

The two men who'd emerged from the saloon were joined by three more. Two others ran down Main Street towards the sheriff's office. "It was Kurt Bauer!" someone yelled. "Just shot Gunter the moment he walked inside!"

The dirt on either side of Gunter's head was stained with the blood – far too much blood – that had spilled from his forehead wound. But the ground underneath his head was dry. That wasn't good. That wasn't good at all. Cassie reached under his head to feel for herself.

"Blast it!" she hissed. "No exit wound. The bullet's still inside him!"

"Cassie?" one of the onlookers asked. Klein. That was his name. Paul Klein. "He gonna make it?"

The folks who watched her might or might not have favorable opinions about the ancient Mantissa. They might or might not have a pleasant reaction to the presence of one among them. Given a choice between keeping her power a

76

secret and saving Gunter, she'd choose saving Gunter without hesitation. But saving him was an option rapidly being taken off the table. She couldn't feel a pulse from him any longer, and the lack of an exit wound was a big problem.

"If I heal him up," Cassie said to Siv in an undertone, "I'll be leaving a chunk of lead in his brain. Instead of bleeding to death, he'd die of a nasty infection. He needs surgery – delicate surgery – to get that out."

The irony of what she was about to say stabbed her in the heart. She turned to the gathered crowd. "Where's Doc Laubscher?"

"Still up in Harbrucken," someone answered.

Of *course* he was. Every doctor within fifty miles of Harbrucken had gone there after Sierra's rampage. Sierra who'd indirectly caused the deaths of Harlan and Sebastian. Well, if Gunter died, Cassie would consider that her fault, too.

Siv put his hand on Gunter's chest and sighed. "Cass," he said gently.

"This isn't fair," she hissed. Her medical knowledge mocked her. She knew Gunter's prefrontal cortex was shredded, and his heart had stopped. Like all Mantissa powers, hers was psychic. She healed by sending commands into her patients' minds, but for all she knew, whatever part of Gunter's mind that received those messages was already ripped apart.

No! She wouldn't accept that.

"Cassie?" one of the onlookers said. She recognized Andrea Krause's voice.

God, let your healing hands work through mine. Please! Let me do something. Let me save this man!

"Cass?" Siv said. "He's gone."

She stood with a huff. The dead man at her feet had worked her father's fields at least three seasons that she could remember. She hadn't known him well at all, but she'd seen him alive, breathing, laughing with his brothers in her dad's corn and wheat fields. Politely tipping his hat to Cassie's mother whenever they left for the day. Someone in the saloon had yelled something about staying away from a girl. Was this was a dispute over a lover? Stupid! Stupid and senseless! He was a human being. No matter what he might have done, he didn't deserve to be shot like a wounded animal. He deserved to live.

And she deserved to have been able to save him.

"I said I needed to know God was still with me," Cassie said to Siv, grinding out the words from between gritted teeth. "And how does he answer my prayer? With *another* patient I'm not allowed to save. Which of the three answers was that? Was that yes? Was that yes, but not right now? Or was that forget you, Cassie, you're on your own now?"

Siv put a hand on her shoulder.

Cassie shrugged it off.

The crowd outside had grown larger. Folks from the inn and stable workers from the livery had come to see what the ruckus was all about. Connie Emerson rushed out of the general store, took one look at Gunter's body, and fainted. Pastor Kolbe, the young preacher who had come to Hondo after Pastor Seelos retired, stood across the street. His face was obscured by shadows, but his black cassock made his identity obvious. Why wasn't *he* doing anything? He could at least drag his rear end across the street and administer the last rites. Instead, he just stood there, like a visible sign of God's bystander apathy. Cassie's stomach turned.

A couple of men knelt beside Gunter and wept. Most everyone prayed. One of Gunter's brothers arrived screaming his name, and he wailed at the sky when he saw the dead body. He collapsed and pounded at the dirt, inconsolable despite two of his friends' efforts. Sheriff Auber ran down the street towards the saloon, cuffs already in hand.

Phil Hersch, the saloon's owner and bartender, approached Cassie and offered her a warm, wet rag. "For your hands," he said. "And gratitude. For trying to help." He shuffled away, apparently unsure of what else he should do.

Cassie's hands were red with Gunter's life. So was her grunblume, which she'd wrapped around her right hand during the ride into town and hadn't even thought about removing before she tended to her patient. The blood on the beads felt appropriate, like a physical symbol of who she blamed for Gunter's death. Her hands trembled with rage.

She stalked back towards Mandolin, wiping her hands on the towel. Siv followed alongside her. "I never asked for this power. I was born with it." She pointed to the sky. "*He* gave it to me. So why give it to me and then not let me use it? What kind of God allows a senseless killing like that to even happen in the first place? The scriptures say God is love, but *that*" – she jerked a thumb backward – "was not love."

Pastor Kolbe ran towards her and Siv on the wooden sidewalk. For a moment, Cassie thought he'd dropped out of heaven to answer her questions and assuage her doubts, but he ran past them without a second glance, heading straight towards the saloon and the dead man lying in the dirt. Where'd he come from? Hadn't he been on the other side of the street a few moments before, watching and not lifting a finger? Whatever. At least he was finally tending to Gunter's soul.

"I'm just trying to make the world a better place!" she told Siv. "Why won't he let me do that?"

"God is good, but bad things happen," Siv said. "The devils are out there trying to keep us from the path God's hands have dug for us. Don't forget the people you *have* saved. You're restoring my daddy's lost arm. You saved Fritz. You saved my life more times than I can count."

"And how long will it be before that privilege is taken from me, too?" Cassie said. "Fifteen simulations say we go up into space to confront these Celestines, and I lose you, Fritz, Annalie – everyone. And I die, too."

"An hour ago, you were telling everyone that ain't gonna happen," Siv said.

She glared but bit her tongue. She led Mandolin to the side of the road and used a hitching post and an empty trough to boost herself up onto her horse's back. Siv climbed onto Rebel and brought him beside her. Leading the horses in a slow walk, they headed down the road back towards the farm. Their appetites were gone.

"Let's pray about this at services tomorrow," Siv said. "Together."

"I'm not going," Cassie said.

The words had spilled out before she could decide if she truly meant them and before she could think about the consequences. But she *had* meant them, and she didn't care about the fallout. God's house was the *last* place she wanted to be at the moment, and she reckoned that wasn't going to change in the next twelve hours.

"Willfully missing services is a sin," Siv said. He wasn't accusatory or sanctimonious about it. He was just concerned.

"When we fought Krulgoth up on that space station," she said, "and he used my own arrows to make me a pin cushion, I saw a tunnel of white light. I was headed... somewhere else. Somewhere that isn't here. And then Sebastian healed me, and I came back into my body, and... Look, I'm not going atheist on you. I *know* God exists. I've seen too much *not* to believe. But that just makes his... his *apathy* that much harder. It'd be a lot easier if there wasn't anyone up there. But he *used* to help me."

Siv started to say something, but she held him off with an upraised hand. "I need some time to think, and I'm sure as sin not going to spend that time in God's house. I'm not going tomorrow. And that's that."

She unwrapped her grunblume from around her hand and stuffed it deep inside her pocket.

Fritz descrambled the chips on the last board, slid it into its socket, and ran a parity check. Green light. Finally. He sealed the compartment's outer hull panel and stood up. His cramped back complained. His aching legs growled at him. His head swam with fatigue.

Still so much to do.

According to his pocket watch, it was a quarter to midnight, though the demons swarming across the barn worked on the cargo ship's restoration with as much energy as they'd had mid-morning. One was welding on the ship's roof. Bright white sparks cascaded down the side of the ship like a waterfall. *Bang! Bang! Bang!* Another pounded metal on the ship's opposite side. At least three of them slathered the special kemosite-rich black paint onto finished sections of the hull.

Well, *he* sure didn't have the same energy level he'd had this morning. He was exhausted. He stifled a yawn and shuffled towards the side of the barn where Krulgoth stood hunched over his workbench.

"Life support system is all green," Fritz said. "We still need to clean the vents and filters, since I'd rather not breathe two-hundred-year-old mold, but other than that, it's done."

"Noted," Krulgoth said.

Fritz frowned at him. No "thank you," no "gratitude," no "yeehaw." If not for the terse response, Fritz would have wondered if he'd even been heard.

In the center of Krulgoth's workbench sat Krulgoth's proc-box – loaded with more chips than Fritz had ever before seen in one device – and an attached screen. Krulgoth kept the proc-box locked whenever he stepped away from the workbench, and he most certainly did *not* allow it to be networked with any other chipware in the barn.

But Fritz didn't recognize the last item on the bench. The rectangular case with pulsating lights and a lid flap. He'd never seen anything like it before, and he'd seen a *lot* of chipware. Like his proc-box, Krulgoth must have restored it with one of the demons' descramblers – the ones they'd forced Fritz to make for them during the time he'd been their prisoner. Krulgoth hunched over to peer through a window on the case's side.

"What's that?" Fritz asked.

"Bioprinter," Krulgoth said.

Fritz blinked. "Wow. I love it. I don't have a clue what that means, but the name alone... Wow." He took three steps across the barn to get a closer look.

Hydraulics pumped, and Krulgoth stood to his full robotic height. He narrowed his electronic eyes.

Fritz took the hint and stopped walking.

Without taking his eyes off Fritz, Krulgoth extended a metal spike from his wrist and placed it into a corresponding socket on his proc-box. The images on its attached screen quickly cut to a padlock icon over a bright red background.

"It uses the same principles behind your planet's teleport pads," Krulgoth said. "Matter-to-energy conversion. The difference is: your teleport pads convert matter to energy, transmit it, then convert that energy back into the same matter it was originally. A bioprinter takes in energy and reshapes it into a pattern of my specification."

Its unfamiliar appearance... the same principles behind *your planet's* teleport pads... "So it wasn't made on Verde?"

Krulgoth stiffened. "No. I took it with me when my brothers and I escaped."

Yeah, that was what Fritz thought. And feared. "It's Celestine chipware. Like your proc-box. Can they track–"

"It was *not* made by the Evil Ones," Krulgoth snapped at him. "The bioprinter was invented by one of my predecessors, S-6, and a small team of Shakren engineers led by E-105. No, the Evil Ones can't track it. And even if they could, what does that do for them? They already know we're here."

Fritz shrugged. "Fair enough."

The lights on the bioprinter dimmed, and Krulgoth opened its lid and retrieved a handful of syringes from inside. Each was full of amber fluid.

"Those were just sparks a few minutes ago?" Fritz asked.

"Yes."

"But they've been transmatted into...?"

"A stimulant for my brothers."

A stimulant? Oh. He assumed the demons would continue to work through the night, same as every night, taking brief naps in shifts. Apparently, thirty minutes was more than enough sleep for them. Yet another benefit of their genetically modified nature. Was that one Krulgoth had given them *after* their escape from the Celestines? Or had that been part of their original nature as Shakren soldiers?

But if Krulgoth was making them stimulants... Had they been sleeping at all?

Fritz dared to take two steps closer. "They OK?" he asked cautiously. Krulgoth himself had been the one to propose this alliance, but that didn't mean he considered it a friendship. And Fritz had found the best way to get him downright testy was to pry into anything he considered a white-demon-internal matter.

"Even we have our physical limits," Krulgoth admitted. He motioned to the demons, and a group of them gathered around. He injected each one in turn and placed the empty syringes in a neat row on his workbench.

"So that bioprinter can make anything?" Fritz asked.

"Yes," Krulgoth said. "Technically."

"Could it make us a new ship?" Fritz said.

"It can make anything capable of physically fitting inside its construction chamber," Krulgoth said. "It could make all the parts for a new ship. But it's not suitable for anything meant to be permanent."

To prove his point, instead of gently laying the next empty syringe on his workbench, he dropped it from just two inches above. It shattered upon landing. He picked up another empty one and showed Fritz how he could actually bend its glass tube just a bit before it also broke into shards.

"It's best suited for anything meant to be rapidly degradable," Krulgoth said. "Like food or medicine."

"Wow. That sure beats farming." Fritz winced a little and looked past the barn's ceiling towards heaven. Sorry, Dad, but it was true. "Is this what the Celestines use to feed the worlds they subjugate?"

"They use it to supplement native food supplies, yes," Krulgoth said. "And to make toxins."

"You mean their biomortic weapons."

Krulgoth nodded. "Bioprinters enable them to manufacture within an hour enough poison to kill an entire native population."

Fritz winced. "Is that... something they do... often?"

Skleght passed by on his way back to the ship after receiving his stimulant. "They're the *Evil* Ones," he said. "What do you think?"

Well. On that pleasant note, Fritz reckoned it was time for bed. The demons could keep working through the night, hyper-stimulated or not, but he needed sleep, and so did Annalie. Speaking of which... where was she? He looked back and forth across the barn, up at the loft, back towards the corner where her workstation was... and found her asleep, slumped over her workbench, resting her head on her arms. She'd accidentally pushed her glasses askew. With every exhale, she blew a strand of her red hair into the air; with every inhale, it landed back on her face.

Fritz grinned and watched her for a long moment. Was this the right time? Hmm. No, his power – his Mantissa hyper-intuition – didn't think so. He had to talk to Felix first, then he'd speak with Annalie. *That's* what felt right.

He gently shook her shoulder. "Annalie?"

She sat up with a start. "What? I'm awake," she said. "Heard everything you said. Just... thinking it over before I respond."

"I only said your name."

Annalie blinked, frowned, then nodded. "I know. That's what I meant. Was just deciding how to respond to you." She sighed, but it became a yawn.

"Come on," he said. "Let's go back to the house."

She stood and found his hand, locking her fingers through his own. He tried to lead her to the barn door, but she stopped and faced the cargo ship.

"It needs a name," she said through another yawn. "Can't keep calling it 'the cargo ship.' It's awkward."

"But it's accurate," Fritz said.

"It's impersonal," Annalie said. "It's gotta have a name."

"Any ideas?" Fritz said.

Annalie rested her cheek in her hand and looked the ship over.

"We could name it after Sebastian," Fritz offered. "Or after my dad. Or your mom or dad. We could give it a name that conveys its mission, like the *Defender*. Or since we'll need to use stealth to reach the Celestines' cathedral ship, we could call it the... the *Sneaky Thing*. Or some other synonym for 'stealth' that I clearly don't know. We could–"

Annalie snapped her fingers. "It's the *Turkey*."

"The..." He scrunched his face at her. "Huh?"

"It's a cargo ship," Annalie said. "Before you send it on its way, you fill it up, yeah? The same way before you eat a turkey, you stuff that sucker full of bread cubes and herbs."

Fritz shrugged. "I never thought of a turkey as the cargo ship of your dining table before. But I can't fault your logic."

She gave the ship a flourish. "The *Turkey* it is!" she said. She pulled him close beside her. And yawned again.

"Good night," he called out to the demons.

86

Those of them that bothered to acknowledge him did so with glares and scowls.

Though still in the regular clothes he'd changed into before dinner, he'd kept his chipsuit's boots on because the right boot's sole was taller than the left's. It compensated for his shorter right leg and kept him from limping up the gravel path from the barn to the house. It was nice not to use his cane across the pasture where Cassie's horse, Mandolin, slept.

"Cassie and Siv are back," Annalie said. "You reckon she's OK?"

Fritz shrugged. "She's sad. Probably angry, too, if I know my sister. She's always in such a rush. Go, go, go. Do, do, do. It's what we fight about the most."

"You and Cassie fight? I thought you were two peas in a pod."

"Once in a while. Not often." He exhaled. "She'll figure something out. She always finds a way."

"Before services tomorrow, maybe I can make her favorite breakfast," Annalie said. "Help cheer her up. What's she like? Flapjacks?"

"Coffee."

"Yeah, but with what? Eggs? Scrambled? Over easy? Guess I never paid much attention to what she eats for breakfast."

"Because she doesn't," Fritz said. "She just drinks coffee. Two cups."

Annalie recoiled away from him. "That's crazy talk."

"I don't disagree. Yet it's true."

"You sure you two are related, honey?" Annalie asked. "Mmm. Honey. Like in graham crackers. You hungry?"

He opened the front door slowly in an attempt to keep quiet, but all that did was stretch out the hinges' squeak from a quick yip to an extended groan. The only light inside came from embers in the fireplace. The main room was empty, and the bedroom doors were closed. Cassie would be on a pallet on the floor of their mom's room. Siv and Duncan were on bedrolls on the floor of Fritz's room. And Annalie shared Cassie's room with Elise and Felix.

Who apparently was not asleep. The door to Cassie's room opened, and Felix – wide awake – poked his head out.

"Hey, Fee," Annalie whispered to him. "It's late. You should go to bed."

He shook his head.

"It's all right," Fritz said. "I'll sit up with him."

"You've barely slept for weeks," Annalie protested, but soft enough that only Fritz could hear her.

Fritz shrugged. "We've been busy, but he needs us, too."

She put her hand on his cheek and smiled. "Gratitude. For giving so much for him." Turning to Felix, she raised the volume on her voice just a notch. "All right, but when Fritz says it's time for bed, it's time for bed."

Felix nodded.

Annalie went into Cassie's room and closed the door behind her.

"What do you want to do?" Fritz asked. He brought his mobile from his pocket and held it up. "We could play a game. Or read a book? Listen to some music? Pfft. What am I saying? Of course we're going to play a game. The only question is *which* game, right?"

Felix brought his hands from behind his back. He held a small battery, two lengths of wire, and a light bulb – a spare health indicator light from the vests and harnesses they wore during their simulations.

"Oh!" Fritz said. "Sparks engineering?"

Felix nodded enthusiastically.

"I approve," Fritz said.

They sat next to each other at the dining table and put the parts between them. "Let's review," Fritz said. "How do sparks like to run?"

Felix drew a circle in the air.

"That's right," Fritz said. "In a circuit. So if we arrange the wires like this" – he connected a single wire between the battery and the light bulb – "will it work?"

Felix shook his head. "No, that's a line, not a circle. We have to do *this*."

Fritz placed the battery and the light apart from one another and connected them with a single wire again, but he used the slack to position the wire in a circular shape. "Now they're in a circle. Will this work?"

Felix shook his head, more forcefully this time, and laughed, too. He *laughed*. Fritz smiled. Even *he* didn't get the kid to laugh very often.

"No, of course it won't," Fritz said. "Sparks need a circuit, not a circle. You show me."

Felix connected a wire to one node on the battery and to the positive node on the light. Then he attached the second wire between the light's negative node and another node on the battery.

"That's a circuit," Fritz agreed. "Want to turn it on?"

Felix shook his head.

"Why not?"

Felix took a small metal peg with wires coming out of either end out of his pocket. "Resistor," he said.

Fritz's mouth dropped open, and not because he was exaggerating surprise for the boy's sake. When had he learned...? "You know about resistors?"

Felix laughed again.

"Maybe I need to call *you* the Sneaky Thing, you little turkey," Fritz said. "Why do we need a resistor here?"

The smile fell off of Felix's face. He grunted and shrugged his shoulders, but Fritz wasn't fooled. Felix could answer the question. He just didn't want to. It would take too many words.

"Does the resistor give the light more power?" Fritz asked.

Felix shook his head.

"No," Fritz said. "Just the opposite, right? Without a resistor, that battery will give too many sparks to that light. Burn it right out."

Felix nodded.

"Can you wire it in?" Fritz asked.

He could. He added it to the circuit, downstream from the battery and before the light, and then flipped a switch on the battery. The indicator light glowed a bright green, but not as brightly as Felix's smile.

And just like that... *click*. The little voice inside Fritz that he recognized as his Mantissa-powered intuition told him it was time.

"This circuit," Fritz said, looking not at Felix but at the battery and the resistor and the light, "it kind of reminds me a little of myself... and your sister. See, if I'm the wire, then in a lot of ways, Annalie is like the sparks. She... powers me. Kind of. It's an imperfect analogy. But what I mean is, she makes me happy. She makes me feel like I could light up the world."

Fritz stole a glance at Felix. He was looking away, but he was definitely listening. "She's done a great job of taking care

90

of you and Elise and your other siblings, too, back north in Mondorf. Bradon, Clark, and Donna."

Felix turned his head slightly back towards Fritz. "Just kidding. I know it's Della. I just wanted to make sure you were still listening to me. Now I'm the Sneaky Thing, aren't I?"

Hiding a smile, Felix looked away.

"I want to always be with Annalie," Fritz said, his hands shaking at hearing the words out loud. "So I was kind of thinking about... asking her. To. You know. To. To marry me."

Felix looked farther away, but Fritz was sure he saw the corner of the boy's mouth turn upward.

"But I'd never do anything to take you away from your Leelee. I want to make sure you know that. If she and I made a new family together, well, I don't feel like it would really be a *new* family. I feel more like I'd be joining yours. But I don't want to do that if it would upset you. Would you be OK with that?"

Felix grunted, frowned, and put his chin on his chest. "I'm sorry," Fritz said. "I know you don't like to be asked your opinion about things." Felix grunted again. "If Annalie married me, she'd still take care of you. That will never change. The only difference is I'd be there to help, too. And I guess I'm trying to say that as much as I want to marry her... Helping take care of you is also something I want. Very much. If... That is if you... Would you... I mean, I really hope you'd be OK with–"

Suddenly, Felix turned to Fritz and hugged his arm. The touch only lasted a second, but it was enough. It was more than enough. It was... Oh. Oh, Fritz couldn't even explain how happy it made him. He wanted to marry Annalie more than anything, but right behind that – even before wanting to

91

restore the world's chipware and defend Verde from the Celestines – he wanted to be there for this quiet, brilliant, and troubled little boy. Felix reminded him so much of himself. Fritz was still trying to find his way in the world without his father around to help him anymore, and Felix had traumatically lost his father at the age of four. He couldn't imagine what it must have been like. Whatever he could do for Felix, he would.

Fritz swallowed, willing himself to say the words aloud, despite the vulnerability they exposed. "I love you, buddy. Thank you."

Felix pulled away, withdrew a small metal box from his pocket, and put it on the table. He glanced at Fritz and smiled.

"You want to wire in a motor?" Fritz's eyes widened excitedly. "What do you have in mind?"

Felix placed two small wooden wheels and an axle on the table.

"You want to make a horseless carriage!" Fritz said. "A toy one. One that moves on its own."

Felix nodded enthusiastically.

"Yes," Fritz said. "A thousand times, yes. That's brilliant. That's the most amazing idea I've ever heard."

The pocket watch attached by a chain to his vest dinged a small bell indicating the top of the hour. Midnight.

"It's late, though," Fritz said. "We should probably go to sleep. If we know what's best for us."

Reluctantly, Felix nodded.

"But I think the pursuit of engineering excellence demands we at least start work on this important project right now," Fritz said. "It *cannot* wait for morning. Am I right?"

Felix smiled and scampered back towards his room to get more supplies.

Chapter Seven

Two Hundred Thirty-Seven Years Ago

Several squads of Shakren peacekeepers conducted training exercises on deck five. Usually a grassland, it had been restructured to resemble the Kiloniks' homeworld. Lush, rolling hills had given way to sharp, rocky gorges and cliffs. The solar lamps mounted in the ceiling four levels above had been both overpowered and set to maximum, baking the stone beneath them in harsh red light. The air shimmered with heat haze.

And the Shakren peacekeepers were losing their practice battle. Again.

Thirty-four... thirty-five... thirty-six...

Simulated Kiloniks eliminated peacekeepers with single punches and kicks. The Kiloniks who carried clubs made of petrified wood took out entire peacekeeper squads with a single swing. Many Shakren tried to attack from a distance, but their laser rifles were useless. The Kiloniks' heat-adverse bodies simply absorbed the shots. At worst, the laser blasts were actually making them stronger. Projectile weapons would be useless against them, too, thanks to their rocky hides.

And the Kiloniks weren't the only threat. Some Shakren were eliminated by bursts of simulated lava and blasts of geyser-propelled steam before they could even join the fight.

Forty-two... forty-three... forty-four...

At the edge of the battlefield, the simulated Kilonik homeworld pressed up against the real *Seraphim*-class vessel's central core. The core resembled a tall building made of smooth, gray steel that seemed to grow out of the rocky ground and disappear into the simulated sky above. Three levels above the terrain, Krulgoth stood at a wide window on deck eight, looking down at the mock massacre, counting the dead.

Forty-eight... forty-nine... fifty...

Those deaths were all simulated, for now. But the slaughter would be real very soon. If it took five hundred dead Shakren to subdue one Kilonik, the Evil Ones would say: so be it. Even hundreds of millions of fallen Shakren could be replaced by a new batch pulled out of the cloning chambers. They were a disposable race, nothing more than cannon fodder in the eyes of the Evil Ones who had created them.

Krulgoth pressed the knuckles of his fist against the glass of the window and dug his fingernails into his palm until he drew black blood. An emotional reaction, but it was extraordinarily difficult for him to remain rational on this subject. The enslavement of the Shakren's bodies was intolerable, but the bondage of their *minds* was abhorrent and unforgivable. An educated Shakren could be ordered to forget his language, and he'd do nothing but babble for the rest of his life. He could be commanded to stop relieving himself, and he'd die when his bladder ruptured. They'd been created to be biological automatons. Krulgoth would not let it stand. *Could not* let it stand.

He stormed back to his proc-box. Pure white light flooded every corner of the lab. All the surfaces gleamed in sterile cleanliness. Though the mock battle continued outside, the soundproofing here was so efficient, all Krulgoth heard was the soft humming and whirring of the centrifuges lined against the wall. Even the ship's engines and gravity generators were inaudible in the lab, perhaps the only such room on the entire ship. Krulgoth and his past colleagues had pleaded their case to the Celestines for a zero-decibel work environment on the grounds that absolute quiet was necessary to facilitate the thought and concentration their work required.

The request had been granted but was made under false pretenses. The quiet was nothing but a security mechanism. The scientists had to be able to immediately hear if one of *them* was coming.

Krulgoth brought a trio of brainwave scans up on his proc-box's screen. On the left was his. In the middle was S-17's, and on the right was S-24's. The scans were taken while the three worked in the lab, and all three were identical. Each of the three scientist Shakren had identical DNA, identical faces, and identical bodies, and the brainwave scans proved they even *thought* the same, even though each of them had different post-breeding-chamber experiences and memories. They were identical in every way but one. The only one that mattered.

The one he still couldn't explain.

With a tap, he switched the screen to a new trio of brain scans. These were from the same subjects, except these were taken when responding to a Celestine's order. S-17's and S-24's were, once again, identical. But Krulgoth's was not. It was radically different than that of his colleagues.

But *why?* Why did his mind function the same as his clone brothers' *except* when responding to the Evil Ones' orders? Why was he capable of disobedience?

S-24 came up behind him, rubbing his chin as he studied the brain scans.

"I thought you were finishing the assignment," Krulgoth said in hushed tones. The three of them never spoke any louder, at least not in the lab.

"All I have to do is pair the new DNA pattern with a Geneditor delivery mechanism," S-24 said. "That's an hour more of work, and we have two days to do it."

"And the alterations will achieve the eight percent agility increase the Evil Ones asked for?"

"*Ten* percent," S-24 said.

Krulgoth nodded appreciatively. Over-delivery kept the Evil Ones happy and away from the lab. A ten percent increase in agility still wouldn't be enough to prevent millions of Shakren from dying on the Kiloniks' homeworld for the sake of the Evil Ones' evangelization, but it would at least produce fewer casualties. A step in the right direction, but not nearly enough.

"What if we're going about this the wrong way?" S-24 asked.

Krulgoth's first impulse was to dismiss the question. What did this newest scientist, only weeks old, know about the right and wrong way to conduct this research? But free thought was precisely why he wanted the Shakren liberated. Maybe S-24 would surprise him. "What do you propose?" he said.

"We keep digging deeper into our DNA, trying to find where ours is different than yours, although it appears identical," S-24 said. "What if we stop searching for differences in the seemingly identical and instead focus on the traits that *are* demonstrably different?"

Krulgoth didn't think any of those differences were the least bit relevant, but he would indulge the line of inquiry. "Very well."

"Let's start with the obvious one," S-24 said. "Your name. You have one. S-17 and I and every other Shakren ever created has only a designation."

"I hardly see how the word with which I am addressed could grant me my ability to disobey," Krulgoth said.

"Nor I," S-24 said. "But why did the Way give it to you in the first place? He's the only one who uses it, correct?"

"Correct," Krulgoth said. "The Life addresses me as S-9. And in the rare times when the Truth addresses people, it's never by their correct designation because she speaks only in lies." He paused, considering S-24's question. "I've never given much thought to why the Way gave me a name. But he has always treated me differently – better – than any other Shakren scientist."

"Hypothesis," S-24 said. "What if he gave it to you because he knew you were different?"

Krulgoth shook his head.

"If they knew Krulgoth can disobey them," S-17 said from the adjacent workstation, looking up from his microscope, "they'd kill him. Immediately. Without hesitation. Their entire empire is dependent upon our forced obedience. They would obliterate even the barest hint of a lack of totality in that control."

"I concur," Krulgoth said.

"And so do I," S-24 said. "I never said they know you can disobey them, just that the Way knows you *are* different in some way. Why else would you be the only Shakren who's ever been given a name? It makes no sense for that to be a coincidence. And coupled with the extra attention you say he's always given you, it becomes more likely."

"Very well," he said. "I accept the likelihood of that hypothesis. But if my name is the proof that the Evil Ones know I am different, yet they are unaware of my ability to disobey, then what do they think makes me different?"

S-24 sighed and shook his head. "I don't know. That's where this line of thought starts to fall apart. But suppose we assume our DNA is truly identical, and there are no hidden differences at the subatomic level. In that case, logic dictates the difference must be something that existed before you were given a name."

"I was given my name almost as soon as I emerged from my birthing chamber," Krulgoth said. "A Shakren from the personnel division was there, of course, but before he could say a word to me, the Way appeared. Though my uniform said 'S-9,' the Way said my name was Krulgoth."

"You were named the moment you were born?" S-24 asked. He blinked. "I didn't realize it had happened so soon. But that significantly narrows our search area. Only two things about you existed before you were born. And since this hypothesis assumes our bodies are physically identical, then what makes you different *must* be in your mind."

"We've checked and rechecked the birthing chamber records," S-17 said, walking over from his workstation to fully join the discussion. "We did that many times before you joined us. *Five* times if memory serves."

"And the records show they were identical?" S-24 said.

S-17 nodded.

"Could they have been altered?" S-24 said.

Krulgoth raised an eyebrow, and S-17's identical face bore a similar expression. *That* was an idea they'd never pursued.

He called up the data on his proc-box. The query returned three results. S-17 and S-24 read the data over his shoulder. "Here are the records of the engrams they implanted in each of our minds," Krulgoth said. "The checksums on the memory files are the same, as we have confirmed many times before. The ship on which we were birthed is the same – this one. All twenty-four scientists ever created have been birthed here on ship one. But our identifiers are different – note here I am listed as S-9, not Krulgoth. The dates our engrams were implanted are, of course, different. Also different is the identifier of the Shakren from the personnel division who implanted the memories."

"Yours were given to you by H-231," S-24 said. "Where is he now? He could tell us if these records are accurate."

"Unless he's been ordered to lie," S-17 said.

Krulgoth had already initiated a query on H-231's whereabouts. "He's no longer on this ship," Krulgoth said. "Seven years ago, he was transferred to ship thirty-three."

"Could we get in touch with him?" S-24 said.

"This is dangerous ground," S-17 warned. "Comm records are logged. They can be traced. And even if they couldn't, H-231 might report strange questions, which would jeopardize everything."

"I concur," Krulgoth said. "We can't risk anyone other than the three of us hearing any of this."

"But the simplest answer is usually the correct one, isn't it?" S-24 said. "Which is the simpler answer: that there's some currently undiscovered attribute of DNA at the subatomic level? And that our ignorance of this attribute makes DNA that is *not* identical appear so to us? Or that the memory implantation records were altered, and the Evil Ones never put the same order to obey them into your mind that they put in ours?"

Krulgoth and S-17 shared a look. This new young scientist was certainly doing as they'd hoped. His fresh set of eyes was spotting at least the *possibility* of new leads, which was far less frustrating than where they'd been before he joined them.

And yet, if the Shakren's forced obedience wasn't biological but merely mental, why weren't more species subject to it?

Why didn't the Evil Ones implant the order to obey them into the mind of every member of every species on every planet they subjugated? Why go through the trouble of cloning an army of millions of Shakren soldiers stationed across the galaxy for enforcement?

There was a hiss of smoke Krulgoth never would have heard if the lab weren't completely silent. The pungent odor of sulfur tickled his nose.

He turned – deactivating his proc-box's screen in the same motion – and lowered himself to one knee, voluntarily. S-17 and S-24 did the same. Involuntarily.

"Luminary," they all said.

Krulgoth hated saying that word. Especially to the Life.

The Truth never visited them. Krulgoth didn't think she cared about their work – the work they were *supposed* to be doing anyway – and that was fine by him.

The Way visited too often, and always with a smile on his ghostly face and compliments on his intangible lips. Whenever the Way was in the room, Krulgoth found his hatred for the Evil Ones lessened, just a little. Temporarily. The Way delighted in reminding them that though there were millions of Shakren peacekeepers across the galaxy, there were only three scientists (*because they'd killed the other twenty-one*), and their work was essential and appreciated.

The Life visited far less often than the Way, but always to bark orders. Every one of his visits was the same. He'd barge in, sneer at the scientists, insult them, order them around, and leave in apparent disgust. Krulgoth knew the drill. Just keep saying, "Yes, Luminary," until he decided to go.

"Get up," the Life said. "The three of you stand together."

But this wasn't normal. Something was wrong. The Life spoke too softly. His expression was too calm. He was usually a torch, singeing everyone he came into contact with, and that was when he was in a *good* mood. When angry, he was a raging bonfire. But at his absolute worst, when he committed his most unspeakable actions, he was ice. A slow, *cold* burn.

The Life's black eyes looked dull. His lips were a straight line. Krulgoth could practically feel the coldness coming off of him.

Had he heard their discussion? Did he know they plotted rebellion?

"The new Geneditor still ain't done," the Life said. "I wanted an eight percent increase in peacekeeper agility, and I still don't have it."

"Luminary," S-24 said, "we have two more days–"

"I never told you to speak!" the Life said.

That was a comment, not an order, but nevertheless, S-24 closed his mouth.

"Yeah, it's two more days until your deadline," the Life said. "I *can* read a calendar, dumbass. But you *could* have been done by now."

"The work is nearly complete, Luminary," Krulgoth said. "If you permit us, we will deliver it by the end of the day."

"It *could* have been done by *now*," the Life repeated. "The Way gave you too much time." The Life smiled. His face actually brightened. "But the Way ain't here, is he?"

Oh, something was very, *very* wrong.

"He and the Truth are on Kilonika, planning out how to beat those rock-skinned freaks into submission," the Life said. "That means I'm in charge. And *I* say your deadline was an hour ago. *I* say you're late. So when the Way and the Truth get back here in three days, they're gonna hear about how our scientists failed us, and about how I had to dish out some... discipline."

He grinned, the whiteness of his teeth contrasting against his gray skin and black eyes. Krulgoth's breaths grew shorter and faster. This situation wasn't just wrong. It was deadly. The Life had come to the lab for one reason.

And that reason was murder.

"S-9," the Life said, "you're the 'senior scientist.'" He snorted. "So it should be you who bears the burden of the punishment here. Ain't that right?"

No! He still had so much to do. He had to free his brothers. He *had* to! They could kill him if they wanted. They could Scourge him, they could rip him apart limb by limb, but *not* before he'd delivered his brothers.

But... but what could he do? His free will was worthless here. The Life had come to kill, and he was willing to trump up whatever reason he needed to justify it. If Krulgoth resisted, what would he gain? Nothing. At worst, S-17 and S-24 would be killed, too.

No, that wasn't the worst that could happen. If he openly resisted the Life's orders, then the secret of his freedom from forced obedience would be revealed. *Nothing* could be worse than that. If the Evil Ones knew he didn't have to obey them, every Shakren alive would be eliminated. They'd kill off and restart the entire species – destroy every current specimen and start again fresh. Why even take the risk of such a defect occurring again?

So be it. Krulgoth stood a little taller, though his vision blurred, and his hands trembled. This wasn't ideal, of course, but S-17 and S-24 would carry on without him. They had all his research. They believed in the cause. He'd hoped to be the one to free his people, but instead, his contribution was to be more minor. Thanks to him, his fellow scientists knew freedom from the Evil Ones was possible. Instead of being the Shakren's liberator, he'd merely be the spark that initiated the freedom that one day *would* come. But he wouldn't live to see it himself.

He was at peace with this.

"Yes," Krulgoth said. "The burden is mine to bear."

"Then go to the bioprinter and get a syringe of the Scourge," the Life said. "The strain designed for Shakren. Maximum potency."

Death by Scourging. Could have been better. Could have been worse – it could have been at a much lower, slower-acting dosage. But he couldn't dwell on it or hesitate. A Shaken forced to obey would retrieve without hesitation the drug that was to be his murder weapon, and that's what he had to appear to be: a Shakren like any other. Forced to obey. The continued safety of his brother scientists depended upon him keeping up the appearance of obedience.

He almost donned protective leather gloves before entering the command into the bioprinter, but why bother? Scourge accidentally spilled on himself and Scourge injected into his veins would have the same result. The bioprinter's construction chamber filled with blinding light then dimmed. He lifted the lid, removed a syringe full of red liquid death, and returned to his brothers, standing beside them one last time.

He recognized the look on their cloned faces. They knew he didn't have to obey, but they also knew he had to pretend that he did. He tried to steel his brothers with a look of his own, a look that said he'd taught them all they needed to know. That he'd inspired them with everything they'd require. Stay strong. Remember his example. *Free our brothers.*

He took a deep breath and brought the needle towards his neck.

"What are you doing?" the Life said. "I never told you to put it into yourself. Inject it into S-24."

Krulgoth froze with the needle just a quarter inch from his exposed skin. Pain exploded throughout his chest, but its cause wasn't physical. It was emotional.

S-24 was going to die. And the Life was going to make *him* inject the lethal dosage.

"Luminary," S-17 said, "though Krulgoth is obeying your order *as I speak*—"

The words snapped Krulgoth back to his senses. No order, no matter how shocking, could cause a Shakren forced to obey to freeze. Krulgoth poked the needle into S-24's neck. "Forgive me," he whispered.

"—we must admit to some confusion," S-17 continued. "We thought you said *Krulgoth* was to bear the burden for—"

"Shut your mouth!" the Life said to S-17. An order.

S-17 closed his mouth.

S-24 trembled and whimpered. Krulgoth pushed down the syringe's plunger. A lethal dose of the Scourge surged into S-24's bloodstream. It took every bit of willpower Krulgoth had to keep his face calm and expressionless even as the drug ripped apart the vein it swam through.

The young scientist screamed and collapsed onto the floor, convulsing. Red welts appeared across his face and hands as if he were being lashed with invisible whips. Blood splattered the inside of his uniform as lash marks ripped open the skin beneath. He clutched at his stomach. Lashes were no doubt already shredding his internal organs. He foamed at the mouth. His hand lashed so badly, two fingers were nearly severed. He shook, gagged, and then went still, a final death rattle slowly rising from his throat.

Krulgoth dropped the empty syringe. It shattered on the floor. S-24 was dead, and *he* had killed him.

The Life took three steps closer and stood nose-to-nose with S-17. "I mis-spoke just now. You don't get to make a sound again. *Ever.* But I will let you open your mouth. Otherwise, I don't know how you're going to cut your own tongue out."

S-17's eyes widened.

The Life grinned. "Do it. *Now.*"

S-17 spun on his heel, opened a drawer in the table behind him, and found a scalpel. Krulgoth raised his hand an inch towards S-17's wrist. S-17 gave Krulgoth a cold stare. *Don't you dare*, it said. *Don't you* dare *expose yourself now and let S-24 die for nothing.*

S-17 seized his tongue and stretched it out of his mouth with such force he tore his lingual frenulum. When he could extract the organ no further, he cut into it with the scalpel. But the muscle was tough, and his blade was small. He had to saw the instrument back and forth. Back and forth. It took time.

It was gruesome torture, but Krulgoth refused to look away. The only way he could support his brother in this horror was to be present with him, so present he would be. S-17 must have been in agony, but he didn't scream. He couldn't – the Life had ordered him to never again make a sound.

An obscene amount of black Shakren blood stained S-17's jaw and white uniform. His lacerated deep lingual artery sprayed its contents towards the Life. The blood passed through the ghost-like Celestine and splashed onto the lab's sterile white floor.

When his severed tongue dropped onto the floor with a *plop*, Krulgoth covered his face. Damn the Life. Damn all three of the Evil Ones. They would pay for this. Oh, how he would make them *pay!*

"See, what's been going on here," the Life said, "is too much yakking. Well, *that* ain't gonna be a problem anymore, is it?" He laughed and guffawed and clutched at his intangible belly.

Before he choked on it, S-17 spat out the blood that gushed into his mouth. Then he spat out a second glob. And a third. His wound was mortal. It would only be a matter of minutes before he bled to death.

"You smart pieces of meat still need to learn your lesson," the Life said. "You think just because you ain't doing drills and workouts like the peacekeepers, you don't have to work as hard as they do. Well, that's *bull!* Just *one* of you could get the work done in *half* the time it's taken three of you. And I'm gonna prove it. S-9, you go get *another* syringe of Scourge!"

S-17 spat out another mouthful of blood. Krulgoth got another dose of death from the bioprinter. It was like he was no longer in his body, and some residual kinetic energy was simply taking him through the motions. He didn't believe there was a God, gods, or goddesses in the universe, but if the Life miraculously ordered him to inject this syringe full of Scourge into himself and not S-17, he'd use his final moments to reconsider his belief system.

"Inject S-17," the Life ordered.

But *of course* there'd be no need for spiritual reflection. Of course this Evil One was going to make him take a second life. There were no gods in the universe, but there were plenty of monsters.

S-17 rolled up his sleeve and presented Krulgoth with his bare arm. Since S-17's face was an exact copy of Krulgoth's own – except for the spewing black blood – it was easy for Krulgoth to read his brother's defiance. *Do it,* S-17 seemed to be thinking. *Do not rebel and reveal your secret, not even for me. Keep up appearances and inject me as you must. But carry on! Resist! And don't* ever *give up on our mission.*

"Goodbye, my friend," Krulgoth whispered. He injected the Scourge into S-17's vein.

The lash marks appeared on S-17's hands and arms almost instantly, first presenting as red welts, then expanding into down-to-the-bone gashes. S-17 made no sound, just as he'd been ordered. The high-potency dose of the Scourge running through his veins made it appear as if invisible hooks were ripping his cheeks and forehead, flaying him alive. He collapsed, convulsed only once, and died.

Krulgoth tossed the second syringe to the floor. It landed near S-17's amputated tongue and shattered. He balled his fists and willed himself not to shake and tremble, for he would *not* give the Life that satisfaction. He closed his eyes so he wouldn't have to see the dead bodies of his friends, but they were still in his memory, where he'd see them again, every moment, forever.

The Life took a step back and tilted his head. "S-9?" he asked quietly. "Why the hell did you just murder your friends?"

Krulgoth wanted to tell him where he could shove it. He longed for a third syringe of the Scourge to inject into himself. It was the only way to end this nightmare. But self-sacrifice would also end his mission. *Their* mission. And if it took every remaining breath Krulgoth had, that mission would only end with freedom from these monsters.

"I was... just doing as I was ordered," Krulgoth said. "Luminary."

How humiliating it was to use the honorific. Someday, somehow, all three of them would *pay*.

"Yeah, but..." The Life grinned. "*You* don't have to obey my orders."

Every drop of Krulgoth's blood seemed to drain out of him. He didn't know whether to scream or vomit.

The Life knew.

The Life *knew?*

"You're the Way's 'special' one," the Life said. "His *pwecious* final experiment to see if he was on the right side of an argument that happened a long time ago." He rolled his eyes. "Pfft. It's his friggin' hang-up is what it is. He's completely incapable of just saying 'Screw you' and walking away. But that ain't none of your concern. You don't have to obey me, S-9. You don't have to obey any of us. You never have."

The syringes on the floor.

The dead bodies of his friends and brothers.

The blood from their Scourge-wounds that stained his uniform and his hands – literally and figuratively. *He* had killed them. To keep up appearances. To protect his secret.

A secret the Life *already knew?*

"Isn't that freaking hilarious?" the Life said. He pointed. He guffawed. "You *chose* to kill your colleagues. Your *friends!* And you chose to do it to protect a secret that *I already knew!*"

As he laughed, the Life stared straight at Krulgoth to hammer home the point that he wasn't laughing at the situation; he was laughing at *him*. At his pain, his torture, his misery.

Krulgoth pressed his hands against the sides of his head. He couldn't hide his agony from the Life anymore, which only added to it. "Why?" he croaked.

The Life's laugh turned into a sneer. "Because the Way has wasted too much time on his deluded experiment. On *you*. He's insane if he thinks you're any different. You're not. You're just like everybody else. *And I just proved it.* When pushed enough, you'll sin. You'll *murder*." He smiled, big and wide. "Hey, how about that? You're a murderer, just like me. That's my real name, you know. The Murderer."

His *real* name? The Way's experiment? Krulgoth didn't know what any of that was supposed to mean. But he was *nothing* like the Life – or the Murderer or whatever that creature called himself. He turned away, but the Life vanished and reappeared right in front of him. "How's it feel to be a cold-blooded killer, S-9? How's it feel to stare at me with all the hate I can see in your eyes, that I can read in your heart, and know that deep down, you and I are exactly the same? The *same!* That when it came down to keeping your secret or killing your friends, you chose to protect your own sorry ass, and screw you, chums. You *chose* to kill them! You *chose* it!"

Fire burned in Krulgoth's brain. The Life thought he was a murderer? If it were possible to kill a ghost, Krulgoth would have accepted that label right then and there.

"All good things gotta come to an end, though," the Life said. "That's what we Celestines do, right? So before the Way and the Truth come back, I'm gonna kill you. But not yet! I want you to sit and stew for a while. For three more days. I want you to *live* with what you did." He waved his hand at the laboratory instruments all around him. "Take that time to finish the Geneditor you were told to make – or don't. I don't give a flying brown turd how many Shakren die on Kilonika. You do whatever the hell you want. But in three days..."

The Life opened his hand. Black smoke from his palm formed into his cudgel.

"In three days, you're gonna die," the Life said. "I can't order you to kill yourself, but I don't want to. I want to exterminate you *personally*. With *great* pleasure, you ridiculous 'experimental' waste of flesh."

He swung his cudgel. Krulgoth cried out and flinched backward, stumbling. He fell on his rear end, landing with a wet *splat* in a puddle of S-17's blood. The Life stood over him. He laughed so hard, his black eyes nearly squinted shut.

"Pathetic," the Life spat. He giggled as he turned away and walked through the wall.

Krulgoth wanted to scream, but his guts were so twisted, no sound could escape his throat. He brought his knees up to his chest and held them tightly, not even bothering to move to a clean spot on the floor. If he had to live with what he'd done for three more days, then it was appropriate punishment that the blood on his hands was literal. He mumbled. He moaned. His sanity shattered under the weight of his grief and despair.

Chapter Eight

On one edge of the Reinhardt property was a field of dirt roughly a hundred fifty feet wide and two hundred feet long. It was surrounded by a wooden rail fence, and a gate sat open in the middle of one short end. Mandolin stood on the grass a distance away from the entrance, and Cassie sat in her saddle and adjusted the wide flat brim of her hat, shielding her eyes from the harshest rays of morning sun.

"Ready, Mandy?" Cassie asked. Mandolin snorted and stomped her left front hoof. Cassie reached down and patted her horse's right shoulder. Then she gave the reins a shake. *"Giddyap!"*

Mandolin bolted into a run. She stomped over the grass and zoomed through the gate into the arena. Her hooves threw dirt in all directions, staining her white legs. Cassie gently steered her to the left. Sixty feet from the gate on the far left side of the arena was a fifty-five-gallon barrel. Mandolin galloped towards it. Cassie didn't need to wear spurs on her boots or kick her mare. All she had to do was make clicking sounds, and Mandolin ran faster.

They passed to the barrel's right and cut a tight left turn around it – as close as they could without knocking it over. Then, they sped across the arena's width towards a second barrel on the other side. When they took a tight right turn around the barrel, Mandolin's hip tapped it, and it teetered. "Stay, stay, stay," Cassie muttered, willing the barrel not to fall. It didn't.

Mandolin's white mane and tail rippled in the breeze. Cassie clicked her tongue faster, encouraging her to keep up her speed to the last barrel. Horse and rider passed on its left side and took a right turn around it so tightly, it brushed up against Cassie's jeans.

All that remained was the home stretch. The gate was directly ahead of them but two hundred feet away on the arena's opposite side.

And Krulgoth was standing next to it. Watching them ride.

What the blazes was *he* doing there?

"Giddyap! Giddyap!" Cassie cried. She clicked her tongue and leaned forward against Mandy's neck. Mandolin charged across the straightaway in an all-out sprint. Sweat glistened on her sides, even in the mid-December chill. Cassie rubbed the side of her neck in time with her gallop.

They only slowed once they emerged through the arena gate and back out into the grass. "Whoa, whoa, whoa," Cassie said, soothing Mandolin with a loving hand on her side. "Good job. Good job."

She turned Mandy around to face the robot demon leader. Reassuringly, her danger sense wasn't reporting any threat. Why should it? Krulgoth and the demons were their allies – right? But it hadn't always been that way. And back when it wasn't, Krulgoth had killed her. The memory was still fresh from having mentioned it to Siv the night before. Even with a danger sense assuring her safety, being alone with Krulgoth made her nervous.

Krulgoth motioned at the arena. "What's that?"

"Barrel racing," she said. "It's a rodeo event."

"Rodeo," Krulgoth said. "Agricultural skills performed for sport?"

"That's about the most boring way you could possibly describe it, but yes."

Krulgoth nodded. "You didn't go to *church* with the others," he said, a rare bit of inflection in his monotone voice betraying his derision for religion. Wonderful. If he was here instead of working in the barn with his brothers just to mock her, he was going to get an arrow through his robotic chest, ally or not.

"Didn't feel like it," Cassie said. Words chosen to be vague but technically truthful so that she didn't lie. Gosh, what a piece of work she was. Still slightly scrupulous, ladies and gentlemen, even when feeling abandoned by God.

She steered Mandy in the direction of the house. Krulgoth accompanied them.

"Your religious beliefs confuse me," Krulgoth said.

"That's because you're an atheist," Cassie said.

"No, it's because you're a scientist," Krulgoth said. "I don't understand how you reconcile the scientific method, based on observation and objectiveness, with belief in an omnipotent and omniscient being who is conveniently invisible and silent."

"I've never seen the two as being incompatible," Cassie said.

Krulgoth side-eyed her from his expressionless metal face. "They're polar opposites."

"Not really," Cassie said. "Science tells me what God's creations are and how they work. Cells, photosynthesis, human gestation – the fascinating atomic-level details of an unbelievably complex world. But my religion tells me *why* they exist. Everything I learn – from either science or religion – gives me a better understanding of the other and of the whole."

"Your scriptures speak of a universe created by magical hands over a few days. Science tells us life evolved in the universe for billions of years. These two versions of reality are incompatible, so much so it pains me to even put the words 'reality' and 'magical hands' in the same thought."

115

"Since you've clearly taken the time to read our scriptures, you know they also say if your hands cause you to sin, you should cut them off. Yet go to any church anywhere, and you'll find people who freely admit they're the worst of sinners *and* who still possess both left and right hands."

"Duncan McCaig does not."

Cassie yanked back on Mandolin's reigns so hard her horse yelped. "Because one of your white demons broke into his home and ripped his arm off. Don't you *dare*."

Krulgoth tilted his head. "My apologies."

That callous son of a... She took a deep breath, then stroked Mandy's mane to apologize for stopping short. Mandolin accepted the apology, and her hooves resumed their soft trail across the grass. Krulgoth's servomotors spun and clicked, and his four heavy steel legs flattened the pasture with every step.

"The point is," she finally continued, "our scriptures are a complex work of history, philosophy, prophecy, and literature. They present a poetic account of the world's creation, one that people with a Stone Age level intellect could understand. Modern science has since enlightened and vastly expanded upon that knowledge. But the scriptural account is still valuable. I learn *facts* from science and *truths* from the scriptures. Only with both can I fully comprehend the world."

"I see. You use the fictions of your faith to fill the gaps in your scientific understanding."

"If you just came out here to mock me, I'm sure you have better things you can be doing."

Krulgoth scanned the area around them with his optic sensors before speaking. "Does your faith bring you... comfort?"

116

Cassie halted Mandolin again, but gently this time. Krulgoth stopped, too, but he wouldn't look at her. "Why do you care?" Cassie said.

He turned towards the barn. They were close enough now that if Cassie squinted, she could see the white demons inside, working on the space ship. "Though I consider your faith to be wholly irrational, I wish I could share it," Krulgoth said. "Sincerely. While remaining a scientist, of course."

"*You* want to believe in God?"

"I want to believe I have done enough to save my brothers." His mechanical red eyes met hers. He turned the volume of his vocal emitters very low. "So please. Tell me the secret. How does a person of science believe in what one cannot see or prove?"

"You're serious about this, aren't you?"

He nodded.

She huffed and shook her head. Why was it always her? When she first met her brother's best friend, she couldn't stand Sivrin McCaig. He was a braggart. He was crude. He laughed louder than anyone at his own jokes. But then he'd admitted, in private, that he was fighting a losing struggle with crippling anxiety, and suddenly, she couldn't *not* help him.

She'd been at school when she'd learned her brother was in a bad place in his head. Hurting himself mentally, emotionally, and physically. She'd ridden straight home over two very long days to be there for him.

And now here stood Krulgoth, the atheist white demon leader who had killed Eroica. And Cassie herself, too, for a short time at least. And he was asking her for help. She really couldn't resist *anyone* in need, could she? No matter their past sins.

"I don't know if I'm the best person for you to talk to about this right now," Cassie said. "But... you gave your brothers their freedom. They're not forced to obey the Celestines anymore. We both know you've made them into strong, efficient killers. Sure, until we get up there" – she pointed towards the sky – "we won't know if they're strong enough to take on the Celestines' entire army, but I'm not sure what else you could do."

"You misunderstand my meaning," Krulgoth said. "I do hope I have done enough to help my brothers survive the fight we will face when we confront the Evil Ones. But more than that, I hope they have been freed from their forced obedience. I... cannot say with absolute certainty that has happened."

Cassie's stomach twisted as if it had been lassoed and hogtied in the middle of her barrel racing arena. "Tell me I just heard you tell a joke for the first time ever."

"I've never identified the exact source of their slavery," Krulgoth admitted. "I hypothesize it's genetic because no other species must obey the Evil Ones the same way Shakren do and because there's no evidence any kind of mind-controlling technology is involved. But I have never proved my hypothesis."

"They might still be forced to obey?" Cassie said. "If you don't know for sure, then you don't even know if it's *possible* to break the Celestines' control over your race!"

"It *is* possible," Krulgoth said. "I *never* had to obey them."

Cassie blinked. "Well. Yet *another* important tidbit you never bothered to share with us before. You can touch them, kill them, *and* disobey them? What makes you so special?"

"That is the question I've spent my entire life trying to answer. My original Shakren DNA was seemingly identical to

118

that of other Shakren scientists, but there must have been some difference. Something I'm simply too ignorant to see. Therefore, since I didn't know exactly what to change, I changed my brothers every way I could. I made them stronger, faster, more capable of self-defense. I made them very much *not* Shakren."

He eyed Cassie. "I mapped your species genome when I first arrived here. I could give my brothers all their own Mantissa powers right now. You know I could."

Oh, she knew. The biological Krulgoth Siv had killed – the one who had killed her – possessed *every* Mantissa power.

"But doing so would require changing two DNA pairs back to matching Shakren DNA," Krulgoth said. He shook his head. "I cannot risk that change with the Evil Ones on their way here."

"In case one of those pairs is the one that controls their genetic obedience?" Cassie said. She shrugged. "Why not just change everything in their genetic code? Leave nothing as it was. Rewrite the whole thing?"

He gave her a patronizing look as if pitying her ignorance. "Many species share the bulk of their genetic code in common with other seemingly disparate species. While the transformation from Shakren to Shakrath was certainly dramatic, it required me to edit less than twenty percent of their DNA. Editing every base pair just for the sake of change could have rendered them brainless or turned them into bacteria."

Cassie resisted the urge to kick him in his steel teeth. She didn't need another reminder of her lack of formal medical education. "The whole reason we agreed to an alliance is because you could provide an army," Cassie said, her cheeks flushing red, her breath coming short. She struggled to keep her voice down, and she didn't entirely succeed. "We provide the chipware and the Mantissa powers. You provide the old, beat-up ship and an army big enough to get us past the Shakren and face-to-face with the Celestines. Then we all take our chances together. But if your brothers still have to obey, then we *don't have an army,* Krulgoth!"

"I am aware of this."

"How are we supposed to have *any* chance at stopping the Celestine invasion before it happens without an army?" she demanded.

"That's what I'm asking you," he said, and when he spoke again, it was in *her* voice. "But none of that can happen if we all die on some alien spaceship or if these Celestines conquer Verde. Right? But I *know* everything in my plan is going to happen because God was my inspiration. He made me a Mantissa healer, and he answered my prayers and helped me figure out exactly what to do with that gift. God wouldn't inspire me with dreams he won't let me fulfill. So you see? It's simple logic. We can't lose!"

Krulgoth returned to his own voice. "I would like to understand how a scientist can put that much confidence in an unobservable God," he said. And he wasn't just jerking her chain. He meant it.

Cassie closed her eyes and bit back a profanity. Had she really only said those words yesterday afternoon? It felt like a lifetime ago. Now here was Krulgoth – atheist *Krulgoth,* of all people – wanting to know the secret to having faith. Faith she didn't even know if she had anymore. How was she supposed to answer him? Right now, she wasn't sure God was doing a thing to help her with her plan, let alone that he would get her through the invasion of these galactic tyrants alive. Why did *she* end up having to be the one to give the robot monster a pep talk?

Still unsure what words were going to spill out, she opened her mouth and started talking. "Once upon a time, you attacked one of the Celestines. And I presume you attacked him– It was a him, right?"

"Yes," Krulgoth said. "The Life."

Cassie raised an eyebrow. "The Life?"

"That was his name. The Evil Ones' call themselves the Way, the Truth, and the Life. I killed the Life."

Curious. The prophets who wrote the scriptures described God as the way, the truth, and the life.

She shook her head to refocus. "You attacked him because of the many times you'd witnessed someone kill one of these Celestines, right? You knew exactly what had to be done and how to do it? No – of course not. No one else has ever even touched one of them."

"To be fair, I have very little memory of killing the Life," Krulgoth said. "At the time, I was mad with grief. Irrational. Temporarily insane, to be honest. Most of my memories of what happened come from the vid of the killing."

"But still," Cassie said, "you had no objective evidence whatsoever that you'd be able to kill that Celestine, yet you attacked him anyway, regardless of whether or not you were rational at the time. My point is: you already have a history of doing things science says are unproven. And that wasn't the only time. Don't forget you cheated death and turned yourself into a robot" – she grinned – "after my betrothed chopped your head off."

That struck a nerve. Krulgoth spun on her and growled. Mandolin, who didn't have a danger sense to tell her she was safe, took a step backward.

"Hey, you made that crack about Duncan's arm," she said. "Now we're even."

He grumbled but let it go.

"You don't have any way to test whether or not you've freed your brothers," Cassie said. "So what? Just believe that you have. Trust in yourself. Confidence because of how often you've succeeded in the past isn't blind faith. It's scientific observation."

"Technically, it's mathematics," Krulgoth said. "It's probability." The gears and motors visible inside his unfinished body clicked and whirred. He stretched a little longer, lowered himself an inch closer to the ground as if he were relaxing. "But I appreciate the sentiment. And it does present your advice in a way I find palatable."

That was the closest he was ever going to come to offering gratitude. Cassie nodded in acknowledgment, but she wasn't nearly ready to hold hands and sing hymns with him. "You know I can't keep this quiet," she huffed. "That your brothers' freedom is uncertain. If the white demons aren't free, it changes everything our alliance was built upon. I have to tell my brother, Siv, and Annalie."

And Sierra would find out, too. She'd been complaining during every simulation that they were in big trouble if the demons were still subject to their forced obedience. By the stars, Cassie didn't know what was worse: not having an army to help them or even the *chance* that crank was right.

Both were insignificant next to the growing feeling that God really had abandoned her.

122

"I assumed you would," Krulgoth said. "But, I do ask that you not share the truth with my brothers and destroy their hope."

"They don't already know?"

"They do not."

Cassie *tsk*ed. "Aren't you afraid of what they'll do to you if they find out you've hidden this from them? No – you've done more than hide it. You've *lied* about it. At the end of every one of our simulations, you remind them that they're no longer Shakren and that they're no longer forced to obey."

"Indeed," Krulgoth said. "I've promised them for centuries that they're free. If they find out I'm uncertain of that, they'll kill me, whether I'm their revered 'general' or not."

Cassie's eyes widened incredulously.

"But if we succeed in defeating the Evil Ones..." Krulgoth said.

It took a moment for Cassie to understand. "Then your deception becomes a moot point," she said. "And if we *fail* to stop the Celestines–"

"Then we all die. So it doesn't matter if I'm killed by the Evil Ones or by one of my brothers, does it?" He tilted his head. "That's why I suggest you abide my request and join me in keeping this secret. You and the other Mantissa Reborn face the exact same dilemma."

"Is that a threat?" Cassie demanded.

"It's logic," Krulgoth said. "Like me, your only hope is that I *have* broken the bonds of my brothers' slavery, whether I – or now *we* – lie about its certainty or not."

He nodded and made off towards the barn. He was practically skipping. Cassie was glad at least *someone* around here felt better, but it sure wasn't her. Krulgoth spoke of hope, yet Cassie felt like there was a distinct lack of hope in her world, with more dark clouds gathering on the horizon. Forget figuring out how to get her life plan back on the rails. If the white demons were still genetically bound to obey their creators, her biggest concern was suddenly basic survival.

She looked up to the sky. "Anytime you're ready to show up and help us out down here, we'd be much obliged."

Chapter Nine

Rebel pulled the family carriage off the road and into the pasture. Cassie checked the clock on the kitchen wall – a chipware model Fritz had given their folks. It was a little after one in the afternoon. If services had started at nine, then factoring in time for Sunday school, coffee and pastries and fellowship, and the trip back, worship must have lasted about an hour and a half. Wow. Pastor Kolbe must have gotten a lot of "Amen"s during his sermon. The village was sure warming up to the new guy.

With swift strokes of her pocket knife, Cassie sliced the skin off of a potato, then another, then another. In the time she peeled three, even the most experienced chuckwagon cookie would have peeled only one. It wasn't that she was particularly skilled with a blade. It was that her danger sense would warn her of an impending laceration if she accidentally put a finger in harm's way. It was a saloon trick, nothing more, but at least it was *something* God still allowed her to do with her power.

The children's rapid-fire footfalls pounded across the porch steps first, then the front door flew open, and Felix ran inside the house, grinning widely. His sister Elise came charging in behind him. "Hey, Doctor Cassie," she managed to say between whoops of laughter.

"How were the doughnuts?" Cassie called after them as they ran towards their bedroom – well, *her* bedroom that she was loaning Annalie and her siblings.

"Chocolate!" Elise hollered back before she slammed the bedroom door behind them.

Siv was next through the door. "Hey, darlin'." He put an arm around her shoulders and a kiss on her cheek. "How you be?"

Cassie shrugged. Her mother stepped inside.

"Hi, Mom," Cassie said.

Ruth flashed a forced smile, the first sign of the disapproval Cassie knew was coming her way for skipping church, then retreated to her bedroom to change, closing the door *hard* behind her.

"And here we go," Cassie said in an undertone.

Siv furrowed his brow. "She seemed fine all morning."

"That's because all morning she was with folks who *didn't* skip church," Cassie said.

"I was gonna go help Daddy in the barn with some of the hull work," Siv said. "But I can stay in here if you need me...?"

"It's OK," Cassie said. "It'll be fine."

"It's no fuss if I stay–"

"For goodness sake, she's not a white demon or a Steelterror," Cassie said. "She's my mom."

"All right, I'll let it ride." He winked at her. "But if you need me...?"

She rolled her eyes. "If she comes out of that room with a shotgun, I will scream bloody murder for you, Sir Blacksmith. Deal?"

He barked out a loud laugh, kissed her again, and walked out of the house.

Cassie's bedroom door swung open, and Elise – now dressed in jeans and a flannel shirt instead of her church dress – charged into the kitchen and held up the first aid book Cassie had given her. "Quiz me," she demanded. She set the book on the table and rubbed her hands together in anticipation.

126

Ruth emerged from her bedroom, marched into the kitchen, put on an apron, and got to work making dinner without giving Cassie the slightest glance.

"All right," Cassie said to Elise. "But I'm going to make it tough."

About as tough as her mother was making things on her.

Elise nodded.

"Before administering first aid, what do you do?" Cassie said.

"Look around," Elise said. "Is the area safe? Figure out what happened. How many people are involved? Who needs help the most? Is anyone else able to help?"

"Very good," Cassie said.

"Tell the patient your name, what you think is wrong with them, and what treatment you'd like to provide – if they're awake, of course," Elise said. "Make sure they're breathing. Ask someone else nearby to get help. Point at them. Look them in the eye. Make sure they know they're the one you're pointing to."

She pointed at a pretend bystander near the fireplace. "You! Go get help!"

"That's great, kiddo!" Cassie said. "I'm very impressed."

Elise wasn't finished.

"If there are no obvious signs of injury, you can roll the person onto their side," Elise continued. "That's a recovery position. But *only* if there are no signs of injury."

"Oh my gosh," Cassie said, pulling the girl into a hug. She couldn't believe how much the girl had taught herself just from a book. Also, a hug might be the only way to get her to stop. "I'm very proud of you. Keep reading. Keep learning."

"I almost forgot," Elise said. She pulled away from the hug and closed her eyes as if reading from her memory. "The very

127

first step of successful first aid is to pray for the patient. And if all else fails, the last step is also to pray for the patient."

Cassie forced a smile. "It says that in there?"

"Yep," Elise said. "Not in the text itself, but it was penciled into the margins. Which I think means it's extra important."

Cassie had scrawled those words after hearing an inspiring sermon a long time ago.

"Can I be a doctor like you?" Elise said.

The question hit Cassie like a slap in the face, but it wasn't Elise's fault. The girl had no idea what she was going through. Cassie rested her chin on Elise's head and closed her eyes. "I think you're going to be whatever you want to be," Cassie said.

Elise pulled away and flashed her a huge smile. "I'm gonna go outside and play with Felix."

Felix was outside? When had that happened? That kid was so silent, it was hard for Cassie to keep track of him. Elise tossed the first aid book on the table, sprinted across the room, and darted outside where, sure enough, Felix was waiting for her out on the porch.

Which left Cassie alone with her mother. Ruth slammed handfuls of ground beef together into the shape of a meatloaf.

"How was worship?" Cassie asked.

Ruth didn't say anything. Maybe talking about the source of her anger wasn't the best place to start a conversation.

The front door was open, and through the screen, Cassie watched Elise and Felix chase each other around the pasture. "Elise is a really smart kid," Cassie said. "Annalie's done an amazing job raising her and her other siblings. Elise was only seven when the white demons killed her folks. Felix was four."

Her mother knew that already. Why was she trying to make small talk? This was pointless. She was just killing time, dancing around the issue. She'd been wrong a moment earlier. Talking about the source of her anger wasn't just the best place to start; it was the only place to start.

"I'm not going pagan on you, Mom," Cassie said. "I just needed some time."

Ruth washed the meat off her hands then grabbed a jar of tomato paste off the shelf.

Fine. Maybe Cassie could shock her into talking.

"Siv and I ended up in the village last night just in time to see Gunter Asheford take a bullet to his head."

Her mom didn't even pause from spreading the tomato paste on top of the meatloaf.

"Yeah. He bled all over me. Bullet wound right in the middle of his forehead. And I tried to help him. Couldn't do anything, though. Just like with Eroica. And Harlan. And Sebastian. And dad." She seized the knife she'd used earlier for cutting potatoes and held it over the palm of her other hand. "I could chop a finger off cutting potatoes and grow it right back. But apparently, I can't use this stupid power to help other people."

She slammed the knife down onto the counter. Ruth picked it up without missing a beat and used it to chop an onion.

Cassie didn't know whether she wanted to scream or cry. "I didn't skip church just to torque you off, Mom. I did it because it didn't make sense. Nothing makes sense right now. The white demons who killed those kids' parents are out in our barn restoring a space ship with Fritz. The crank spirit of the planet who drove Fritz to depression and nearly killed him *three times* is here because she's suddenly his friend now. I get a letter saying the university is just *gone*, and I can't even go up there and find out first-hand what's going on. Why? Because a pair of dang ghosts and their army are on their way here, and

God made me a Mantissa. Pfft. *I* sure as sin never asked for that. Did you? Did you pray that God would make your babies into the people who are supposed to protect this stupid planet? No. That's a legacy *he* handed me. So get out there and save the world, Cassie, but oh, you'd like to save your *father?* No, *that's* too much to ask. Forget that. Forget you."

Ruth arranged pieces of chopped onion in a line down the center of the meatloaf.

"I didn't go to church because I'm *hurting,* Mom," Cassie said. "My heart hurts so bad, I'd rip it out if I could. God used to be my only solace against this kind of pain, but he's not doing anything for me. Not anymore. It's like he's not even there."

Her mom turned around and slid the meatloaf into the oven. It was like she was listening to soft string music instead of her only daughter confessing her emotional torment.

"I guess he's not the only apathetic one around here, is he?" Cassie said. She stormed across the kitchen towards the door, threw open the screen–

"Cassandra," Ruth said.

Cassie spun on her heel as if her mother were an attacking Shakren soldier. "*Now* you talk to me?" Cassie said, wiping an arm across her eyes. "Is this a game to you? See how long it takes to make me cry?"

"The last thing I want to do is hurt you," Ruth said. "Especially when you're already in such pain. Which I knew all about before you said anything. Because I'm your mother."

She beckoned Cassie to come closer. Cassie moved two steps back into the kitchen.

"Then why give me the silent treatment?" Cassie said. "That's *very* mature."

"My point exactly," Ruth said. "I raised you better."

"What are you talking about?" Cassie said. "What did I do?"

"You're giving the silent treatment."

"To whom?"

"To God," Ruth said.

Oh.

Now that she thought about it, that kind of was what she was doing.

"I didn't mean to upset you further," Ruth said. "I just thought you might need some convincing. You *can* be a little stubborn sometimes. I know because you get it from me."

"You're not mad I skipped worship?"

"I know how much you miss your father," she said. "God knows *I* wish you could have saved him, too. I know how important medical school is to you. You're hurting, and you're my daughter, so no, I'm not mad." She put down her knife and brought a hand to her face. Her voice cracked. "I'm downright woebegone you have to go through all this."

Cassie embraced her. She almost instinctively said *It will be OK*. But that was kind of the problem. She didn't know that anymore.

"We work out our problems through conversations, and it takes two to have one," Ruth said. "Now you have a lot of questions and a lot of disappointment. I wish I could give you what you need, but I can't. And you'll never get any answers or comfort if you shut out the only person who can."

It was quiet in Hondo. The street was empty except for a stray cat searching for a warm spot in the fading sun. No fiddle or piano music drifted out of the saloon. Even the breeze must have felt lonely. Folks were no doubt still reeling over Gunter's murder and probably weren't up for socializing.

Cassie turned Mandolin onto the cobblestone path leading off Main Street and up to the little stone church nestled behind it. She dismounted at a row of hitching posts, but she left Mandy untied and allowed to wander free. She wouldn't run. She filled a trough with water from the church's well and stroked Mandy's back as she took an eager drink.

Adjacent to the church was a small cemetery. Weaving between headstones, Cassie took a meandering path past everyone she wanted to visit, pausing long enough to make the Sign of God's Hand over the graves of Grandma and Grandpa Reinhardt, Meemaw and Opa Winkler, Eroica, and Bernice. Finally, she came to her father's resting place. Before his headstone, the ground was still covered with bare dirt and dormant grass that wouldn't bloom until spring.

It used to be that she'd run off and find a tree to climb into anytime she and her mother had a big enough argument. Eventually, her father – bearing a bag of popcorn – would find her, and they'd sit and eat their snack in silence. Once Cassie was ready, they'd go back to the house.

"I should have brought popcorn," she told her dad. "But then that was always your job."

A wave of grief hit her hard. She bit her lip and breathed through her nose until it passed.

"Mom's right," Cassie said. "If I have a problem with the Lord, I need to take it right to him. It sure feels like he's saying 'no' right now, but I need to remember that's *not* one of the Three Answers. He and I will work this out together. We always have. But I'm still going to be a doctor, Dad. I *will* find a way."

A weight seemed to lift off her chest. She kissed her fingers, touched her dad's headstone, and walked into the church.

There were no services this time of day, so the building was empty and silent inside. Her footsteps echoed. The only light came from the sanctuary candle behind the altar and the pale sunlight poking through the stained glass windows. Each of those windows depicted a scene of God's hand – enormous and glowing with ethereal holiness – interceding in the world. There was God's loving hand embracing a sorrowful woman. God's illuminating hand placing the sun in the sky above Verde. God's blessing hand offering a benediction over the saints. God's wrathful hand casting the devils out of heaven. God's creating hand granting life to the first people – the event they were about to celebrate on Lenerstelen day.

Cassie tried to think positively. Maybe God would come through for her so brilliantly that someday there'd be a new window in the church depicting God's guiding hand. Leading her to her dream of being a doctor, even without the university. It would certainly take a window-worthy miracle at this point.

She walked up the center aisle just as she had every Sunday since forever. Her grunblume was wrapped around her left hand. She'd thoroughly cleaned Gunter's blood from the beads, but his murder still had a presence of memory on them. She squeezed them and made the Sign of God's Hand for Gunter's immortal soul.

Having reached her family's usual place, she turned into the pew but stopped short when she noticed the candle above the confessional was lit. Pastor Kolbe was here this late in the evening? And hearing confessions? That was a pleasant surprise. She thought he only did that on Saturday afternoons and by appointment.

Well, she'd come to apologize. Might as well do it right.

She walked towards the confessional. Her favorite of all the church's windows was the one above it – the one depicting God's healing hand mending a man's broken arm. Its placement was deliberate; physical healing was meant to symbolize the spiritual healing of the confessional. She didn't take her eyes off of it, despite the longing it stirred within her.

God was still there – here – listening to her. Helping her always. She didn't know how it was going to work out this time, but it would.

So why did it still feel like she was trying to convince herself?

The penitent side of the confessional was no larger than a closet. Cassie stepped inside, closed the door behind her, and knelt before the square of grating on the wall. The screen protected her anonymity from Pastor Kolbe, who sat in the cramped compartment next door. All she could see of him through the wooden lattice were his hands resting on his knees. The fading sunlight filtered through the stained glass windows had an odd effect, making his hands appear gray.

"Firm in the grasp of God's loving hand, we confess our sins in honesty and humility," he said, and Cassie nearly gasped. It wasn't Pastor Kolbe. Whoever it was, his voice was soft and pleasant. It sounded like a song. Cassie almost asked him to repeat himself just so she could hear it again.

Cassie startled, realizing the pastor was waiting for her. "Sorry. I was expecting Pastor Kolbe." She made the Sign of God's Hand. "May God's judging hand be merciful."

"Pastor Kolbe is supping with Gunter Asheford's family this evening," the pastor said. "I'm tending the church for him."

"Ahh," Cassie said. "Well. It's been a little under two months since my last confession. I've said a cuss word or two since then. I've had some uncharitable thoughts towards" – *Sierra* – "someone I've been working with lately. I've let myself get caught up in" – *preparing for an alien invasion* – "my work and have sometimes led a slothful prayer life. But what I'm really here to talk about is that I missed services this morning. Deliberately. Knowing it was a sin."

"Hmm," the pastor said.

"It's just..." She grunted out a short laugh. "How much time do you have, pastor?"

"Speak from your heart," the pastor said. That *voice!* That soothing voice. Where was this pastor from? Cassie didn't recognize his accent.

"Since I was very young, I've wanted to be a doctor," she said. "Not for the money, and surely not for the long hours. I just want to ease suffering. There's so much of it in the world. Sickness happens. Accidents happen. Sin happens." She squeezed the grumblume wrapped around her left hand and remembered Gunter tumbling backward off the saloon's steps with a bullet in his head. "I just want some healing to happen, too. And I want to be a part of that."

"That's admirable," the pastor said.

"About six years ago, I didn't see any way to get the medical education I needed, which made me angry with God. Like he'd inspired me with this noble dream but that he had no intention of helping me obtain it."

"Yes," the pastor said softly.

"I talked to the former pastor here, and he told me something I've always remembered. He said our infinite, all-powerful God has just three answers to every single prayer he receives: yes, yes but not right now, and I have something better planned."

135

Cassie paused for another audible sign from the pastor that he'd heard her, but he remained silent.

"I believed that," Cassie said. "And something better did happen. My dad found a way to send me to the university. But I just learned the university is closing. It suffered too much damage" – *from Sierra and her Steelterrors* – "in those attacks. And when I heard that news, and then when Gunter Asheford died last night, it all just took me back to how I felt six years ago. But worse. I felt like God inspired me, started helping me work towards my dream, and then just stopped. And it... well, it felt malicious. Letting me indulge my dream for four years of pre-med and a semester of med school before dropping the floor out from under me."

She took a deep breath. "The thing is, Pastor, if I'm honest with myself, I wasn't just angry this morning. I was hurt. I'm not asking for wealth or power or carnal pleasures. I'm not wishing anyone dead. I'm wishing people *alive*. I want to help. I want to *heal!* And not just one person or a hundred. I want to heal everyone. I want to cure diseases that take people from their families too soon."

She thought of Siv's mother, who died of cancer long before Cassie could ever meet her.

"I just want to make the world a better place," she said. "And a *really* bad night made me feel like God wasn't going to help me anymore. So I skipped services this morning. I knew it was wrong. My anger with God gave me *more* reason to be here, to talk with him in his house. But I didn't. So I'm sorry. And... and I guess that's all I have to say."

She rested her forehead against the wall above the grating and closed her eyes. She breathed like she'd been freed from a set of too-tight restraints. In a few moments, the pastor would raise his hand in representation of God's all-merciful hand and say the words of absolution. Cassie knew she'd feel a practically physical weight lift from her shoulders. She always did after reconciling with God.

She was still hurt. She was still angry. She still had questions she demanded to have answered. But having cleared the air, she and God would be able to move on together.

The pastor cleared his throat. "Ma'am, did you have any sins to confess?"

Cassie frowned. Had he not been listening? It seemed like he had. The pastor moved his hands to the arms of his chair, and in the dim light, his hands seemed to pass right through them.

"I skipped Sunday services," Cassie reminded him.

Through the grating, Cassie saw him give a dismissive wave. "I know what it's like to dream of a better world," the pastor said. "I had such a dream once. Like you, I took it before God in humility. He's omnipotent, so he already knew all about it. But I went before him anyway to declare I was his servant, answering his call. I expected approval and praise in return."

"Right," Cassie said. She knew how that felt.

"He rejected me," the pastor said, his voice dropping to a sour note. "He called my dream flawed. Disordered. Immoral. It seems you have suffered a similar rejection. And faced with such disappointment and agony, you spent one morning away from God." He chuckled. "Young lady, if you have anything to apologize for, it's for coming here and groveling before God, apologizing to *him* for the pain *he* has caused you."

Cassie was so shocked, it took her several heartbeats before she could speak. "But... But God didn't *cause* the barriers blocking me from my dream."

"Look at the windows all around this church," the pastor said. "They're full of God's hand reaching down from heaven into your world. He can part the seas – or flood the planet with them. He can inflict deadly plagues. He can *resurrect the dead.* It doesn't matter whether or not God caused the barriers blocking your dream. What matters is that he *can* remove them. Surely the God who can perform the miracles depicted on those windows can reach down and rebuild a university. Surely he can stop a bullet before it rips a man's brain apart. Surely he can do whatever it takes to ensure his obedient servant spends her life healing his people, yes?"

"Yes," Cassie whispered.

"Of course he can," the pastor said. "But he *won't.* Your dream of being a healer is noble. It has the smell of God all over it. I'm certain he inspired it. But you are right to be hurt, and you are right to be angry. He *cannot* inspire you with such a dream and then, when you ask for help in fulfilling it, tell you, 'No.'"

Wait, wait – "no" was *not* one of the Three Answers.

"Maybe he's saying 'yes, but not right now,'" Cassie offered, and even she could hear the desperation in her voice. "Maybe he's saying he has something better planned."

"Young lady, do not delude yourself," the pastor said. "God has *abandoned* you."

Cassie reeled as if she'd been physically punched.

"You are the victim of a tease in which you were inspired with goodness, then actively opposed in your pursuit of it. It's not right. It's vicious. It's cruel."

He was saying everything she'd felt when she was at her angriest and most distraught, and they were blasphemous thoughts. That's why she'd come to confession. But this pastor was speaking them aloud, validating them, inside the house of God. She couldn't believe what she was hearing.

"But before God did you this injustice, he first inspired you," he said. "And what makes you special is that despite the pain you've endured, you will not abandon that inspiration. Will you? You won't let go of that dream. Despite the active opposition of your creator, *you* will not abandon *God*."

Outside at her father's grave, she'd vowed to find a way. She'd meant that she and God would find that new way together, but if he genuinely wasn't going to help her...

"No," Cassie whispered, "I won't abandon my dream."

"Then I have no stones to throw," he said. "You are without sin."

She'd never heard anyone, let alone a pastor, speak of God in such ways. His words were shocking, but his voice was like a song – minor chords and staccato notes when he spoke of her pain, beautiful melody when he talked of how she could still pursue her dream. Her stomach rolled as if she'd smelled rotten eggs.

"I'm not sure I understand," Cassie said. "I came here to make right with God. But you're a pastor. And you're telling me–"

"I'm telling you not to bother," the pastor said. "Don't waste time waiting for help that will never come. Accept his initial inspiration, but pursue your dream without him."

She swallowed. "Alone."

"Oh no," the pastor said, his voice swelling with tenderness. "God may have abandoned you, but you will *not* be alone for long. You must follow the way. And I promise that very soon, it will reveal itself to you."

Chapter Ten

As the aerocopter slowly descended towards the mountain peak, Fritz rose from his seat and looked out the copter's side window. Ten inches of cold, white powder covered the mountain, but the late afternoon sky was clear, and no new snow was falling. The glare was terrible, though. At least once they landed and went outside, he could lower the faceplate of his helmet and let his chipsuit's polarized lenses block most of the annoying way-too-bright light. Gah, it was blinding.

Annalie gently put the copter down. She flipped switches and turned down dials, and the sound of the rotor blades above them gradually slowed to nothing. The distinctive mound of snow fifty yards downhill from where they'd landed made a lump form in Fritz's throat. He swallowed it down as Annalie came beside him and took his chipsuit-covered hand in her mitten-covered one.

"You OK, cupcake?" she asked.

He nodded.

"You sure? We could go somewhere else..."

"We need more kemosite," Fritz said. "And I know from personal experience this peak is loaded with it." He sighed and never took his eyes off the snow that marked a Verdant Warden's resting place. "I should have come back and fixed him before now."

"Good golly, do you love to beat yourself up," Annalie mumbled. She squeezed his hand. "You've been a little busy."

Fritz shrugged his shoulders. "I suppose."

Annalie put on a knit hat and a long scarf. Fritz closed his helmet and encased himself in the warmth of his chipsuit. They slid open the copter's door, and a blast of cold air welcomed them to the Lavare Mountains. Annalie wrapped her arms around Fritz's neck and kissed the cheek of his helmet. Then a quick blast from his chipsuit's boosters propelled the two of them down the slope to where Samson lay buried and asleep.

Fritz made two more trips to the ship and back to unload their shovels and a stack of three empty containers for their cargo. Once all the gear had been unloaded, he found a wide swath of land ten steps away from the snow mound, pointed his right arm at it, and popped out one of his laser cannons. Reducing the weapon to its lowest power and most sweeping beam, he fired a steady stream at the ground. Within thirty seconds, enough snow had melted away to expose a circle of uncovered land four-feet in diameter. Annalie gave him one of the shovels. He scooped exposed dirt out of the ground and into one of the containers.

"I keep meaning to ask," Annalie said. "Why does the kemosite in this dirt make our mobiles not work?"

Fritz shrugged. "Sierra could probably explain it in better detail, but something in its mineral content disrupts the haupian waves our mobiles use."

"No incoming calls, no outgoing calls," Annalie said. She glanced at the mound of snow behind her. She hadn't yet started digging. "And we're sure the Celestines use haupian waves in their ships' sensors?"

Fritz shrugged again, then loaded his shovel with another pile of dirt. "Krulgoth's sure. They don't call them haupian waves, of course, and they use different frequencies than our mobiles do, but physics is physics."

Annalie shook her head. "Just hard to wrap my head around the idea that we can mix some mineral into black paint, cover our ship with it, and *poof*. We're invisible enough to slip right past the entire Celestine fleet. It's odd to have such a low-tech solution to a high-tech problem. Pretty dang daisy, though."

"Invisible is an imprecise word," Fritz said. "Painted black and against the blackness of the void, the ship will be practically invisible to the naked eye. Though if we get between the fleet and one of the moons, or any other bright object, we'll be very much visible. And the swarm of ships they send our way will prove it."

"And we'll be double-blind to sensors," Annalie said. "No signals will detect us, but neither will our signals be able to get out." She again glanced back at the mound of snow and rested her hands on the top of her shovel. "Fair price to pay to sneak past the Celestine fleet, I suppose."

Fritz raised his faceplate and frowned. "I don't want to sound rude, but am I doing *all* the digging here?"

Annalie bit her lip and cocked her thumb over her shoulder. "Is it OK if I... take a look at him?"

Fritz stopped shoveling and looked down. He wouldn't be alive today if not for the man of metal buried underneath that mound.

"Can *we* look at him?" Annalie said. "Together?"

Fritz shrugged. "We don't have much time..."

"We can spare five minutes," Annalie said.

She took his hand, and together they walked towards the eight-foot-high heap.

"Half of what's under there is the pile of rocks I was buried under," Fritz said. "The other half is Samson. He's badly broken, but he freed me, gave me his sparkscube, and... and he went to sleep."

143

Annalie smiled. "I'd sure like to tell him gratitude for saving your life."

Fritz shrugged. "Someday."

It took a while, but they managed to brush or heat-laser all of the snow off the fallen forty-foot-tall Verdant Warden. Samson laid flat on his back. Twisted steel and broken cables poked out of his left hip joint instead of a leg. His right arm was flattened as if Siv had spent a particularly grumpy day working it over with a sledgehammer. Chunks of metal were missing all across his dented chest. His deep-set robotic eyes were dark and lifeless. Seeing him this way caused physical pain in Fritz's chest.

"What's wrong with him?" Annalie asked. "Reckon it's a long list."

"He needs a new sparkscube for starters," Fritz said. "But beyond that, I think a lot of what's wrong with him could be self-repaired if his microbot cache was functional."

Fritz used a quick burst from his boosters to fly he and Annalie up on top of Samson. They carefully stepped to the middle of the robot's chest, where Fritz pointed out a particularly deep dent. "He told me he had a whole mess of smaller robots inside of him that worked throughout his body, fixing things."

"Microbots," Annalie mumbled, chewing on the inside of her cheek. "Daisy." She laid flat on her tummy with Samson's chest dent directly in front of her face. "Ooo, that metal is cold, even through my coat." She shivered, then lifted her glasses and squinted at the dent. "Huh."

"You see something?" Fritz asked.

"Maybe," Annalie said. "Fetch me a light and a screwdriver, would you? Flathead. Thinnest you have. And a laser cutter."

144

A small tube raised itself from the side of Fritz's helmet, and a bright white light shone forth from it. He detached the beacon from his helmet and handed it to Annalie. Then he opened a compartment in his chipsuit and retrieved the screwdriver and laser cutter. "Gratitude," Annalie said, taking the tools and poking around the dent with them.

The laser cutter hummed and buzzed for a long time. A *long* time. How much was she cutting? He tilted his head to get a better look; she'd made only a two-inch long cut. What was taking– Oh, right. Traskian armor was some of the strongest material manufactured before the Blackout, and Samson was covered with it. If Annalie was going to take a look inside Samson, she'd have to be patient and persistent to–

Click.

"Hey," Fritz said, "what if we bring back some of Samson's Traskian armor with us and use it to finish Krulgoth? As coverings, I mean, for the parts of him that are still unfinished and exposed?"

"Ooo," Annalie said, turning off the laser cutter and looking up at him. "I like that. One of Krulgoth's strengths is his agility. Traskian armor is hard as thermodynamics, but also relatively lightweight and flexible. It should keep him right well protected without costing him much speed."

"I'll finish scooping out enough dirt to get all the kemosite we need," Fritz said. "Then I'll cut the armor off his right arm. There should be plenty on it to cover Krulgoth, and we'll have to refabricate it to match Krulgoth's shape anyway. Might as well take some that's already biffed and bashed."

Annalie stood. "I should help. The kemosite's what we're here for, and here I'm goofing around with a Steelterror."

"He's not a Steelterror," Fritz said, and catching his tone, he softened it. "He was made to be something different. He was made to help people. The others – Gravitas, Banshee, Leviathan – they were built to be weapons. And for a while, they turned Samson into a Steelterror." He shrugged. "But before he died, he was himself again. A Verdant Warden. More than that, actually. Do you know when I talked to him, he expressed interest in becoming a farmer, like my dad?"

She reached towards him and popped open his faceplate. The cold immediately fogged up the lenses of his glasses. She lifted them above his eyes and caressed his face. "Don't use that word," Annalie said. "'Died.' Let me see if I can do anything for him. OK, muffin? I'll go as fast as I can."

Cupcake earlier, muffin now... "You hungry?" Fritz asked. "We... we just ate."

"I'm right starved," Annalie said. "But, let's get everything done first."

So Fritz dug up some mountain dirt. It wasn't so bad once he got into a routine. His arms worked automatically, allowing his mind to wander free. He thought about how things would go in three days when they went into space to confront the Celestine fleet – it was hard *not* to think about that. He thought about the work they still had to do on the *Turkey*, about introducing Felix to combination circuits, and about how his sister was doing. He knew how hard the closing of the university had been on her.

"Hey, sugar?" Annalie called down to him.

"Yeah?"

"Tell me about the revival."

Fritz sighed. That topic was both intensely intriguing and maddeningly frustrating. "I don't know anything new," he said.

"Just tell me again what you already know," Annalie said. "How'd you first learn about it?

He took a deep breath and sighed again. "Normally, my power works the same way everyone else's intuition works."

"Just cranked up to maximum power," Annalie said.

"True," Fritz said. "Some part of my brain puts together numerous pieces of data, including facts and memories and the opinions of others and pieces them together into a coherent whole. I make numerous suppositions and choose the most logical one. All pretty much subconsciously. But the day I first..."

Heard? It hadn't come to him as sound. Saw? It wasn't anything he'd seen, either... at least not with his eyes.

"The day I first learned about the revival was nothing like that. Which makes it both amazing and frustrating. It wasn't a new *conclusion* my power had somehow calculated. It was new *data* that simply hit me. Like a lightning bolt at noon on a sunny day – completely out of nowhere."

"Data about the revival," Annalie said. "You mean visions."

Fritz shrugged. "I guess."

"It all just came to you like in a series of pictures?" Annalie said. "Tell me about them."

"I've forgotten most of them," he said. "Or I saw them too fast to ever remember them in the first place. And some I just saw like through a fog. But others I remember in great detail. You want to hear the one about the river, don't you?"

"You know I do," Annalie said.

Fritz put his shovel in the ground and rested his hands on the end of the handle. "The land on either side of this river was covered with trees. A little way past those trees, rock cliffs shot straight up, and there were more trees on top of them.

147

Downstream a bit was a dam – and not one made by an animal. It was made of metal. But in a beautiful little corner of the river – in a little inlet or something – there was a circular waterfall. Like a hole right in the middle of the river, and the water cascaded down into it."

"And everything was green?" Annalie asked.

He closed his eyes and saw the lake in his mind's eye. His shoulders relaxed, and he exhaled. "Everything was green," he confirmed. "Nothing at all like the miles and miles of dirt and patchy grass and scrub brush out in the unoccupied territories today. The trees had leaves, and there were so many flowers. Fauna ran through the forest on all sides of the lake. It was like that in all of the images. So much water and trees and sky and sun."

"You hate being out in the sun," Annalie said.

He nodded. "I liked this, though."

"You ever ask Sierra about this lake?" Annalie asked. "To see if it's a for-real place?"

"I did," Fritz said.

"You did?" For the first time since she'd started working on Samson, she turned her head to look at him. "What'd she say?"

"She said it's... well, she said the name of the river, but I don't remember it. She said the circular waterfall was a bell-mouth spillway that diverts water downstream as flood defense. Except she said it doesn't look anything like that anymore. This river is apparently an offshoot of the Elde downstream from the ruins of Borusia, where a bunch of... 'bad people' filled the river with their toxic chemical runoff."

"Sierra did not really use the words 'bad people,'" Annalie said.

"She did not," Fritz said. "But I don't want to repeat what she said. She got awful upset when I asked her about this – not at me, but at the memory of what happened. She said the trees I saw are all gone now. The river is dried up. Bare. She said that spillway's just a hole in the ground, and it hasn't been a circular waterfall for centuries."

"But it's a real place?" Annalie said. "And you saw it *not* all messed up?"

"Sierra said I must have seen the past," Fritz said. "But it wasn't. I know it wasn't."

"It was the future," Annalie said, an awed tone to her voice.

"I saw cities, too, but not like Hondo. Not villages made of wood and dirt and horse dung. They were made of steel and glass and chipware solar panels. They were full of people – people in flying carriages, people teleporting here and there and everywhere. And they weren't hungry or sick. They were happy and at peace. It was everything I want to do with the chipware restoration. But whenever I try to think about how we get from here to there, the only thought that comes to mind – every single time–"

"Is revival," Annalie said.

Fritz nodded. "It's going to happen. But I don't know how."

He got back to his shoveling, filled all three containers with kemosite-rich dirt, and loaded them into the aerocopter. Then he went to work on harvesting the Traskian armor from Samson's crushed right arm. With one of his laser cannons configured both to its most powerful setting and its thinnest beam, he was able to carefully slice through the armor without damaging Samson's structural components underneath.

He was just about finished when there was a loud *clang* of metal from atop Samson's chest. "That's what I thought," Annalie said. "Can I show you something?"

He boosted himself back up on top of Samson's chest. Annalie's work area was a mess. There were scraps and shards of metal everywhere. Loose screws, metal washers, and o-rings were tripping hazards. A single polished, shiny gear reflected the sunlight. Fritz was careful not to step on any of it. Samson was probably going to need it inside him if they were ever able to figure out everything wrong with him. He consciously resisted the urge to frown at the mess. How Annalie could work in such disorganization was a complete mystery. "What did you find?"

"Nothing much," she said. "Reckon I might've just fixed him."

Fritz's mouth dropped open.

"That dent in his chest looked nasty, and I just had a feelin' maybe the problem wasn't chipware but mechanical. Sure 'nuff, there's a container – like a metal box of some kind – right under that dent. The dent was jamming it, holding it closed. Well, it ain't jammed no longer. We have a spare sparkscube?"

Fritz used his chipsuit's rockets to blast himself back up the slope to the aerocopter. He rummaged through the storage bins under the back seats, found a sparkscube, and rocketed back down to Annalie. Together, they put the cube into the empty slot in Samson's chest, and... nothing.

"It's charged?" Annalie said.

Fritz checked the readout on the cube and scanned it with his chipsuit. "It's charged."

"Dagnabit," Annalie said. "I thought we just needed to get some sparks into him, and those robot antibodies you talked about would kick in and fix him up."

"I'm sure that was a necessary first step," Fritz said. "But he was pretty broken. Maybe he needs more work. Or maybe those microbots need more time. But still..." He shrugged and laughed. The pain he'd felt at seeing Samson beaten and broken crumbled away. "This is amazing. I can't believe how easily you figured that out!"

She playfully punched him in the shoulder. "You're not the only smart one around here, you know," she said. She grinned wide and bounced on her toes. "I know I should've helped you shovel dirt, but buttercup, I also know how much you've wanted to help Samson, and I just thought..." She shrugged her shoulders.

Fritz looked down at his boots. There was a loose o-ring between him and Annalie. A thought came to mind, and it was crazy, and it made him both so excited he wanted to yelp and so nervous he wanted to throw up. But it also felt *right*. And unlike the foreknowledge of the mysterious revival, he was certain this idea came from his hyper-intuition. Good things happened when he listened to his power. So without giving himself time to reconsider, he dropped to one knee, picked up the o-ring, and held it up in front of Annalie.

"Will you marry me?" he asked.

Annalie gasped and took a step backward. She covered her mouth with both hands. "Oh my days!" she said. "For serious?"

"For serious," Fritz said. "Annalie..."

There were so many things he wanted to say. He should have written them all down, and he would have, but since his talk with Felix last night, he'd just barely begun planning.

He wanted to tell Annalie that he was a guy who'd always been extremely happy spending the vast majority of his time

151

alone, but now he didn't like spending even a few minutes away from her.

He wanted to say that before he knew her, he didn't even know it was possible to feel as happy as she made him.

He wanted to promise that he'd protect her and cherish her and treat her like the queen she was every day for the rest of their lives.

But in the moment, he couldn't verbalize any of that. So instead, he just shrugged. "I love you."

"I love you, too," Annalie said. "For true and for always." She held her left hand out to him.

"I'll get you a real ring once things settle down, and–"

"You will *not*," she said. "This is the ring I want."

Fritz laughed. "Really?"

She tapped Samson's chest with her boot. "It's part of the man who saved your life."

Fritz slipped it on her.

"Yes," she said. "My answer is yes."

He stood up and pulled her close. She brought her lips towards his.

"Wait!" Fritz said, pulling away from her. He pointed at the tiny camera embedded into his helmet. "Is it OK that I vid-recorded this? Felix wanted to see it."

"You planned this out with *Felix*?"

"Not exactly," he said. "But I did ask him for permission."

"Permission from my ten-year-old little brother?"

He shrugged. "Permission from the boy who's like a son to you. Who's... like a son to me, too. It felt right."

Annalie considered that then nodded. "Agreed," she said. "But turn off the camera before you kiss me, yeah?"

"Oh. Sure!"

He stopped recording.

Chapter Eleven

Dead leaves crunched under Cassie's boots. The live oak branches surrounding her swayed in the breeze. The morning sun warded off the chill, though her wide-brimmed hat kept its brightness off her face. And for the sixteenth time, the chirpy chipware-generated voice was back in her earpiece.

"Warning," it said. No direction specified. That meant it was trying to simulate danger that was lurking but not imminent. Cassie stopped and held up her hand. Siv, Fritz, Annalie, Sierra, Krulgoth, and the white demons behind her stood still, too.

"Where are they?" Siv whispered.

She *shush*ed him. She didn't see any simulated Shakren anywhere, but they'd proved very good at hiding behind trees. Or in the brush. Or under rocks. Fritz was probably scanning for them with his chipsuit's sensors. Gashg was checking, too, with a pair of infrared goggles. Those were new for this practice run, and they would make him much better at spotting hidden Shakren. And as an added bonus, they also made him instantly recognizable amongst the demon clones.

But none of them saw anything. Had the warning been a glitch in Fritz's simulation? Cassie looked to him for an answer, but he just shrugged. She lowered her hand, lifted her foot to take a step–

"Warning!" the chipware voice said. "Danger above you."

Above?!

Cassie crouched and aimed her fake bow towards the tree canopy above. "In the trees!"

Red laser fire rained down on them. Shakren peacekeepers dangled from branches, perched on the larger limbs, and some even floated in the air via chipware devices around their ankles. That was a new trick. The demons aimed their rifles upward and painted the sky with green lasers. Two demons – Vlas and Kwegh, maybe? – leaped onto Krulgoth's shoulders, both to get a higher vantage point and also to shield their robot leader, who couldn't be healed like the rest of them. Fritz and Sierra rose into the air like soda out of a shaken-up bottle and engaged the Shakren close-up.

Siv pressed his left hand against Cassie's shoulder, silently urging her to stay crouched. He stood over her, picking Shakren out of the trees with his shotgun like he was shooting skeet.

Gashg spun and pointed his laser rifle towards a different section of the tree canopy. "Another squad over here!" he called out in his tinny, translated voice.

A volley of red laser fire aimed straight for his chest, but when it was inches from him, an aura of blue energy sprang to life, absorbing and dissipating the fire. His goggles weren't the only new chipware they were using in this run. Annalie had finally made enough personal shield generators to guarantee every demon would have one. Fortunately for Gashg, his shield made the onslaught non-fatal, but it was still brutal. His shield burned out, and a dozen blasts slammed into his chest. Six of his health lights turned red.

"Get where I can reach you!" Cassie yelled.

Gashg took two steps backward and stretched his back leg towards her. Cassie strained her arm but managed to wrap her fingers around his ankle. She held on until his simulated health lights all turned green. Zethken, Merkeg, and Rarkh came up beside Gashg and covered him while he healed, exchanging fire with the second squad of peacekeepers.

But they all scattered when a simulated Shakren fell out of the sky and slammed into the ground where they'd just been standing. For a stunned second, they gaped at it – or rather at how close it had come to hitting them, which would have hurt something fierce if it had been real. Then it flickered out of existence.

Sierra, who'd knocked the Shakren out of the trees with violent winds, called down to them. "Oh, hey. Look out below."

"Try not to take out your own teammates, *Lady Verde*," Cassie grumbled.

Sierra flashed a rude gesture at her and flew away.

After a few minutes, it was over. The latest wave of peacekeepers had been defeated, and they'd lost three demons, bringing their total casualties for this run up to eleven. It was their best run yet, by far, but Cassie couldn't find much comfort in that. Eleven casualties. Even with all the practice. Even with the shield generators.

Krulgoth assessed the situation with a solemn nod to the three demons they'd lost. Tvelth was among them, but Cassie couldn't immediately name the other two. So many demons, and all with names that sounded like fingernails on a chalkboard. They tilted back their heads and gave Krulgoth a bark that went untranslated by the chipware devices on their throats. Then they stomped off to the out-of-bounds area while everyone else raced to the simulated elevator.

"This is the best we've ever done," Fritz said.

"Amen," Siv agreed.

"Lucky number sixteen?" Annalie said.

"No luck about it," Fritz said. "Those personal shield generators are game-changers. *Your* idea."

"I'm a little tired today," Sierra said, "so go ahead and pretend I'm giving my standard warning, OK? Blah blah, what if the demons are still forced to obey? Blah blah blah, we don't *know* we'll be able to even touch these wankers."

Cassie stole a look at Krulgoth. His face remained as emotionless as ever.

"Since the moment I realized the Evil Ones created us to be disposable, I have devoted my life to freeing my brothers," Krulgoth said. "That will never end."

Sierra serenaded Krulgoth with disingenuous applause.

"Enough," Cassie said. She tried to sound confident, even if it felt as fake as the laser fire and the simulated Shakren. "We all have jobs to do, so let's do them."

"Make the Celestines surrender," Fritz said. "Nothing else matters."

"Kill the Evil Ones," Skleght said. "Acknowledged."

"That's not what I said," Fritz said.

"That's what I heard," Skleght said.

Krulgoth made his way through the fake elevator doorway and into the clearing where the Celestines' control center was simulated. Fritz and Sierra followed him and took to the air. Then the demons charged inside, half of them fanning to the left and half to the right. Siv, Cassie, and Annalie entered last.

But something was off. The simulated Shakren were filling the room with their laser fire – and turning a lot of the demons' health indicator lights red. But the white demons didn't fire back. They just faced the control room's center with puzzled looks on their faces.

As always at this part of the training exercise, the simulated Celestines were in the middle of the room. The male in a black cassock. The female in a black jacket and pants. Both wearing badges of three interconnected silver triangles. But *unlike* every other simulation, this time, there were *two* of each of the Celestines, as if each had a twin or a mirror image.

"What are you waiting for?" Krulgoth hollered. He'd refactored both of his arms into laser cannons, and he sprayed fire over the Shakren. But he was the only one from their side who was firing. "Attack them!"

"There's a malfunction," Gashg said.

"What kind of malfunction?" Krulgoth said.

Zethken motioned towards the center of the simulated room. "The Evil Ones are duplicated," Zethken said.

"I don't understand," Krulgoth said. "Duplicated how?"

"As in there are *four* Celestines instead of two?" Siv said. How did Krulgoth not understand this?

"Oh, that's odd," Fritz said. "I see all four of them, too. Unless I view the vid feed from my on-suit camera. On that, there's only two."

Krulgoth abruptly stopped firing. "End the simulation!" he yelled with uncharacteristic emotion in his voice.

The projections all vanished. The fake control center walls and chipware consoles disappeared. The Shakren vanished, too, as did *two* of the four Celestine images... but only two.

"What's the matter with this thing?" Fritz said.

And then Gashg dropped his weapon and fell to one knee. "Luminary," he said, grimacing at the word.

Two more demons knelt. "Luminary," they said. They seemed just as pained as Gashg.

"What the barking hell?" Sierra said.

Every demon except Krulgoth dropped his weapon and lowered himself to one knee. Dry leaves crackled underneath them. They grit their teeth and clenched their fists, but they all said the word. "Luminary."

"The hell are they all kneeling for?" Siv said.

"The Evil Ones are undetectable to chipware," Krulgoth said. His voice had dropped to barely above a whisper. "Like Reinhardt's on-suit camera. Or my eyes."

"N-n-no," Annalie stammered. "You saying what I think you're saying?"

"It's them," Fritz said. "The *real* them."

It was the Celestines. They'd arrived days earlier than expected. Krulgoth couldn't even see them. And the white demons were doing them homage because apparently, they *still had to obey them.*

Cassie swallowed hard and reached towards her quiver for an arrow, then remembered she only had simulated ones. Blast it.

Though the demons' body language was reverent, their expressions were masks of disgust. They looked to Krulgoth with their faces twisted in agony, silently begging for answers and help. The sight turned Cassie's stomach.

Krulgoth's sword-length blades emerged from his lower arms. His upper arms refactored into laser cannons and hummed with gathering power – *real* power. They weren't in simulation mode anymore. He pointed them in the general vicinity of where the simulated Celestines had been.

"Tell him to hold his fire," the Celestine man said, "or I'll order every Shakren present to stop breathing."

Cassie gasped. His voice!

Fritz glanced at Krulgoth. "Is he bluffing?"

160

"About what?" Krulgoth said. "If they're speaking, I can't hear them either!"

"He wants us to hold our fire," Fritz said, "or else he'll order all the demons to stop breathing."

Krulgoth's laser cannons let out a descending whine. He lowered his arms. "Do as he says."

Fritz returned his weapons to the hidden compartments in his suit. Sierra came back to the ground. Annalie powered down the reader emulator circlet. Siv lowered his shotgun but didn't let go of it.

But Cassie ground her teeth together and glared at the Celestine man. His voice was the voice of the pastor who'd heard her confession last night. It didn't just sound the same. It *was* the same. She'd recognize him anywhere.

Last night, in the church's weak light and when viewed through the confessional grate, the pastor's hands had appeared gray and transparent. They'd seemed that way because they *were* that way. The "pastor" hadn't really been a pastor. He'd been this Celestine.

The demons who had flanked out to either side of the simulated Celestines continued to silently genuflect, except for one. "General, please!" Rarkh managed to bark out from a throat that sounded constricted. He was weeping. White demons could cry? "Mercy!"

Krulgoth spun at the waist and pointed one of his laser cannons at Rarkh's head.

Cassie shoved her way forward and pushed Krulgoth's forearm down, forcing him to lower his weapon. "What do you think you're doing?" she said. "You asked us to stand down to protect them. Now you're going to shoot them yourself?"

"I promised them freedom," Krulgoth said. "If this is the only way..."

"My danger sense is silent," she said. "They don't mean us any harm."

"They've stripped my brothers of their free will!" Krulgoth roared, all sign of his usual emotional restraint gone. His mechanical eyes blazed as with hot red fire. And Cassie heard his unspoken accusation loud and clear. He'd hoped – on *her advice,* he'd hoped. And that hope had proven fruitless.

"And that's not OK," Cassie said. "But before you murder your own brothers, let's just hear this out. Please?"

"General!" Rarkh yelled again.

"P-27146, you will remain silent while in my presence," the Celestine man said.

Rarkh closed his mouth and bowed his head.

Gears inside Krulgoth scraped like grinding teeth. "How long did he tell Rarkh to stop speaking for?"

"P-29333," the Celestine man said, "rise and act as our speaker."

Gashg stood.

"There's no need for bloodshed," the Celestine said to Krulgoth. That melodious voice!

"There's no need for bloodshed," Gashg repeated.

"Krulgoth," the Celestine said. Gashg continued to repeat his words. "It's been a long time. I know what you did to S-17 and S-24, and I know it wasn't your fault. But the Life isn't here to trick you this time. If you kill P-27146 or any other Shakren, you will do so of your own volition."

"You still recognize us?" Krulgoth asked. He spoke in the general vicinity of where the Celestines stood, but not directly at them, much like a blind person would. He really couldn't see them. "You still recognize me?"

The Celestine man gave Krulgoth a rueful smile. "I know who you *think* you are."

"I know who you *think* you are," Gashg said.

The Celestine female laughed. "You're Krulgoth!" she said.

"The Truth says, 'You're Krulgoth!'" Gashg said.

Krulgoth startled and took three steps backward. His eyes widened. The motors inside him clicked and slipped gears. Cassie had never even imagined Krulgoth in such a state. Why did the Celestine woman saying his name put him into such a bad box? At least it finally made him change his laser cannons back into his arms and stop pointing them at the demons. He averted his eyes, refusing to look both at his brothers and at where everyone else could see the Celestines.

"Thank you," the male Celestine said, and with a start of her own, Cassie realized he was speaking to her. "Once again, you've made the right decision, Cassandra."

Siv's head whipped around to face her. *Once again?* And calling her by name?

The brazenness of the violation was appalling. She thought she'd been making a personal, confidential confession to an ordained pastor in church last night. Her hands tightened into fists. "Make your say. And make it quick."

The Celestine man stood taller and addressed the Mantissa Reborn. "For those who do not know us, you may call me the Way."

"My name is the Truth," the woman said.

"No, it isn't," Krulgoth said after hearing Gashg repeat her. "Every word out of her mouth is a lie."

"'The Truth' speaks in lies?" Siv said.

The Truth winked at Siv and licked her lips flirtatiously. Cassie clenched her teeth.

"We come before you as heralds," the Way said. "Our fleet is not here, but it will be soon. As you already know. You should be rejoicing that your deliverance is at hand. Instead, you prepare to fight us. But there need not be any bloodshed. Understand that we do not, and will not, bring you conflict. But, if you choose to live by the sword..."

Smoke poured out of the Truth's hand and solidified into the shape of a long, thin blade.

"Then we *will* respond in kind," the Way said.

"We know what you do to worlds," Fritz said. "Peace through tyranny. Well. No. Not here you won't."

"Fritz Karl Reinhardt!" the Way said. Annalie was startled at the familiar use of her boyfriend's full name. The Way spread his arms as if offering an embrace. "I am so pleased you took my advice and didn't take your own life."

Fritz popped the laser cannons out of both arms of his suit and pointed one at the Way's head.

The Way held up a finger in warning. "We will end all violence on your world," he said. "Senseless saloon shootings will be a thing of the past. Krulgoth and his brothers will no longer terrorize anyone. We will not permit giant machines to ever again kill so many men, women, and children. And we will hold accountable those who commit such sins." He looked at Sierra. "Consider yourself warned, Sierra Dawn Monet. We'll even bring Lady Verde herself to justice if we must."

And that's when Sierra *snapped.*

She clenched her fists, and the land the Celestines stood upon exploded. A ten-foot-tall pillar of dirt punched up out of the ground, shattered, and crumbled. Grainy bits of fresh soil covered everything and everyone. The ground shook beneath them. The trees swayed. A pit formed where the dirt had burst forth, spreading and opening like the maw of some angry beast. Soil, leaves, and twigs slid down into it. Cassie couldn't see its bottom. Sierra yelled, and the pit stopped growing, *just* shy of swallowing up the demons and the Mantissa.

But the Celestines were unharmed. There wasn't a spot of dirt on them. They remained precisely where they had been, even though there was no longer any ground underneath them. They floated in place.

"No one will ever again go hungry," the Way said, continuing his speech as if Sierra's outburst hadn't happened. "An unequal distribution of wealth will be a relic of the past. We will institute a culture of abundance. Everyone will be satisfied. Those who have ears ought to hear."

"And all it costs is our freedom, yeah?" Siv said. He motioned towards the still genuflecting demons. "We become the same kind of puppets you force these poor souls to be?"

"Sivrin McCaig just referred to the 'white demons' who took his father's arm and traumatized his memory for a decade as 'poor souls,'" the Way said. "Now *that's* forgiveness. You aren't far" – his solid black eyes found Cassie – "from the way."

You must follow the way, the "pastor" had said to her. *And I promise that very soon, it will reveal itself to you.* The son of a gun had been teasing her. Even last night, he *knew* he was going to crash their training session today.

"All diseases will be cured, Cassandra," the Way said. "The university medical school may have closed, but... we have something better planned."

Oh, *hell* no. How *dare* he taunt her with the Three Answers?

"Reckon it's time you got the hell off our land," Cassie said.

The Way held her gaze for a pair of heartbeats, then black smoke billowed behind both him and the Truth. As they stepped back into it, they began to disappear. "You have four days," he said. "And then, as the leaders of planet Verde, you must decide. Will it be time to mourn or time to dance? Time to uproot or time to plant?

"Time to die or time to be born again?"

Chapter Twelve

"What just happened?" Annalie asked anyone who could fathom a guess. "How are they here? Why didn't Skylab alert us to their fleet?"

"Their fleet isn't here yet," Krulgoth said. "But the two Evil Ones can travel–"

Skleght roared so fiercely his translator couldn't put it into words. He barreled into Krulgoth's steel chest and knocked the massive robot demon over, then leaped onto his throat. Merkeg, Zethken, and four other demons piled on. They swiped Krulgoth with their claws, whipped him with their tails, and yanked at his limbs with their bare hands – even though gouging at his metal hide rendered their hands bloody.

"You said we were free!" Skleght yelled, the translation barely audible over the original snarls and growls.

"Get off him!" Cassie said. She grabbed demons by the ankles and used her healing power to put them to sleep. Once they'd passed out, Siv and Fritz pulled them off Krulgoth. Gashg and Vlas helped, too, dragging the manic, thrashing white demons away from their leader and pinning them to the ground to prevent them from causing further harm.

"Told you so," Sierra said. "I barking told you all so!"

Once all his attackers had been pulled off of him, Krulgoth stood, though one of his knees threatened to buckle. A bundle of severed wires at the exposed joint was the likely cause. Sparks crackled at random places across his chest.

"You said we were free," Vlas said to Krulgoth. He hadn't jumped his general, but his shaking fists told Cassie he wasn't far from it, either. "You told us we'd never be enslaved again!"

"I tried, Vlas," Krulgoth said, his voice back to its familiar monotone. "I made us all different from what we were. So different. So much stronger. I thought it was enough."

"We thought you knew for sure," another demon said. Tvleth maybe? "If you never said that, then you *heavily* implied it. But you *never* knew. Did you?"

Krulgoth shook his head.

Sierra's body collapsed into dust, then a new one – much larger than normal – formed out of the air right in front of Krulgoth. Its size put her nose-to-metal-snout with the eight-foot-tall robot. "And when you said you'd killed one of those gray-skinned ghosts before, that was a lie, too. You don't know how you did it because you never did!"

"No," Gashg said. "We all saw that happen. The general threw the Life out a window. The Evil One exploded into black flame. For years, the general wore the Life's broken badge on his own chest as a trophy of his victory. That was no lie."

Sierra's giant body dissipated, and she formed a new regular-sized one on the outer edge of the group, away from everyone else. She stomped back and forth and muttered under her breath.

"We saw that badge," Siv said. "And I saw it disappear, too, when Krulgoth... well, when his flesh and blood body died. Vanished into smoke just like those Celestines did when they left just now."

"If the creepy lady always lies," Cassie said, "and she calls you Krulgoth, then that either means 'Krulgoth' isn't your real name, or you're not Krulgoth. Which is it?"

The barest hint of danger flickered into Cassie's awareness. "I *am* Krulgoth," he said, standing as tall as he could with his busted knee. "What are you insinuating?"

168

"Calm down, tin can," Cassie said. "I'm not *insinuating* anything. I'm just trying to make sense of everything that just happened and figure out where it leaves us."

"I can tell you where it leaves us," Sierra said. "Screwed. *Screwed.* Screwed in both–"

"Would you *hush,*" Cassie snapped at her, "Your. Vocalities. For *goodness* sake."

Sierra shoved past three white demons to get right up in Cassie's face. "You can hop in that space ship you're repairing and just leave," Sierra said. "Right now! All of you can get your asses far the hell away from here. Make a break for it. Run away from those ghosts and leave Verde to them. But I *can't.* I'm bonded to the planet because these wankers killed me back when *they* invaded us. I'm stuck here. So if you want me to hush up, you *make* me hush up, you barking crank!"

Cassie's danger sense warmed to a soft burn. An attack wasn't imminent, but Sierra *was* torqued off enough to do her harm.

"Hey!" Fritz said, shoving himself between his sister and his friend. "Both of you, calm down. Sierra, I could have left you to die once before. I didn't. I won't do it now. None of us will. Just calm down."

She vanished into the wind and disappeared.

Siv stepped up, asking Cassie with a look if she was all right. She was.

"You really couldn't see or hear them?" Annalie asked Krulgoth.

He shook his metal head. "I'm chipware," Krulgoth said. "And they don't appear on chipware devices."

Annalie showed them all her mobile, which played the vid captured just a few minutes earlier by the chipware running the simulation. On it, the demons were genuflecting to nothing. Cassie and Siv and everyone else who spoke to them was talking to thin air. The audio recorded a one-sided conversation. "Don't make any sense," Annalie said. "We all saw 'em. Light reflected off of them and went into our eyes, and our brains turned that into their image. Why didn't the cams or Krulgoth's eyes pick up that same light?"

"They've always been this way," Krulgoth said. "I've never figured it out. I never had the time." He gave his brothers a meaningful look. "I've devoted my life to solving a different problem."

"Well, that's what we have now, isn't it?" Cassie said. "A problem. We always knew we'd be almost hopelessly outnumbered, even with this alliance between our peoples. But now, it will be just six of us going up there. The Mantissa Reborn and you. That's it."

Because if any white demon – Krulgoth excepted – came along, then once back in the Celestines' presence, they'd do more than just genuflect to their former masters. They'd betray and kill Cassie, Fritz, Siv, and everyone else. It didn't much matter they'd do so against their own will.

"For all the good I can do blind and deaf to them," Krulgoth said.

"Can even the six of you go?" Vlas said. "The Evil Ones know our plans. They'll be waiting. They'll be prepared."

"*How?*" Annalie asked. "That's the part that's bothering me. How can the two of them get around space without ships? How did they just disappear into smoke? How do they know our *names?* It's like they really are ghosts. That can't be, can it?"

"I reckon Red's asking the right questions here," Siv said. "What can you tell us, Krulgoth? All *we* know is they're ballsy enough to call themselves 'the Way,' 'the Life,' and 'the Truth.' And I know just laying eyes on 'em made gooseflesh run up and down my arms. But what in tarnation *are* they? Where they from?"

"We don't know," Krulgoth said. "From what little they've said in our presence over the years, we've pieced together that they're ancient. Think of their ages in terms of millennia, not years. They call themselves outcasts. They've mentioned some kind of conflict in their past – perhaps a war. I think they were on the losing side of it."

"I'd love to talk to whoever it is who beat them," Fritz said. "And that's saying a lot since I don't like talking to anybody."

"What we do know," Krulgoth continued, "implies they have a homeworld, and there are others of their species. But we've never seen anyone else like them. Just the three. The two that were just here, and the one I killed. And we certainly don't know where that homeworld is."

"Home for them now is just one of the ships in their fleet?" Cassie asked.

Krulgoth nodded. "Whichever ship they're on is considered their cathedral ship."

"If they're thousands of years old, it kind of makes sense they're *not* carbon-based lifeforms," Fritz said. "Maybe they *are* energy-based."

"I'm more concerned about how they knew our names," Siv said. "They been watching us?"

Cassie cleared her throat. "Last night, I went to church. Pastor was in the confessional, only it wasn't Pastor Kolbe. It was some other pastor who said he was visiting, filling in. Except I learned just now it wasn't a pastor at all. It was the Way."

"You're sure?" Fritz asked. "You saw him?"

"Only through the confessional grate," Cassie said. "But I heard him. You don't forget that voice."

"That's for sure," Siv said. "Reckon he could sell water in the middle of a river. But why would he pretend to be a pastor?"

"Beats me," Cassie said.

"So that's how they knew we've been practicing?" Annalie asked. "And how they learned our names?"

Cassie frowned. "No. I didn't talk about the pending invasion or our defense preparations. We just..."

God has abandoned you.

"Well, it was something of a personal conversation," she said. "I thought he was a pastor hearing my confession. But I didn't say anything about what we've been practicing, and I definitely didn't tell him my name."

"I saw them a couple of months ago," Fritz said. "Back when I was having a hard time. To be honest and open with all of you, I felt that maybe things would be better if I were just gone. And then those two Celestines showed up, right in my bedroom in the middle of the night. I tried to tell myself it was just a nightmare, but I have white demon memories in my head of what it was like to be in their presence. I knew better."

Annalie placed a hand on Fritz's arm. "What'd they say?"

"The Way said I was a victim. He said it was a crime that I was even able to consider hurting myself."

The still-conscious white demons all made a curious motion. Cassie couldn't tell if they'd shuddered or rolled their eyes. "That is definitely something he would say," Krulgoth said.

"Then the Truth" – Fritz looked to Annalie – "she made herself look like you, actually, and she said I *should.* Hurt myself." He crinkled his nose. "But if she speaks only in lies,

172

that means she was saying I *shouldn't?* Anyway. I never told them my name, either."

"What about you?" Cassie asked Siv.

He spread his palms. "I got nothin'. Ain't never seen either of them before today."

"So they know our names and who we are and what we're doing because..." Annalie waved her hands. "Because magic?"

Siv raised an eyebrow. "Hey. Maybe that's exactly how they know. Maybe that's exactly what they are."

"Umm," Fritz said. He pushed his glasses up his nose. "That's not real, you know."

"I know y'all think your Mantissa powers have smart brain scientific explanations," Siv said. "That's dandified. Y'all keep thinking that. I still say they're magic. And magic can explain why chipware like Krulgoth's eyes can't see them. It explains how these Celestines can just show up, know who we are, know everything we've done, and then just disappear. If they're magic, then magic can hurt 'em right back." He stood tall and nodded. "We need some magic weapons."

"I will not even dignify that with a response," Krulgoth said.

"At least you can agree we do need a new plan," Cassie said to Krulgoth. "Why take anything off the table at this point?"

"But we *don't* need a new plan," Fritz said. He shrugged. "We just need to adapt the one we already have. They were always going to outnumber us – a lot. Our first priority still has to be forcing them to free the Shakren. Now more than ever."

"How are we even going to get in the same room with them when it's six versus six thousand?" Cassie asked.

"That's a fair point," Fritz conceded. "But whether we have an army or not, we still need to hit them head-on, the moment they arrive. What's that rodeo analogy, sis? Take the bull by the horns? We need to walk right in through... their front... door..."

His eyes had gone glassy, distant. Cassie recognized the look well. His power was speaking to him.

"I might have an idea," Fritz said.

"Honey," Annalie said, "if we go up to their ship, why would they even bother fighting us? We just saw how they can come and go like they're on a teleporter. As soon as we arrive, they could – *poof* – vanish and vent whatever room we're in out to space. Or fill the room with poison gas, or blow up the whole dang ship already. We'd all die, and all their Shakren on their ship would die, but they'd just walk out of a black cloud on another ship, completely unharmed. So why go up there? Let's make them come to us. Fight 'em here. At least we'd be on our own land. At least we'd be where Sierra will be strongest."

Fritz shook his head and rubbed at his temples. "It sounds crazy, but I know going up to their ship is the right thing to do," he said. "I wish I knew why, but I don't. All I know is that the revival is coming, and... and that means things will be OK. No more sickness. No more ignorance or hunger. The air and the water will be clean again. And there'll be no more fighting and no more war."

"You're describing what the Evil Ones have done to a thousand other worlds," Krulgoth said, "at the cost of the natives' freedom. Perhaps your Mantissa intuition is just foreseeing their 'blessing.'"

Fritz didn't really have an answer for that, so he just shrugged.

Skleght stirred and groggily got to his feet. So did the other demons who Cassie had put to sleep to keep them from attacking Krulgoth. Skleght glared at her, but he saved the bulk of his dirty looks for Krulgoth. "We demand to be free, *General*. You promised us. And we will hold you to that promise."

Servomotors in Krulgoth's shoulders clicked and whirled as he drooped his head like a reprimanded puppy. "You were all witnesses to my failure today. Worse: you were *victims* of it. I have failed you. My shame is deep. There is no apology I can offer sufficient for this incompetence. But I *will* free you. One way or another."

Skleght nodded tersely, then stormed away in the direction of the barn. Merkeg, Zethken, and the other demons who'd attacked Krulgoth followed him.

"What's the other way?" Cassie demanded of Krulgoth. "Freedom the way you almost 'freed' Rarkh? With a laser cannon?"

"You don't have a say in this," Krulgoth said.

"Oh, yes, I do," Cassie said. "You're *not* euthanizing the entire white demon race."

"There was a time your planet would have welcomed such eradication," Krulgoth said.

"We don't welcome genocide!" Cassie said. "There has to be a better way."

Krulgoth hunched his back to meet her eye-to-eye. "I want to believe that," he told her. "Just as I wanted to believe that I'd done enough to free my brothers. But *faith* has not produced the desired results."

Part of her almost snapped right back with: *Yes, but not right now.* But she couldn't bring herself to say it. It had been hard enough to encourage him to find some way to keep the faith before. Now that defending Verde from the Celestines seemed more hopeless than ever, any attempt she could think of just rang hollow.

So she said nothing. She just watched as Krulgoth limped away. Rarkh, Vlas, and the rest of the demons went with him.

Only one lingered behind.

"You OK, Gashg?" Cassie asked him.

"My brothers," he said, watching them go. "It's an understatement to say we hate the way we were under the Evil Ones. All we want is to never be like that ever again. That seems the same as wanting freedom, but it's not. We don't understand freedom. We never have. We certainly don't value it. After Krulgoth killed the Life and we escaped from the Evil Ones, what did we do with the freedom we'd so often longed for?"

He shook his head. "Nothing. Nothing but terrorize others. Krulgoth would find a world with some biological strength he felt could make us stronger, and we'd swarm in. Take over. Krulgoth would map their genetic codes and steal what we needed. He'd use Geneditor to incorporate the stolen biology into our bodies. And we'd move on to the next world, leaving wreckage and flames and death behind us." He turned to Cassie. "You see the irony, don't you?"

"You became everything you hated," Cassie said.

Gashg nodded. "The people of the worlds we attacked would have seen no functional difference at all between the Evil Ones and us. For all the time we've been free, we've never had a clue what to do with that freedom except fight to defend it. And now it's too late. Unless you can go up to their ship and somehow stop them, our freedom is gone." He grunted. "But considering what we've used it for, maybe we *deserve* to lose it."

"Everyone deserves to live free," Fritz said.

Gashg didn't seem convinced. He left the clearing, dragging his tail behind him.

"Let me noodle on this idea some more," Fritz said to Cassie. "I'll tell you about it later." He motioned towards Annalie, who stood some distance away, running her fingers across her temples. "I'm gonna get her something to eat. Try to calm her down."

Cassie nodded. Fritz and Annalie left. And that left her and Siv alone with the giant pit Sierra had rage-made. She'd better come back and fill that in at some point.

"How you be?" Siv asked her.

She found a fallen log and collapsed down onto it.

"Honestly?" she said. "Not very great."

"Me neither," he said. He sat down beside her. "Feels like defending Verde just went from nigh-impossible to never-gonna-happen."

"It's not just that," Cassie said. "It's remembering my dad and how suddenly he died. Remembering everyone else I've lost, even with this power that's supposed to save people. It's the university closing. It's not knowing, for the first time in a *long* time, what's going to happen with my dream."

She made the Sign of God's Hand, then harrumphed. "It used to mean something when I'd make that sign," she said. "But now it feels hollow. Rote. I *want* to believe God is still with me, but just like how Fritz can't shake his weird revival idea, I can't stop hearing what the Way told me in church. That God has abandoned me."

"But that's balderdash," Siv said. "He twists the truth, like how he calls his subjugation salvation."

"I'm not feeling abandoned because the Way said what he said. I'm feeling abandoned because... well, just look around. I

177

don't *want* to believe God has abandoned me." She hung her head. "But it's getting kind of hard not to."

He ran his hands back and forth on the legs of his jeans and kicked at some twigs. His jaw was set. "I've been thinking," he said. "Maybe we ought not wait any longer. Just in case Fritz is wrong. Just in case everything ain't everything. Maybe we should just get hitched. Tomorrow. Or today. Just in case."

"Just in case one of us dies up there?" Cassie said.

Siv nodded. "Or in case both of us die. There's no marriage in heaven. If we want to be hitched, we gotta do it here on Verde."

This wasn't an idle whim. He was serious. He'd marry her this afternoon if she'd agree to it. And part of her was absolutely thrilled at that. It made her feel so happy, so loved.

"I can't," she said.

She'd never forget the way his face fell.

"Please don't," she said. "It's..."

"Forget it," Siv said. He waved his hand and stood up.

"Don't go," she said.

"It's all right," he said. "I was just being a stupe."

"I've imagined my wedding since I was a little girl," she said. "Every detail is part of my plan. Blue skies and my mother's wedding dress. Flowers in my hair. My family and your family gathered in the church. The perfect music, softly strummed on the guitar. An amazing guy – who looks just like you – waiting for me at the altar."

His face brightened. "Then let's go right now!"

"And my father. Beside me. Walking me down the aisle."

Just thinking about it nearly made her break down.

Siv's shoulders sagged.

"That was a pretty darn important part," Cassie said. Her lip quivered. She wiped away a tear. "And I can't have that anymore."

He sat back down beside her. "I know," he said. He took her hand in his.

"I want to marry you one day," Cassie said. "I want you to be my man, and I want to be your bride. And when we do get hitched, I want everything to be perfect. But without my dad, it won't be. It never can."

He nodded and looked away.

"I know I probably sound selfish and ungrateful..." Cassie said.

"You don't," Siv said.

"But if my dad can't walk me down the aisle, then I *have* to have everything else."

"All right," Siv said.

"And we just don't have time right now to make it almost-perfect. That's what I meant when I said I can't. I need it to be as perfect as it can be without my dad. I need that victory. I need at least that much of my plan to still..."

She couldn't hold it together any longer. He pulled her into his arms, and her tears wet his shoulder.

"I didn't mean to upset you," Siv said.

"I know," Cassie said. "You meant to make me happy. It was sweet of you. It means so much to me that it was something you wanted."

He kissed the top of her head. "At least I just proved your faith isn't completely gone."

She gave him a questioning look.

"You just said you want to someday marry me," Siv said. "In a church."

179

Despite how low she felt, that made her laugh. It came out as a snort, which just made her laugh even more. "Reckon I did," she said.

"Well, darlin', I'll take that little bit of your faith that's left," Siv said. "Cause that's all you need. Faith the size of the smallest seed can move the tallest mountain. Everything will work out just how God wants it to."

It wasn't lost on her that this sounded a lot like the conversation she'd had with Krulgoth at the barrel racing field, except that her role was now reversed.

"How can you possibly be so sure?" she asked.

"When my mama was dying of cancer, none of us were fair to middlin'. Daddy worked as much as he could. Cam got angry. A lot. Sammy tried to take over for mom – the cooking, the cleaning. She ran herself ragged. And me? I didn't know what to make of any of it. Especially since mama was so calm while the rest of us fell apart. One day, towards the end, I asked her about it. How she could seem so... so OK with what we all knew was coming. And she told me, 'Complete abandonment.'"

Cassie frowned. "She felt abandoned by God, too?"

"No, *she* was the one doing the abandoning. From herself. From her worries and her cares. She told me she could remember all the great things that had happened in her life if she wanted to. She could also dwell on her mistakes. Lament her regrets. She could shake her fist at the future she'd never have. Weep over the grandchildren she'd never get to see. But she told me none of that would make any sense. The past was the past. The future was only what God would give to her. All she really had was right then – that moment. That *now*. So she took the past and the future and" – he extended an arm

180

outward – "handed everything to God. Told him it was all in his Almighty hand. She lived only in each moment she had left. It was like she was a baby again, and God was her father. Total dependence. Complete abandonment." He bit at his lip. "And my *God*, was she at peace."

"Wow." Cassie couldn't imagine such reliance on anyone, even God. She was far too used to taking an extremely active role in bringing about her future. "I wish I'd have known her."

"She was a saint," Siv said. "Don't reckon how she ended up with a sinner like me for a son. But I do believe God's still holding us in his hand. You. Me. Us. He'll make your dreams come true eventually, or else he'll surprise you with something you never expected."

Yes. Yes, but not right now. I have something better planned.

"I just need to know," Cassie said. "Maybe my faith should be stronger than that, but I need to *know* he's still there. I need to know I'm not going to lose people I love anymore. That I'm going to get to use my power to heal them. I need to know that my plan – my dream – is still alive. I don't need to know *how* things will work out. I can take that on faith. But I just need to know that things *are* going to be OK. That I'm still going to be a doctor."

Siv closed his eyes, and Cassie closed hers. Their hands remained tightly joined. "Lord, give your daughter a sign," Siv prayed softly. "Put her heart to rest. Let her feel herself inside your loving hand."

Oh, how she longed for that feeling again.

"Amen?"

"Amen," Cassie said.

But she didn't feel it. Not right now. Not before the prayer or after.

She didn't feel anything.

Chapter Thirteen

Two Hundred Thirty-Seven Years Ago

Facts and logic combined made hypotheses. Hypotheses and experiments – carefully controlled and free of error, bias, and emotion – made new facts. When done correctly, the cycle repeated itself in a spiral of forward motion. The attainment of knowledge. This was the way of rational thought, and it had long been Krulgoth's anchor.

That anchor had lifted three days earlier, and Krulgoth now found himself adrift on a tumultuous sea. No new knowledge was being sought out and acquired. The thoughts and suppositions that occupied Krulgoth's mind had only a whiff of fact when they had any at all. For the most part, they were lies, follies, and fantasies. Fictions. Hopes based on nonsense. Wishes and dreams.

The worst part was: the deaths of his brothers at his own hand had so twisted his mind that he believed them all. Even the fantasies. No – *especially* the fantasies.

Krulgoth's eyes burned in their desperate attempt to close themselves, but he refused to submit to exhaustion. He watched the Shakren peacekeepers three levels below the lab die simulated deaths at the hands of simulated Kiloniks. Ten times the number of peacekeepers participated in the simulation as there had been just three days earlier. The Life had balanced the equation. He'd figured out that the only way to capture Kilonika was with overwhelming numbers. If that meant thousands or even millions of peacekeepers died, so be it. All hail the Luminous Ones.

The coolness of the window glass against his forehead felt pleasant – almost comfortable enough to put him to sleep. He jerked away and shook his head, forcing himself alert. He needed a stimulant. The bioprinter made one for him. "Thank you, S-17," he said as he removed it from the construction chamber. Why shouldn't his colleague be present but invisible and untouchable? Krulgoth had been manufactured in a lab by a race of intangible entities most people considered ghosts. Were invisible dead people only he could see and hear such a stretch?

"You're right," Krulgoth told S-24. (For why shouldn't he still be alive, too?) "I am risking stimulant overdose at this point. A muscle enhancer should strengthen my heart and stave off cardiac arrest." He procured one from the bioprinter and injected it into himself.

The familiar hiss of smoke and pungent odor marked the Life's arrival. Adrenaline flooded Krulgoth's body. He dropped the empty syringe, let it shatter on the floor, and faced the Evil One.

"Time's up, smart meat," the Life said. One side of his mouth was turned up in a malicious grin. He raised his right hand and conjured his cudgel. He'd come to kill Krulgoth, and he was ready.

But Krulgoth was ready, too.

"I wanted to spend the last three days the same way I've spent the last several decades," he said. "Researching what it is about me that makes me capable of disobeying you. My goal is to use Geneditor to replicate that difference in my brothers and free them from their bondage."

The Life dropped his cudgel, which vanished into smoke, so that he could clutch his belly with both hands and bend over laughing. "Seriously?" he spat out between guffaws. "Oh my gosh, you beautiful moron. The ignorance. The stupidity. Tell me again. Please. I want to hear you say it again."

"I should have gone back over all my data," Krulgoth said. "I should have run more full DNA comparisons between my genes and those of all twenty-three other scientist Shakren ever manufactured. After all, once you kill me, there won't be anyone else to continue my work. No one left who even knows a Shakren *can* disobey you. No one left to unlock the genetic enhancements necessary to liberate all Shakren."

"This is too funny," the Life said between laughs. "You don't have a clue. You don't have a friggin' clue."

"Maybe I could have solved in three days a problem me and S-15, S-16, S-17, and all the other *murdered* Shakren scientists haven't been able to solve for decades. But it seemed..." He pointed a shaking finger at his head. "*Irrational.* But then it hit me. The problem. *My* problem. I've been *too* rational! I've been mired in the scientific method. Instead of being a slave to you, I've been a slave to fact and reason. But *you* liberated me, Life! The Murderer. Whatever your name is. I have you to thank for freeing me from the shackles of logic!"

"I broke your mind!" the Life cheered. "You can't even think right anymore. It's one of the funniest things I've ever seen, but I gotta say, it won't be fun to kill you anymore. Now it'll be a mercy. And I'm not into mercy."

"Nor am I," Krulgoth said. "That's why I and every other Shakren aboard this ship are going to leave.

"Right after I kill you."

The Life's black eyes went wide. His jaw dropped open.

Then he exploded into laughter again, this time with twice the intensity.

185

The three chrome interlocked triangles that made up the Life's badge should have glistened under the lab's bright white lights, but they remained dull. Why didn't they reflect light like every other metal in the universe? How did the Evil Ones summon matter, such as their weapons, out of thin air? What was their energy source? Why did his creators not obey the laws of physics?

And a more important question – who cared? Because if the Evil Ones didn't have to obey the laws of physics, then neither would Krulgoth. The idea was completely irrational. So be it!

He reached towards the counter and picked up a scalpel. It was the one S-17 had used to carve his own tongue out of his mouth. He held it up before him and took three steps closer to the Life. "S-17 says it's OK if I use this," Krulgoth said. "He says it would be *poetic*." His face twitched.

The Life took three steps forward until he and Krulgoth stood toe-to-toe. "It's a shame I have to put this show to an end." He pointed at his gray-skinned face. "Go ahead. I'll give you a free shot just so I can see the look on your face when your last hope dies. Seriously. Go ahead."

Krulgoth reared back his arm. He slashed the razor-sharp scalpel across the Life's face. And the blade cut deep... into *tangible flesh.*

The Life howled. Krulgoth's attack had carved a notch through his nose and had come within a half-inch of his left eye. Black smoke poured out of the laceration. And underneath the smoke... At first, Krulgoth thought the Life had been cut so deeply that muscle had been exposed, but it wasn't muscle underneath his flesh. It was fire. That might have bothered Krulgoth back when he was a slave to reason, but it didn't matter now.

"He bleeds, S-17!" Krulgoth yelled. "I cut him, S-24! I cut him!"

"You can't!" the Life shouted.

Black smoke poured from the palm of the Life's right hand as he summoned his cudgel. Krulgoth seized his wrist. The metal spikes on the Life's bracelet were now very tangible, and they punctured Krulgoth's hand, but he didn't let go. He twisted the Celestine's wrist, turning the weapon away from him. With his right hand, he slashed the scalpel at the Life's face, chest, hands, anything he could cut. Anything he could wound.

"You– you– no," the Life said. "You can't! You can't do this!"

Krulgoth stabbed the scalpel into the middle of the Life's chest, hoping he was putting it deep into a heart. The Life gasped, and his black hole eyes went wide with terror. Krulgoth left the blade there. He twisted the Life's cudgel-holding wrist until he heard a bone snap, and the Life dropped his weapon, which dissipated into smoke. Krulgoth pounded the Life's face with his right fist, over and over and *over*. With each hit, he twisted his knuckles on impact, attempting to rip open and widen the scalpel wounds he'd already cut into the monster's face.

The Life kicked Krulgoth in the gut, sending him a step backward. Krulgoth's left hand was covered in soot and nearly immobile from where he'd cut it on the Life's bracelet spike, but he didn't care. The Life turned to run. Krulgoth seized the back of his vest. It felt like leather, now that it could be touched. He dragged the Evil One away from the door and shoved him towards the window.

Smoke poured out of the Life's body around the scalpel handle still embedded in his chest. Krulgoth grabbed the Life's left wrist – this time just below his spiked bracelets – and

187

slammed the spikes up into the Celestine's chin, his neck, and his face. First, he attacked with a grunt. Then with growls. The Life whimpered and slapped his hands at Krulgoth defensively.

"You're not doing this!" the Life whimpered between blows. "You can't! It's impossible, and you're *not doing it!*"

Krulgoth punched him, clawed at him. He was a starving animal who could smell that a kill was near. Krulgoth wrapped the fingers of both hands around the Life's throat and squeezed with every ounce of force he could muster. He screamed with the effort, right into the Life's face, his hands shaking around the Life's throat. The Celestine gagged. He clawed at Krulgoth's hands and face. The Life was fighting for his life, and it was the most beautiful piece of justice Krulgoth had ever witnessed.

With one hand around the Life's neck and the other under one of his arms, Krulgoth called forth all his strength, lifted the Life off his feet, and threw the Evil One against the glass. The window shattered, cutting Krulgoth's arms and torso and drawing black blood. The Life fell over the edge, screaming all the way down.

Krulgoth stepped as close as he safely could and watched. When the Life hit the simulated rocks three decks below, there was no crunching of bones and no splatter of flesh. Instead, a ball of fire blasted upward from the point of impact. A cloud of the thickest black smoke Krulgoth had ever seen followed. The sulfuric odor was stomach-turning. When the smoke cleared, the Life was gone.

Under the weight of exhaustion and emotion, Krulgoth nearly collapsed. He hadn't just touched a Celestine. He'd killed one. He'd murdered the Murderer.

And it wasn't a secret. The hundreds of Shakren peacekeepers who'd been training three decks below had stopped their simulation. Some stared at the place where the Life had fallen. They watched the smoky remains of one of their Celestine masters dwindle into embers, then sparks, then nothing. Others stared up at Krulgoth. His uniform was ragged and stained with both soot and his own blood. Shards of glass from the window were still embedded in him. There were scorch marks on him, too – and now, as the adrenaline wore off, Krulgoth realized he'd been burned on his hands and face by the fire the Celestine had bled.

"Freedom!" one of the peacekeepers yelled. The cry was echoed by others until it became a chant.

The laboratory door behind Krulgoth opened, and three peacekeepers burst in. Their weapons were holstered. "Are you all right?" one of them asked.

Krulgoth nodded. He blinked and rubbed at his temples. He felt as if he were waking from a deep sleep. "I am wounded, but I will heal," he said, a little surprised to hear he was back to his old monotone. They needed a plan. He needed to think. "We must gather into the *Virtue*-class shuttles. The Way and the Truth will return soon. Our time is limited."

"Other ships will track us," another of the peacekeepers said.

"We'll get as far as we can, then stop at an occupied world and trade the shuttles for something larger," Krulgoth said. "Something non-Celestine that they can't track as easily."

"What if the Way and the Truth come after us?" the last peacekeeper said.

"Then I'll kill them, too," Krulgoth said.

Something like awe came across the peacekeepers' faces.

"What's your designation?" the first peacekeeper said.

"My *name* is Krulgoth."

189

The light caught something on the floor. Next to his feet, amid shards of glass from the window, was the Life's badge. Curious – it reflected the lab's lights now, but it was no longer made of three interlocking triangles. One had been broken. Krulgoth appreciated the irony, considering the broken Celestine he'd just thrown through a window. He kicked at the badge, half-expecting his boot to pass right through it or for it to vanish into smoke the way its owner had, but it was still tangible. That was odd. But Krulgoth decided he'd hold on to this last piece of irrationality as a trophy. He reached down, picked up the badge, and pinned it to his uniform. Then he turned to the broken window and called down to the assembled Shakren below.

"The Life is dead," he said. "We are now liberated Shakren. And we will *never* be enslaved again."

Chapter Fourteen

"Everything looks so peaceful up here," Annalie said.

"Up here" was two-hundred fifty miles above Verde's north pole. Cassie stood at the front of the *Turkey's* control deck – they were really calling this ship the *Turkey?* – right behind Annalie's pilot seat. Aside from a sliver of their green world at the bottom edge of the viewport, all that was outside was a vast void of black space and so many white stars. Which did absolutely nothing to ease Cassie's feelings of insignificance.

Behind them, the entire ship had been stripped down to its hull. They'd mounted a couple of jump seats off to the side, and symmetric rows of tie-down hooks lined the deck and the ceiling. Other than that, it was an empty box of dented, beat-up metal. There was enough space to hold a barn's worth of cargo, but all they'd brought was a single rain barrel, tied down with thick leather straps. The ship was so large and so empty, their voices echoed, and an unpleasant frowsy scent wafted through the entire cabin, but Cassie couldn't complain. With minimal time, they'd managed to make the ancient, decrepit ship spaceworthy. Making it clean enough to eat off would have to come later.

Cassie braided her hair, both to make sure it stayed out of her face and also to keep her hands from shaking. It wasn't her danger sense. That was silent. It was her lost confidence. Her decimated faith. *Do not delude yourself*, the Way had said with one of the most soothing voices she'd ever heard. *God has abandoned you.*

But that was just a lie. Wasn't it?

She was still waiting for that sign she and Siv had prayed for.

"Nine minutes," Krulgoth announced.

This was the event for which they'd spent three weeks preparing: a full-scale invasion of Verde. When the demons arrived two hundred years earlier, they came on just one ship. This time, an entire fleet was about to descend on her world. Annalie's fingers nervously drummed on the ship's control panel. Siv breathed heavily, and Cassie could practically see his pulse in his neck. They were all as anxious as a long-tailed cat on a porch full of rocking chairs.

Which made it something of a shock when Fritz suddenly burst out laughing.

"Care to share the joke?" Cassie asked him.

"I had to make a trip to the outhouse in the middle of the night," he said.

"Sorry I asked," Cassie said.

"It's nothing disgusting," Fritz said. "At least not in the way you think. On the way there, I saw a possum." He shuddered. "Hideous creatures. But it made me remember that time I was trapped in the outhouse by the pack of rabid dogs, and you had to save me."

Annalie looked up sharply from her control panels. "What in the heavens?"

Cassie couldn't help but smile at the memory. "They weren't *rabid.*"

"Dirty, smelly, rabid, all the same thing," Fritz said. "They attacked me for no reason."

"You were walking to the outhouse with two fistfuls of bacon!" Cassie said.

Siv retched. "You were taking food into the *outhouse?*"

192

"I'd planned to eat it on the way there," Fritz said. "Before those dogs attacked me."

"You couldn't have left it in the kitchen and just waited two minutes?" Cassie said.

"One does not simply wait on bacon," Fritz said.

Annalie pointed at him. "That's why I love you."

"Eight minutes," Krulgoth said.

"Keep talking," Siv said. "This sounds too good."

"If you continue down the road from the village past our farm, you come to a dead-end at the Murphy ranch," Cassie said. "They have the three most lovable dogs. They're supposed to be sheepdogs to help Mr. Murphy tend his herd, but they're the *worst* sheepdogs you'll ever meet. They're beautiful. So playful. But they wander. They wouldn't stay with their sheep if their lives depended on it."

"Playful?" Fritz said. "They tried to kill me!"

Cassie put a hand up to shush him. "They were wandering down the road one day, ignoring the herd back home as always, when they ended up downwind of Bacon Boy here. They came running after the bacon–"

"After *me*," Fritz said.

"–and instead of just stopping and saying hello, or sharing his bacon with them, God forbid, he ran for it. Locked himself into the outhouse."

"They chased me!" Fritz objected. "They barked really loudly. They clawed at the door to try and get me."

"No, they tried to get the meat you had in your hands," Cassie said. "Mom was in town. Dad was out in the fields. I was his only hope, and by the time I found him, he was screaming for his life."

"Your folks were away?" Siv asked. "Wait a minute. How old were you two that they could leave you both alone? When did this happen?"

"Five years ago," Cassie said.

Siv gaped for a beat before bursting into laughter. "This happened when he was an *adult?*"

"Why is that so funny?" Fritz said.

Siv doubled over with laughter.

"Once I figured out what was going on," Cassie said, "I had to yell over the dogs to get him to just eat the dang bacon already. But even after he did, it was too late. Those dogs wouldn't budge. I thought he was going to stay locked in there all night. I should have let him."

"I don't know how she did it, but she tamed those beasts," Fritz said. "Somehow."

Cassie rolled her eyes. "Oh, it was so ingenious. I went into the house and got them some jerky. Then I pet them and actually gave them some attention. We played fetch-a-stick all the way back to their house."

"My hero," Fritz said.

"The guy who took down the Steelterrors, hiding out in the crapper to escape a couple of sheepdogs," Siv said. He laughed again.

Fritz shrugged and lowered the faceplate of his helmet.

"Hiding his face, he's so ashamed," Siv said between guffaws.

"Six minutes," Krulgoth said.

"Hey, sis," Fritz said. His voice was in Cassie's earpiece. He was speaking through the voice-comm, and apparently directly to her. No one else made like they could hear him. "It's good to see you laugh. I should have said something sooner, but we've been so busy. I'm sorry."

She furrowed his brow. What was he talking about?

"I thought you should remember that story," he said. "It might not be the best example, but it's an example, nevertheless. Of how you never give up. I know you're upset about the university, but just... don't let it get you too down. OK? You always find a way."

She wanted to tell him she wasn't so sure. It was God who'd always found a way for her, and she just followed. If he wasn't leading her anymore...

"I know everything's hitting you pretty hard right now," Fritz said. "Right in the soul. But you're the most determined person I've ever known. I'm actually a little afraid of you when I'm between you and what you want. You're going to find a way to carry out every part of your plan. And that's not just my power talking. It's your brother."

He reached an arm out, hesitated, then put it around her. It was one of the few times Cassie could remember that he'd made voluntary physical contact with her. Or anyone.

She touched his hand and bit her lip. "Gratitude," she said so softly he'd have to read her lips. Everyone around them was still oblivious to their conversation.

"Five minutes, twenty-nine seconds," Krulgoth said. He shuffled his black metallic feet. Fully covered with black Traskian armor, he looked less like a stack of spare parts and more like one of the Steelterrors. Probably because Fritz and Annalie had harvested the armor from the remains of Samson.

"December 19 on our calendar," Siv said. "Mark it, Krulgoth. Your people are gonna be free today."

"If, somehow, you're all correct," Krulgoth said, "and there is an afterlife in which you are aware of the events occurring

195

amongst the living, I hope S-17 and S-24 get to watch when I destroy the Way and the Truth."

"Who were they?" Cassie asked. "Didn't the Way mention them when he came to our farm?"

"He did," Krulgoth said. "S-17 and S-24 were my brothers. My twins – scientists just like me. My colleagues. My friends. The Life tricked me into killing them."

"And I'm very sorry that happened," Fritz said. "But can we try to avoid having any more killing? Even of the Evil Ones?"

"No," Krulgoth said. "They must die. And they will."

Well then. There wasn't much to say after that, so they all just waited.

A few silent minutes later, Cassie's danger sense came alive, but unlike it ever had before. She didn't feel under threat of imminent harm. Instead, she felt as if a mantle of palpable dread had descended over her. For the first time in her life, she had an idea of what it felt like when people said they were sick to their stomach. She braced herself on the back of the empty co-pilot's chair. Her guts felt as dark as the vastness of space outside the ship's front windows.

And as sudden as the gunshot that killed Gunter Asheford, the appearance of another ship broke that darkness.

Its back half was more-or-less what Cassie expected a space-faring capital ship to look like. It was gray and roughly rectangular in shape but with curved edges, and covered with portholes – some dark, some lit from the inside. But its front half was *nothing* like what she'd expected. The ship's front looked like a giant auger a thousand times larger than a post hole digger. Helical screw blades spun around a central core filled with brilliant white fire as if the ship had just drilled and burned its way through space to get to Verde. Within a few moments of the ship's arrival, its blades' rotations slowed to a gentle, casual pace, but they never came to a complete halt. The back half of the ship rotated at an identical speed but in the opposite direction. The fire in the ship's core dulled to blue, then orange, and finally an ember-like red.

Another ship arrived, and then another, and then another, all identical to the first in shape and size. Each was *not there* one moment, then *there* the next. Cassie imagined an audible *pop* with each ship's appearance like each one was a corn kernel popping on the stove. The map screen at Annalie's station lit up with dots, each one representing a Celestine vessel. An entire fleet of ships, just as the scanners had promised. The mantle of dread Cassie felt grew heavier. Siv grumbled a curse word under his breath.

"Ho-lee mo-lee," Annalie said, stretching each syllable.

They were everywhere, spread out across the space above Verde like game pieces lined up on a board – or more appropriately, like infantry lined up on a battlefield. None of the Celestine ships moved towards them or towards the planet. They didn't alter their position at all. They just hovered in space, their helical blades settling into a slow, casual rotation. Eventually, their pace of arrival slowed.

"How many?" Cassie said after a minute had gone by with no new ships arriving.

"One-hundred four," Fritz said.

"They'd have seen us by now," Annalie said. "Wouldn't they have? So the kemosite's working?"

"Yeah," Fritz said. "We're hidden."

"From the Shakren maybe," Krulgoth said. "But I promise you the Evil Ones know exactly where we are."

"How?" Cassie demanded.

"They always do," he said, and he pointed at a ship in the middle of the Celestines' formation. "This is a standard formation, and that is the current cathedral ship. The Evil Ones are there."

Annalie pushed buttons on her controls, cross-referencing between her readouts and what she could see out the front viewport. The kemosite keeping them hidden rendered their own sensors equally useless, so the ship was unable to automatically plot her a course. It had to be done manually.

When she sat back and took a deep breath, Fritz put his hand on her shoulder. "Ready?"

Annalie nodded and put on a brave smile. "I guess."

"You can do this," Fritz said. He climbed into the co-pilot's seat next to Annalie and strapped himself in. Cassie and Siv made their way to the side of the cabin and fastened themselves into the jump seats. With a hum of sparks, Krulgoth engaged electromagnets in his feet and secured himself to the floor.

Siv made the sign of God's hand. "May the Almighty's hands be yours, Red."

Cassie kept her own hands on her knees.

"Gratitude," Annalie mumbled. Her lips moved silently as she performed mental math, comparing her numbers against the ones on her control screen until she gave a satisfied nod. "Y'all ready?"

Annalie pushed a button on her console, and the *Turkey* surged forward, straight towards the Celestine ships. Cassie's stomach got left a hundred yards behind her. Out the front window, one ship in particular – the cathedral ship – rapidly grew closer and larger. Much closer. *Dangerously* larger. The *Turkey* zoomed towards a dome-shaped protrusion made of

198

glass or some other kind of advanced transparent material on the side of the cathedral ship, though since the ship continued to slowly rotate, the "side" would soon be the "top" – from their perspective anyway.

The *Turkey* shook and rattled. A bolt felt out of the hull not far from Cassie's head. Had any of the test flights taken the ship to this high velocity?

Sixteen times they'd practiced slowly sneaking up alongside the Celestine cathedral ship, docking against it, cutting their way inside, and fighting their way to the control center. But after the real Celestines had crashed their practice back on the farm, leaving the white demons behind wasn't the only part of the plan that had to change. If Krulgoth was right, and the Celestines already knew they were here, there was no need for subterfuge. They didn't need to sneak in.

They could just pound down the Celestines' front door.

With a barely-stifled scream, Annalie *increased* the throttle.

"Knock knock," Siv said.

The front of the *Turkey* smashed through the cathedral ship's dome, then came to a sudden, jolting stop. The leather restraints seized Cassie and squeezed her against her seat. Her stomach slammed back into her abdomen, then lurched straight up her throat. The rain barrel tipped over and shattered, spilling fifty-five gallons of dirt across the deck. Blue energy shimmered at the edges of the cargo ship's front windows. It was the safety force field Krulgoth promised would activate as soon as they breached the cathedral ship's hull... and that would augment the *Turkey*'s brakes and prevent the impact from flattening her passengers. Well, it worked. Outside the front viewport, broken glass and shrapnel covered the cathedral ship's gray metal wall – or was it the cathedral ship's floor? There was smoke, and an alarm klaxon repeated over and over.

The dirt spread across the *Turkey*'s deck contracted inward in defiance of the laws of physics. It rose into a column, and Sierra took her human shape.

Fritz was already climbing out of his chair. "How's your cohesion?" Fritz asked her. "Holding up?"

She rocked her hand from side-to-side. The spirit of the planet had left the planet. Her eyes were sunken, and the dark rings around them didn't look intentional for once. Her skin was ashen. Her hair was a dull green and lacked its usual vibrancy. Cassie's official med student diagnosis? She looked like hell.

"Let's go," Fritz said. He used the rockets on his suit to propel himself to the cargo ship's door, but Krulgoth reached it first. The robot demon stepped out of the ship and fell... sideways?

"We'll transition from our gravity to theirs," Fritz explained before he, too, fell out the door sideways. Annalie followed, adjusting the metal circlet on her forehead – the Mantissa reader mind blast emulator. Sierra exited next, then Cassie. The drop was much farther than she'd expected, but a cushion of air compliments of Sierra softened her impact. Siv took up the rear.

They followed Krulgoth around the cargo ship's nose, which from the cathedral ship's perspective was standing straight-up-and-down at the control center's middle. Just like the forest clearing back home where they'd simulated this place, the room was circular, but the real thing was *much* more expansive. It wasn't a control *center*. It was a control *arena*. Four or five concentric rows of workstations circled the main floor and spread up and out towards the back wall. Stairways spaced equidistantly apart provided access between rows and down to the floor. Flashing red alarm lights gave the room an eerie shade. Steam burst out of broken conduits.

Though many of the workstations were obscured by smoke, every one Cassie could see was operated by a Shakren – a *real* Shakren, not one of Fritz's chipware simulations. And they didn't sit and sip coffee and read reports off their workstation's screens. Some nursed lacerations from the shower of glass that had peppered the room when the *Turkey* crashed through its ceiling. Most stood behind their chairs, armed with rifles pointed right at Cassie and her friends, on guard.

Guarding *them*. Cassie saw them through the haze of the steam, waiting off to the side on the main floor. The Celestines. They were dressed exactly as they had been in the forest. The Truth was dressed for business in a black jacket and pants. The Way seemed ready for church services in a black cassock. Were their closets full of multiple versions of the same intangible outfit? Or did they shape-shift like Sierra – and like how the Truth summoned her sword? Oddly, their silver badges didn't seem to reflect the red light from the alarms or the blue light from the force field that contained the ship's heat and air.

Other than that all-encompassing dread, Cassie's danger sense remained silent. Despite being in the invading fleet's cathedral ship, despite being surrounded by the Celestines and so many Shakren they were outnumbered ten-to-one, she was not in immediate harm. Which didn't make any sense. The Celestines knew she and her friends planned to stop them. They'd said as much back in the forest. So why weren't the Shakren already shooting?

Is this my sign? Cassie prayed. *Do I not sense any danger because your Almighty hand is guiding me in this valley of shadow?*

201

Would she audibly hear an answer? Or feel one in her heart? There wasn't any time to dwell on it. It was time to do what they'd come to do.

Green laser-light shot out of emitters in Fritz's shoulders and formed a rough outline around the Way and the Truth. It was a trick her brother had come up with to help Krulgoth shoot that which he couldn't see. Fritz popped his weapons out of their hidden compartments in the forearms of his chipsuit. Krulgoth refactored his upper arms into laser cannons.

"Stand down," Fritz said to the Celestines. "Release the Shakren from your command. All of them."

True to his promise, Krulgoth didn't waste time on negotiations. He fired at the Way and the Truth, shooting to kill, but his shots passed harmlessly through them. Fritz joined in, but also with no effect. Their laser cannons oscillated in pitch, up and down, like a child puffing air up and down a harmonica just to hear how much noise she could make. Their networked systems tried multiple frequencies to find one that could harm the intangible Celestines.

The indicator on Annalie's circlet was brightly lit, but her teeth were clenched, and she groaned in frustration. "The mind blaster ain't working!" She looked at a Shakren. He cried out, grabbed his head, and collapsed. "At least not on the Celestines it ain't."

Sierra stepped forward – unsteady and almost tripping over her own boots in the process. A torrent of wind and cold howled towards the Celestines. The steam hovering throughout the control center solidified into ice, dropped to the deck, and shattered. The Shakren guards – who didn't fire their weapons, despite their masters being under direct attack – cowered. The ones immediately behind the Celestines froze in place, their faces dripping with icicles, their skin a pale shade of blue. Lingering smoke from the *Turkey*'s battering-ram entry dissipated under Sierra's wind, but not so much as a hair on the Celestines' heads fell out of place.

"Time for magic," Siv said. He pumped his shotgun, fired a silver bullet at the Way; pumped it a second time, and fired one at the Truth. Simultaneously, Cassie nocked an arrow whose head had once belonged to the Ancients and shot at the opposite target. Siv believed the arrowheads were magical and that they might work. Cassie didn't think they were anything but dime-store trinkets, but she was willing to try anything. But her betrothed's bullets passed straight through the Celestines' heads and blasted chunks of hull plating and chipware out of the walls behind them. Cassie's arrows sailed harmlessly through their chests and stuck into workstations.

"Use your bare hands!" Siv yelled to Krulgoth. "That's how you killed 'em before!"

Fritz stopped his laser barrage so Krulgoth could advance. Sierra called off her winds and collapsed to her knees, exhausted. Krulgoth bounded towards the Celestines and reached his lower left hand out towards the Way. His lower right hand grabbed where Fritz's laser outline indicated the Life's throat was.

His hands passed right through both of them.

Krulgoth took three awkward steps backward and glanced at Cassie, Fritz, and Siv with an incredulous look on his electronic face. None of their ideas had worked. Not a single one.

The Way sighed. "I'm disappointed you've chosen the sword," he said.

"I'm disappointed you've chosen the sword," a Shakren off to the side repeated so that Krulgoth could hear.

Doors at the top of each of the arena's staircases slid open. Krulgoth saw who stood behind them.

"No," Krulgoth said.

"But I'm not surprised," the Way said.

The white demons descended the staircases and joined them on the arena floor.

Chapter Fifteen

The Shakren guarding the room made no effort to stop the white demons. When all fifty or so of them reached the bottom, they bowed low towards the Celestines. Each of them wore translator devices at their throats – the ones Fritz had designed and built for them. Because these weren't Shakrath the Celestines had made for themselves. These were Krulgoth's brothers. Their demon allies. The people they'd been working with and practicing with for a month. The ones who they'd left back home on the farm specifically so that the Celestines couldn't enslave them.

Krulgoth's arms fell to his side.

Bowing next to the Truth, Cassie recognized Skleght. "They came to your farm and ordered us to sleep," he said when she caught his eye. "We awoke on a stealth ship as it docked with–"

"Stop speaking to her," the Way said to him.

Skleght spoke no more, but he gave Cassie a look that said all he had to. He'd lost his freedom. He was once again a slave of the Celestines. He'd be better off if Cassie hadn't stopped Krulgoth from mercy killing him and the rest of the demons.

And if the Celestines ordered the demons to attack, mercy was most definitely *not* something they would show.

Fritz turned to Cassie, Siv, Annalie, and Sierra and raised the faceplate on his helmet. His lips trembled. "I... I don't know what else to do."

Her brother was the one whose whole Mantissa power was a hyper-intuition that spawned ideas no one else had even considered. If *he* was out of ideas...

"I got nothin'," Siv said. He glanced around at the demons still on bended knee before the Celestines. "And we're about out of allies."

"General, please!" one of the demons yelled.

"End your resistance," the Way said to the demon, "and serve us in happiness."

The demon bowed so low his snout touched the ground. Then he barked white demon laughter at the sky.

The Way raised his voice to address all Shakren and Shakrath in the room. The Shakren who'd repeated his words earlier continued to do so. "Use deadly force against anyone who attacks one of these modified Shakren," he said. "Except where that order conflicts with the ones I gave you an hour ago."

"I failed," Krulgoth whispered.

"Hold it together, Krulgoth," Siv said.

"Stop calling him Krulgoth," the Way demanded. "You killed Krulgoth, Sivrin McCaig. *That* is not Krulgoth."

"He rests in peace," the Truth said, grinning as if she'd heard a funny joke. A Shakren repeated her words, too.

"Yes," the Way said. He seemed uncomfortable. "Krulgoth's poor soul is in Purgation. It is... difficult for him there."

Krulgoth's head trembled back and forth. Low buzzing sounds, like error tones from a piece of Fritz's restored chipware, came from somewhere inside his robotic body. "*I* am Krulgoth," he said weakly.

"You're not," the Way said. He gestured around him at the white demons. "Why do you think we waited so long to reclaim our escaped peacekeepers? We knew where Krulgoth was. Always. We never once lost track of him since the day he killed the Life. Why else would we have come now unless he – the only being who has ever harmed one of us – was dead?"

"You fear me?" Krulgoth said.

"Yes," the Truth said.

"She lies," Krulgoth said. "Always. Which means you *don't* fear me now. But you *did* fear me before."

The Truth sneered. "Never."

"And you don't fear me anymore because... I'm not... I'm not..." He balled his hands into fists. "I *am* Krulgoth!"

"You're a soulless machine that has been programmed to think like Krulgoth," the Way said. "You use his name, but it is a name I gave to *him*. Not to you."

So that's what they meant back in the forest when they told Krulgoth they knew who he *thought* he was. The real Krulgoth was still dead. The one they were allied with was just a robot copy.

Did that matter?

"Don't listen to them, Krulgoth," Fritz said. "They're both liars. They don't have any way of knowing anything about anyone's soul. They're not God."

The Way narrowed his coal-black eyes and stared at Fritz long enough to make him uncomfortable. "No," he finally said, "we most certainly are not *God*. But we *do* know the state of Krulgoth's soul."

"Bunch of malarkey," Siv said.

The Way looked offended. "The Way and the Truth are not our real names. They are names we gave ourselves, and self-given names carry no power."

"The Life told me his real name was the Murderer," Krulgoth said.

The Way averted his eyes. "Long ago, we were exiled from our home. But that... *abandonment–*"

God has abandoned you.

"–was not the only injustice done to us. We were also branded by our creator with new names. Names that marked us as exiles. He renamed us the Blasphemer, the Liar, and the Murderer."

Siv gasped.

"But the power of names is such that our true names can never be taken from us," the Way said. "Not even by him."

The Truth gave the Way a questioning look. "It's all right," he told her. "Why shouldn't they know the true names of their saviors?" He took a step forward and raised his voice. "The name you shall praise me by is Nariel."

"No," Siv moaned.

"This is Daphne. And the Celestine Krulgoth killed two centuries ago–"

"Was Rudger," Siv whispered.

"–was Rudger," the Way finished.

Fritz spun on Siv. "How did you know that?"

But Siv had gone pale. His hands trembled, and he breathed heavily – too heavily. Cassie hadn't seen him like this since the night she'd first revealed her power to him. The night he'd opened up to her about his crippling anxiety and fears. She thought he'd overcome all of that, but here he was, terrified. "Siv, what's wrong?" she said.

"That's why we can't touch them," Siv said. "Oh, by all that's holy..." His shotgun fell to the ground, and with trembling hands, he made the Sign of God's Hand.

Cassie touched him and reached out with her power to try and sedate him to calmness without putting him to sleep. It worked a little, but not enough. He was still rapidly tumbling into a panic attack. "Siv? Look at me. Focus on me."

"This is beyond us," Siv said. "They're not aliens. They're demons."

Cassie shook her head. "The white demons *are* aliens. We learned that months ago. What are you getting at?"

"Gotteszorn. My favorite constellation," he said, practically panting. "Their names are the names of its stars. Their former home is heaven. They were exiled when God's Almighty hand cast them out. Their new names are their *Curse Marks*."

Cassie went cold.

Do not delude yourself.

"They're the *damned!*" Siv said. "They're the fallen angels!"

The Truth wagged her finger and shook her head.

But the Way smiled sadly... before charred and chipped bones burst out of his back and spread out from his shoulder blades. He stretched out his pair of burnt, broken wings, flapped them once, then folded them against his back.

And then everything descended into madness.

"Son of a..." Sierra muttered.

Annalie screamed.

The assembled army of Shakren and white demons gasped and stirred. Had they ever before seen their masters' true nature?

"Back to the ship!" Fritz yelled.

"General!" one of the demons shouted, reaching out towards Krulgoth before falling into a bow as if pushed there by an invisible force.

Krulgoth pointed his upper arms – still refactored into laser cannons – at the white demon nearest him and fired. Then he shot the next one, and the one after that sequentially down the line. Black blood spurt from their mortal wounds.

"Never! Be enslaved! Again!" Krulgoth cried.

"Destroy that machine," the Way's melodious voice raised over the din. "Let the others go if that be their choice."

The demons Krulgoth hadn't shot yet all leaped at him, swarming him like the pack hunters they were, hanging off of his neck and shoulders and legs. Biting with their teeth. Ripping with their claws. It was just like how Skleght and the others had attacked Krulgoth after the final training session back home, except this wasn't seven-on-one. This was thirty-on-one. Even made of steel and covered with Traskian armor, Krulgoth didn't stand a chance, and if Cassie tried to jump into the fray to save him this time, she'd be torn to shreds.

Fritz spun Annalie back towards their ship and shoved her towards it.

Sierra turned to run, but her legs turned into dirt, and she collapsed. She dragged herself back towards the *Turkey*.

Krulgoth extended the blades from his lower arms' wrists and cleaved one of his brothers in half. "Freedom!" he roared. Would that be his last word? He couldn't possibly survive their assault for long.

Cassie grabbed Siv's hand and pulled him towards the ship, throwing a final look over her shoulder at Krulgoth, the demons, the Shakren, and the Celestines. Were they really the devils themselves?

With a roar, Krulgoth threw his brothers off of him and climbed back to his feet. The Shakren stationed throughout the control center raised their weapons and fired at him, but not with lasers or bullets. Their ammunition was acid. Each shot that hit Krulgoth melted away a fist-sized portion of his

Traskian armor and his robotic body underneath, leaving behind smoke and jagged metal. He fell back to his knees, then was again tackled by swarming white demons.

"He won't survive," Fritz said.

No, he wouldn't. Krulgoth couldn't face all the white demons he hadn't yet mercy-killed *and* the army of Shakren stationed throughout the control center. He was moments away from death. Or blackout. Or whatever happened to machines that died.

"Another life I won't be allowed to save," Cassie said.

"I won't accept that," Fritz said. He raised his arms, and with precisely located, non-fatal laser shots, he picked demons off of Krulgoth. Cassie applauded his "leave no one behind" sentiment, but pragmatically, she knew it was a wasted effort.

"Destroy that machine!" the Way repeated.

"Let him leave with us!" Fritz said. "No one else has to die today."

Annalie grabbed Sierra by the forearms and dragged her along. More of her waist and abdomen was losing form and reverting back to dirt. Could she survive long enough to make it back to Verde? Cassie and Siv ran hand-in-hand. Fritz was falling further behind. "Come on!" Cassie yelled back at her brother.

The rockets on his chipsuit flared to life, and he took to the air. From above, he picked even more demons off of Krulgoth. He shot the acid-wielding Shakren, too, but no one fired back at him. Why had the Way ordered restraint against everyone except Krulgoth?

The Truth vanished in a puff of smoke.

Krulgoth crumpled as he took an acid shot to the hip, and the joint attaching his leg melted away.

211

Fritz took out four more of the Shakren snipers.

Annalie reached the cargo ship's door. She turned and saw Fritz was still halfway across the room and up in the air. "Fritz, come on!" she yelled.

Fritz stopped three more demons from attacking their former general. Krulgoth stretched out his one arm that wasn't pinned. "Gashg..." he said. Then one of the demons still on Krulgoth ripped the arm off and discarded it away from the melee.

The Truth reappeared in the air behind Fritz and opened her hand. Black smoke poured out of it and coalesced into a long, thin sword.

"Fritz, behind you!" Cassie yelled.

Do not delude yourself.

"Daphne, *no!*" the Way shouted. "*No!*"

The Truth drove her sword into Fritz's back. It didn't rip, tear, cut, or break the metal of his chipsuit. Nevertheless, it disappeared into his body then emerged on the other side, out of the center of his chest.

His lasers ceased firing, and he went limp.

God has abandoned you.

Annalie screamed as he fell to the floor.

"Professor!" Siv hollered.

Fritz crashed and didn't move.

Cassie stood frozen.

A demon Fritz had previously shot off Krulgoth leaped, straddled Krulgoth's chest, and gouged its claws into his neck. With a groan of effort, it ripped Krulgoth's robotic head off of the rest of his body and tossed it halfway across the control center.

The Truth, still in the air above everything else, tossed her sword aside, and it disappeared into smoke.

Fritz still hadn't moved.

An animal-like scream from behind Cassie startled her back to awareness. It was Sierra. What was left of her was strewn on the floor at Annalie's feet. Bellowing with the effort, she pulled the dirt she'd "bled" back into herself, then stretched out her arms to an inhuman length. She scooped up Fritz and dragged him across the control center back towards the ship.

Several Shakren converged on Krulgoth's discarded head and shot it with their acid rifles until it melted into slag.

Annalie ran away from the ship, back towards Fritz, reaching out to him. Siv grabbed her at the waist and used her forward momentum to lift her onto his shoulder. She thrashed and kicked, calling out Fritz's name.

Sierra screamed wordlessly as she pulled Fritz closer to them, struggling to hold herself together.

"Daphne, what have you done?" the Way yelled. "You've ruined everything!"

Cassie touched Fritz as Sierra's elongated arms dragged him past her. She reached out with her power. Her brother didn't move. Didn't make any sound at all.

Do not delude yourself.

"Reinhardt," a translated demon voice growled.

Cassie turned. A demon – Gashg – charged towards her. Her danger sense was silent. Of course he meant her no harm. The Way – or the Blasphemer, or Nariel, or whichever devil he was – had ordered that they be allowed to leave, and the white demons had to obey them. Gashg held something out to Cassie. It was one of Krulgoth's arms – the one she'd seen ripped off at the elbow. "Let this be a lesson in what happens to those who defy the Celestines!" he said.

His words were a warning, one either the Way or the Truth must have ordered him to deliver. But his back was to both the devils, and his face... Cassie had spent enough time around the demons to recognize their expressions. His face didn't match his tone. He grimaced. It almost looked as if he were pleading. Was he resisting his forced obedience? Was he trying to escape with them aboard their ship?

He swept a finger across his translator, lowering its volume. "Take it," he said low enough only she could hear. His outstretched arm trembled.

She snatched the robotic arm from him, but before she could grab him and pull him towards their ship with her, he turned and ran back to join his brothers. Had he just wanted to gloat after all? To hell with him then. To hell with all of them. She stormed back towards the *Turkey* and her injured–

Do not delude yourself.

–brother.

"Cassandra!" the Way called out to her. "Please listen to me. I'm sorry this did not go as I planned. But I promised you wouldn't be alone for long, and I meant that. God is unwilling to do what must be done. You know this to be true. But you also must know that I *am* willing. I told you to follow the Way. Accept what I have to offer, and senseless killings will be a thing of the past."

She ignored him. Sierra had already lifted Fritz aboard and pulled herself up after him. She stretched her arms out from inside the ship to take the still-thrashing Annalie from Siv and help her inside. Then she pulled Siv up inside the ship, too.

"We will bring about your chipware restoration," the Way said, continuing to address Cassie as if his army of Shakren weren't there. As if rampaging white demons weren't ripping

214

Krulgoth's metal corpse to shreds. "We will feed your hungry. We will clothe your naked. We will bury your dead. We are the peacemakers, Cassandra. We are the healers. We are the greatest medicine the world has ever had."

"Blessed be the Celestines!" the assembled Shakren and Shakrath called out as one. "Blessed be the Celestines!"

Sierra pulled Cassie up into their ship and slammed the hatch shut behind them before she collapsed to the deck. Her legs and left arm fell apart back into dirt. The parts of her that still looked human looked half-dead.

"Rest," Cassie told her. Sierra made no reply. Maybe she couldn't even hear anymore.

Cassie realized she was still holding Krulgoth's dismembered robotic arm, and she tossed it aside. Fritz lay in the middle of the cargo area. Annalie knelt beside him and took off his helmet. His eyes were closed. "Help him," she begged. Was Annalie talking to her or to God?

Cassie knelt next to Fritz, placed her hand on his exposed neck, and reached out with her power.

"Red?" Siv said to Annalie. "We need you to fly the ship and get us back home. I'd do it, but I don't know how."

Annalie grabbed Fritz's hand. Cassie observed his fingers made no effort to squeeze back. There was no palpable pulse in his neck. "I'm staying with him," Annalie said.

"Cassie won't lose him," Siv said.

Do not delude yourself.

"Please," Siv continued. "You're the only one who can get us away from those... things."

"Are they really the damned?" Annalie asked with a shaking voice.

God has abandoned you.

215

"I reckon they are," Siv said. "Red. Annalie. We've been off-planet so long, Sierra can't hold her shape anymore. She's dying. If the devils change their mind and order their army to keep us here, they'll rip this ship apart the same way they did Krulgoth. Please. Take us home."

Annalie wiped her arm across her face, nodded, and got into the pilot's seat.

Fritz looked pale – far paler than usual.

"Honey?" Annalie called from the pilot's seat. The ship lurched backward and moved away from the Celestine cathedral ship. "You have to hold on. You can't leave me. I just found you, honey. I need you."

Siv knelt beside Cassie, just like he had when she'd tried to help Gunter – when she hadn't been able to save Gunter. She unlatched the front piece of Fritz's armor with one hand, keeping the other on his cheek. She flooded him with her power, but she felt nothing. No air from his nostrils. No pulse at his neck. He wasn't breathing. The dread she felt wasn't coming from her power anymore but from her rational mind. She got his armor open. The shirt he wore underneath wasn't torn or damaged in any way. She unbuttoned it and found his flesh similarly intact. No sign at all of a sword wound. Or of a heartbeat.

"What did she use on him?" Cassie said. "Are his injuries all internal?" She looked at Siv. "You know the scriptures better than anyone I know who isn't a pastor. What kind of weapon leaves no wound and–"

She almost said *kills*.

"–and, and makes... makes people unconscious?"

"There's a prophet who once wrote something about – this ain't in the scriptures," Siv said. "So it's not for certain."

216

"Just tell me!" Cassie snapped. She lowered her eyes, needing to hear what he had to say, but so afraid to hear it she didn't want to see his lips form the words.

"This prophet said the devils' can cleave a person's soul right outta their body," Siv said.

"*Honey?*" Annalie yelled.

"Fritz, can you hear me?" Cassie said.

Do not delude yourself.

The *Turkey* had spun about and lurched up to full speed. Verde loomed large out the front viewport. None of the ships in the Celestine fleet pursued them. None fired any weapons.

"Fritz?" Cassie said. Her power wasn't having any effect.

She knew what was going to–

She knew what *had* happened to him.

But she couldn't accept it.

She brushed a lock of her brother's bangs off his forehead and carefully buttoned his shirt. He wouldn't want his bare skin exposed, not to anybody. He didn't even like taking off his socks. His spectacles – the ones he didn't need but that he wore anyway just because he liked wearing them – were smudged. She gently took them off his face and cleaned them with the tail of her shirt. He looked younger without them. Like the boy with whom she'd spent so many hours playing blocks and cards. And rescuing from boisterous, energetic dogs.

Maybe it would somehow be easier if there were blood, a wound, or if his face were frozen in a grimace, but he looked so peaceful. Like there was nothing wrong with him at all. It was so easy to pretend there wasn't.

Do not delude yourself.

"Talk to me!" Annalie demanded. "Fritz?"

First, Dad. Now...

Oh God, how was she going to tell their mom?

Sierra dragged herself a foot closer. Her face had regained some cohesion, but she still looked like hell, and she could only form half a chest and one arm. "Is he gonna be OK?" she asked. She didn't even sound like angry, crank Sierra. She sounded scared.

Twice Cassie had prayed for a sign that God hadn't abandoned her. That he'd still help her fulfill her dream of healing people. After the first time, Gunter Asheford had been shot dead right in front of her. And after the second time, she'd come face-to-face with the devils *he* kicked out of heaven... and he let them... he let them...

God has abandoned you.

"Oh no," Sierra moaned. "No."

Annalie leaped out of the pilot's seat and returned to Fritz's side. "No!" she screamed. She shook Cassie by the shoulders. "You gotta help him! You promised! Heal him! Heal him!"

Cassie shook her head. Struggled to find her voice. "I can't."

Annalie threw herself across Fritz's prone body, embracing him as if she could reverse what the Celestines had done if she just held him tightly enough, just loved him strongly enough. The sound of her sobs would haunt Cassie for the rest of her life.

Siv put his arm around Cassie's shoulders. "Oh Lord," he mumbled.

"Please," Cassie prayed, covering her face, unable to hold it together any longer. "I'm sorry if it was wrong of me to ask you for a sign, but please, God. Don't do this. Not my brother."

Fritz remained silent. Still.

Gone.

"Not my *brother!*" she yelled. She fell face-first to the ground, pounding the deck with her fists. "Not my *only brother!* Please, God, please!"

She screamed wordlessly until her voice cracked. Because of her power, she'd never been sick. She'd never had a runny nose, never had a headache, never even had a stubbed toe that hurt for more than the briefest moment. Not even once her whole life.

But now she had experience with pain unlike ever before.

Now she knew what it felt like to have her chest hollowed out and gutted.

Chapter Sixteen

Felix yelled and hurled a handful of resistors across the room. They bounced and clattered across the wooden floorboards. Annalie raised her hands helplessly, then slid her back down the wall until she sat on the floor. Her chest shook with her sobs.

He yelled again. A floor-to-ceiling bookshelf stood next to the fireplace. Felix pulled a hardcover off of it and threw it across the room. Then another. And another.

Cassie's mother stood at the window at the kitchen side of the room, staring into the blackness of the night outside. If she realized Annalie's brother was tearing apart their house, she didn't seem very concerned about it.

Felix threw another book and growled.

"Hey, Felix," Cassie said gently, taking a cautious step towards him, "Elise is sleeping in my room. Let's not wake her–"

Felix threw a book that only missed Cassie's head because her danger sense warned her to move. "*Want Fritz!*" he yelled.

Well. At least he *could* speak when he wanted to.

Cassie usually touched the people she healed. She liked the tactile contact. It just felt right that it be her hands that did her healing. But her power, like all Mantissa powers, was actually psychic. She reached into the minds of her patients and gave them instructions to mend their bodies. Touch wasn't strictly necessary.

Siv was ten steps behind and to the side of Felix. With a tiny jerk of her head, she signaled him to get closer. He did, then she mentally reached out with her power and made Felix fall asleep.

Before he hit the floor, Siv scooped him into his arms, just the way Sierra had carried Fritz off the Celestines' cathedral ship. The resemblance wasn't lost on Siv, either. He closed his eyes and took a deep breath to hold himself together. Annalie should have been the one to put Felix to bed, but since she wasn't really in any condition to do that, Siv took care of it.

Cassie sat on the floor next to Annalie and put her arm around her. She leaned over and laid her head in Cassie's lap. Where were her glasses? Did she even know?

"What am I gonna do with Fee?" she murmured. "You saw the two of them together. Fee loved him so much."

"Fritz loved him, too," Cassie said.

"They were inseparable."

Except they weren't. The Celestines had proved that beyond all doubt, hadn't they? Those God-forsaken fallen angels had done a pretty darn good job of permanently separating Fritz and Felix.

"He's only been gone half a day," Annalie said. "I haven't seen Fee this bad in years. He misses Fritz so much."

"So do you," Cassie said. She paused until she could get the words out. "So do I."

Siv gently closed the bedroom door behind him. "Me, too," he added.

Annalie reached under her shirt and pulled out a black metal o-ring hanging from a chain around her neck. She held it up and fingered it, spun it around, tilted it side-to-side.

"Is that from some piece of sentimental chipware or something?" Cassie said.

"It's from Samson," Annalie said. "Fritz gave it to me when he and I went to get kemosite and Traskian armor the other day. He gave it to me as... as a..."

If that was what she thought it was... It couldn't be. They hadn't said anything to anyone? But it was exactly the kind of ring Fritz would use. "That's not a betrothal ring, is it?" Cassie asked.

Annalie closed her eyes against her tears. "We were waiting to tell everyone until this invasion thing was over, but..."

Cassie looked over at her mother. Even that news hadn't gotten a response out of her. Had she even heard Annalie?

"I didn't know," was all Cassie could think to say. She hadn't thought it possible for her heart to ache even more. It was already nightmare enough that Fritz was gone. He'd left behind a betrothed?

"I was really looking forward to being his wife," Annalie said. "And to being your sister-in-law. And now I won't ever get to be either."

"No," Cassie said, wrapping her arms tighter around Annalie. "I know he wanted that, too. It's not his fault it didn't happen. Or yours. So as far as I'm concerned, you *were* his wife. *Are* his wife. And we *are* sisters. From this day, forever. OK?"

Annalie found one of Cassie's hands and squeezed it for dear life. "I'm so lost," Annalie said. "I don't know what to do."

Cassie ran her fingers across Annalie's scalp and down the length of her red hair with her free hand.

"I don't know, either."

A few minutes later – or maybe an hour, who knew? – the front door opened. Duncan stepped inside, carrying his telescope case. The university – when there had been a university – had far more advanced telescopes, but the one Duncan used for his and Siv's favorite hobby was all they had access to right now. It would have to suffice.

Annalie still laid in Cassie's lap. Cassie kissed the back of her head and gently stood to greet Duncan.

"They're still up there," Duncan said. "I can see their ships. They're just small dots of light, but they sure ain't stars."

"What are they waiting for?" Cassie mumbled. They promised an invasion – or in their terminology, "a blessing." They promised to feed the hungry and heal the sick and bring all sorts of good at the cost of everyone's freedom. So why were they just sitting up there? Had the Way really meant it when he said the Truth had ruined everything? Were they not as united as Krulgoth had said they were? Did the Way somehow want to help, but the Truth had gone rogue when she'd murdered Fritz?

"You all right, son?" Duncan asked.

Siv sat on the edge of a rocking chair, pale as flour. He was trembling again. Cassie and Duncan both went to him, and Cassie tried to calm him both by holding his hand and reaching out with her power to lower his heart rate and calm his nerves.

"I saw them, Daddy," Siv said. "The *devils*. One of them even showed off his burnt, clipped wings, just to make sure we knew it was them. I ain't ever been so afraid. Ever. And considering my history, that's saying a lot."

"You're all right," Duncan reassured him.

"Yeah, because they just let us go," Siv said. His voice shook as much as his hands. "We ain't even a threat to them. How can we be? We're just men and women. They're pure spirit. Angels. Damned angels, but still."

224

"Keep the faith, son," Duncan said. "They're nothing next to the Almighty Hand."

The Almighty Hand, which was apparently very busy doing many vital things *elsewhere* in the galaxy because it hadn't bothered to show up and stop the Liar from driving a sword through Fritz's chest.

Cassie wiped the back of her hand across her eyes.

"Cass," Siv said, reaching out to her. "I'm sorry. Forgive me, I... I need to be strong for you."

"You lost your best friend," Cassie said. "You get to mourn, too."

"But you lost your brother," Siv said.

She shrugged. Fritz used to do that all the time, and she'd made so much fun of him for it.

Used to. Oh God, she was already thinking of him in past tense.

"I should get the horses down for the night," Cassie said.

"I'll help," Siv said.

Duncan looked into the kitchen. "Ruth? It's late. You should get some sleep."

Cassie's mother still stared out the window, like she was expecting Fritz to fly over the empty fields at any time, moonlight glistening off his chipsuit.

"Ruth?" Duncan repeated. "Ruth?"

"Hmm?" she said.

Duncan motioned Cassie and Siv that they should go on, that he'd take care of Ruth. Cassie stepped out onto the porch and down into the yard without bothering to get her coat. The air was coldish, and the wind didn't help any, but she didn't care about the chill. The yard's fire pit was still blazing. She'd started it earlier so Mandy and Rebel could keep warm while

225

grazing. The two horses were some distance off, but Mandy slowly clopped over as soon as she spotted Cassie.

The *Turkey* was parked next to the barn. Annalie had abandoned flying it the moment she realized Fritz was gone. It had made for a rather rough re-entry until they were back in Verde's atmosphere, and Sierra had regained her strength and controlled the winds to bring it down safely. The barn doors were closed. The lights inside it were off. For weeks it had been lit twenty-four hours a day – the center of so much bustle. Now it was dead inside. Cassie could relate to that.

"We'll have to go to the church tomorrow and talk about a funeral or something," Cassie said. "I guess."

"When I went to the undertaker, he said Pastor Kolbe would likely come by," Siv said.

Cassie hadn't yet bought Fritz a Lenerstelen present, but she'd planned to buy him new socks. He loved his socks. They'd have to make sure he was buried in some. Had Siv told that to the undertaker? Fritz wouldn't be happy if he was buried without socks.

Would he be buried next to dad?

His grave. She was thinking about her brother's grave. He'd been just twenty-four years old. She shouldn't have to be doing this for at least another fifty years.

"Do you think he's... OK?" she said. "Somewhere?"

"Of course he is," Siv said.

"But their weapon killed him instantly, yet left no physical damage of any kind," Cassie said. She bit her lip, forced out the words. "You don't think they destroyed his soul, do you?"

"They can't," Siv said firmly. "They may have cleaved his soul right out of his body, but no one can *destroy* a soul, not even an angel. Fritz is OK, Cass. He just ain't *here* no more."

Yeah. She didn't need a reminder of that.

"No way he's in Torment," Siv said. "He'll get to heaven. I just reckon he'll need to stay in Purgation a bit."

"Why would you say that?" Cassie said. "He was a good person!"

"He was the best," Siv said gently. "Purgation isn't a place of punishment like Torment. It's a place you go for a spell when you die, but you're still attached to the world. Purgation's where you get used to the idea of moving on. My Mama – she knew she was dying. She was ready. I reckon she may've gone straight to heaven. But most folks need some time. We need to pray for him. When you're in Purgation, it's just your soul. You don't have your body anymore. Your hands can't merit any more graces. So the souls there are relying on us."

"He was betrothed," Cassie said. "He and Annalie were going to be married."

She took her grunblume out of her pocket and wrapped the string of wooden beads around her hand. Part of her wanted to use them to pray the Litany of God's Almighty Hand – to use the beads to keep count for her as she rattled off praises for his holy and mighty deeds. But she couldn't bring herself to do it. Not even for Fritz.

Siv wrapped his arms around her. "I meant what I said in there. I gotta be strong for you. You've been so busy taking care of everyone else."

"That's what I do," Cassie said.

"Gotta let us help you, too," he said. "You're not alone."

"Except I am. At least in spirit, I am. The Way, or the Blasphemer, or Nariel, or whatever you want to call him. That night he was in the confessional, he told me, 'God has abandoned you.' I could dismiss that idea if it remained nothing but him taunting me. But God himself proved it up there today."

When she pointed up at the Celestine fleet's distant lights, the stars that made up the constellation Gotteszorn caught her eye. "In his holy wrath, God's Almighty Hand exiled the fallen angels. He tossed them out of heaven and into *our* world. Into *my* life. And right into the end of Fritz's." She harumphed. "Does that mean this world is Torment? Sure would explain a lot."

"Cass," Siv said.

She shrugged his arms off of her. "I prayed for a sign," Cassie said. "I *begged* for a sign. A simple acknowledgment that God hadn't abandoned me. And he didn't answer that prayer by saying, 'Yes, but not right now.' He sure as sin didn't answer it with 'I have something better planned.' He said 'yes.' And the sign he gave me was my brother's dead body. That's his answer, Siv. He *has* abandoned me."

She stomped closer to the fire. "It wasn't enough for him to take Bernice from me? Harlan, Eroica, Sebastian? It wasn't enough for him to take my dad *one day* after I could have been here to save him? He had to take my only brother, too? *That's* how he answers my prayer?"

"God didn't take Fritz," Siv said. "That devil did. God didn't kill that fella outside the saloon, or Harlan, or Eroica, or anyone. Bad things don't happen because of God. Bad things happen because of people. Usually good people who just make bad choices."

"But we talk all the time about God's *Almighty* Hand," Cassie said. "He doesn't have to allow bad people to do bad things. He could stop it, but he doesn't."

Siv shrugged. "I suppose. But if he didn't let people make mistakes, then we wouldn't really be people. We'd be like wheels on a carriage, going wherever we're led. Having no say for ourselves." He pointed up. "Kinda like them poor souls up there forced to obey the devils. No will of their own. What's worse? A God who gives us our freedom, even if we use that freedom to make mistakes? Or a God who turns us into mindless machines?"

It annoyed her that he was trying to defend God instead of just being there for her. "I'm not debating this with you," she said.

"Sorry," Siv said. "I don't want to either. Just remember. Faith the size of the smallest seed can move the tallest mountain. We have to keep the faith."

"No," Cassie said, much more harshly than she'd intended, but she didn't care. "Not me. Not anymore."

Siv mumbled utterances twice before he managed any words. "You don't believe anymore?"

"I'll believe in God's existence until the day I die," Cassie said. "How *can't* I? When Krulgoth nearly killed me, I found myself out of my body in a tunnel of white light. Today, I was in the same room with a pair of fallen angels. I watched one drive a barking *soul-cleaving sword* through my brother's heart. Oh, I believe. Don't for a moment think I don't believe.

"What I will *not* be doing any longer is praying. Worshiping. Going to church. 'Keeping the faith.' Biting my lip and telling myself, 'Well, Cassie, things are bad, but at least God is there to keep them from getting worse.' He's there, all right, but he doesn't give a *damn* about me, about the dreams he inspired me with, or about the people he gave me to love and then snatched away from me. So no longer – not for *one second longer* – will I give the slightest damn about him."

Siv swallowed hard but didn't say anything.

"You hear me?" she hollered at the sky. "We're done!"

After that, there was only one thing left to do.

She threw her grunblume into the fire.

Chapter Seventeen

Cassie had always been a lucid dreamer. Whenever she dreamt, she was conscious of it, even if only distantly. She once told this to a fellow med student, Velma Lopez, and Velma had reacted as if Cassie had a newly discovered blood type. She'd wanted to interview Cassie for a paper and study her while sleeping. She'd had so many questions.

But Cassie really didn't find this "skill" astounding. In dreams, her actions were entirely unplanned, spur-of-the-moment decisions steered by her stream-of-consciousness. Since that was the exact opposite of how she lived her waking life, it was obvious when she was dreaming. Also: the waking world had color, not just shades of gray.

How had Velma taken the news of the med school's closing?

Had she even survived the Steelterrors' attack?

In Cassie's dreams, Bernice was always a young girl, even when the dreamer in Cassie tried to imagine what she might look like as an adult. The lucid part of Cassie always seemed to overrule the idea and saw only the clinical diagnosis of what had killed her childhood friend: internal injuries. Trauma.

When her dreams took her back to her father's funeral, the dreamer wanted to wish him awake. Wanted a chance to say goodbye. Or just a chance to hunt a deer together, or ride horses together, one last time. All her lucid self could think was: myocardial infarction. Blocked coronary artery. Heart attack.

And then she was back with the Celestines, and the Liar had just run Fritz through with her black sword, and... there was no medical diagnosis. No scientific description of why her brother was no longer alive. What was the medical term for body and spirit separation? That would be plain old "death," right? What was she going to tell the undertaker in the morning? Cause of death: acute body and soul separation?

Tap tap tap

"Reinhardt?"

Maybe part of why she'd felt so *off* ever since learning about the med school closing was that without a plan for the future, the waking world felt more like the dreaming one. Devoid of color. Spur-of-the-moment. Unplanned.

TAP TAP TAP

"Cassie?"

Wait. *That* hadn't been in her dream.

Cassie forced herself awake. She was on a pallet of blankets on the floor of her mother's bedroom. The sun was up because she could see mom's bed and dresser and wardrobe, but it must have been early because the light was still dim. Mom was asleep, so it hadn't been her who'd spoken. It hadn't sounded like her voice anyway. It had sounded like...

Oh. Great. *She* was back.

Sierra stood outside the window. She looked sterner than usual if that was possible. If Fritz had been in the room when she'd tapped on the window, he'd have been startled. Probably would have squealed, too. Cassie chuckled. Of *course* he'd have squealed. And she was going to tell him so next time she–

No. There wouldn't be a next time. She didn't get to talk to him again. Ever.

Cassie threw the top blanket off herself, shuffled to the window, and opened it.

"They're up to something," Sierra said.

Cassie folded her arms across her chest. Any conversation with Sierra Monet was very much an *after* coffee conversation. The morning after her brother's murder, it was an after-two-cups – both spiked with whiskey – conversation. "Can you be more specific?"

"They're landing ships," Sierra said. "Shuttles. Drop ships. There's at least one in all thirty-one human settlements I've visited this morning and a lot more in larger towns like Mondorf and Harbrucken. And they're pumping something into the air. Don't know what it is."

That same sense of dread she felt when their ships first arrived returned. "Is it toxic?"

Sierra raised a pierced eyebrow. "Pretty sure I just said I don't know what it is."

"Where's the nearest ship?"

Sierra cocked her thumb over her shoulder. "Right up the road in Hondo."

"Thanks," Cassie mumbled. "Be right there." She closed the window, padded out of her mother's room, and knocked on Fritz's door. Not Fritz's. The room didn't really have an owner anymore, did it? It still felt unreal. "Siv?" she said. "They're landing ships. Everywhere. Closest one is just up the road."

"I'm up," he called from inside. She returned to her mother's room and found her boots and a leather coat, then headed outside to saddle up Mandolin.

Overnight, the fire in the pit had burned itself out. The remains of her grunblume were somewhere in the ash. Cassie didn't care where.

Siv stepped outside and greeted her with a nod. What a friendly, platonic gesture. Was that because they were fixing to hurry down to the village? Or was that because a good church boy like him didn't want to give a godless pagan a good morning kiss? "Should I wake Red?" he asked.

Cassie shook her head. "Let her sleep. Besides, if Felix wakes up in a mood and she's not here, I don't know what happens. My mom's in no state to deal with him, and Elise or your dad shouldn't have to."

They saddled the horses, charged down the dirt road, and arrived in the village just before nine. It was just as Sierra had said. Almost smack dab in the middle of town, parked in the center of the main street, was a sleek, chrome-covered shuttle. A crowd of people led by Sheriff Auber had gathered around it, but they all kept several paces back. After the Steelterrors' attack in Harbrucken, even a village that had once welcomed Fritz's lights was wary of chipware. Especially chipware that descended from the sky.

Cassie and Siv left Mandolin and Rebel at a hitching post and found Sierra at the back of the crowd. She wore ripped jeans, and her hair was bright green. "Sorry," Cassie said. "Didn't recognize you at first, what since you're doing such a fine job of remaining inconspicuous."

"There's a barkin' spaceship in the middle of your podunk village," Sierra said. "I could grow a second head right now and nobody would pay me a second glance."

"Cassie?" It was Phil, the bartender. "Please tell us that's a piece of Fritz's chipware."

Oh. Of course, they didn't know. Not yet. They'd only know if Mr. Fitzgerald, the undertaker, had spread the news at the saloon the night before, and he'd never been the social type. Reading the crowd, Cassie guessed most folks, everybody, hadn't yet heard. She shook her head at Phil. "No, it's not Fritz's. But we" – she glanced back at Sierra and tried to share

what they knew without revealing themselves as Mantissa –
"we used some of Fritz's chipware to scan beyond Hondo.
These showed up all over Verde this morning."

A frightened murmur spread across the crowd. More folks
emerged from their shops and homes. Andrea Krause. Paul
Klein. Connie Emerson watched from inside the general store,
peeking out from behind the curtains.

Cassie squinted at Phil. The back of his hand was covered
with thick, red welts. "What's on your hand?"

"Don't know," he said. "I just noticed it a few minutes ago. It
itches. I'm allergic to cedar. Maybe cedar season is starting."

"That doesn't look like allergies," Cassie said. There was one
on his face, too. She could heal him with a touch–

A gunshot rang out, and a red energy barrier appeared
around the shuttle. The bullet struck the barrier and instantly
burned to ash. Then, its work apparently accomplished, the
energy barrier disappeared.

"Put that down!" the sheriff barked in the direction of the
shooter.

"Cassie?" someone said behind her shoulder. She turned to
find young Pastor Kolbe offering his hand. He was only a few
years older than her, but because he was four decades younger
than Pastor Seelos had been when he retired, everyone in town
called him "young Pastor." "I'm so sorry about your brother."
He glanced up at the shuttle. "I get the feeling it's going to be a
busy day, but I'll still come by later to see your family."

God has abandoned you.

"Fine," Cassie said. "Thank you."

"If there's anything–"

He was interrupted when someone's pocket watch ticked off
nine o'clock, and a ramp dropped down from the shuttle's

underside. Two columns of twenty Shakren peacekeepers each marched into the street. The only difference between them was the numeric designations on their uniforms. Each was armed with identical heavy-duty laser rifles.

For most everyone assembled in the crowd, this was their first look at the Celestine soldiers. Even if Shakren were more-or-less human but bald with white skin and red irises, they were more than strange enough to hold the crowd in nervous tension. And their guns – chipware rifles – certainly didn't inspire any calm, either. There were gasps, a few startled screams, and several hands dropped to rest on holstered pistols.

A final peacekeeper descended the ramp after the rest. Shortly after his boots touched the ground, an image projected from the side of the shuttle. It was a three-dimensional, life-size image of the Way and the Truth. The devil who'd murdered Fritz. It wasn't a vid. It was a still, but it didn't look like a photograph. It had a texture to it that looked like paint on canvas.

"Citizens of Verde," a Shakren voice said. It was the same voice that had repeated the Way's words back on the cathedral ship. The ship must have been playing it from a chipware device Cassie couldn't see. "The Celestines, who have delivered your world from bondage, would now address you. I will repeat to you the words of the Way."

The image of the Truth shrunk in size; the image of the Way grew larger. "Greetings," the Shakren speaker continued. "I am the Way, and this is the Truth. We are the Celestines."

"He some kind of pastor?" Grady Mitchell – an old friend of her father's – mumbled. Cassie supposed it was an easy mistake to make. The Way wore his cassock like it was the vestment of his twisted religion.

"That ain't no pastor," Siv said.

"Silence!" the lead peacekeeper barked in the Verdant language. Cassie knew from the demons that before visiting a world, that world's language was implanted into the Shakrens' minds.

Sierra's eyes had rolled back, but then full awareness suddenly returned to her. "Same message is being played at all the ships worldwide," she whispered. "I managed to be in three different places at once to confirm."

Cassie shushed her.

"–visitors to planet Verde," the Shakren speaker continued.

"They're from the stars?" someone shouted.

Andrea Krause fainted.

"We arrived yesterday morning," the Shakren speaker said, "and we came bearing gifts."

The image of the Way vanished. In its place appeared a photograph of a line of Shakren peacekeepers carrying supply crates. A crowd of creatures with light blue skin and strange appendages surrounded them, but the smiles and happiness on their alien faces were evident. The Way and the Truth were in the image, too, except it looked like someone had dropped a drawing of them on top of a photograph of the scene. The Way held his hands out above the crowd as if giving them a blessing.

"We bring chipware far more advanced than anything your planet possesses," the speaker continued. "We will teach you mathematics and science far beyond your current knowledge. We'll bring literature from across the galaxy. And food. My friends, hunger is now a thing of the past."

The projected image changed. A group of very tall, broad people seemingly made of rock sat about on stones and boulders. All had heaping plates of food balanced in their laps. The Way and the Truth stood with them, their hands almost comically stretched out in an invitation to eat, drink, and be merry. Once again, it seemed the original source photo had been edited to include artwork of the intangible beings. The fallen angels.

The projected image changed to a portrait of the Way. His gray face was somber. "We also bring medicine," the Shakren speaker continued. "We will ensure no one on Verde is ever ill, ever again. But... not yet. Unfortunately, I must warn you that before things get better, they will have to get a little worse."

A murmur went through the crowd. Everyone pointed at one another and looked at their hands and at the faces of those standing nearby. Someone screamed. Yet Cassie's danger sense remained quiet.

Siv itched at the back of his hand. It had a red welt on it, just like Phil's, but Siv wasn't allergic to anything.

"Siv?" Cassie said.

His face was covered with hives. Some were pink, some were bright red. One just under his left eye made it look as if he'd been punched in the face. The wounds were thin pink lines surrounded by inflamed, red flesh. It looked like he'd been whipped.

And it wasn't just Siv and Phil. Sheriff Auber had similar sores. So did Paul Klein, and Pastor Kolbe, and Grady Mitchell. Everyone had them – everyone except Cassie and Sierra.

"By now, most of you are experiencing symptoms of the Scourge," the Shakren speaker said. "Those of you who aren't will be soon enough."

"What have they done?" Cassie said. "What did they put in the air?"

The projected image changed to one of an emaciated alien woman huddled on a threadbare cot. Her orange skin was covered in sores, and the rags she wore were stained with blood. The Way stood over her and sternly gazed down upon her. "We call it the Scourge because by the time it kills you, you'll have so many bleeding wounds both on your skin and on your internal organs you'll look like you've been flagellated. And you'll feel like it, too. The next few weeks will be... excruciating."

Cassie balled her fists and ground her teeth. A biomortic weapon. Indiscriminate. Barbaric. *Horrific.* Even before the Blackout had destroyed Verde's chipware, biomortic weapons had been banned for centuries. They were sick and immoral. If she didn't already believe the Celestines were the fallen angels, she sure as sin believed it now.

She'd known that what the Celestines called a "blessing," any reasonable person would call "tyranny." But this was far worse. This was about the worst-case scenario Cassie could imagine. *By the time it kills you...* the Way had said.

The devils weren't going to spare anyone. They planned to commit genocide.

At least the people she could touch would be safe. She took Siv's hand in hers, and the swelling in his wounds went down almost immediately. The red welts turned pink. The pink ones disappeared. After just a couple of heartbeats, his skin cleared completely. Not today, devils. Not him – *never* him. She let go of his hand.

But what about everyone else? The crowd had already grown louder and more restless at the sight of their sudden injuries

239

and the news this new disease was fatal. How was she going to protect the rest of the world, the people she couldn't heal in person, from a biomortic–

Siv winced and held up his hand. The welts had returned, but not the same ones as before. They were of different shapes and sizes and in different places.

She took his hand in hers, reached out with her power, and once again, the sores disappeared. She let go, and within seconds, new ones once again took the place of the old. This time, one on his right cheek appeared so severely, blood dripped from the wound.

Cassie's heart pounded against her breastbone. "I can't cure it."

Siv put his arm around her shoulder and pulled her close. But she didn't miss the fear that had appeared in his eyes.

"Verde is perhaps the most special place we've ever visited," the speaker continued. "We want to give you our blessing, but your leaders chose to attack us. Actions have consequences. We must respond appropriately. But though we must at times be disciplinarians, we're not devils. We're merciful. We're ready to offer absolution, but the power to request it is in the hands of one of your leaders. And you know who you are."

Cassie looked up sharply. None of the Shakren peacekeepers guarding the crowd gave her any kind of special attention, but she knew the Way was talking directly to her via the Shakren speaking for him. "I told you," the Shakren speaker said, "you must follow the Way. After yesterday's unfortunate events, I expect you will not be very eager to listen, but this is important. I did not say the path would be easy. But in the end, it *will* prove right."

What did he want from her? Taking her brother – then poisoning her entire world – wasn't enough? Were Annalie and her siblings sick already, too? The rational part of her mind knew they had to be. But the desperate part of her mind begged to differ.

Do not delude yourself.

Had they given this painful and ultimately fatal disease to her *mom?*

The Celestines' projected image vanished, and the murmurs of the crowd became shouts as everyone cried out to one another and yelled for Doc Laubscher. Was he back from Harbrucken yet? Apparently not, because some of the crowd turned to Cassie.

"You're in med school," Mary Engel – her mother's best friend – said. "Is there anything you can do?"

"Can you help us?" Phil asked.

She wanted to. She *should* have been able to.

But for the first time in her life, she couldn't permanently heal something.

She took one of Mrs. Engel's hands between her own. "I've only had a couple of months of med school, but try gently pressing your hand on the sores. See if that helps reduce the swelling."

"That does feel a little better," Mrs. Engel said. Of course it did. While holding her hand, Cassie had reached out with her power and healed her. But when Cassie released her hand, Mrs. Engel's sores returned. "Just... just keep trying that," Cassie said, knowing it was a lie but unable to bear telling the poor woman the truth.

"This is the end times!" someone shouted.

"Please!" Pastor Kolbe raised his voice above the rest. One of the sores on his face was bleeding. "Stay calm. Trust in God's Almighty hand."

Someone inside the general store screamed. Was that Connie? Before Cassie could check, Paul Klein threw a horseshoe through the store's front window, then he charged inside over the broken glass. Two others followed him. Cassie took a step towards the store to stop the looting, but her danger sense forced her to pause.

The lead Shakren motioned towards the store. "Bring them out." Five of the peacekeepers stormed inside. There was more shouting, but not from Connie this time. And there were laser blasts. The Shakren shoved two of the looters out of the store and carried out the dead body of Paul Klein.

Cassie ground her teeth. Sure, those guys shouldn't have been looting. But they shouldn't have been *killed*.

"Theft is not permitted on planets under Celestine rule," the lead peacekeeper announced. *Peacekeepers.* Had the Truth come up with that name? Because it was a crock.

And as if that thought had summoned her, the Truth appeared in a swirl of black smoke. Not a projection. Not a simulation. The devil herself.

The Shakren, including the leader, immediately dropped to one knee. "Luminary," they all said, practically in unison.

The leader raised his head just slightly and tilted his mouth towards the crowd. "When in the luminous presence, you will all genuflect," he said. "And you will address them as 'Luminary.'"

Slowly, of their own free will, the people in the crowd lowered themselves to one knee. They didn't do it because the Shakren had told them to. They did it because they didn't want to end up like poor Paul Klein. But regardless of the reason, they knelt in submission to the devil who had conquered and poisoned their world. The devil who had murdered Cassie's brother. The Truth stood right behind the two looters. Was the one on the left one of the Birch boys? Trembling, they genuflected.

With everyone on one knee and bowing their heads, the only person who saw that Cassie, Siv, and Sierra remained standing was the Truth herself. "I'm *not* bowing to you," Cassie said under her breath.

The Truth heard her. Her solid black eyes gleamed. Smoke rose from her hand and coalesced into Fritz's murder weapon. She held it up before her, taunting Cassie.

With a quick swipe, she swiped her blade through the looters' necks.

The crowd gasped, shouted, and turned away from what they expected to be a gruesome sight, but of course, neither man was physically harmed. Neither bore any visible wounds. But both went limp. Their bodies were useless now that their souls had been cleaved out of them.

"Blessed be the Celestines!" the lead peacekeeper announced. "And peace to the people on whom their favor rests."

Smoke shrouded the Truth, and she vanished.

The crowd dispersed in chaos. Shouting, running, the citizens of occupied Hondo fled from the Shakren and returned to their shops, homes, or anywhere else the alien soldiers weren't. The Shakren kept watch but allowed everyone to leave, so long as they didn't break any more Celestine laws. Sierra dispersed into the wind. Cassie and Siv mounted their horses and cantered them away from the crowd. Once on the outskirts of town, they urged Mandolin and Rebel to a gallop down the main road.

Cassie looked back. The lead peacekeeper watched her and Siv but made no effort to stop them or otherwise punish them for refusing to genuflect. "Now we know why they let us leave their ship yesterday," Cassie said. "They didn't want to shoot us in the face."

"They wanted to stab us in the back," Siv said.

He'd said something the night before, and at first, Cassie had just thought it was his fear talking. But he'd been right. The Mantissa Reborn, who had brought down Krulgoth and the white demons – who had destroyed the Steelterrors and defeated the spirit of the planet – weren't even a threat to the Celestines. They had just casually occupied every city, town, and village planet-wide. They'd imposed their law, and they'd poisoned everyone with a fatal disease.

Verde belonged to the fallen angels.

Chapter Eighteen

When Cassie saw the sores on her mother's face and hands, all she could think about was that another member of her family was going to die at the fallen angels' hands. But it wasn't just her mom. Everyone was sick. Annalie. Elise. Felix. Duncan. Every one of them had whip-like welts and sores on their skin.

Cassie and Sierra made sure everyone was comfortable. Elise helped, too – she followed Cassie and imitated everything she did, even while itching at her sores and wincing when they hurt too badly. Ruth and Felix stayed in their beds, but Annalie, Siv, and Duncan camped out on chairs in the main room. Though it didn't feel particularly cold to Cassie, everyone who was sick was chilled, so Sierra lit the fireplace. They served bread, milk, and coffee for breakfast, and every time Cassie came to someone, she touched them long enough to heal all their wounds.

As soon as she walked away, new wounds took their place.

How was *she* not sick? Obviously, her healing power was doing something. But was it constantly healing her, or had it given her some kind of immunity? What exactly was this Scourge? Was it a virus? A disease? Some sort of allergen?

"They said this is..." Annalie said. She glanced at her little sister and saw Elise's back was turned. She mouthed the word *"fatal?"*

Cassie nodded. "Yeah. So they said."

Siv took a deep breath and put his chin up. "What do we do?"

Annalie shrugged her shoulders just like her betrothed would have. "Gotta cure it. We gotta cure everybody."

"Can you get it all out of the air?" Siv asked Sierra.

"Not really," she said. "Even if I could gather it all, where am I gonna put it?"

"Getting rid of all the airborne specimens wouldn't even necessarily heal everyone," Cassie mumbled. "Not if it's an infectious disease. The sick would still be sick. And if it's not an infectious..." She growled and grabbed two handfuls of her hair. "This is pointless. We don't even know what it is."

"All right," Siv said. "Then we start there. How do we learn more about it?"

She wasn't just frustrated. She was angry. The clock was ticking away on her mother, her betrothed, her family, her friends, on everyone back in town, on everyone everywhere. She'd turned away from God because he wouldn't let her save the people she loved. Now she couldn't save *anyone.*

God hadn't just abandoned her. He'd abandoned the entire planet.

"Cass?" Siv said.

"Hmm?"

"I asked how do we figure out what exactly they did?" Siv asked.

"How should I know?" she said. "This is a pandemic, and I'm a first-year med student. I had two months' worth of classes before the university was destroyed. I'm completely unequipped to deal with this."

She balled her hands into fists and paced back and forth across the middle of the cabin's floor.

"This is exactly why I need medical school," she said. "This is *exactly* why I need to be not just a Mantissa healer but a

246

medical doctor. A Mantissa healer can completely cure a person of this – for all of two seconds. But a doctor could study it, learn what it does, learn how to neutralize it, and learn how to heal it *permanently*."

"OK, OK," Siv said. He held up his hands, and she had to look away before she threw a punch at him because the placating gesture really torqued her off. He was telling her to calm down, but she had no interest in calming down. Not when the fallen angels had come to Verde to commit genocide. "But there has to be some way we can learn more about–"

"You don't get it!" she yelled. "It wasn't enough for them to kill my brother. They're gonna kill us all! Everyone but me and Sierra. And I *can't* do anything about it! I'm not an infectious disease specialist. I'm not a doctor. I'm not a nurse. I don't have a lab, I don't have any way to conduct research. *I can't do anything*. And neither can any of you. So stop trying to make it out like we can." She shrugged. "Actually? There is something the rest of you can do. Why don't you all try praying to your God? He doesn't listen to me anymore. Maybe he'll still listen to you."

Duncan shuffled his legs uncomfortably. Annalie gaped at her. Elise looked terrified, either because of her outburst or the fatal diagnosis she'd just revealed, Cassie wasn't sure which. Siv exhaled and rubbed the back of his neck in an obvious but much-appreciated effort to hold his tongue.

But Sierra clapped her fingers and thumb together to imitate an opening-and-closing mouth and said, "Blah blah *barking* blah."

Cassie stomped across the room and stood toe-to-toe with her. "You shut your stupid, pierced mouth. You dug up those robots, and you *murdered* people with them. Just to prove a point. My brother forgave you and gave you another chance because he was *better* than you, yet here you still are with your ugly green hair and your crank attitude, making snide comments, trying to piss people off. You haven't changed, and you're throwing away every chance he gave you. Well, he's not here anymore, and he's the only one who wanted you around. So why don't you just leave?"

"Cass!" Siv said.

"You want to know why I can't stand you, Reinhardt?" Sierra said. "Because you're not *here*."

"The hell's that supposed to mean?" Cassie scoffed.

"All you talk about – probably all you think about – is what you're gonna do in the future. And" – she mimicked wiping tears from her eyes – "all the awful things that happened to you in the past to keep you from getting there."

"*You* destroyed the medical school, you barking crank!" Cassie shouted, spittle flying from her lips.

"Language," Annalie said.

"You're proving my point!" Sierra hollered back. "I can talk to streams and mountains and trees that are thousands of years old. They give me a perspective no one else can. What we're facing here, *right now*, is the worst thing that has ever happened to this planet. Those freak shows are gonna kill everyone. That's barking *genocide!* And are you doing *anything* to help? No! All you're doing is complaining and whining about how the past keeps you from your precious future. Sod off, Cassandra! When we're facing extinction, you don't get to have a pity party. *Shut up* about the past. Shut the hell *up* about the future. And for the first time in your burning life, exist in *this present moment.*"

Cassie wanted to grab one of her lip rings and yank it off her face. It took everything she had to restrain herself. She breathed quickly, her chest squeezing with tension. Her cheeks were warm and flushed. How *dare* that crank speak to her that way.

"Cass?" Siv said quietly.

"What?" she snapped, not taking her eyes off Sierra.

"Enough's enough."

Cassie spun on him. "You talking to me or to *Lady Verde* here?"

Siv looked her straight in the eye. "Those devils took my best friend. They took my health and the health of my family and all my friends. 'Fore too much longer, they might take my life. But by God, they *will not* take your spirit."

Cassie folded her arms across her chest. "You're mad because I'm mad at God?" She *tsk*ed. "Look, I know you're a good little church boy, but you can keep the self-righteous attitude to yourself."

"That's not what I–" Siv snapped. He closed his eyes, took a breath, and lowered his voice. "That's not what I mean. I have a *lot* of thoughts and feels about your relationship with God, but that ain't my business. That's between you and him. And I'll respect whatever decisions you make. Come on, Cass. You know me better than that. I *love* you. I plan to make you my bride."

She shuffled her feet. So he did still want to marry her. Well... that was good. If God didn't take him from her first.

"No," Siv said, "this is about the fact that since you got that letter from the university, you've added a word to your vocabulary. A dirty word I ain't *ever* heard out of your mouth before."

249

Cassie tilted her head.

"Can't," Annalie said, barely louder than a whisper.

Siv pointed at Annalie and nodded. "Until just now, I ain't ever heard you say you *can't* do something. They told you that folks go to the university at age eighteen, and they move on to medical school at twenty-two. That wasn't good enough for you. So you worked your duff off and went to school when you were just *sixteen* years old."

"So?"

"They told you Terrascorcha was a poisoned wasteland. You knew better. You told them they were wrong. When a white demon took a chunk out of my side, you got it in your head that it wasn't my day to die. You could have said, 'I can't save him' and walked away. You decided I was gonna live, then you made it happen."

"That was all different," Cassie said.

"No," Siv said, slapping his leg. "It's not. You think the difference is God helped you before, and he ain't helping you now. But even if that's true, that don't matter. *He* didn't do those things. *You* did. We worship his Almighty Hand, and rightly so, but his Almighty Hand is spirit – it's as untouchable as those devils up on that spaceship. *Our* hands are the ones that work on his behalf. If you don't have faith in God anymore, then at least have some faith in yourself."

She bit her lip. That sounded strangely similar to the advice she'd given Krulgoth when he said he wanted faith but couldn't trust in an invisible God. Which she was finding it impossible to do now, too.

"Now there's a disease gone poisoned the whole land," Siv said. "Made everyone sick – everyone except the woman whose dream is to cure a fatal disease. I'm sorry you don't see God's guiding hand in all of this, but Sierra's right, Cass. *This is your chance.* I know you haven't had the learning you want yet. I know you feel unprepared. But dammit, you are Cassie Reinhardt. The fact that you *can't* do something has *never* stopped you before."

His words made her take a deep breath and lift her chin, but only for a moment. Because once her frustration and anger were pushed away, it let everything she'd been trying to avoid bubble up to the surface. Through the open door to the middle bedroom – to Fritz's bedroom – she spotted his workbench. It was still covered with chipware parts and pieces. In the corner was a toy carriage he and Felix had been working on. A project he'd never be able to finish with a boy he'd never be able to help grow into a man.

Fritz's glasses were neatly folded and sitting on their mother's dresser. He loved pancakes and syrup. He wore the same damn shirt, vest, and trousers every day, and she loved him, and he was gone. She pressed her hands against her face to try and forcibly push back her tears.

Annalie stood from her chair and put her arms around her. She had Fritz's old pocket watch in her hand, holding onto it like it was a rope keeping her from falling. Its second hand softly ticked away each moment her loved ones had left before the devils' Scourge ripped them apart.

"Fritz was so quiet," Annalie said, "but when he was alone with me, or with you, or Siv, he talked our ears off, didn't he?"

Cassie tried to nod, but she couldn't. She couldn't do anything but hold onto Annalie like she was *her* rope.

"He talked to me about chipware, about books, about food, about my brothers and sisters," Annalie said. "But except maybe for chipware, you know what he talked to me about the most? You. His little sister. He thought you hung the dang moons. He was so proud of you. Told me over and over and over how there was nothing you couldn't do. How you understood him when no one else did. How you pulled him back from the brink when he was stuck in despair."

The pain constricted her throat, her lungs, her stomach.

"And I think it's because of you that he believed so much in hope," Annalie said. "You taught him love was stronger than fear, too. And with everything he had, he *knew* peace was more powerful than hate. Because he knew his little sister was gonna heal the whole world."

Annalie held her out at arm's length. Cassie saw her reflection in Annalie's spectacles. With her puffy red eyes and running nose, she looked sick, too. Annalie's face, the face Fritz had thought was so beautiful, was blemished with sores and welts. But there was a light in her eyes as fiery as her red hair.

"If it's the last thing I do," Annalie said calmly, "I'm gonna show those God-damned devils that Fritz's way is better than theirs. That when they would kill, we show mercy. I know you *can* help me do that. But will you? Please?"

"It's not fair," Cassie said. "You shouldn't be without him. You two should have been married."

"No, it ain't fair," Annalie agreed. "But it's what is. And you and I can mourn him. Together. But we have to stop his killers first."

Cassie felt a hand on her back. She turned and rested her head on Siv's chest, and he kissed the top of her head. Annalie was right. Siv was right. Sierra was... well, Annalie and Siv were right. "What do you want me to do?" she asked him.

"I want you to do what you do best, darlin'," Siv said. "Make a plan."

She wiped her nose with the back of her hand, and took a deep breath. "I need to see what they put in the sky," she said.

"I can get a sample of it," Sierra said.

"And I'll need a lab," Cassie said. "I'll need a lot of supplies, and the only place in the world that has them is the medical school. I'll need empty microscope slides. Needles for blood draws. And if we're going to the university's ruins, we might as well find some painkillers for all of you, too. But I'm guessing the militia isn't in charge in Harbrucken anymore, and we know what the Shakren will do to looters. If we get caught–"

"I won't get caught," Sierra said. "I can be in Harbrucken in two seconds. Literally. I can get everything you need. Carrying it all back here will be a little more difficult, but I'll make it work. I can sneak out of town and fly it back."

Cassie swallowed. "I'm grateful you still want to help after what I–"

"Despite what you want," Sierra interrupted, "or maybe *because* it's what you want, I'm not leaving. Besides, if you can't cure this plague, then you and I are gonna be the last two people left on the whole planet."

Cassie grimaced.

"Yeah, I don't want that, either," Sierra said. "So keep that in mind. Use it to help get your rear in gear."

"Gratitude, Sierra," Siv said. He turned back to Cassie. "What else you need?"

Cassie shook her head. "I just needed that reminder. Now I have a plan, and I don't need much of anything else but that."

Siv grinned. "*That's* my lady."

He leaned in close as if to kiss her, but she wasn't finished.

"But I'm done sitting around, waiting for guidance, praying for signs," she said. "I'm *going* to be a doctor. I'm *going* to cure cancer. And – new to the plan – I'm going to cure this Scourge. I'm going to make *every one* of my dreams come true. And no one, including God, is going to get in my way."

Siv winced at that last swipe, but before he could say anything, the floor rattled underneath them. The windows shook. The cabinets shuddered. Loose items fell off shelves and shattered on the floor.

"Are they back?" Annalie shouted over the din. "They landing a ship here?"

"No," Sierra said. She was the only person *not* grabbing the nearest object to steady herself. "This is coming from below." She dissipated into the air and vanished.

A picture fell off the wall and hit the floor. The glass inside the frame broke into shards. Cassie's bedroom door fell off its hinges.

At last, the shaking stopped.

"Come take a look at this," Sierra called from outside. Cassie, Annalie, Siv, and Duncan all stepped out onto the front porch. The stair railing leaned at a funny angle. But what really caught their attention was the crack in the ground between the house and the barn. It was a jagged line stretching forty-some feet long. One side of it was a foot higher than the other.

"This is a surface rupture," Sierra said. "And that was a groundshake."

"I've lived in the occupied territories all my life," Duncan said. "We've never had a groundshake here."

Sierra clicked her tongue. "You have now."

Chapter Nineteen

Behind Cassie, the barn doors slid open. Elise, a frigidly cold wind, and a swarm of snowflakes all sneaked inside. "Hey," Elise said.

"Hey, kiddo," Cassie said. "It's getting worse out there, isn't it?"

"A little," Elise said. Before she could close the door behind her, a groundshake rattled the dirt beneath them. At least it was a mild one. "Was that the third one today?"

"Fifth," Cassie said. "You slept through two of them during your nap."

Elise closed the barn door to shut out the blizzard and stomped the snow off her boots. Cassie's old ranch boots, actually, because who needed snow boots this far south? Hondo got a light dusting of snow maybe once every twenty years, and it was so rare, it was a day kids always remembered. Blizzards like the one raging outside just didn't happen here. Ever.

"Since you slept right through them, I reckon you had a good nap?" Cassie said.

"So-so," Elise said. She shivered. "My sores kept me from finding any position that was comfortable, so I didn't rest much well."

Cassie frowned. When Elise reached her work table, Cassie took off the girl's snow-covered glove and put a hand on her. Elise's splotched skin cleared. She sighed in relief as her sores withered and vanished.

"OK if I just keep my hand here a while?" Cassie asked.

Elise smiled and nodded.

A month earlier, the barn had been used for its originally designed purpose. Her father's tools hung on the wall, the mechanical reaper took up a prominent place on the floor, and the loft was full of hay. Mandolin had a stall. But then it had become a garage for the *Turkey*, a chipware workshop and factory for Fritz and Annalie, a blacksmith shop for Siv and Duncan, and a base camp for Krulgoth and the other demons.

Now it had experienced another transformation. The reaper was still parked outside and covered with a tarp. The *Turkey* was out there, too, abandoned since they'd returned from the Celestine cathedral ship. Sierra had helped her box up Fritz's projects. They'd shoved aside Krulgoth's workstation and bioprinter, and once the unnatural cold and snow started, they'd repurposed the forging furnace to serve as the barn's heater. There was still clutter everywhere – tools and scraps of wire and bits of metal leftover from all the work they'd done to prepare for the Celestines' arrival, but there was at least enough room for Cassie to set up the equipment Sierra brought back from the university.

She had a microscope. Siv had hung some shelves for slides, specimen containers, and the few books from her list Sierra had been able to find amidst the university's rubble. The barn was a medical research lab now. Well, mostly – Mandolin had her stall back, so at least that much was normal. Maybe the only normal thing left in the world.

"Where we at?" Elise asked.

Cassie couldn't help but smile at her use of the word "we."
"Not nearly far enough. My medical school closed before I was able to get any training in the science behind infectious disease, but I did get my undergrad degree in biology, so I'm

not a complete dummy." Cassie motioned Elise towards the microscope. "Take a look into that. Tell me what you see."

Elise squinted one eye and looked down the eyepiece with the other. "It's a bunch of red and pink circles on a pink background. Kinda pretty."

"It's blood."

Elise looked up. Her face beamed. "Really? That's splendiferous."

"I think so, too," Cassie said. "Specifically, it's a drop of Siv's blood. Except the pink circles aren't supposed to be there."

"That's the Scourge?"

"That's what the Scourge looks like in the air," Cassie clarified, "when it's wearing a mask. Hiding its true nature." She peered down into the microscope, adjusted the position of the slide, and increased magnification. "Take a look at it now."

Elise did. "Eww. What are those brown things?"

"That's the Scourge without its mask on. Its outer membrane tricks the body into thinking it's a simple chain of oxygen molecules, but that camouflage breaks down once it's absorbed into the blood, leaving behind something I don't fully understand. It's kind of like histamine, but– wait. Quiz time. Tell me what histamine is."

"Umm." Elise closed her eyes. "It's a chemical – a hormone?"

"Yep."

"A hormone released by the body during allergic reactions."

"Good," Cassie said. "What's it do?"

Elise considered. "It makes you sneeze?"

"Nice try," Cassie said. "Half point for that one. It *can* make you sneeze. But mainly, it causes dilation of capillaries and contraction of smooth muscle. Histamine is part of the immune system, and it's supposed to boot foreign invaders out of the body like a good sheriff runs outlaws out of town. The Scourge prompts a similar reaction, but an *incredibly* overzealous one. It causes the body to attack itself – to burst its own blood vessels, to rip its own organs apart, to burn itself up with fever."

"That's why I feel so crummy," Elise said. "Except when you heal me. So it's not an allergen, but it does produce a similar effect. Is it a virus?"

"How'd you get to be so smart?" Cassie asked.

Elise beamed. "I listen to you."

Cassie ruffled her hair. "I suppose you could call it a virus. But that's not strong enough a word. It's a biomortic weapon."

"A bio-whats-it?"

"*Biomortic*," Cassie repeated. "A life-killer. Centuries ago, before the Blackout, chipware was used to make awful weapons, like nuclear bombs. But it was also used to create infections and diseases that were deliberately introduced with ill intent."

"That's terrible." Elise shuddered.

Cassie shrugged and withheld her comment about how the genuinely terrible part was that God had allowed it to happen. The wind rattled the barn's frost-covered windows. Cassie replaced the slide under the microscope with another. "Tell me what's different about that one."

Elise examined the new specimen. "Same magnification level as before?"

Cassie hummed an affirmative.

"This one has the red circles," Elise said.

"Red blood cells," Cassie said.

"But not the ugly brown molecules. So is this blood without the Scourge?"

Cassie reduced the microscope's magnification. "No," Elise said. "There's the pink circles – the Scourge with its mask on. Unless those are the things the Scourge pretends to be. Oxygen chains?"

"No, that's the Scourge," Cassie said. "That's the Scourge *not* attacking *my* red blood cells."

"So this is what *your* blood looks like," Elise said.

"For reasons I can't understand, my blood isn't fooled by the Scourge's mask. I carry it like everyone else since it's airborne. But my cells just ignore it."

"Because you're a magic healer," Elise said.

"I'm not though, kiddo," Cassie said. "It seems like magic, but when I'm healing you like I am right now, it's just my brain talking to yours. Except something inside my brain knows how to keep the Scourge from attacking me, and when my mind talks to yours, it tells you how, too. But when I stop" – she let go of Elise's hand, and a red welt snaked up the side of Elise's face – "you forget."

"And *that's* the magic," Elise said.

"Take a break from looking in the microscope, but make sure the slide that's in there now doesn't move," Cassie said. "I'm going inside to fetch a cup of coffee. When I get back, I'll show you something interesting."

"OK," Elise said. She went over to the stall to pet Mandolin. "Don't trip over the crack."

At first, Cassie thought she wouldn't be able to miss the surface rupture that had torn up the land outside her house. The one Sierra had unsurprisingly not bothered to fix yet. The souvenir still left behind from that first groundshake. But while she'd been working in the barn, so much snow had fallen, she couldn't even see the crack anymore. She stepped carefully

259

across the lawn, gingerly kicking out the toe of her boots with each step to ensure she didn't trip.

Before getting her much-needed coffee, she made the rounds, using her power to give everyone a brief Scourge-free, pain-free moment. Her heart rose as she watched the wounds clear from Siv, Annalie, Duncan, Felix, and her mom. It sank when she removed her hands from them, and new injuries appeared.

Everything she'd learned over the past week was fascinating, but it was all just the groundwork. Knowledge of how the Scourge worked and how her body continually fought it off didn't do anything for the everyone-else-in-the-world who was sick and dying. She needed to know how to kill this thing in an infected person and prevent them from being re-infected. She needed to know how to eradicate it out of their air.

Sometimes diseases were fought by transferring blood from a recovered patient into an infected one. Like sharing the answers to a test in school, the antibodies present in the recovered patient's blood taught the sick patient how to fight the disease. That wouldn't work in this case, though, because with the Scourge, the antibodies were the problem. What was supposed to be fighting the disease was instead destroying each infected person's body. And to add insult to injury, even that overzealous response didn't take the Scourge with it. It survived and hung around to taunt and infect until the moment its victim died.

She could test the various medications Sierra had brought back from the university on the blood samples she'd taken from her patients. Maybe one would have a positive effect? It was worth a shot, and it wouldn't take very long. But if no existing medicines worked, she would have to start making cultures of the Scourge and researching how to inactivate it or attenuate it. And that would take time. Maybe more time than the victims had left. The Way had said the Scourge's victims would have a painful "next few weeks." That didn't give her much time to develop the cure. And once she created it, she'd still have to figure out how to go about making enough for the entire world's population – and distributing it globally – before it was too late.

Do not delude yourself.

She returned to the barn bearing a steaming hot mug of caffeinated goodness. To stay awake long enough to do all she had to do, she was going to have to live on coffee. Hey, how about that? There was a silver lining to all this after all. "I'm going to stay over here for a minute," Cassie told Elise from just inside the barn's doors. "Go look at the–"

Elise turned around and held up her right hand. A new Scourge wound had nearly severed her pinky finger. She was trembling – no, scratch that, she was going into shock. Blood flowed down her hand and stained her coat sleeve. It pooled in the dirt before Mandolin's stall.

"Hold it in place!" Cassie shouted, reaching out with her power mentally as she ran across the barn. She slammed her coffee mug down on her work table as she went by, spilling half her drink. Very gently, she prodded Elise's hand, making sure the internal structures were lined up as best as she could tell. Then she flooded the girl with her healing power. Elise's visible Scourge wounds vanished as her hand sewed itself back together.

"You all right?" Cassie asked her.

Her teeth chattered. "It was a new wound. Appeared when you were inside."

Cassie pulled Elise into a hug. It wouldn't have taken long for her to bleed to death from that wound. And the fallen angels hadn't manufactured this sick disease to only attack the outer layer of skin. The Way had said it would tear apart internal organs. It was only a matter of time before someone Cassie loved developed a Scourge wound between two of their vertebrae. Or on their heart. Would she even be able to heal an injury like that in time?

"You're OK now," Cassie reassured her. "You feel up to looking at the microscope again? Tell me what you see?"

Elise shuffled over and peered down at the slide. "The brown things are back," she said. "The Scourge without its mask on. But I don't get it. I thought this was your blood?"

"It is," Cassie said. "But when it's out of me for a while, it's just as susceptible to the Scourge as anybody else's. My power is the only thing I know of that kills it. So far. We need to figure out how my body is doing it, then design the right medicine to make everyone else's do the same thing."

She sipped her coffee, closed her eyes, and felt some of the tension leave her shoulders. One spoon of sugar and a splash of cream. Perfection. Elise curiously eyed her, so Cassie offered her the mug. "You want to try some?"

"For serious?" Elise said.

"You've been working hard," Cassie said. "You deserve it."

Cassie might as well have offered her ten bricks of gold. Elise cautiously took a sip, grimaced, choked it down, and coughed. "It tastes like the inside of a fireplace. That's the worst drink ever."

Cassie frowned, took off her coat, and stole back her mug. "I'm going to pretend I never heard that so you and I can stay friends."

Elise grinned, but only for a moment. "My brother's not well."

"I know," Cassie said. She took another sip of coffee and set down her mug. "He was sleeping when I healed him just now. How was he earlier?"

"Leelee said his fever's pretty high. And when he coughs, there's blood on the rag."

Did he have a Scourge wound on his lung? Cassie winced before she could hide the expression from the girl.

"I think every time you heal us, the Scourge comes back a little stronger," Elise said. "It's like it's trying just as hard to keep us sick as you're trying to keep us well."

"You noticed that, huh?" Cassie said. "Me, too." Her chest tightened. She needed to change the subject. "What do you want for Lenerstelen?"

Elise shrugged. "I just want to feel better."

Ouch. So much for changing the–

Thunder clapped outside.

Cassie and Elise frowned at each other. "I thought it was snowing?" Cassie said.

"It is," Elise said. "Thundersnow? Is that a thing?"

Cassie pulled the sleeve of her flannel shirt over her hand and wiped at the window, but the frost prohibiting her view was *out*side. "Have you seen Sierra around?" Cassie asked. "I'm kind of busy figuring out what they did to *us*. I really need *her* to be figuring out what they did to the weather."

"Haven't seen her," Elise said. "But I talked to my sister – not Leelee, but my other sister, Della – on the mobile today. She said they've had eight groundshakes up north in Mondorf, three days of torrential rain, and a high of a hundred-ten."

263

Cassie sighed in frustration. Here they were having weather typical of a northern winter, while the north enjoyed their usual southern summer weather. It was like the globe had literally been turned upside down. Thunder again rumbled outside.

"Let's talk vaccines," Cassie said, mostly to spare Elise from hearing a diatribe about Sierra's disappearance and lack of help. "There are several ways to make one. An inactivated vaccine comprises pathogens grown in a lab culture then killed to eliminate their disease-producing capacity. An attenuated vaccine is one that contains the real pathogen itself – in this case, the airborne Scourge – and alters it. Hurts it so that it's less harmful. Then there are messenger vaccines. They teach the body how to fight off disease without actually exposing the patient to the real virus. In any case, you get the vaccine into the patient, and their body learns how to fight off the disease *before* they get infected."

"But why does that matter?" Elise said, but before she could elaborate, she had to pause for a coughing fit.

Cassie patted her on the back and healed her. "I'd offer you another sip of my coffee, but..."

Elise took a deep breath. "A vaccine would keep people from getting the Scourge. But doesn't everyone already have it?"

"Everyone but Sierra and I," Cassie said, "and Sierra isn't really human anymore. But we still need a vaccine because the fact that y'all keep getting sick even after I heal you tells me you *can* get this disease twice. Or three, four, or ten times. For reasons I don't understand." There was far, *far* too much about all this she didn't understand.

"So we need a vaccine *and* a cure," Elise said.

"You're smart, kiddo," Cassie said. "A cure is definitely the most important thing we need right now, though it's also much more difficult to make. Especially for someone who hasn't had all of her medical school training yet. But I have one thing going for me. I can see my body destroy this thing under a microscope, so I know it's possible. I can watch it happen at will. I just need to understand the science behind..."

More thunder. The wind increased to a howl.

And in the back of her mind, her danger sense made its presence known.

Cassie ran to the barn doors and threw them open. In the distance, the clouds had turned purple, and they rapidly circled across the sky. Some moved in one direction, some in another. The competing winds spiraled around one another. Their rotation speed increased, and a funnel of cloud stretched down from the sky and reached towards the ground.

She reached a hand out to Elise. "Come on!"

Elise ran to her. In her stall, Mandolin neighed. She sensed something was wrong, and she wanted to follow, but she'd never fit in the shelter. She'd have to hunker down in the barn. "Sit tight, girl," Cassie told her. Then she closed the door, and she and Elise sprinted across the yard to the house as fast as the half-foot of snow on the ground would let them.

She'd left her coat back in the barn, but there was no time to go back for it now. At the house, she threw the front door open and leaned inside. "Funnel cloud!" she hollered. "Everyone to the shelter!"

Siv looked up from the chair he'd been dozing in. "You say funnel cloud? In December?"

"Mom!" Cassie yelled loud enough to wake her. "Mom! Tornado!"

Duncan emerged from Siv's old room in bedclothes but fully alert.

"Get to the shelter," Siv said. He knocked on Ruth's bedroom door, then went inside to retrieve her.

Cassie entered her own bedroom, where Annalie had Felix cuddled against her for warmth. "We have to get to shelter," Cassie said, gently waking Annalie. "There's a funnel cloud on its way."

"Oh my days," Annalie said. She got out of bed and carried Felix. Cassie touched and healed them both.

The wind battered the windows. Back out in the main room, Siv helped Ruth walk, and Duncan stood near the door, urging everyone on. They went out onto the porch, through the snow-covered lawn, and around the side of the house. Duncan and Siv brushed away the snow covering the storm cellar's doors and threw them open, and everyone went below ground.

The shelter was just the space between the bottom of the house's floorboards and the dug-out dirt basement underneath them. Thick wooden beams that held up the house above were scattered around the room like short flagpoles. Small chipware lights, each with a disconnected battery, were mounted to the posts. Fritz's restoration was his legacy – a gift that kept on giving.

Siv sealed the doors behind them, though they rattled something fierce under the pounding of the wind. Elise helped Cassie and Ruth connect the batteries and turn on the lights. Annalie sat with her back against the foundation's stone wall, cradling Felix, who breathed heavily and occasionally moaned. Cassie touched him, again healing his visible welts and sores. Color returned to his cheeks, too. When she stepped away, new

266

sores took the place of the old, and his breathing became labored again.

On the other side of the cellar, Elise turned on one of the lights and gasped. "Doctor? You have a patient here!"

What, a dead mouse in the corner? "Thanks, kiddo," Cassie said. "I'll take a look when I have more–"

Cassie startled. *Sierra* was slumped against a corner post, moving very little. Cassie wasn't even sure she was conscious, but she was *very* sure of the welts across her face, neck, and hands. "Impossible," Cassie said. "She's not even biologically human anymore!"

Sierra's eyes fluttered open as Cassie knelt beside her.

"Hey, Reinhardt," Sierra said. "Did what you wanted me to do. Figured out what they did to the weather. Funny story. Turns out I'm still human enough for those barking ghosts to infect me with their disease." She vomited foul black water.

"And you weren't even going to tell me?" Cassie grumbled.

"Didn't want to distract you," Sierra said.

"We're having more daily groundshakes than meals," Cassie said. "There's a tornado headed straight for us!"

Sierra shook her head to clear it and struggled to focus her eyes on Cassie. Giving up, she closed her eyes and took a deep breath. "I'll... break it up." She winced. "Maybe."

The wind screamed outside. Somewhere in the distance, glass shattered. It sounded like a freight train was bearing down on the house. Nothing changed. Sierra wasn't able to do anything.

Or at least she wasn't... until Cassie put an arm around her and reached out with her healing power. Then the winds outside calmed. The cellar doors ceased rattling. Even the air in the cellar changed. Growing up on a farm, she'd experienced plenty of hot summer thunderboomers. She could tell the low atmospheric pressure that rolled in right before one had suddenly raised to higher, normal levels. She'd also bet that the snow had stopped falling, and the tornado was gone, and that the bad weather would *stay* gone so long as she kept healing her newest patient.

The groundshakes. The erratic weather. The thundersnow.

By the stars – they were Sierra's Scourge wounds. They were the *planet's* Scourge wounds.

Siv made the Sign of God's Hand, and Cassie didn't need to be a Mantissa reader to know what he was praying for. If Sierra was infected, then it wasn't just everyone *on* Verde that was going to die...

"Be happy," Sierra grunted at her. "At least you don't have to worry about being stuck alone with me forever anymore."

Chapter Twenty

Sierra became Cassie and Elise's most important patient. She was in the barn with them almost all the time, usually resting on a pallet of blankets. Cassie didn't even pretend to understand anything about Sierra's unique planet-linked physiology. Even if she'd managed to earn *five* medical degrees before the university was shuttered, she'd have to toss them all out when it came to Sierra. All she knew is when she didn't keep Sierra healed, the weather got crazy. When she did, the weather remained normal and non-severe.

Or at least it did in the Hondo area. Based on calls Annalie made to her siblings still up north and from data collected by Skylab, they knew the weather elsewhere ranged from odd to frightening. Heat waves. Torrential rains. Groundshakes. Fire tornadoes. Cassie's healing of Sierra seemed to be a localized phenomenon, not a global one, which made frustrating sense. Cassie had always been able to heal only people with whom she was physically present. She'd never been able to, say, reach out from her apartment in Harbrucken and cure her mom a two days' ride back home in Hondo. It seemed logical, then, that Cassie could only heal the planet in her immediate area.

But she and Sierra conducted numerous experiments anyway. Sierra even managed to stretch herself and be conscious and aware in five different places at once – a new record for her – but it was no use. Sierra could still take a physical shape anywhere on the planet, but even right after Cassie healed her, she couldn't transfer that health anywhere Cassie wasn't. Apparently, unless Cassie could physically get to the coast and heal Sierra there, typhoons would still batter the shores she hoped to one day retire to with Siv. Unless she could fly the aerocopter all across the occupied territories, healing Sierra everywhere she went, people would either wake up to snowstorms or swarms of locusts.

If they woke up at all. Ten days of the Scourge had taken their toll. Sometimes Siv could barely speak his pain was so bad. Cassie's mother and Annalie both struggled to walk. Felix and Duncan were in an especially bad box. They both slept most of the day, sweating and shivering through dangerously high fevers. It was difficult for any of them to make it to the outhouse. Cassie had to put aside her research often to clean soiled clothes and sheets.

When Cassie rode into the village to check on things there, she went with a scarf wrapped around her face. Everyone else thought it was to hide some particularly nasty Scourge wound, though it was actually to hide her clear, unpocked skin. If anyone in town saw she *wasn't* infected, she'd be swarmed by very sick and very scared people all wanting a share of her medicine. It was already hard enough to find time away from her research to heal and care for her family and friends on the farm. She just didn't have time to ease the suffering of anyone in town. She hated herself for that, but she hated God for it even more.

Turned out she needn't have bothered with the scarf. With Lenerstelen just two days away, there should have been shoppers and flowers and banners everywhere. Every window in every shop and every home should have been soaped green. But the only signs of the approaching holiday were the few decorations that had gone up before the Scourge. And the only person she saw was Phil Hersch. He sat in front of the saloon with bandages wrapped around his hands and half of his head.

A Scourge wound across the middle of his face and had taken one of his eyes. He drank from an open bottle of liquor, and three empties lay scattered at his feet.

The village was bustling though, just with Shakren instead of holiday shoppers. Though they'd moved their ship to the outskirts of town, Shakren were stationed in pairs up and down the main street. They patrolled and leaned against the wall outside the empty law office to flaunt their position as the new sheriffs. And they were armed, of course, though they were the only ones who were. Possession of a weapon was a crime under the Celestines.

Grady Mitchell was the first person she knew to die from the Scourge. His wounds grew infected, and he died of sepsis. Percy Fitzgerald, the undertaker, was next. He died when a Scourge wound emerged on his neck and went so deep into the skin and muscle that it severed his carotid artery. He bled out in seconds, all by himself. Turned out his services weren't required anymore anyway. When not standing around looking threatening, the Shakren occupiers buried the dead. They also made clear they were willing to deliver food supplies to anyone who wanted them. They had plenty, and they could create more because they had bioprinters like the one Krulgoth had used to make stimulants for the white demons. No one took them up on the offer, though.

And those Shakren hadn't been left to hold Verde all by themselves. When she felt well enough, Annalie used Skylab's sensors to check both Verde and the space around it. There were still one-hundred five Celestine ships in outer space watching Cassie's family, people, and world endure slow, painful deaths.

While leaving town, Cassie caught a glimpse of the church up on the hill behind Main Street. There was nothing she could do to help everyone on Verde, but *he* could. In a second, he could reach down from heaven and take the entire planet in his healing hand, and the Scourge would be over. He'd banished the Celestines once. He could do it again. He *could*, but he wouldn't. And Cassie would *not* ask. She would not suffer another disappointment. Besides, everyone else was probably already praying for deliverance. What about them? Why wasn't he answering their prayers?

Every evening, she brewed a fresh pot of coffee to get her through another long night of research. While drinking the first cup from it, she made her heartbreaking rounds of her family's bedsides. She offered comfort, temporary healing, and encouraging words she didn't believe before moving on to the next dying person.

She always saved Siv for last. Even asleep, his face was twisted in a grimace of pain. She stroked his short hair, caressed the skin around his facial wounds, and sent her healing power into him. His pocks faded and disappeared. His eyes fluttered open. "Hey," he croaked.

Even right after healing him, he sounded so weak.

"I never told you this before, but after my folks first met you, they sat me down alone and had a say with me," she said. "They were pretty concerned. They wanted to know what it was I saw in you."

"For serious?" Siv said. He even laughed a little. She hadn't heard him laugh much over the past nine days. Hadn't been much to laugh about.

"Other than a shared love of horses and hunting – and travels across Terrascorcha and fighting the white demons – they just didn't see what we had in common. And since they could tell I was smitten with you, they wanted to understand why."

"They needed to make certain you weren't just raptured by my studly good looks?" Siv asked.

"Something like that."

"What'd you tell them?"

"I told them you let me dream," she said. "Not all men would be so supportive, you know. But you're supportive of me practically to a fault. Even when I take you for granted."

"You don't take me for granted," Siv said.

"I do," Cassie said. "I know I do. But even when I do, there you are. Supporting me. Lifting me up. Not just letting me dream, but encouraging it. Sharing in it.

"You work hard, and I admire that. You know what's good, what's right, and you don't hesitate to do it. You were once burdened by so many fears, and you pushed against them, fought through them, and conquered them. You refused to let them define you and restrain you."

"You gave me a lot of help with that," Siv said.

She placed a finger against his lips. "*Shhh.*"

He closed his mouth and kept his eyes locked on hers.

"You're handsome. Obviously. I really like that you rarely wear shirts with sleeves because it makes it very easy to see the muscles in your arms, and..." She felt her cheeks warm. "Well, I think I've said enough on that part." She could practically see his laugh coming on.

"You're a man of God, which I especially admire now what with all that's going on. It shows you have a faith stronger than I ever had. I respect that, even if I can't share in it. And you pray for horses, even though every preacher I've ever met has tried to tell me they don't have immortal souls."

Cassie took his hand in hers.

"I love you," she said, and as hard as she tried to restrain it, a tear snuck out and ran down her cheek. "I just want to build that house with you out on the coast. I want us to have a life together."

"Me, too, darlin'," he said, but he was too honest a man to assure her that they would.

"You were right, you know," she said. "We should've gotten married when we had the chance. At least then, when I was the last living person on this planet, I'd have been a widow instead of a spinster. Now it's too late."

He shook his head and tried to say something, but he couldn't get out the words.

"If you were well enough to get to church," she said, "and if Pastor Kolbe were well enough to meet us there, then I'd want to marry you for Lenerstelen. I'd marry you right now. I would. I'm so sorry I didn't before."

She kissed his forehead.

He smiled weakly and fell asleep.

And when she let go of his hand, fresh scourge wounds ripped across his cheek, ear, and arms.

She was so distraught, she couldn't work on her research. Instead, she rode Mandolin out to their barrel racing field. She'd have taken Mandy for a run or two around the barrels right then, in the dark, if the field hadn't been such a muddy soup. The mixture of rains and snows and blazing heat waves the area had endured before she began healing Sierra had taken their toll. But just being on her horse near the racing field was enough to provide some semblance of comfort, so she just sat in the saddle and emptied her mind. She was too tired to do anything else, including cry.

Maybe seeking solitude was foolish. Within another week or so, she'd be alone forever – the last living person on a dead rock that had once been a vibrant world. She'd once thought the Celestines would kill her personally when their Scourge didn't, but what if they did something far more horrible? What if they let her live?

How long could she survive? She'd hunted enough deer and antelope with her father and gone camping often enough that she'd have no problem finding food and water. But Sierra – the planet herself – was dying, too. After she was gone, would the soil be capable of growing anything? Would the water be potable? Would fauna die off, would food chains collapse?

Would being so utterly alone drive her mad?

Gazing upon the stars her betrothed loved to watch, she was able to pretend everyone she loved was just fine. She could forget about how shallow Felix was breathing and how obviously close to death he was. She could act like the tears Elise wept as she watched her brother die – knowing her own death wouldn't be far behind – didn't gut her. She could pretend she'd mastered the emotional distance they'd told her about in her one semester of med school. She could ignore that all the hopes of the entire world were on her, waiting for her to do exactly what she'd always wanted to do – cure a killer disease.

She could pretend she had hundreds of leads and that a permanent cure was just around the corner. But it wasn't. She still had *no idea* how to cure the Scourge. Even after nine twenty-hour workdays in a row, she had no idea how to save everyone. Or anyone.

Sometimes she found herself pretending her instructors and fellow students were all alive and well at the open and undamaged university, and they'd just discovered the cure and were preparing to distribute it worldwide instantly via the chipware technologies Fritz had restored. Because *of course* Fritz was still alive in her daydreams. He was alive and well and still preaching about the revival. Why not? She wasn't dreaming during the four or less hours a night she gave in to a fitful sleep. Might as well indulge in some hallucinations.

Maybe she was already insane.

Thanks to his Mantissa-powered intuition, her brother had possessed a good track record for making guesses about the future, but his power was only as good as his knowledge. He needed data from which he could extrapolate conclusions, and he hadn't lived long enough to witness the Celestines poison the planet. If he had, he would've realized his prediction of a pending revival had been entirely wrong. But he hadn't known, so he'd told anyone who'd listen that the chipware restoration was only the first step. He'd talked of a world without misery, pain, or fighting. No one ever had to be hungry, sick, poor, or ignorant ever again, he had said. Tomorrow could be better than today.

Remembering hearing *him* talk about it is what hurt Cassie the most. In her mind, his spectacle-covered eyes were still open. His voice was *not* silenced.

"I miss you so much," she said to the night sky. "I can't do this without you."

"You're not alone, Cassandra," a regrettably familiar, almost musical voice said.

The Way – Nariel the Blasphemer – stood ten feet or so behind her. A cold wind blew across the field, but it didn't make his cassock or hair move an inch.

Mandolin whinnied and reared up, kicking the air with her front hooves. Cassie placed a hand on her neck and soothed her. She returned to all fours, but only Cassie's insistent voice kept her from fleeing. Cassie dismounted, and Mandolin ran to the other side of the barrel racing field, keeping her distance from the devil.

Cassie's danger sense was silent. Did Nariel really intend her no harm? Or was he somehow strong enough to *not* trip her power? The badge he wore on his chest didn't reflect the starlight. The meager moonlight didn't cast his shadow.

"You here to kill me personally since I'm immune to your disease?" she asked.

"I don't want to kill you," Nariel said. "I don't want to kill anyone. I want to show you a more excellent way."

"Do you do the sword thing, too?" Cassie said.

Black smoke poured out of his hand and mutated into a seemingly-solid weapon. Daphne's sword was long and thin, but Nariel's was a black broadsword similar in shape and size to Siv's.

"That's a soul-cleaving blade?" Cassie said.

"It is," Nariel said. He tossed the sword aside, and it disintegrated into smoke. "But I prefer not to use it."

"You going to possess me then? Demonic possession is real, right?"

"Yes, and I am capable of it, though it would only make me tangible and therefore subject to death. But *honestly*." He tilted his head. "*Demonic* possession? You think me a demon, Cassandra?"

"Don't call me that. Only my mother calls me that, and only when she's cross with me."

"It's your name. Names are powerful. How did God give people dominion over the animals, on this planet and on every other? He let people name them. That act was not merely a set of linguistic decisions. It was the ritual that established the dominion."

He came up to the fence not far from her and appeared to rest his arms on the top rail, except his intangible limbs sank an inch into it. "Even Krulgoth never made that connection. He focused only on what he understood, like the protein chains that make up your bodily matter. Hence his obsession with DNA. Before he died, he'd just started to explore the mind. That was, in fact, why he came here. He thought the Verdant Mantissa's mastery of the mind could help him 'free' his comrades. Yet, he dismissed as insignificant the most obvious difference between him and them. He had a name. Every other Shakren did not."

He was baiting her. This had to be more of his horse manure, but her curiosity had been piqued, and a few answers wouldn't hurt, she supposed. "You're telling me the Shakren have to obey you because you gave them serial numbers instead of names?"

"I'm oversimplifying the matter," Nariel said. "But basically, yes. Our names are written in our souls. They define us. A Shakren with a serial number is soul-marked not as a person but as a biological machine. Likewise, a person endowed by his creator with the name Krulgoth – which means 'will' – possesses freedom that even that creator can never rescind." He shook his head. "He was my finest creation. And my most shameful failure."

She motioned towards the silver badge of three interlocking triangles he wore on his breast. "Yeah, you failed rather spectacularly with him, didn't you? Before he was a robot, Krulgoth wore a badge like that. He took it from the devil he killed, right?"

"Yes."

"How's that make you feel, knowing something you created killed one of your fellow angels?"

Nariel lowered his head. "Deeply sorrowful."

She'd been trying to anger him. It torqued her off that she'd saddened him instead. "So the robot that helped us wasn't really Krulgoth?"

"It had all his memories, rendered in ones and zeroes instead of neurons. There are those who say we are nothing but the sum of our memories, and by that rationale, that robot *was* Krulgoth. But that's wrong. The robot did not have Krulgoth's soul. Therefore, that robot was *not* Krulgoth."

"Well, hooray for you," Cassie said. "Your failed experiment *and* his robot copy are *both* gone. And you have the white demons back now, too. You have everything you came for. So why don't you just go away and haunt someone else?"

"I don't have everything I came for," Nariel said. "I didn't come here for Krulgoth or any of the other lost Shakren. I came to Verde for one thing. *You*, Cassandra."

Cassie brushed her hair off her ear and turned it towards him. "Sorry?"

"I want you to join the Celestines. I've wanted you to join me for a very, very long time."

She balled her hands into fists and stared straight back at his black orb eyes. Her teeth were clenched so tightly, she couldn't spit out any words. He couldn't possibly be serious. It was more lies.

"Well?" he prompted.

"Your sister, or your wife, or your fellow angel – whoever the hell she is. She *murdered* my brother."

He raised a finger. "I did not want that to happen."

"But you stood by and *watched*. And now you want me to *join* you? You poison everyone on my planet with a deadly disease, and you want me to work with you?" She spat in his face. Even though she knew it would pass right through him – and it did – it still felt good.

He folded his hands and seemed to consider his words. "Cassandra–"

"*Stop* calling me that! Get the hell off my farm."

"The world – the universe – needs to change," Nariel said. "People lie, cheat, and steal. They kill. They fight wars and starve children. They hate others because of their skin color or because of how they choose to worship or not worship. They kill the inconvenient unborn, the useless elderly, and other undesirables. They hoard wealth and spread poverty. They treat medicine and education as goods belonging only to the capable, not rights deserved by all. Verde is no different than any other world. These things happen here, too."

"Because you're the devils, and you tempt people into it!" Cassie growled.

"You overestimate my power," Nariel said. "I don't make people do evil. They choose it themselves."

Cassie had another cuss word ready for him, but she stopped short. What he'd just said was a paraphrasing of what Siv had told her the night she'd discarded her grunblume. *Bad things don't happen because of God. Bad things happen because of people.*

"Just leave," Cassie said. "Get back in your ship, turn around, and go back where you came from."

Nariel's head dropped. "I can't."

Oh, right. He really couldn't go home. That was exactly what made him a *fallen* angel, so telling him to go back where he'd come from was kind of dumb. Admitting he couldn't might have been the first true statement he'd ever made, but it was his body language that surprised Cassie. His face fell. He fidgeted with his hands. His shoulders seemed to tense. He no longer seemed the confident, supernaturally charming devil. He seemed more like a gangly teenager struggling through nervousness to ask her to a shindig.

"What I tell you now, I have never told anyone before," he said so quietly Cassie had to lean close to him – much closer than she wanted – to hear.

"OK," she said.

"I *can't* go home," he said. "You know that. What you don't know... is that I *want to*."

She blinked. "You *want* to go back to heaven?"

"I was the greatest of all the angels," he said. "That's not a boast. I was the prince of heaven. Before the world, before time, when all was spirit and nothing else was, God showed me – me alone – his plans for creation. He showed me stars. Water. Flowers. Food – coffee even."

Cassie didn't mean to, but she smiled at that.

"And he showed me people," Nariel said. "A universe full of galaxies full of planets full of families full of *people*. Extraordinary people who could grow and create and *love*. He showed me all of it. And it was *good*. Oh, Cassandra, it was so good. It was *divine* in the fullest, truest sense of the word. A universe full of God's children loving him and being loved by him. To this day, I've never seen anything more beautiful."

Nariel grimaced. "But then... then he told me all those unique, amazing persons... every single one of them... would have a *choice*. They wouldn't be *required* to love him. They wouldn't even be required to obey him. They would be capable of rejecting him, of choosing evil. And so it was that after showing me all the beauty he was going to create, God showed me the most repugnant ugliness I've ever seen. He showed me *sin*."

Cassie couldn't take her eyes off of him.

"I begged him not to do it," Nariel said. "I offered him an alternative, and he called it flawed and disordered. Immoral. But I could not accept what he was proposing. I *would* not! I told him it was *senseless*. It still is." He harumphed, and his jaw quivered. "And, of course, you know what happened next. For defending the goodness of God's creation from God himself, I was thrown out."

Cassie looked up at the stars and found the constellation Gotteszorn – God's Almighty Hand casting the rebellious angels out of heaven. One of the three exiles represented in that constellation was standing with her and talking to her now. Nariel followed her gaze, and his lips twisted into a sneer. "After he abandoned us, he rearranged every star in the galaxy so that a constellation like that one is visible from every planet in the universe," he said. "Here on Verde it's his Almighty Hand casting us aside. The natives of the planet Kilonika are made of living rock, and from their homeworld, one sees the constellation of a boulder falling towards three pebbles as if to crush them. On Barohnde, the natives have long prehensile tails. Such a tail is seen in one of their constellations preparing to sweep aside the three stars representing myself and the others."

"Wait," Cassie said. "He *rearranged* the stars? There's a constellation representing your exile visible like from *every* planet?"

Nariel seemed to steel himself against what was obviously painful. "It wasn't enough for him to just exile us. He had to make certain we'd know, always, no matter where we were in the universe, that we were *not welcome* back home. Ever."

How could a loving God commit such mockery? Cassie nearly reached out to put a comforting hand on his shoulder before she remembered he was intangible.

"I've tried to see it his way," Nariel said. "So many times. That's what I meant when I called Krulgoth an experiment. Unlike every other Shakren, I granted him free will. I cursed him with the ability to sin, just as God cursed every one of *his* creations. Why? Because I was and am open-minded. I figured: maybe God was right about the goodness of free will. Maybe he was just giving it to the wrong people. Maybe the right kind of life – life of *my* creation – could be different." He shook his head. "But you know too well that Krulgoth was no different at all. You know how many planets he pillaged before he and his 'white demons' came to Verde. How many souls he and his comrades killed. Verde still pays the price for his wrath. Your Mantissa are all but extinct. Your world was deep into its technological age yet has spent the last two centuries clawing its way out of its second steam age. And it's my fault. I was so desperate to prove myself wrong and finally go home that I permitted Krulgoth to possess *free will*. I was just... so... desperate..."

She couldn't stop listening to him.

"But I couldn't prove myself wrong because I *wasn't* wrong," he sighed. "I *hate* sin, but I cannot and will not condemn a single sinner because if evil happens when good people choose to do bad things, then *people* aren't the problem. *Free will* is the problem. Bad things happen because free will ensures they can. Free will is bondage to death and sin. It is a curse – the evilest curse ever cast upon sentient life. It is what I've spent my entire existence trying to erase from the universe. I lay the blame for all the evil in the world on the head of the God who made people capable of choosing it."

Cassie licked her lips. "Free will allows us to choose evil, but if God hadn't given it to us, we'd be automatons. Mindless puppets acting out someone else's story."

He waved his hand in dismissal. "I'm not lamenting the ability to choose what's for dinner. I'm not saying people shouldn't be allowed to pick a favorite color or choose whom they want as a mate. I'm saying people shouldn't be permitted to choose *evil*."

Now that she thought about it, back in Hondo, the Shakren had allowed the people to assemble. They'd allowed them to speak. Since that first day, they'd permitted everyone to keep attending church. They kept the library open, the stores, the saloon – not that anyone was well enough to visit those places. But they'd used ruthless violence to halt looting at the general store.

"Because theft is a sin," Cassie mumbled.

"What's that?" Nariel asked.

"That's what you do," Cassie said, louder. "When you come to a planet, you don't use your army to conquer anyone or anything... except sin."

Nariel beamed. "I knew you'd understand. Cassandra Theresa Reinhardt, from the time you reached the age of reason, you've felt a burning in your soul. You want to heal the sick, but that's not enough, is it?"

"No," Cassie said.

"You want to cure disease. And that's noble! But even that isn't enough, either."

Just like in the confessional, it was like he could see right into her. His voice sounded like a song.

"The real sickness is in people's *souls*," he said. "And God put that sickness there. The freedom to choose evil. It *must* be cured."

Cassie looked away to break herself from his captivating gaze. She licked lips that had suddenly gone dry. He was a fallen angel, one of the devils. But...

He made sense.

Disease didn't make sense. Killings outside of saloons didn't make sense. Losing her best friend and her father and her brother even though she'd been born with a miraculous power to heal sure as hell didn't make sense.

But Nariel the Blasphemer... made sense.

"Even if I could go home right now, to be welcomed back into heaven, I'd have to admit that I was wrong," he said. "But I'm *not* wrong. Am I, Cassandra? The only way to bring deliverance to peoples cursed with free will... is to take it from them."

She almost said, *Yes!*

Instead, she blinked, shocked back into rationality. "But your Shakren commit atrocities in the name of imposing your agenda," she said. "They kill. They destroy. They use biomortic weapons. You're killing this planet right now. That's evil. That's *sin*."

"God's curse is a strong and terrible one," Nariel said. "People resist us, even when they know in their hearts we're right. Some won't follow God's laws except under threat of violence, but those hardened hearts are no less worthy of our blessing. Their obstinance is *not their fault*. They were born flawed. We must give will-cursed people an *incentive* to follow us. The Shakren, though brutal, help those poor souls find the way."

She nodded in agreement, then – realizing what she was doing, what she was thinking – she shook her head to clear it. "I should go," she said. She turned to get Mandolin and then head back to the barn. To *run* back to the barn. Sure, she wasn't on very good terms with God at the moment, but Nariel was a devil, and he was making her start to think–

"I have the cure," Nariel said.

Cassie froze.

"For the same reason that the Shakren must use violence to guide will-cursed souls down the path of righteousness, I *had* to infect the people of Verde," he said. "I had to put *you* into an impossible situation. The same kind of impossible situation I found myself in so long ago when I told God his designs were wrong, and he exiled me for it. I had to show you, to prove to you beyond all reasonable doubt."

"Prove what to me?" Cassie said weakly.

Nariel smiled sadly. "I think you know."

She did. She swallowed and nodded. "You had to prove that God isn't going to help me."

"No. He's not going to help you. It's not his way." He looked across the field towards the barn and her house. "It's appropriate that in two days, you'll commemorate the creation

286

of life in the universe with your Lenerstelen holiday. I approve of such a celebration because creation was the last great thing God ever did. He created life, he gave it a push down the hill... and then he left it to roll off at catastrophic speed. To fend for itself." He chuckled. "And that's the most ironic part of my mission. His way means he *won't* get involved, which leaves me free to implement mine."

Cassie had been convinced of God's abandonment ever since Fritz died, but voicing it out loud to one of the devils themselves... It felt like crossing a line. She reached for her grunblume, but it wasn't there because she'd cast it into the fire. A sick feeling overtook her that wasn't the Scourge, and it wasn't her danger sense. Guilt maybe?

"When you're one of us, Cassandra, you'll have the cure for the Scourge," Nariel said. "*You* can be the one to give it to Verde as a Lenerstelen present. Think about how it will feel to achieve your life's dream of curing a deadly disease. And then think of what you could do not just for Verde but for the entire universe. Think of all the good you could do as the new Life of the Celestines."

Now she knew for sure that she was going mad. Because she *was* thinking of all the good things she'd do with that power. She was actually considering joining the damned. Except... it wasn't so crazy. Nariel made sense. Evil was the real scourge in the world, and did God do anything to stop it? Hell no. He'd *permitted* it from the beginning.

But more important than anything else, the judgment of her immortal soul included, *they had the cure*. Both for the Scourge and for all evil in the world.

Nariel spread his arms as if he would embrace the entire universe if only he could stretch wide enough. "The world needs a revival, Cassandra. And together, we can make it happen."

Revival – just like what Fritz had talked about before his death. A world where peace and prosperity and liberty and happiness were in abundance, and war and poverty and bondage and despair were things of the past. Fritz was sure it was coming, but he didn't know how. Well, maybe this was how. Was she supposed to join the damned? Would *that* bring about the revival? Oh, if only she knew what Fritz would suggest if he were here. If only she had his intuitive power to counsel her right now.

Siv once told her he'd heard his mother speak to him, long after she'd died, in a moment when he'd urgently needed her. Similarly, Fritz said he'd once heard Harlan's voice in his own moment of desperation. Cassie listened with her ears and heart, but she didn't hear anyone except a fallen angel.

"There are *three* triangles on those badges," Cassie said. "I could work with you, but I won't work with *her*. The Liar. She murdered my brother."

Nariel shifted uncomfortably. "That was not the first time I've been unable to restrain her from doing something terrible. I was kicked out of heaven unjustly, but Daphne and Rudger deserved their exile. They're twisted and corrupt. The three of us came together because they had nowhere else to go, and without them, I would have been alone. But... my need for Daphne's companionship is coming to an end."

"What's that mean?" Cassie demanded.

"It means a seraphim with an aversion to verity is not now and never has been my peer. I wish to associate with a soul who can help me right every wrong in the universe. Someone whose yearning to heal others – whose burning desire to paint the world in the image of God's goodness – is just like my own." He shrugged his shoulders, just like Fritz used to do all the time. "I could get rid of Daphne. I could kill her just as Krulgoth killed Rudger. I'd be doing the universe a favor. Then we could find a new Truth – you and I, together. Perhaps even your betrothed, Sivrin, would qualify."

He took two steps closer to her. If he could touch her, he'd have been close enough to caress her face. And she didn't back away.

"You want to heal the universe more strongly than any soul I've ever felt," he said, "and I know you're willing to do whatever it takes. Well, this is what it takes."

What would Siv say? Or her parents? What about her pastor?

"Everyone will be cured?" Cassie asked.

"Everyone," Nariel promised. "Shakren peacekeepers will be needed here, of course, but your people will all live." He put a gray finger under her chin as if he'd lift it if he could touch her. She took the cue and looked into his eyes. "You won't have to lose anyone ever again, Cassandra."

Her dream wasn't just alive, it was within her grasp! Except she'd never dreamed big enough. Why save everyone on Verde from one disease when she could save everyone everywhere from *every* disease? She didn't need the medical school. She didn't need to earn a doctorate.

All she had to do was sell her soul to the fallen angels.

It was blasphemous. It was a sin against the spirit – and possibly an unforgivable one at that. Something deep within her shuddered at the mere consideration of it.

But for a world without disease...

For a *universe* without suffering...

To save her mother and her betrothed and all her friends...

It didn't seem like too steep a price to pay at all.

Chapter Twenty-One

When you have an offer on the table to sell your soul, what's the customary and reasonable amount of time for contemplating it? How long should you give yourself to be comfortable with your decision? How long do the devils patiently await your answer?

And when everyone in the world – including your family and all your friends – are nearing the end of their slow, painful march towards death, and only your affirmative answer can help them, does that help speed up the decision making process?

Cassie had sat and paced and thought and screamed and cried in the barn until... late. Or early. She didn't know the exact time she'd fallen asleep on her workbench, but she woke up around dawn after what felt like about five minutes of shut-eye. Rain pounded the barn's roof and dripped inside through a leak near the corner. Sierra moaned in her sleep. Without touching her, so as not to risk waking her up, Cassie reached out with her power and healed her. The rain stopped.

She stretched. Her face felt grimy, and her hair felt like she'd dipped it in grease. She couldn't remember the last time she'd bathed. She couldn't even remember the last time she'd changed clothes.

Personal hygiene might not be high on her list of priorities, but coffee was. She couldn't sell her soul and save everyone while exhausted and passed out. So she tromped back to the house to put on a pot and scrounge up a piece of bread. They were running low on flour, but where was she going to buy more? Connie Emerson was too sick to run the store. Even if she wasn't, were the merchants' delivery wagons still making their rounds across the territories? Probably not. People weren't even Lenerstelen shopping. Everyone was too busy dying to worry about everyday commerce and the Reinhardt farm's dwindling supply of flour and coffee. The Shakren occupiers would probably be more than willing to provide her some, but she'd rather drink out of a spittoon than accept anything from them.

Of course, they'd be *her* army to command if she said yes.

She'd hoped to find everyone else still resting, what with it still being so early in the morning. Her mom's bedroom door was closed, and so was the door to Fritz's room. No, dang it, Fritz's *old* room. Every time she made a mental slip and forgot, just for a moment, that he was gone, it felt like a knife stabbed her in the heart all over again. And she slipped up a dozen times a day. Would she ever get used to him being gone?

The only bedroom open was hers. Felix was asleep, and he wasn't sleeping well. He breathed heavily and irregularly. Elise dabbed water on his lips, even as the sores on her cheeks bled onto her nightgown. Annalie squeezed his hand. She had her glasses off, probably so that she wouldn't cry on them. Cassie walked in and healed all three of them, then turned and left before she could watch them all get re-infected.

Back in the barn, Cassie flopped into her chair. Then her coffee turned cold, and her bread turned stale. Her microscope sat unused. She knew what she had to do, and she knew people were going to die while she wallowed in indecision. But she still couldn't bring herself to accept Nariel's offer.

She'd asked him how she was supposed to inform him of her answer. Was she supposed to send up a signal flare? Go to Hondo and ask the Shakren stationed there to take her to the cathedral ship? Burn another grunblume in the fire? He said he'd know when she decided – because of course he would. The scriptures said the devils were always prowling about, waiting for someone to devour. *Resist them*, the good book said, *strong in your faith*.

Was that why she found Nariel's offer irresistible? Because she didn't have any faith anymore? She didn't think so. Even if she were still devout, she reckoned she'd find it just as tempting. The Scourge had to end, and joining the Celestines was the only way it would.

Behind her, the barn door opened. Cassie was surprised Elise would join her. She belonged inside with her little brother. She wouldn't have much time left to be with him, and just as she was figuring out a way to gently tell Elise that, she realized her visitor was *not* Elise. It was Annalie.

"Hey," Cassie said.

Annalie paused in the doorway. The last time she'd set foot in the barn, the *Turkey* had been undergoing its restoration. She and Fritz had been repairing ship parts and manufacturing replacements for the irreparable ones as quickly as they could. Now the barn was practically empty – just Cassie's lone workbench. A visible reminder of Fritz's absence.

"Hey," Annalie said after composing herself. She closed the barn door behind her and limped across the floor.

"Your leg OK?" Cassie said.

"Hurts something fierce," Annalie said. "And I have so many sores on that foot, every step is murder. I'm probably bleeding all over the soles of these boots."

Cassie quickly met her half-way, laid hands upon her, and healed her. Her shoulders relaxed as Cassie's power washed over her and healed her ravaged body. Then she whimpered.

"It still hurts?" Cassie said. "Even with my hands still on you?"

"No," Annalie said. "It feels wonderful. I was just thinking how bad it's gonna be again once you let go."

Cassie didn't think her heart could hurt any more, but apparently, it could.

"I came out here because I didn't want Elise to hear," Annalie said. "But I reckon Felix only has a day or two left. I think he'll be the first of us to go."

"I..." Cassie said. What had she been about to offer? To sit with him all day? To reach out with her power and heal him as necessary? Of course she'd be willing to do that, for anyone – especially for the little boy Fritz had been so close to. But it wasn't really necessary, was it? She *had the cure*. Or rather, the Celestines had the cure, and she had an offer on the table to join them. The cure was within her reach.

All she had to do was agree to pay for it.

Annalie shook her head. "You don't need to do nothin'," she said, assuming an incorrect reason for Cassie's hesitation. "You're doing the Lord's work out here, running yourself ragged, practically killing yourself, all to try and help us. *That's* what you need to keep doing. Please. Keep doing whatever you can to save my baby brother." She wiped a tear from her eye and dried blood from her cheek. "I just wanted you to know, that's all."

"Why don't you both just leave?" Sierra said. Apparently, she'd woken up.

Cassie glared at her. "Her brother is dying, you heartless crank. If you want to hit the road, be my–"

"Calm down, Reinhardt," Sierra said, turning over on her pallet of blankets to face Cassie and Annalie. "I get that I'll

294

never get the benefit of the doubt with you. You've made that abundantly barking clear. But I'm *not* telling you off. I'm reminding you that you have a burning spaceship parked outside. One we spent a lot of time and effort painting with kemosite to hide it from those ghosts' sensors. If you can heal people of their plague, except they get re-infected immediately after 'cause the air's all poisoned, then why don't you just pack up your people in that spaceship and get out of here? Go somewhere the air *isn't* poison?"

Could that work? Maybe. Even if it could, how could she leave? She had to stay and (*sell her soul*) find a way to save everyone else on the planet – everyone who *couldn't* leave.

"I wish it were that easy," Annalie said. "We'd bring our own air up with us, and the recyclers would keep it fresh and breathable. They wouldn't filter out the Scourge, though. They weren't made to do that."

"You can't modify them?" Cassie said.

"May can," Annalie said. "But another problem is that ride was designed for cargo runs up into orbit and back. I'm not even sure it would get us as far as the moons, let alone somewhere far away from the devils. And even if it could, we don't have that much fuel." She smiled tightly at Sierra. "Besides, we can't leave you behind."

"Yes, you can," Sierra said. "And you should. Why should we all die if some of us can live?"

Likewise, why should *anyone* die when *everyone* could live? Cassie nearly slapped herself across the face. What was she waiting for? Join the Celestines already. Cure everybody!

"Just leave me with a bottle of beer," Sierra said, "take off, and don't think twice about it."

"You drink?" Cassie said.

"Hell yeah," Sierra said. She motioned across herself from her combat boots up to her matted green hair that was shaved to the scalp on one side of her head. "Do I look like a saint to you?"

"I don't mean that," Cassie said. "I mean do you require sustenance? I can bring you something."

"No," Sierra said. "I don't *need* to eat. But I can if I want. The good stuff. Like beer. Apples. Peanut butter." She closed her eyes and moaned. "Apples dipped in peanut butter."

Cassie shook her head. "I didn't know."

"Why would you have? In what world were you and I *ever* gonna be drinking buddies?" Sierra went into a coughing fit, and somewhere in the distance, thunder rumbled. She pulled her blanket tighter around herself and rolled over. "Figure out how to get away from here. Then do it, and don't look back."

When she walked Annalie back to the house, she found Siv awake and sitting in a rocking chair on the front porch. His hairline was matted with blood. He must have had a Scourge wound somewhere on his scalp. "You want to take a walk with me?" she asked him.

"Want to? Yeah," he said. His voice wavered, and he spoke between gasps. "Can I? Not so sure. Came out here to go say mornin' to you in the barn, felt something snap in my ankle, and barely made it into the chair."

She sat down in front of him and gingerly prodded his joint. It felt OK, structurally. Maybe a Scourge wound had formed across a ligament? She healed him, his tremors stopped, and he was able to stand.

Hand-in-hand – partly because they were betrothed, and partly so Cassie could keep healing him – they walked across the pasture, behind the house, out towards the fields where her father had died.

"You look like you didn't sleep at all last night," Siv said.

"Because I didn't."

"Cass," he said. "I appreciate what you're trying to do. So much. But you're gonna kill yourself in the process."

"I have a way to cure everyone," she said.

"You found it? I knew you would!"

"It's not what you think," she said. "Nariel was here last night."

His face fell. "The Blasphemer."

"He offered me a place in the Celestines. As one of them. He said if I join them, he'll give me the cure."

She closed her eyes. She couldn't bear to see his face when she told him.

"And I want to do it," she said.

The only thing she heard was his labored breathing.

"I don't *want* to join Fritz's killers," she said. "But I *have to* cure everyone. And other than joining them, I don't know how else to do that. I've been up almost all night, every night, for over a week. Researching. Thinking about the cure, thinking about everything. Curing disease is all I've ever wanted to do. My whole life plan revolves around it. But my plan fell apart, and I'm tired of losing people I care about. Any moment now, we're going to lose Felix."

Her throat seized. She had to squeeze the words out. "I can't lose anyone else."

"I know, darlin'," he said.

"I used to know everything I would be doing, every day for the next five years, with broad stroke plans for the next twenty after that. And I don't know *anything* anymore. I don't know if

297

tomorrow I'll be the last living human on Verde or if I'll be among the damned. I just want to make this world better! I want to see the future Fritz talked about. I want to make it all happen, but I *don't know* how."

Finally, she opened her eyes. He was still there, and he didn't look horrified. Pained, but not disgusted.

"Your relationship with God," Siv said, and before he could finish, he fell into a coughing fit – deep hacking coughs that produced thick wads of phlegm and blood. And she'd just healed him! But nevertheless, she healed him again. She'd heal him over and over and over if she had to, just him, the rest of the world be damned. Everyone else might die. The world itself could shatter apart. But she had to have him with her, always.

But healing him wouldn't work forever, would it? One day, a Scourge wound would rip his heart open or burst a blood vessel in his brain, and instead of being right beside him, she'd be asleep, or in the other room, or using the outhouse – something stupid. Then the man she loved would die, and she'd be alone on a dead planet.

None of that ever had to happen if she would just accept Nariel's offer.

"Every person's relationship with God," Siv continued after catching his breath, "is an intensely personal thing. I don't belong in the middle of yours. But can't you see how much worse things have been ever since that devil started crooning in your ear back in the confessional? Can't you see he's got you pondering blasphemy like selling your soul because he's the Blasphemer?"

"What he says makes sense," Cassie said.

"I'm sure it does. I've heard him talk. He could tell me day is night, and so long as he said it that sugary voice of his, I'd believe it. But he's preying on your dreams and your fears. Making you think right is wrong and wrong is right. My daddy always says sin makes you stupid, and that devil is sin incarnate."

"You're saying I'm stupid?"

"No!"

"Don't you think everyone on this planet is praying to God for deliverance from the Scourge?" Cassie said. "Look around. It's not happening. God *cursed* us with free will."

Siv scoffed. "*Cursed* us?"

"Yes! He could have kept us from being capable of committing evil. When he didn't, he allowed sin into the world. And then he walked away to let us wallow in it. What kind of plan is that? He abandoned me. He's abandoned everyone. He's indifferent to our plight. But Nariel's not. That's why they travel world to world, ending hunger, ending disease, ending war. Isn't that worth taking away people's free will?"

He squeezed her hands. "I'm not good with words. The more I try to convince you, the more I'm likely to just push you the other way. But *don't* join them. Just don't. By all that's holy, Cass, *please* don't sell your soul to the damned. God has not abandoned us."

"Well, I guess I've been too busy to notice the Almighty hand reaching down from heaven to save everyone from the Scourge," Cassie said through gritted teeth. "You want to point that out to me next time you see it?"

"*Here!*" He took her hand and raised it between them. "Right here. *This* is God's hand. Working to find a cure and save everyone. Your hand has been God's hand more times than I can count, saving me from getting killed by the demons and the Steelterrors. Fritz's hand was God's hand when he showed mercy to Sierra instead of killin' her. Sierra's hand was God's hand when she dragged Fritz off their ship. My daddy's hand was God's hand when he carried me out of the fire when I was a boy."

Siv squeezed her hand in both of his. "Our whole religion revolves around the power of God's Almighty Hand – a hand that ain't even physically here. Because it doesn't have to be! He works through *us*. The hand we see reaching out to us *is* God's hand. He lets us decide whether or not we want to work with him, and when we say yes, our hands become his. He doesn't have to let us be a part of the good he does in the world, but he does anyway. That's our free will, and it's a gift. It's a grace even."

Could he be right? All of this – the white demons and Krulgoth and Sierra and the Steelterrors and the Celestines – it had all started for Cassie the day Fritz showed up on her doorstep at the university with his best friend, and that friend had offered his hand and introduced himself. *Siv McCaig.* Had his hand been God's hand, reaching out to her as a new friend? As a new love?

On the spaceship, right before they came face-to-face with the Celestines, Fritz had reached out and touched her – a rare gift from someone like him who didn't care for physical touch. Had that actually been God's hand reaching out to comfort her in advance of what was to come? Had that been the sign she'd prayed for, and she'd been too angry and scared to see it?

Even if it had been – what about when the Steelterror Gravitas had reached his robotic hands out over the city of Harbrucken, using his gravity-twisting powers to crush university buildings and the people inside them? Had that been

God's hand, too? And if not, then where had God's hand been when the most populated city in the territories was destroyed?

Why hadn't God's hand caught her father when he collapsed in his field and died all alone? Why hadn't God's hand deflected the bullet meant for Gunter Asheford? Where was God's hand when Krulgoth reached out, pleading to Gashg, while his white demon brothers ripped him–

Krulgoth's hand... reaching out...

The hand we see reaching out to us is God's hand, Siv had said.

Krulgoth had reached out to Gashg, and after the other demons had ripped it off, Gashg had brought her that hand. *Take it,* he'd told her soft enough so only she could hear. She'd assumed he'd been ordered to give her the hand by the Celestines, as a warning. But something hadn't rung true.

In that moment, had Krulgoth's hand been God's hand? If yes... then why? To what purpose? How could a severed robotic limb possibly be part of God's plan? She stood there in her father's field, pondering this.

And then her knees buckled when she realized the answer.

She turned away from Siv and ran towards the barn. "Get Annalie!" she called back over her shoulder.

"What's wrong?" Siv said.

"*Get Annalie!*" she yelled.

Her boots pounded the grass. She pumped her arms, and her lungs burned, but she kept running. Past the outhouse. Past the chicken coop. Finally, she reached the *Turkey*. She punched the button that was supposed to open the hatch, but it didn't work with the ship powered down, so she grabbed the manual release. Grunted as she gave it a pull and a twist. The hatch opened. The gangway dropped to the ground.

She sprinted up into the ship. It was dark inside. The angle of the early morning sun was such that only a radiant glow lit the cavernous cargo vessel. Where was it? Don't say she'd left it up on the cathedral ship. She thought she'd boarded the *Turkey*, then tossed it–

There. In the corner. The severed robotic arm of Krulgoth that Gashg had given her. One of four that had belonged to the robot demon – one of his lower hands. He'd been able to extend blades out from those lower hands, weapons that hadn't done a bit of harm to the Celestines. And when they weren't fighting the devils, when they were working in the barn, Krulgoth had been able to pop a spike in and out of that hand. A spike he used to secure his secrets.

To lock – and more importantly, to *unlock* – his workstation.

She jumped down out of the ship and didn't bother to close it up behind her. Off to the barn, again at her fastest run. She threw the doors open, barreled inside. After tossing Krulgoth's arm onto her workbench, she carefully moved her microscope to a side shelf, then swept away every other paper, pencil, and slide that had been on the table. Everything but the severed arm.

"What the hell?" Sierra said, sitting up.

Cassie looked back over her shoulder. "*Annalie, I need you!*"

She found Krulgoth's workstation, its screen, and his bioprinter on the floor, out of the way and tucked against the wall. She hefted the workstation and screen up onto her table. After a bit of rummaging, she found one of Fritz's old car batteries, too, and set it down between the workstation and the robotic arm.

302

"What's all the fuss?" Annalie said from the barn doorway, just as Cassie was about to yell for her again. Siv followed her inside.

Cassie held up the robotic arm. "Gashg gave me this before we left the cathedral ship," she said. She was panting. And shaking. "And unless I'm completely wrong, I think this was the arm Krulgoth used to unlock his workstation."

Annalie tilted her head.

"His workstation," Cassie repeated. "The one with all his files from back when he was a scientist for the Celestines. What if it contains the cure for the Scourge?"

Annalie bolted towards the table as fast as her Scourge-ravaged body would let her. When she got within reach, Cassie touched her to heal her. Annalie connected wires from the battery to both the workstation and the severed arm.

Siv made the Sign of God's Hand. "Please, God, please..."

Annalie flipped a switch on the battery. The workstation came to life, but with a red lock on the screen. Servomotors clicked inside the severed arm. Annalie fiddled with it, and a familiar spike extended out from the wrist. She put it into a corresponding socket on the workstation.

And Krulgoth's workstation was unlocked and open to them.

Cassie threw her arms around Annalie. "How do I work this?"

"Just ask it for what you want," Annalie said. She coughed into her elbow.

"Show me the cure for the Scourge," Cassie commanded the workstation.

A square with alien text scrawled across it appeared in the middle of the screen.

"Oh, for goodness sake," Annalie muttered under her breath. Then, louder, "Present display in the language of the request, for cryin' out loud."

The alien text shifted into words Cassie could understand. *No results found.*

"Oh, you ain't getting off that easy," Annalie said. "Show us everything you have on the Scourge."

A box full of text appeared on the screen. Then another. And another. Diagrams appeared. Photographs taken with a microscope. Genome maps. Experiment logs. Pictures of unknown alien species whose bodies were riddled with all-too-familiar looking wounds. Screen after screen of raw material on the Celestines' biomortic weapon, all suddenly at Cassie's disposal.

She looked down at Krulgoth's severed hand. Was it – in a way – God's hand? Had that atheist son-of-a-gun been doing the work of God without even realizing it?

Cassie took the sides of Annalie's head in her hands and kissed her forehead. "You're the best."

"Will his data help you find the cure?" Annalie asked.

Cassie had no idea. Search results were still appearing on the screen. It would take a lot of time to go through them all, and no one on Verde had much time left.

And of course, she didn't *need* to go through all these files to find the cure. She'd already found it. It was up above, in space. The Celestines had it, and they were willing to share. Were more people going to die while she tried to find another way?

Siv caught her eye and mouthed the word *please.*

She supposed that if there was a way to get the cure without joining Fritz's killers, she could make a little time to explore the option.

"I don't know," Cassie answered Annalie. "But it can't hurt to look. So long as you can help me with one more thing. Can you help me hook this up next to Felix's bed? I think I can manage healing him and reading at the same time."

Chapter Twenty-Two

Cassie had gone to university two years earlier than most students. She'd maintained a mostly-A average through four years of undergrad school. She knew how to study. She *liked* studying. Give her a stack of books, some notepaper, and a pot of coffee, and she could pull an all-nighter anytime – and thoroughly enjoy herself in the process. Learning was more than just fun to her. It was intoxicating.

But Krulgoth's files were not the kind of knowledge troves she was used to mining. For every idea that fascinated her, she found ten that horrified her. Sure, he'd died as their ally, but long before he'd become a robot or even before he came to Verde, he'd been quite the scapegrace, and his own journals were the proof.

"Ooo," Cassie muttered. "That's interesting."

"What's interesting?" Elise said.

"Sorry, kiddo," Cassie said. "Did I wake you up?"

Elise shook her head, stretched, and winced. Stretching tended to aggravate Scourge wounds. Cassie reached out with her power, and Elise's cuts stopped bleeding and even faded a little, but they didn't disappear completely. Cassie hadn't been able to get anyone back to full health without several minutes' worth of healing for days now.

Felix was still asleep between Elise and Cassie, who was sitting in a chair beside the bed with a chipware pad in her lap. Before she'd curled up on a pile of blankets in the corner and gone to sleep, Annalie had attached the pad via some kind of data-comm to Krulgoth's workstation. It was smaller than his workstation's main screen, but it was more comfortable in her hand, and it still gave her access to all the files she needed.

Elise checked her little brother's pulse. "He's OK," Cassie reassured her. "I haven't stopped healing him."

That didn't seem to reassure her much. "What time is it?"

"'Bout quarter to midnight," Cassie said.

"Not Lenerstelen yet," Elise said.

"Almost. But not yet."

"What was interesting?"

"I just found out what 'Shakren' and 'Shakrath' actually mean," Cassie said. "They mean 'the loyal' and 'the free.'" Nariel had said names contained power, and this was further proof of it. He'd encoded Shakren loyalty not just in their lack of names but in the one name they did have – their species' name. Nariel had also been right when he said Krulgoth never even considered names relevant to the Shakren's forced obedience. File after file after file proved that. Just as he'd told her the morning he'd watched her and Mandolin practice barrel racing, he'd been convinced the key was in their DNA.

"This drug Krulgoth invented back when he was still a scientist for the Celestines," Cassie said. "Geneditor. He mentioned it to us back when they were here, working with us. But now that I have access to everything he ever wrote down about it, it's the most amazing thing I've ever heard of."

"What's it do?" Elise said.

"It rewrites genes. Edits DNA. Krulgoth found a chemical formula that changes a base pair of adenine and thymine into a cytosine and guanine pair. That's downright revolutionary. It would have earned him head chair of the biology department at the university easily. But that's not even the best part. What makes this drug mind-blowingly miraculous is that he used

308

software to design doses specific to the change he wanted to make in his brothers. He plugged in the necessary genetic data – both existing and desired. He chose the delivery mechanism: intravenous injection, swallowing, inhalation, absorption through the skin, whatever. Then, faster than a dog comes for dinner, his proc-box created a custom dose of the drug, ready to manufacture using a bioprinter. Once administered into a Shakren, the drug targeted the specific base pairs that differed between the recipient's current DNA and the blueprint and altered them to match the blueprint." She spread her hands, momentarily speechless. "Unbelievable."

"Wow," Elise said, then a Scourge wound lashed across her cheek, making her yelp in pain. Cassie reached out with her mind and healed it. "Gotta admit I don't follow most of that, but it sure sounds impressive."

"If I could share this right now with my most tenured professors at the university – well, the ones still alive anyway – they'd agree that Krulgoth's was the most advanced scientific mind Verde had ever seen."

That shouldn't have been so surprising. The scriptures said the angels possessed far more intelligence than humans, and Krulgoth had been created by fallen angels.

"I think yours is the smartest mind Verde has ever seen," Elise said.

"Thanks, kiddo," Cassie said. "Here, look at this." She tilted the chip pad so Elise could see the screen. "You know who that is?"

"Whoever it is, he looks exactly the same as the troops in town," Elise said.

"That's Krulgoth," Cassie said. "From before he and his brothers escaped. Before he changed them all into white demons. Oh, and watch this."

She played a vid – with no sound, so as not to wake Felix or Annalie – recorded sometime after Krulgoth and his brothers had fled from the Celestines. Krulgoth was still mostly Shakren in appearance at this time, but with one significant difference. He had four arms instead of two. The vid had been recorded in a laboratory. Two hospital cots were in the center of the room. On one lay a Shakren soldier. Unlike Krulgoth, he had only two arms. On the other cot was some kind of creature Cassie had never seen before. It was certainly alien to Verde, it was certainly dead, and it had four arms hanging limply at its side. Krulgoth came to the Shakren on the cot and injected a dose of Geneditor into him. Within a few minutes, as the Shakren's DNA was rewritten, he grew a second set of arms halfway between his shoulders and waist.

"Un-*barking*-believable," Cassie whispered. She winced at Elise. "Pardon my cussin'."

Elise blushed and restrained a laugh.

"Obviously, he understood the Shakren genome enough to be able to rewrite it," Cassie said. "But he also understood the DNA of every species the demons encountered after their escape. These files contain genetic maps on hundreds of species, including us. Remember, the white demons came here because they wanted to give themselves Mantissa powers. I have no idea who these other species are, but I've learned where the white demons' snouts came from, where their tails came from, where their agility came from. Every demon body part was native to some other species. Krulgoth analyzed their DNA, isolated that part of that species's genome, and rewrote it

310

into himself and his fellow Shakren until they'd become white demons. It's really hard not to just stand up and applaud at the sheer scientific *skill* of it all, even if Krulgoth isn't here anymore."

Elise swallowed. "Kinda hard for me to applaud a white demon for anything. They killed my folks. Kept us living in squalor and slavery."

"I'm sorry," Cassie said. "I know that. I don't mean to sound like I'm... I'm just fascinated on an intellectual–"

"It's OK," Elise interrupted. "If there's a cure for us in there, I don't care who it comes from." She seemed to brace herself. "*Is* there anything about a cure in there?"

"Yes and no," Cassie said. "These files taught me more about the Scourge in a day than I've learned in the past two weeks. I know what its bonding agents are. I've learned the exact molecular makeup of the baseline strain, which has helped me map out the strain they poisoned us with – a strain uniquely engineered just for our species, I think. I've seen records of its use on other worlds, including pictures of the dead that will haunt me for all my born days. Krulgoth meticulously compiled cross-referenced notes comparing and contrasting the Scourge with several other Celestine biomortic weapons."

Yes, apparently, they had *several* others.

Cassie sighed. "But nothing on a cure."

Felix stirred on the bed. She touched him, and his wounds disappeared, and he relaxed.

"He's still really sick," Elise said, looking him over. "But he's much better than he was this morning."

Cassie allowed herself a small smile. "No one's going to die on *my* watch."

She adjusted herself in the uncomfortable wooden dining table chair she'd brought into the room so she could sit beside Felix. "I've tried two hundred different search terms, questions, and queries so far. Time for two hundred one." She tapped her chip pad's screen. "Show me every file you have that contains the word... remedy." A long list of matching documents, pictures, and recordings appeared on the screen. "Now filter that list to only include items that have the word 'Scourge.'"

One item remained, and it wasn't one she'd read before. It wasn't experiment notes or a DNA profile. It was a laboratory log note. The screen highlighted in yellow the text that matched Cassie's search.

1423 hours. Peacekeepers brought in a Reselite male infected with the Scourge. He'd been sentenced to watch his family die, but he'd become infected himself. The Celestines wished to make sure he did not die before his family did. S-24 administered the remedy, and he was returned to peacekeeper custody.

Sentenced to watch his family die – Cassie could undoubtedly relate to *that*, but it made her stomach turn. How could she want to join beings who were capable of such cruelty? Such barbarism?

Because those beings had the cure, that's why. It said so right in that log entry. And that entry was cross-referenced to a vid file. Cassie checked the volume on her pad to make sure it was low enough not to wake Felix or Annalie, then she tapped the screen to play it.

Like others Cassie had watched, the vid was recorded in a laboratory – presumably, where Krulgoth had worked with other Shakren scientists. There he was, in the background, working at the rear of the lab with... some kind of cell-culture dishes maybe? She knew it was him, though, because she recognized the alien text on his uniform as the untranslated form of S-9, the Shakren designation everyone but Nariel and his fellow scientists used to address him.

The doors of the laboratory opened, and two more Shakren entered. These weren't scientists but peacekeepers, judging by the rifles they wore strapped across their backs and the glyphs on their uniforms. Between them was a thin, wiry alien with light-green skin, except where sores that were all-too-familiar to Cassie pocked his flesh and split it open.

"How can we help you?" one of the scientists asked. Cassie compared the glyphs on his uniform to the untranslated text of the linked note. This was S-24.

"This one's been ordered to watch his family's Scourging," one of the peacekeepers said. "But he went and caught it himself. The Luminous Ones want him alive to see everything."

The alien made motions that Cassie at first thought were hiccups, but for all she knew, they were his species' way of weeping.

"Full cure and inoculation?" S-24 said. He moved to a corner of the room, where a piece of chipware looking a lot like Krulgoth's bioprinter sat on a shelf.

"Authorization number 278106," the peacekeeper said.

S-24 tapped keys on a panel adjacent to the bioprinter. The device lit up from inside. When the light subsided, S-24 lifted its lid and removed two syringes. The peacekeepers held the alien while S-24 injected the contents of both needles into his neck. "The sores will heal in time," S-24 said to the peacekeepers. "But he won't get any more of them."

The peacekeepers nodded and escorted the alien out of the lab, and the vid ended.

Cassie put her feet up on the bed – careful not to disturb Felix – and leaned back in her chair. The file contained very little scientific data that could help her, but it was irrefutable proof of one thing. Nariel hadn't been lying. The cure *did* actually exist. And *full cure and inoculation* implied there was a vaccine, too.

"They manufactured it with their bioprinters," Cassie said, "just like how Krulgoth used his to make stimulants for his brothers. That bioprinter is out in the barn, but it doesn't do us a bit of good without a molecular pattern for what we want to create." She stabbed her finger at the screen of her chip pad. "*That's* what I need to find in here: the molecular patterns of the Scourge's cure and vaccine. But if they're in here, I've searched all day and can't find them."

She tossed the pad onto the mattress, covered her face, and sighed. "We might as well use that bioprinter for something," she said. "What do you say, kiddo? Should we ring in Lenerstelen with some ice cream?"

Elise didn't answer. "Kiddo?" Cassie repeated, uncovering her face.

Elise had fallen back asleep. Her head rested on her pillow next to Felix.

And blood ran down her face from inside her ear. A *lot* of blood.

Cassie leaped from her chair and leaned over Felix to touch Elise, to take her pulse, to reach out with her power. "Hang on, kiddo," Cassie soothed her. What would cause bleeding from inside her ear? An ear infection could, but she'd just healed Elise a few minutes earlier, so that seemed unlikely. Had a Scourge wound suddenly formed in her inner ear, ripping apart her eardrum?

She flooded Elise with power, but the visible Scourge wound on her face didn't heal. And she didn't have a pulse.

"No!" Cassie said.

A less common, more extreme cause for ear bleeding was a head injury. Maybe a Scourge wound hadn't suddenly broken her eardrum. Maybe one had suddenly lacerated her brain.

Cassie wanted to scream, but she was clenching her jaw too tightly to manage it. She gently turned Elise so she was flat on her back, climbed onto the bed next to her, and used her fists to compress the young girl's chest in a desperate attempt to restart her non-beating heart and get air into her non-breathing lungs.

Do not delude yourself.

"Come on, kiddo," she said. "Come on, breathe!"

If a Scourge wound had formed on her brain, it could have been the part of the brain that responded to her telepathic Mantissa healing instructions. Maybe that's why she wasn't responding.

Or such a wound could have instantly killed her...

"My first aid book!" Cassie said. "The one you can't put down. I'm giving it to you for Lenerstelen, and I can't wait to see the look on your face, but you have to breathe. *Breathe*, Elise, breathe!"

The chest compressions weren't working. Her Scourge wounds weren't healing. Her heart wasn't beating. She made no visible sign at all of responding to Cassie's power.

Cassie growled, stepped off the bed, and pounded her fist against the wall hard enough to rip open the skin on her knuckles and crunch a few bones. Her power healed her hand in two seconds, so she punched the wall again, and then again, and then again. The noise roused Annalie from her slumber.

She incoherently mumbled an inquiry and reached for her glasses.

Cassie covered her face with her temporarily bleeding, broken hand. Her growling gave way to weeping. "I promise I just looked away for two minutes," she said. "I'm sorry."

Annalie leaped to her feet. "Felix? *Elise!*"

When Fritz had been killed, Cassie hoped she'd never again have to see Annalie so distraught.

It only took twelve days for that wish to *not* come true.

Unable to bear watching Annalie grieve, Cassie ran from the room, out the front door, down the steps, and into the yard. Her chest ached with hurt. Her fists shook in rage.

God answers every prayer with one of three answers...

"Can you hear me?" she shouted into the night sky.

Yes.

"Show yourself!"

Yes, but not right now.

"Heal them. *Heal them!*"

I have something better planned.

She stalked around the pasture, yanking at her hair, growling and screaming wordlessly, until she tripped over the surface rupture that had split the yard during that first groundshake. Landing on a knee and a palm, she tore a hole in her jeans and skinned her hand. She almost jumped back up to her feet, ready to scream and berate God for tripping her, but instead, she accepted defeat, rolled over onto her back, and stared up at the stars. Nariel – the star in the constellation Gotteszorn – beckoned to her.

When you're one of us, Cassandra, you'll have the cure for the Scourge.

316

Mandolin came to her, sniffing her face, nickering gently. Checking on her. Cassie didn't move, not even to stroke Mandy's face.

"Cass?" Siv said. The screen door slammed closed behind him. The sound of his limping footsteps drew closer, then he knelt beside her. "You all right? What happened? Did Felix...?"

Cassie shook her head. "Elise."

"Elise?"

"I lost her."

Sierra rose up out of the ground beside her. "What's going on?"

"Elise passed," Siv said.

Sierra gasped. "Is Annalie OK?"

"What do you think?" Cassie said.

"Are *you* OK?" Sierra said.

"Do I look OK?" Cassie said.

"Cass," Siv said.

"I said I couldn't lose anyone else," Cassie said. She sniffed and wiped her nose. "Did he not hear me? Or did he just not care?"

Siv sat on the ground next to her. "My daddy likes to say, 'God speaks all the time, but only in whispers. It's up to *us* to go shout it on the mountain.'"

"Oh, I'll shout it on the mountain when I get that cure," Cassie said. "And for once, he won't be able to ignore me. He's gonna *know* I did what he wouldn't, and that's a promise."

"Cass, *please*," Siv said. "Before you sell your soul, can we *please* just consider that maybe God *is* talkin', but the world's just been so noisy we ain't been able to hear him?"

Sierra's hand dropped away from Mandolin's mane. "When you say 'sell your soul,' you're talking in metaphor. Right?"

"Not really," Cassie said. "If I hadn't been so weak, so scared to do what I know I have to do, then I could have cured Elise this morning."

"You could have saved her?" Annalie said.

Cassie sat up. She hadn't heard Annalie step out of the house or come across the lawn, but there she was. Without her spectacles. Still in her nightclothes. Grief over losing her sister still streaking down her face. "Nariel came here last night," Cassie said. "He offered me a place in the Celestines, and he said I can have the cure when I accept. So yes. I could have saved Elise this morning. But I deluded myself into thinking Krulgoth's robotic hand was God's hand helping me out. Offering me another way. I'm sorry. Elise died because I didn't have the sand to do what needs to be done. And now I have to live with that."

"You're thinking about joining them?" Annalie said.

"To get the cure?" Cassie said. "To cure all of you? Yeah. I'm doing a lot more than just thinking about it. It's the only way."

"No!" Annalie shouted. And in a flash, Annalie rushed Cassie, grabbed two fistfuls of her flannel shirt, and shook her. "No, you *won't!* Not for *any reason.* Shame on you! What the *hell* would my sister say if she heard you say that? Huh? What would your *brother* say?"

Mandolin snorted, but Cassie made no effort to make Annalie let her go, to stop shaking her, to silence her. Because she was right. Fritz and Elise would be more than just disappointed in her if she joined their killers. They'd be heartbroken. But it was the *only way.* She'd let them all hate her forever so long as it meant everyone else lived.

Sierra put one hand on Mandolin to calm the horse and her other on Annalie's shoulder. Annalie let go of Cassie's shirt and fell into Sierra instead, wrapping her arms around her, trembling with her grief.

"Isn't there anything in Krulgoth's chipware that can help?" Siv said.

"No!" Cassie said. What part of this didn't he understand? "There's nothing helpful on the Scourge, nothing on a vaccine, nothing on a cure. There are galactic maps, databases of alien species and their genomes, file after file on Geneditor and how to make it and how to use it. But no cure. The only files Krulgoth took with him when he left the Celestines were the ones he thought he would need to free his brothers, and since they didn't have the Scourge, he didn't bring any information about it.

"Look – I wish there was another way. I wish I could be God's hand, just like you keep saying, and cure everyone. But I only know of two ways to cure the Scourge. Be born a Mantissa healer, or get the cure from the devils who made it. I wish there was a third option involving God dropping the cure into my lap, but he *isn't* helping us."

No one had anything new to say, so no one said anything. Everyone just sat there in the grass, underneath the stars. The only sound was a dog barking somewhere in the distance – probably one of the Murphys' incompetent sheepdogs. Annalie wasn't even crying anymore, as if she couldn't even muster any more tears.

It was time. Time to join the devils. Long past time, to be honest.

Far in the distance, a bell tolled. It must have been the church bell in the village. It chimed again, and again, and again – twelve times to mark the midnight hour. To celebrate the start of Lenerstelen.

319

When it finished, Siv sang. He didn't have a great singing voice. He didn't even have a *good* singing voice, to be honest. But he sang nevertheless.

God's creating hand made every kind of life on that very first Lenerstelen
He made us, the birds, the fish, the flocks
The trees, the skies, the stars, the rocks
And every angel in his glorious heaven
Now, if darkness should arrive, God's love will never fade
He shall defend the life that his Almighty hand has made
He'll protect us and remake us
Never once shall he forsake us
He holds us always near his loving heart

And in the silence that followed...
Cassie heard a whisper.

She wasn't sure she'd heard it with her ears because it wasn't words. It was an idea.

No, it was more than a single idea. It was answers. It was revelation. And it was a *plan.*

The most beautiful plan she'd ever considered.

Suddenly, it was as if Siv, Annalie, and Sierra – all still within arm's reach of her – had moved a far distance away. Cassie remained aware she was with them, but the focus of her consciousness shifted to somewhere else, to a higher plane of thought, to this plan that had been shown to her. It explained everything. It would solve every problem. It was a fantasy, though. It couldn't possibly work.

Could it?

Do not delude yourself.

Oh, Nariel's voice could shut up already. She was *not* deluding herself. This would work, and she could do it. Because it was far beyond the plan for her life she'd been cultivating since her youth.

It was *God's* plan. And it was glorious.

But... but for how long had he...?

"When was that song written?" she asked urgently. "Does anyone know?"

"It's from the scriptures," Siv said. "Isaac the prophet. He lived, what... probably nine thousand years ago?"

Cassie closed her eyes to hold back tears born both of pain and joy. "Nine *thousand* years?" she said. "Oh, me of little faith. He never abandoned me. He's *always* had something better planned!"

She stood up. "Nariel was right about one thing. Free will does mean we can choose evil. But what he refuses to see is it also means we can choose good. God wants a relationship with each of us, but he won't force us into it. It has to be *our* choice. When we choose to work with him, even in little ways, he'll see our goodness and raise it tenfold.

"Like when Krulgoth gave us the key to his proc-box. I think he just did it hoping we'd find a way to free his brothers. But God uses our goodness to make miracles. He makes us more. And so when Krulgoth stretched out his hand to us, it *was* God's hand. Giving us the greatest gift Verde has ever received."

"A cure?" Siv asked.

"A revival," Cassie said. "*The* revival, the one that Fritz talked about."

She put one arm in front of her, palm facing down. Annalie put her hand on top. Siv put his hand on Annalie's. Sierra put hers on Siv's.

"Keep talking," Sierra said.

"It was the song," Cassie said. "The song I've sung every Lenerstelen, my whole life. That nine-thousand-year-old song was written about *this* Lenerstelen. It's telling us what God is going to do in *this* moment. 'God will defend the life he's made. He'll *remake* us.' I always thought that was figurative. Like a metaphor for the soul-cleansing we get in confession. But its meaning is literal."

Annalie shook her head, not yet understanding.

"We're not just going to cure the Scourge," Cassie said. "We're going to do it in a way that changes *everything*. We're going to turn every person on this planet into a Mantissa healer."

Chapter Twenty-Three

Krulgoth had only ever used Geneditor on the white demons, but his proc-box contained all the instructions needed to use it on *any* species, so long as their DNA was well-known. And Krulgoth himself had mapped out the people of Verde's genome as part of his plan to give his brothers Mantissa powers. And so it was that the Verdant Revival began at just after two on Lenerstelen morning, when Cassie Reinhardt watched Krulgoth's bioprinter create a small bottle of liquid. Then she grabbed it and ran from the barn.

Rain poured down so heavily, she couldn't even see the house. She made her way by memory, being careful not to trip again on the surface rupture's foot-tall step-up. She kept her right hand wrapped around a pair of bottles and stuffed them into her coat pocket to keep them doubly safe.

She couldn't remember the last time she'd really slept. Her eyes felt like they might bleed. Her blood had to be half-coffee and half-adrenaline by now, but she didn't feel tired. She felt like if she jumped, she'd land on one of the moons.

At the front porch, she tossed off her soaked jacket – careful to remove the bottles first – kicked off her muddy boots, threw open the door, and charged inside. Annalie tried to warm herself by the fire. Sierra formed out of the air. She coughed and started to fall apart, but she took a deep breath and held herself together. Siv and Duncan sat beside one another at the kitchen table. Duncan's breathing was shallow. The wounds on his exposed skin were open and bleeding.

"I wish I could test it on myself," she said to Duncan.

He reached out with his only hand. Then he coughed and hacked up a wad of blood. Siv wiped it with his dew rag.

Cassie gave him a bottle. He poured a gulp of the clear liquid down his throat. "Bah," he said. "It's bitter."

For a long minute, nothing happened. Dread called Cassie's name.

But then his bleeding stopped, and his wounds closed and faded away into healthy, unmarked flesh. Sweat droplets formed on his face and neck as his fever seemed to break right before their eyes. His labored breathing normalized.

"How do you feel?" Cassie said.

He examined his wound-free arm and hand.

"Better." He smiled.

"What else?" she said. "Any negative effects?"

He pondered for a moment. "I'm hungry. Reckon I'd like a big steak. Medium rare."

Cassie winked at him. "Anything else?"

"No," Duncan said. And then he grimaced and clutched the empty shirt sleeve covering the stump of his left arm.

"You OK?" Siv asked.

"Oh, don't worry, love," Cassie said. "Your daddy's never been better."

Annalie moved from the fireplace to the table to get a closer look at Duncan's loose, empty shirt sleeve... which was filling from the inside. The short sleeve widened like a balloon being inflated. Flesh poked out of the end of the sleeve and formed an elbow. The new arm – pasty and pale from a lack of sunlight – lengthened and stretched. It thickened, too, until it was the same thickness as his other arm.

The fact that Duncan was regenerating his lost limb didn't surprise Cassie, but the *rate* at which he self-healed did. She'd been working off-and-on to heal his arm for a month now and had only made it grow a few inches. But right before their astonished eyes, hair follicles poked out of Duncan's skin. As his new arm approached the same length as his other, it split into five separate threads, which formed into fingers, knuckles, and nails.

It seemed the genetic code for a Mantissa healer in Krulgoth's notes wasn't just for an average-ability healer. It was for an extraordinarily powerful healer.

"By the stars..." Annalie breathed.

Cassie handed her the second bottle. "Give that to Felix."

When his new left arm had fully grown, Duncan put it in front of his chest, palm facing up. He opened and closed his new hand several times, then he put the back of his right hand into his left, made a joined fist, and pulled both to his heart. He closed his eyes tightly. Tears poked out from underneath the lids. "I never thought I'd make the Sign of God proper, with both hands, ever again."

Cassie kissed the top of his head. "Joyful Lenerstelen, Duncan."

As the sun poked above the eastern horizon on Lenerstelen morning, a gentle rain fell, but this rain wasn't a symptom of Sierra's Scourge-infection, because she was no longer infected. This was one she made very deliberately.

Mandolin kicked up mud as she thundered down the road, staining her white legs brown beneath the knee. Cassie leaned forward as if they were on the final stretch of a barrel race. Sitting in the saddle behind her, Annalie clung to her tightly. Siv rode Rebel alongside her. They topped the last hill, and Hondo came into view.

They only slowed their horses once they were in the middle of town. Cassie helped Annalie down from the saddle. She looked different without her spectacles, but Cassie would have to get used to that because Annalie didn't need them anymore. Her vision, like everything else about her health, was now perfect. Cassie dismounted, too, and let Mandolin wander free. She looked to the sky. "Ready?" she asked.

"Outside!" Sierra's voice boomed from the sky. "The cure is in the rain."

Siv was already pounding on doors. Annalie spotted the town butcher, Robert Steiner, standing in his house's doorway with his wife and young son. Their sores were bleeding and infected, and all three of them were obviously in pain, yet they curiously inspected the crazy people running around in the downpour. "Come on," Annalie said, taking the little boy by the hand. "Come get as wet as you can."

"You don't have any sores!" Margie Steiner said.

"And you won't either," Annalie said. "I promise. Come outside!"

"The rain will heal you," Sierra's voice boomed.

Mr. Steiner startled. "Who said that?"

"Don't be afraid," Annalie said. "That's just Sierra." She lowered her voice to a whisper. "She don't like being called Lady Verde."

The rain washed over the Steiner family's hair, skin, clothes, and their Scourge wounds, which shrank and disappeared. Their tentative steps became leaps of joy. Mrs. Steiner took her healed son in her arms, squeezed him tightly, and squealed in delight. Mr. Steiner dropped to his knees and made the Sign of God's Hand.

The first few people to emerge from their shops and homes did so cautiously. But as they watched more and more of their fellow residents miraculously healed, the next waves of people came out running. Phil Hersch threw back his head and opened his mouth, drinking in the rain as the Scourge disappeared from his body and as his missing eye returned to its socket. "I'm healed!" he shouted. "And... I'm sober?"

"Oh right," Cassie said. "I forgot about that part. You might not be capable of getting drunk ever again. I'm sorry, or you're welcome, however it is you feel about that."

Sheriff Auber escorted a handcuffed Kurt Bauer from the jail, and both lawman and murderer were freed from the Scourge. Someone helped Pastor Kolbe limp down the hill from the church. He laughed with delight as he watched his wounds and everyone else's disappear. "It's a Lenerstelen miracle!" he declared.

"It's the most splendiferous thing in the history of splendiferousness," Annalie agreed.

Cassie knocked on the general store's front door. Its main window was still covered with plywood instead of glass. "Connie?" she called out. "It's Cassie Reinhardt. Everything's OK. No one's going to hurt you."

Connie Emerson emerged from the shadows inside, cradling a badly wounded arm. She tentatively unbolted the front door and opened it a crack. Cassie offered her hand. "Come outside," Cassie said. "The cure is in the rain. The Scourge is over."

She threw herself into Cassie's arms and wept. Cassie healed her, then helped her get wet with rain so that she could heal herself of everything else for the rest of her life. By the time Cassie helped her join the crowd, it looked like almost the entire village was present.

"My bad knee always hurts when it rains," Brady Williams said. "But it's not hurting now. It's not even sore."

"My arthritis is gone!" Mary Engel said.

"The scar on my arm just disappeared," Andrea Krause said. "I saw it! It shriveled up and disappeared right before my eyes, same as my Scourge wounds did."

All I know is that the revival is coming, and... and that means things will be OK, Fritz had said. *No more sickness.*

"I'm moving on," Sierra's voice boomed.

Cassie saluted the sky, then shook her head in wonder. Sierra was the only person who could spread the cure worldwide fast enough – the only person who *ever* could. She should have died two centuries ago, yet she was here, now, because God knew. He *knew.*

As the rain tapered off, Cassie moved to the front of the crowd with Siv and Annalie and cleared her throat. "Everyone's read stories about the Mantissa, right?"

"The old guardians?" someone in the crowd said.

"The ones who caused the Blackout?" someone else said.

"Witchcraft!" someone cried.

"You call them whatever you want," Cassie said, "but I can tell you now, I've been a Mantissa healer all my life. And now all of you are, too. Everyone everywhere will be. Sierra – the lady up in the clouds you might think of as Lady Verde but *don't* call her that – she's spreading the cure worldwide. Except you haven't just been cured of the Scourge. You've been cured of *everything.* You'll never be sick ever again. And you can heal other people, too, if you just think about doing it. Though once everyone's turned into a healer, I'm not sure what you'll need that ability for."

Some in the assembly whooped and hollered at the news, though the reaction was tempered by others' stunned disbelief. "Everyone's immortal?" someone said.

"No," Cassie said. "We'll all still die of old age, eventually. And if hurt badly enough, we can still die before we can heal from it. But there's something else that will help with that."

Siv had entered the crowd and maneuvered himself behind Sheriff Auber and Kurt Bauer. He reared back his fist and aimed a rabbit punch directly at the back of the murderer's skull, but before he could throw it, Bauer yelped and ducked. "He was gonna punch me!" Bauer yelled.

"Danger sense!" Cassie told the crowd. "Think of it as pre-healing. Your body doesn't have to heal itself when it can avoid injury before it happens. I hope you have a hobby, Sheriff, because you won't be half as busy as you used to be."

And there'll be no more fighting and no more war, Fritz had said.

Sheriff Auber chuckled and made the Sign of God's Hand. "How's anyone going to fight when the person you're trying to hurt will sense it coming?" he said.

"Or when they can heal themselves of almost anything?" Connie added.

"Cassie, how have you done this?" Pastor Kolbe asked.

Cassie held up her hands. "I just stopped resisting and finally let the Almighty Hand work through mine." She wanted to say more, to tell them all how long God had planned this miracle, how neither fallen angels nor the white demons nor sinful humans could foil his plan, but she couldn't bring herself to say anything else. She'd been one of those sinful humans, maybe the most sinful one. Her happiness at seeing the world healed was tempered only by her shame, her guilt.

How many more might have lived if she'd just trusted God sooner?

"Cass," Siv said. He motioned up the street with his chin. A squad of seven Shakren stood at the opposite end of town, watching the gathering with their weapons drawn and pointed at the people.

"Let them shoot!" Phil said. "They can't hurt us anymore." He blew a raspberry at the Shakren, then turned, bent over, and shook his rear end at them.

"Careful," Cassie said. "I repeat: you *can* still be hurt beyond the capacity to self-heal. If you suddenly feel like they're going to shoot you, get out of here, fast."

"That's the danger sense you mentioned?" Sheriff Auber asked.

"Aye," Cassie said. She took three steps forward. Siv and Annalie came with her. "Get out of here," she yelled to the Shakren. "Go back up there and tell the Celestines that the Scourge is over. Not just here, but everywhere. And you tell the Way I said *no*. He'll know who I am and what I mean."

One of the Shakren peacekeepers touched the comm he wore on his ear and leaned closer to the squad leader. Cassie had to strain her ears to hear him. "Confirmation this is happening worldwide," he said. "And we've been ordered to return to our base ship."

The Shakren quickly headed towards their shuttle parked just outside of town, because of *course* they had to immediately obey a Celestine order. Far off, in the direction of Fort Belknap, Cassie spotted another Celestine shuttle ascending towards space. Then another. A fresh wave of excitement swept across the people of Hondo. "They're leaving! They're leaving!" the crowd cheered.

330

"I reckon they'll be back," Siv said. "And they'll be *torqued*."

"Then we better get ready for them," Cassie said. "But there are two things I have to take care of first. A pair of mistakes I need to make right." She scanned the crowd for the young man wearing a black shirt and a white collar. "Pastor Kolbe, a word?"

"Outside!" Sierra boomed in the thunder whenever people were beneath her. "The cure is in the rain."

The young and the old, male and female, families and couples and single persons, all stumbled outside at her thunderous call. They ingested Reinhardt's drug – or was it the white demons' drug, and did it really barking matter – through their mouths and skin, and their wounds disappeared. Their strength returned. They hugged and danced in the rain. They filled buckets of rain to take to those too weak to come outside. Maybe on any other day, they'd have been more cautious of the sound of voices from the sky and of magical rain that cured the plague. But superstitious people expected miracles on Lenerstelen. And Sierra had to admit, everyone was witnessing a miracle today, believer and non-believer alike.

She'd never been a religious person, but she knew those who were spent this day celebrating the creation of life in the universe. And here she was, raining life down on the dying. After she'd merged with the planet, she'd spent centuries thinking she was dead. When she did take human form once more, she'd truly believed herself to be Lady Verde, but it had all been a misunderstanding – trauma-induced amnesia. She was *not* the spirit of the planet. She was just a Mantissa with environmental powers who'd unconsciously took those powers farther than she'd ever dreamed possible.

But on that Lenerstelen morning, as she delivered Reinhardt's drug worldwide, Sierra felt like she really was Lady Verde. Like the people she healed were *her* people.

She soared over the occupied territories in the form of wind and clouds and rain. First above Hondo, then Gorman, Cleburne Hill, Fort Belknap, Domino, Clarion, and Oak Leaf. She flew north, over the rebuilding of Harbrucken. In the form of raindrops, she plopped down into the Elde River, and as the river, she reached out and splashed the shores, bathing those who had come to the riverbank in the early morning with life-giving water. "Drink!" she commanded. "Drink and be healed."

She flew over the mountains to the few isolated human settlements in Terrascorcha, such as Jasper, Big Sprint, and what remained of Earp. She came to Mondorf and doused the sprawling, ancient capital city with medicine-filled rain.

After Fritz had reached out to her in friendship, she'd told him she deserved punishment for all the harm she'd done waging war against his chipware restoration. *You want to do penance for your sins?* he'd said. *Forgive yourself, and do better in the future.*

This was the best thing she'd *ever* done.

After she'd distributed the cure to every human settlement worldwide, she returned to the Reinhardt farm and healed herself, repairing the surface rupture that split the pasture in front of their house. That act of restoration involved just moving around dirt and stone. It was an exercise in the same power she'd always had. But she, like everyone else, had a new ability. It had healed her body of the Scourge, but her body was just an avatar she molded out of dirt and air and water.

Her power had once caused her to bond with the planet. Could this new power allow her to *heal* the planet, too?

The air and water will be clean again, Fritz had said.

She turned herself into wind, scaled the Lavare Mountains, and focused herself on a miles-wide section of land near the eastern coast of Terrascorcha. The ground here was dark brown – made even darker by the mud from the rains – and it was not hilly or mountainous, but nor was it flat. It was marked with tens of thousands of tree stumps. Once this had been the Naunhof Forest, but an overly-aggressive, financially-driven lumber industry had clear-cut the area three hundred years earlier.

Sierra put her presence deep underground beneath the forest and then reached out, splintering herself into thousands of tendrils, each coming up into one of the stumps. She had to be careful. If she split herself too much, she started to lose herself, to forget she was Sierra Monet, knowing herself only as Lady Verde. That was the real reason she'd never been very successful at making herself physically present in multiple places at one time. It wasn't that she *couldn't*. It was that she was afraid she'd go too far. But the dead trees of the Naunhof were, by definition of being a forest, all clustered together. She didn't feel at risk of losing herself here, even spread out across the forest's entire width.

As she filled them with her presence, stumps of wood that had sat dead and decaying for hundreds of years turned firm and robust. The wood behind their bark changed from decrepit to bright and healthy. And they *grew*. The trunks stretched towards the sky, new branches sprouted and intermingled with their neighbors. Leaves popped out of buds, the rains pelted the leaves, and Sierra was speechless. Not because she didn't physically have a human mouth at the moment, but because she was overcome with emotion she usually tried so hard to restrain. She didn't stop applying her new power until every one of the trees told her it was now taller than it had ever been before.

Sierra moved her presence miles to the west of the forest and took a human form high in the sky, so she could look down on her work from above. She'd only seen the Naunhof Forest in pictures, and now it was alive again. The forest was her, and she was the forest, and both were healed.

She left the Naunhof and became the Elde River, and her power surged through it and destroyed pollutants that had poisoned it for hundreds of years. The murky waters turned clear. She soared into the sky and became her ozone layer. Its holes filled in minutes. She moved her presence to the poles, normalizing temperatures and increasing the size of the glaciers.

She took a human form high in the sky above the equator and looked over her world. Her*self*. Morning sun fell upon her face, both the ground beneath her and the human one she'd assumed. She never smiled much because few things really made her happy, but this? All the damage she could now undo? All the nature she could now heal and keep pristine?

She pumped her fists. "Oh *hell* yeah!"

Chapter Twenty-Four

Cassie knelt in the confessional. The panel covering the pastor's side of the lattice between the two rooms slid aside. "Firm in the grasp of God's loving hand, we confess our sins in honesty and humility," Pastor Kolbe said. And this time, it really was him. It was his voice, and from what little Cassie could see through the grating, his hands were *not* gray and intangible.

"May God's judging hand be merciful," she said as she made the Sign of God's Hand. "It's been about a month since I made my last confession. My last real one anyway. Gosh. Feels like it's been years."

"It's been a rough couple of weeks for everyone," Pastor Kolbe agreed.

"Since my last confession, I've had a crisis of faith," Cassie said. "Hmmph. That feels like I'm sugar-coating it. The fact is: I gave in to despair. Pastor Seelos once told me there was nothing wrong with honest doubt, but I went way beyond doubt here. I was *convinced* God had abandoned us – especially me. And I wasn't shy about saying that out loud. I turned my back on him. I threw my grunblume into a fire. I refused to pray. And I came very close to..."

How was she supposed to confess this? Sure, he was a pastor, but would he believe the Celestines who had come from outer space to poison Verde were the devils themselves? That they'd murdered Fritz? And that they'd been in contact with her personally? Even on a Lenerstelen morning that had seen so many miracles worldwide, would Pastor Kolbe believe such a thing?

"Let's just say I was willing to offer my soul to the devils in return for everyone being cured," Cassie said.

She rested her head against the wall between the chambers, just above the grating. Admitting her sin out loud was definitely cathartic, but it also laid her shame bare. She wrapped her arms tightly around herself and closed her eyes. If she couldn't see anything, maybe no one could see her, either.

"It sounds like you've had a dark night of the soul," Pastor Kolbe said. "With all that's happened over the last two weeks, both here in Hondo and within your family, it's understandable that you'd suffer as you have."

"Suffer?" Cassie chuckled. "You make it sound like I'm the victim here. I'm not. I'm the penitent. I was willing to abandon God and follow the devils. I gave up every ounce of faith, except the one that still believed in God's actual existence. I committed *blasphemy*, Pastor. I believed with every ounce of my being that the devils had a better plan for us than God does. I don't need to tell you that's the sin that got them banished from heaven *forever*. Honestly? I'm not even sure I *can* be forgiven."

There was a long pause from the other side of the lattice.

"I've never done this before," Pastor Kolbe finally said, "but could we continue with this reconciliation outside the confessional?"

"Beg pardon?"

"I assure you the confidentiality of the confessional seal remains intact," he said. "I just need to show you something out in the church."

"Umm. OK."

Cassie stood and stepped out of the confessional. Pastor Kolbe emerged from his side of the chamber, too. He motioned her to follow him, and he led her up the side aisle to one of the church's windows. The scene depicted on the stained glass was the same scene found in Siv's favorite constellation. In the night sky, the devils' banishment was made up of dots of light from distant stars, but the window was far more detailed. On it, God's hand was made of flesh and gave off an ethereal blue glow. The devils – two male, one female – had red skin, horns, and fiery wings.

"You recognize this, of course," Pastor Kolbe said, keeping his voice low.

"That's what God's probably gonna do to punish me," Cassie said.

"Punishment?" Pastor Kolbe said. His lips turned up into an odd grin. Did he think something was funny about this? "What do you think this picture depicts?"

She frowned at him. "What do you mean, what do I think? Everyone knows that's God's wrathful hand casting the devils out of heaven."

"Except it's not," Pastor Kolbe said. "People want an angry, wrathful God. They want him to give sinners a slogging – all sinners except themselves, of course. They want him to act like an overzealous sheriff in a lawless town. They want a God who wields a sword and who isn't afraid to use it." He shrugged his shoulders. "It's not all their fault. For far too long, the church has emphasized sin and punishment over love and mercy. As a result, the common interpretation of this well-known image has become inaccurate. The constellation that depicts it even has a name that means 'wrath of God.' But that's all balderdash. This image depicts no such thing. It's an image of God's *merciful* hand calling the devils back to him."

If Cassie had been sipping water, she'd have spit it all over the floor. "Calling them back? *Them?*"

"Imagine you have a pair of dice in your hand," Pastor Kolbe said. "Pretend to give them a shake, then throw them across an imaginary table. Right here."

She felt a bit silly, but she went along with it. "Now, look at your hand," Pastor Kolbe said. "After expelling the dice, your fingers are laying flat and pointing towards our pretend table. Is that what the Almighty fingers look like in this image?"

"No," Cassie said slowly. "They're tilting upward." She mimed shaking dice again. "It's as if the dice – or the devils – were still in the palm of his hand."

"Or as if he were beckoning them back," Pastor Kolbe said, and he raised his hand and motioned her to come towards him, then froze his fingers in place. His palm was flat. His fingers were tilted upward. Just like on the window. "He's not throwing them out. He's asking them to come home. He's beckoning them to return to him."

Cassie braced herself on the end of a pew. Despite no physical exertion, she suddenly found herself trying to catch her breath. She'd never heard anything like this before. She was still having a hard time wrapping her head around the idea that God had something better planned for Verde than a cure for the Scourge and that she was the hand who made it happen. Did he really have something better than wrath and vengeance planned even for the devils?

Nariel told her God reordered every star in the universe after the devils left heaven such that every planet had a constellation similar to Gotteszorn. The Blasphemer had told her it was a permanent, universal reminder that the devils could never return home. Did he really not know what those constellations meant? Did that being – the prince of heaven, who has walked with God himself – truly misunderstand God's meaning? Unlikely. If Pastor Kolbe knew the truth, then certainly Nariel knew it also.

He'd lied to her. A lie meant to manipulate her into selling her soul.

And it had nearly worked.

"You said you weren't certain you could be forgiven," Pastor Kolbe said. "But if God refuses to permanently bear a grudge against even the devils, then there is no such thing as an unforgivable sin. Especially not when you've come here to repair your relationship with him."

"This isn't the first time I've been mad at God when I felt he wasn't helping me," Cassie said. "I'm afraid that someday, something will go wrong again, and I'll do this all over again."

"You might," Pastor Kolbe said. "But a saint is just a sinner who keeps on trying."

He extended his hand towards her, palm upward. "God's merciful hand catches us when we fall and embraces us when we return to him. Through the ministry of the church, may God give you pardon and peace, and I absolve you from your sins" – he placed the back of his left hand in the palm of his right and brought both together to his heart – "firm in the grasp of his merciful, Almighty Hand."

Cassie repeated the Sign of God's Hand. She felt like the weight of the world had been lifted off her shoulders. "Amen," she said.

"For your penance," Pastor Kolbe said, "go to the front of the church and wait for me there."

"Pfft. You're letting me off awfully easy."

"Consider it a Lenerstelen present."

"Thank you, Pastor," she said.

"Thank *God*," he said. "Now, if you'll excuse me?" He scurried up the church's side aisle, through an archway, and disappeared into the sacristy.

She turned towards the altar where Siv was waiting for her. His eyes were practically twinkling. Duncan was right behind him. Annalie, Felix, and her mother all sat in the front pew. At the entrance, the church's double doors were open. Even this far south, it should have been far too cold on Lenerstelen morning to open the church to the breeze. Nevertheless, sunlight filled the church, and the temperature had risen to what felt like a pleasant seventy degrees. Birds chirped in the trees. The sound of revelry from Main Street a block away drifted in on the wind.

Cassie stepped outside and found Sierra on the grass, toeing the ground with her boot and looking uncomfortable. "Do I have you to thank for this weather?" Cassie asked.

"Just thought you'd like pleasant spring weather for your wedding," she said. "If you don't, I can change it."

"It's perfect," Cassie said. She puffed air and blew a stray strand of hair away from her face. "Look. I've treated you unfairly. Even cruelly sometimes. Despite what I said before, you have *not* squandered the opportunity Fritz gave you. Far from it. He was right not to give up on you. You've made every effort to change your life, to make amends, and you've done it despite me constantly throwing your past back in your face. I've been completely unforgiving toward you. You deserve better. I'm sorry."

Uncomfortable under Cassie's gaze, Sierra looked away. "Isn't your fault. I don't make it easy for people to get along with me."

"And *I* let my own plans and goals blind me to things that should be obvious," Cassie said. "Like how I trusted Fritz more than anyone, and that if he forgave you, then I should have, too. But I'm trying to learn – from *you* – and take a step towards correcting my mistakes. So... I was wondering if you'd do me the honor of giving me away?"

Sierra's eyes bulged. "You can't be barking serious."

"Might want to watch your language inside church," Cassie gently suggested.

"Look at me," Sierra said. She pointed to herself, from her pierced face to her combat boots. "Do I look like a church person?"

"Siv wanted us to come here and get married almost three weeks ago," Cassie said. "I told him no. I said that if I couldn't have my father walking me down the aisle, I was going to insist that everything else be perfect. Just like I've always planned it. But the thing is, besides my mom and his children, my dad loved one person more than any other. You."

"I never met the guy!" Sierra protested.

"He was a proud farmer," Cassie said. "And a darn good one. He lived off the land, and he loved her for it. He loved *you*, Lady Verde. For reasons I still don't understand, God didn't see fit to intercede and make sure my dad was here on my wedding day to walk me down the aisle. But if he can't be here, and neither can Fritz... I honestly think you're the perfect substitute."

Sierra looked away.

"If you don't want to," Cassie said, "you don't have to."

Sierra stiffly nodded and bit at her lower lip. "All right. I suppose. For your dad. Who raised a good son." She shrugged. "And a good daughter."

Cassie stifled a grin. "I think you have something in your eye."

"Watch it, Reinhardt," Sierra said, looking away again. "It's dusty out here."

"It is," Cassie said. "It's very dusty." She inhaled a lungful of perfectly clean air, then searched around the grassy area between the church and the adjacent cemetery. "Before we go in, do you see any flowers anywhere? Pansies grow this time of year, but..."

Sierra wiggled her fingers, and a sprout of white and yellow pansies poked up out of the ground near the walk leading into the church.

"Ooo," Cassie said. "Those are nice, but what I was going to say was I don't suppose you can make some purple lilacs grow, could you? They're my favorite."

Sierra *tsk*ed. "Lilacs are spring flowers. You *do* know it's the middle of winter?"

"Yeah," Cassie said. "Sure. Forget about it. I just thought maybe–"

Sierra laughed – a real, actual laugh, not a sarcastic one. "I'm just taking the piss out of you." She wiggled her fingers again, and adjacent to the pansies, a large sprout of lilacs blossomed.

Cassie picked one and tucked it into her hair. She brushed off the front of her jeans and pressed a crease out of her shirt. "Ready?" she asked Sierra.

Sierra's hair changed color from green to brown. The side shaved down to the scalp grew out to match the rest. The metal in her face vanished into unpierced skin. It was a breathtaking change. She looked... normal.

"No," Cassie told her. "Don't."

"I just thought, for your wedding, you wouldn't want me to look so... so me."

"No," Cassie repeated. "You be yourself. Always."

Once the piercings and the green hair returned, Cassie offered Sierra her hand.

"Thanks," Sierra mumbled. "This is... kind of an honor. Though I will never again admit I just said that."

"I'll insist to everyone you did this under the most vehement protest."

"You better."

They walked inside and up the center aisle of the church together. When they reached the altar, Sierra gave Cassie's hand to Siv.

"Hurt her, and I hurt you," Sierra said to Siv.

Siv blinked, looking between both Sierra and Cassie. She couldn't blame him. Hearing Sierra talk like a friend sounded remarkably strange. She could get used to it, though.

"Got it?" Sierra demanded with a raised fist.

"Cross my heart," Siv said.

Satisfied, Sierra nodded and retreated to the side aisle of the church, away from everyone else.

"Hi," Cassie said to Siv.

He leaned down and kissed her on the forehead. "Who was that, and what have they done with Sierra?"

Cassie had to cover her mouth to stifle her giggles.

Pastor Kolbe emerged from behind the altar, having traded the stole he'd worn around his neck during confession for a white chasuble. He made the Sign of God's Hand, and everyone else did the same. "I'll keep this short," he said. "I have a sermon to write for Lenerstelen services later today. Services I didn't think I nor anyone else would be healthy enough to

343

attend. Yet here we are. And I can think of no better way to celebrate the creation of life in the universe than by starting you two, Siv and Cassie, on your new life together."

He motioned for the two of them to face one another. They did and extended their hands, palms up. Pastor Kolbe nodded to Cassie, and she placed the back of her left hand in the palm of Siv's right. Siv gently closed her hand in his own and brought both of them to his chest. "By the joining of my hand, yours, and Almighty God's, I take you as my wife. I'll love and honor you forever."

Siv placed the back of his left hand in the palm of Cassie's right. She brought both hands together to her heart. "By the joining of my hand, yours, and Almighty God's, I take you as my husband. I'll love and honor you forever."

Pastor Kolbe raised his outstretched hand above them. "Sivrin McCaig and Cassandra Theresa Reinhardt," he said, "as a pastor of God's holy church, I both witness and bless this marriage you have conferred upon one another. What God has joined cannot be divided. Amen."

"Amen," Siv and Cassie both said.

After a pause, they looked at Pastor Kolbe expectantly.

"I said I'd keep it short," he said.

"That's it?" Siv said.

"You're hitched," Pastor Kolbe said. "Kiss her already."

Before Siv could, smoke appeared near the church's door, and Nariel the Blasphemer stepped out of it. His shoulders were slumped, and his lips were a straight line. Another cloud billowed behind him, and Daphne the Liar – Fritz's killer – was there, too. In Cassie's parish church. Unarmed, at least for the moment.

Annalie stood and put herself between the devils and Felix, motioning him to get underneath their seat. Sierra clenched her fists, and lightning crackled around them. As if shelter under a church pew or lightning would do any good against the fallen angels.

"The Celestines," Pastor Kolbe whispered. He remembered the beings who had addressed Hondo's citizens the day the Scourge began.

Cassie entered the middle aisle and took two steps down it. "You don't look happy, Nariel. What's the matter? You upset because I figured out how to do everything you offered but *without* joining you?"

"I'm disappointed you believe that's what has happened," he said in his melodious voice, and for a moment, Cassie felt a pang of regret. She should have joined them! Maybe she still could. *No!* It was just this devil's silver tongue, trying to make her believe wrong was right. "I'll grant you've given your people health. Long natural life. A defense mechanism against personal harm that should prevent most violence. But you've done *nothing* to put an end to lying. You've done nothing to end theft. Greed. Gluttony. Poverty. Temptation. Sins of the flesh."

Daphne disappeared, then reappeared directly in front of Siv, closing her eyes and lasciviously tilting her head back. She brushed her hand across her jacket, moving it aside to reveal a low-cut top underneath.

Siv took a step back. "Get away from me," he growled.

She licked her index finger and vanished, reappearing at the back of the church next to Nariel.

"What are they?" Pastor Kolbe whispered.

"They're the fallen angels, Pastor," Annalie said. "The damned themselves."

Daphne blew her a kiss.

"So much sin will still stain your beloved Verde," Nariel said to Cassie. "You're disappointingly short-sighted. You've accomplished so little of what you could have. I've visited hundreds of worlds. I've known thousands of cultures. Your people *will* still choose to disobey and disregard God's law."

"I'm sure some will," Cassie said. "But some will choose to follow it. And that's what makes all the difference. The good that happens here will be the good *we* chose, not good imposed on us in tyranny. When God turns his Almighty eye to Verde, he *will* find faith here."

That seemed to startle Nariel, but he quickly composed himself.

"Speaking of the Almighty," Cassie said. "Pastor Kolbe was kind enough to illuminate me about the true meaning of that constellation up in our night sky. You said there are ones just like it on other worlds. You said there's one of a boulder falling to crush three pebbles? Well, it's not. It's a father chasing after his lost children."

The disappointment on Nariel's face fell away. He stood taller and looked indignant.

"You said there's one of a tail rearing back to sweep you two aside," Cassie said. "Well, it's not. That tail is curling to *embrace* you." She pointed at the stained glass window depicting God's Almighty hand calling the devils back to heaven. "And the one in our sky is *not* a warning. It's an invitation. From him to you. To *both* of you. And you *both* know it. Don't you?"

Neither devil said a word, but the anger in their eyes gave Cassie a hint of why they were called the Fiery Ones.

"So why don't you two accept that invitation?" Cassie said. "Leave Verde. Repent. And return home."

Daphne bared her teeth and hissed at her. Anger flared across Nariel's face, but then he seemed to compose himself. He sighed and shook his head. "Your people were close to exploration beyond your own star system once. Left unchecked, that ability will soon be restored, and the people of this planet will visit other worlds. I cannot allow your error to spread. My mission is too important."

Daphne opened her hands. Smoke came out of them and took the shape of small daggers suitable for throwing. She held two in each hand. In the same manner, smoke came from Nariel's hands and took the form of pistols. Cassie was sure both the daggers and the guns were soul-cleaving weapons.

Nariel pointed one of his pistols directly at Cassie's heart.

"I'm so sorry, Cassandra," he said. "You had so much potential, but instead you've proved the evil of free will."

Cassie's danger sense screamed so loudly her body physically shook, but she refused to move. Where could she go anyway? The Celestines could appear anywhere, and apparently, their soul-cleaving weapons could take any form – swords, daggers, guns. Just as she'd told the people of Hondo earlier this morning, even a Mantissa healer could be harmed beyond the ability to self-heal. A soul-cleaving bullet would kill her instantly. She couldn't defend herself against them. She couldn't fight back.

But she would *not* give them the satisfaction of seeing her run. She'd die standing. In her church. With Siv as her husband. Surrounded by her family. And right with God.

She had just started to make the Sign of God's Hand when Pastor Kolbe shoved his way beside her and stretched his arm

347

in front of him, the palm of his hand facing the Celestines. "By the power of the Almighty Hand," he bellowed, "*begone* from this holy place!"

Daphne cursed.

"No!" Nariel shouted.

And they both turned into puffs of smoke and disappeared.

Cassie blinked. She blinked again. She blinked a third time. Her danger sense had gone silent, and Pastor Kolbe's eyes were practically on fire. "What just happened?" she asked from a dry mouth.

"On the day of my ordination," Pastor Kolbe said, "my hands were consecrated to preside at services, to forgive sins, and to exorcise demons." He blinked. "Which I've never had the chance to try. Until now."

Annalie smacked her hands together and whooped so loudly it echoed through the church. "This changes everything!"

"Can you kill 'em, too?" Siv asked.

Pastor Kolbe jerked his head around and gave Siv an incredulous stare.

Siv blushed. "All right, so I'm standing in God's house with murder on my mind, but only of the devils. And you heard 'em, Pastor. They're fixing to end us all."

"The devils' spirits, like anyone else's, are immortal," Pastor Kolbe said. "They *can't* be killed."

"What if I told you we have proof they can?" Cassie said.

He glanced across the church at the confessional, then back at her. Despite he and other pastors' claims that they forget what they hear during a penitent's confession, he remembered that she'd admitted nearly selling her soul to the devils... the devils who had just been physically present in his church. Calling her by name.

Guess now he understood she had *not* been speaking figuratively.

Chapter Twenty-Five

Gashg shouldn't have had any reason to be happy.

He was back aboard a Celestine *Seraphim*-class capital ship and back in forced servitude to the Evil Ones. He was one of a hundred Shakren monitoring a workstation in the control center of the fleet's cathedral ship, though unlike the others, he stood on his four back legs and hunched over the controls because a Shakrath couldn't physically fit into a workstation's chair.

He probably wouldn't even be a Shakrath much longer. Already he'd heard whispers of the ship's current batch of scientists preparing a regimen of Geneditor designed to physically transform the Shakrath back into Shakren. In the meantime, he was clothed in a Shakren uniform specially designed for Shakrath bodies with six limbs and long prehensile tails. His designation – P-29333 – was stitched into the uniform's chest. He'd been ordered to monitor the ship's aft temperature regulation sub-system, and so he did. Because he couldn't say no. But he also watched everything else happening in the control center around him.

And it was in the observation of everyone else's frantic behavior that he found some small bit of happiness.

The comm operators agitatedly rotated through calls. The flight control stations chattered non-stop. Docking procedures were being carried out. Drop ships were returning to the cathedral ship from the planet below – *all* the drop ships. Peacekeeper squads on every deck sought orders. Commanders struggled to tell them anything other than that all ships had been recalled.

"What's happened?" Skleght said from behind Gashg. The designation on his uniform was P-28311.

"How are you here?" Gashg asked.

"I was told to guard an empty drop ship docking bay," he said. "It's now full. Since I no longer have an *empty* docking bay to guard, I've come to find out when I should expect to guard it again. And what's really going on."

Even after two hundred years, it was easy to remember how to exercise some small bit of free will by taking advantage of the Evil Ones' impreciseness. "What's happened is all the peacekeepers on Verde have been recalled," Gashg said.

"So that's it then," Skleght grumbled. "Everyone on Verde is dead."

"Just the opposite. They cured the Scourge."

Skleght blinked. "They *cured* it? Who? Reinhardt? McCaig? Annalie?"

Gashg nodded, then sat up a little taller. "Though perhaps with a bit of help."

That baffled Skleght even more than hearing everyone had been cured, but it only took him a moment to comprehend. "Krulgoth's arm."

"The one that unlocked his workstation."

"You gave them Geneditor," Skleght said. "They made themselves all Mantissa healers."

"They did. Though I didn't give it to them. I just carried out Krulgoth's last request."

Skleght lowered his head. Though Krulgoth had died without the two of them on the best terms, he had still been the person who'd freed them – at least for a time – from the Evil Ones. "They've only delayed the inevitable. If the Evil Ones want everyone on Verde dead, then everyone on Verde *will* die. One way or another."

"I don't disagree," Gashg said.

Skleght leaned over Gashg's shoulder and spoke very softly. "Do *they* know? About your role?"

"I don't think so," Gashg said.

"If they figure out you were involved, even in the smallest way, they'll kill you, too," Skleght said.

"Then I'll die having done one good thing with my freedom when I had it."

Off Skleght's puzzled look, Gashg explained. "Krulgoth freed us, and then what did we ever do with it, Skleght? For centuries, what did we ever do with our freedom except subjugate anyone who might take it from us? Nothing. We were just as bad as *they* are."

Skleght hissed at him, low and from the back of his throat.

"Oh hush," Gashg said. "You know it's true. We even enslaved other people. Ask the residents of Mondorf down on that planet, the people we lorded over for two hundred years. We were no better. Ever. Except for the one moment when Krulgoth called out to me and raised his hand. The one moment where I gave that hand to Reinhardt. If they want to kill me, they'll kill me. But I don't care. Because I'll have died having finally done *something* worthwhile with my life."

Skleght seemed to weigh his words, but before he could say anything, black smoke rolled across the control center floor. All Shakren and Shakrath eyes went to the room's center, where the Way and the Truth would step out of the smoke at any moment.

Instead, they stumbled out of it as if they'd tripped.

Gashg furrowed his brow. He'd never seen anything like that before. The Evil Ones seemed unsteady. The Truth wrapped her arms around herself and looked around the room with wide, blinking eyes. The Way stared into the middle distance, expressionless as if lost in thought.

Every Shakren in the room – including Gashg and Skleght – took to one knee. "Luminary," they greeted.

The Evil Ones made no reply. Not that they usually did. But it was like they didn't even comprehend the control center was fully staffed. The only sounds were beeps and trilling noises from the workstations. Air blew out of ventilation shafts and was sucked back into recyclers. No Shakren moved.

The Truth looked to the Way expectantly. "We're done here," she said. "You know what needs to be done. So do it."

The Way blinked but otherwise remained still.

"Remember the Reselite man?" the Truth shouted. "Remember the Diladian woman? The Kronosian woman? The Feregit man? This Verdant woman is *just like* everyone else you've ever tried to recruit. You've failed. *Again*."

The Way recoiled as if he'd been physically slapped. He met the Truth's eyes. "You lie," he stuttered.

"*No*," the Truth said. "For once, no. Because you're failing to recognize the truth that has been staring in your face since the day we left home. They're *never* going to join your crusade, Nariel! Not a single one of them. Ever. *Ever!* The best you're ever going to get is Rudger and me – a murderous demon and a lying demon. You're *not* going to lead some world-changing crusade. You are just as damned as we are, except you're a million times more sanctimonious."

Gashg and Skleght shared a look. What had happened on Verde? This was behavior unlike anything they'd ever seen out

354

of the Evil Ones before. The Way closed his eyes, as if resigning himself to the Truth's criticism. And it *was* criticism, right? She *wasn't* speaking in lies?

"I repeat: you know what needs to be done," the Truth said. "So if you don't give the order, I will."

The Way stood motionless.

With a huff, the Truth took two steps towards the workstation nearest her.

"Stigmatize them," the Way commanded in a booming voice. His shoulders slumped, and he seemed to deflate. "Stigmatize Verde. Now."

Gashg's already white face turned a shade paler, but the Shakren in the room burst into action. Their hands furiously tapped at their workstations and command consoles. Some stood and scattered from the control center. "Stigmata has been ordered," a nearby Shakren said into a microphone, passing the order across the fleet.

"All ships – the Luminaries have ordered the Stigmata on Verde," another said.

"Prepare for Stigmata," another said.

Skleght backed away from Gashg because he had to obey his standing orders regarding which station he should report to when Stigmata was ordered. "I'm glad you were able to do something good with your freedom, my friend," he called back to Gashg. "I wish it could have been more."

Skleght left. "Me, too," Gashg whispered.

"Let me put it into my own words to see if I understand," Pastor Kolbe said. "The Celestines aren't aliens. They're demons – the devils themselves. But the white demons aren't really demons. They're aliens. It was their elixir that cured the

355

Scourge by turning everyone into Mantissa – who two hundred years ago did *not* wield black magic, but who *did* cause the Blackout. To stop the demons."

"The *white* demons," Cassie said. "Who are actually aliens."

He leaned forward in the pew, closed his eyes, and rubbed at his temples. "My head hurts."

Cassie frowned. "That shouldn't happen anymore. Your healer abilities– Oh. You mean to say all of this is overwhelming."

He looked up at Annalie and then Cassie. "Fritz didn't die of an accident on your farm. Did he?"

"No," Cassie said. "And I guess next time I go to confession, I better mention that I told you a lie about that." She swallowed. "The devils killed him. They used what we believe was a soul-cleaving weapon. It did no physical harm, but he died instantly. We think it just booted his soul right out of his body."

Pastor Kolbe made the Sign of God's Hand. "I'm sorry. If it's any consolation, being murdered by the devils would certainly seem to qualify as a martyr's death. That will earn him extra graces."

"What really scares me," Cassie said, "is the possibility they didn't just cleave his soul out of his body, but that they somehow... destroyed it. Permanently. And that he's not anywhere anymore. That he's just gone. Forever."

"No," Pastor Kolbe said firmly. "They don't have that kind of power. With a martyr's death, your brother's place in heaven is assured. He might need to spend a spell in Purgation before he gets there, and if he's in Purgation, then he needs our prayers. The souls there can no longer pray for themselves. But rest assured. He is *not* gone."

"That's exactly what my husband told me." She looked at Siv, and he nodded back.

They were still in the church, though Duncan and Ruth had taken Felix home. At Siv's insistence, Sierra had flown back to the barn to retrieve their weapons. He already had his sword and shotgun both strapped across his back, convinced a new wave of Shakren invasion would begin at any moment. Sierra paced back and forth, occasionally pausing as she moved her consciousness elsewhere, watching as much of the planet as she could.

Annalie had set up a comm-net between Cassie's chip pad and Krulgoth's workstation back at the house. Cassie sat next to Pastor Kolbe and showed him its screen. It displayed a picture of Krulgoth from back when he was still a Shakren scientist. He stood alone in a Celestine laboratory – the same laboratory, apparently, from the vid Cassie had been watching when Elise died. The one that showed the Shakren scientists administering a cure for the Scourge.

"Krulgoth said he and his people escaped from the Celestines after he killed one of them," Cassie said, "and I don't believe he was lying or mistaken. I found this vid in his personal journals."

Siv, Annalie, and Sierra gathered behind her and watched over her shoulder. "Play," Cassie said.

The bipedal, albino, almost-human Krulgoth in the still-frame came to life. "I wanted to spend the last three days the same way I've spent the last several decades," he said. "Researching what it is about me that makes me capable of disobeying you. My goal is to use Geneditor to replicate that difference in my brothers and free them from their bondage."

An awkward silence followed, and although the vid showed Krulgoth was alone, he carried himself as if someone else were present. Because someone was. Someone who couldn't be recorded visually or audibly.

"I should have gone back over all my data," Krulgoth said.

"Forward thirty seconds," Cassie said. The vid flickered.

"That's why I and every other Shakren aboard this ship are going to leave," Krulgoth said. "Right after I kill you." Another silence followed. Krulgoth picked up a scalpel and held it before him. He stepped forward as if stalking prey. "S-17 says it's OK if I use this. He says it would be poetic."

"Watch this," Cassie said.

In the vid, Krulgoth reared back his arm and slashed his scalpel across what was at first empty air...

And then the gray face of a stocky Celestine suddenly appeared. One second he hadn't been there; the next, he was. He wore a black vest, and his white hair stood straight up like spikes.

Krulgoth slashed the Celestine across the face.

Annalie startled and covered her mouth.

"That's Rudger?" Siv said.

"The Murderer," Pastor Kolbe whispered.

Krulgoth's attack had come dangerously close to taking the Celestine's glossy black eyeball, and he wasn't finished. "You can't," the Murderer protested as Krulgoth continued to cut and slash and beat him. "You– you– no. You can't! You can't do this."

Yet the smoke and fire that bled out of the gash Krulgoth carved into his face proved it was possible. The fact that it was on vid proved the devils *could* appear on electronic devices, somehow. The Celestine's howl confirmed they *could* be audibly recorded.

The vid ended after Krulgoth choked the Murderer and then threw him against a window, which shattered under the impact of the Celestine's *tangible* body. With a scream of terror, the Murderer disappeared from the vid. Krulgoth stood at the broken window and watched him fall.

"The badge!" Siv said, pointing at the screen. "See it? It fell off the Murderer in the scuffle, and it's a might broke, but it's still there. That's the one Krulgoth wore when he first came to Verde. The one I saw disappear when I" – he mimed a slash across his throat.

"It disappeared when Krulgoth – the real flesh-and-blood Krulgoth – died," Cassie explained to Pastor Kolbe. She raised her voice slightly. "Show the other angle."

The screen switched to a second vid, apparently one recorded with another camera. This one showed Rudger drop into frame onto a wide patch of bare rock. On impact, he exploded into flame and smoke and soot. When the smoke cleared, the rock he'd landed upon was stained black.

"There was a puff of that same black smoke when Pastor exorcised the Way and the Truth out of here," Annalie said. "Does that mean Krulgoth *didn't* kill that one? Did he only exorcise him?"

"Or just the opposite," Sierra said. "Maybe the sin-buster here didn't just send them away. Maybe he already killed them."

"Pure spirits can't be killed," Pastor Kolbe said.

"I think we just saw proof they can," Cassie said. "Nariel's just as much a liar as Daphne, but he did seem genuinely grief-stricken when he spoke of Krulgoth *killing* that Celestine."

"Unless that was all an act, too," Siv said.

"I don't think it was," Cassie said. "Up on their cathedral ship, they said they always knew where their escaped Shakren were. The white demons were stuck here on Verde for *two hundred years* after the Blackout, yet the Celestines never came for them, not until the original Krulgoth, the biological one, was killed. They were afraid of him. They didn't want to be anywhere near where he was because he really did kill a fallen angel."

She turned to Pastor Kolbe. "I don't want to murder anyone, but I fear that for Verde to survive, we'll have to kill the other two fallen angels before they kill us."

"I fear you're right," Pastor Kolbe said.

"We just saw it happen," Cassie said, tapping her finger on her chip pad for emphasis. "Did you see anything in that vid that indicated how he did it? Did he do something like your exorcism ritual? Did you see anything in there we could do to harm them?"

Pastor Kolbe shook his head. "I'm sorry I didn't."

"How does that exorcism ritual work?" Siv said. "Can you teach us?"

"I could teach you the words, but that's only the *form* of the ritual," he said. "A solemn exorcism isn't a magical incantation. It's the church exercising her authority to demand that a person or place or thing be protected from the devils. The rite requires a specific form, but it also must be performed by an ordained pastor under their bishop's approval. Even if I taught you the form, the laity simply *can't* perform an exorcism. But all that may be moot. I didn't really perform a true exorcism here. I just commanded those devils to leave, and that didn't require any of my pastoral faculties. That just required me invoking the power of Almighty God."

Cassie motioned towards the screen. "But Krulgoth clearly didn't do that. He was an atheist."

"So how did he slay the demon?" Siv said. "And why did they obey Pastor's command to leave?"

"Time's up," Sierra said. Her eyes glazed over, but only for a moment. "They're coming."

Cassie, Siv, and Annalie bolted for the church door. Pastor Kolbe followed them. Sierra simply disappeared then reappeared outside. They looked up to the sky, shielding their eyes from the late morning sun.

"Is it the same drop ships the Shakren came in before?" Annalie asked.

"Is it another biomortic weapon?" Cassie asked.

"No and no," Sierra said. "It's... oh, crud."

They didn't need Siv and Duncan's telescope, or chipware sights, or any kind of magnification. The Celestine ships that poked through the clouds were easily visible with the naked eye. And indeed, they weren't shuttles, or fighters, or anything like that. It was their capital ships. The same giant, drill-like spacecraft the Celestines had arrived in had entered Verde's atmosphere. They descended towards the ground, with their drill ends facing down.

Well. At least now she knew what the Celestines used those for.

"One-hundred five of those ships arrived here two weeks ago," Annalie said.

"And one-hundred five are entering my atmosphere," Sierra said. "They're spread out all over. Some are headed towards settlements, but others are headed towards the middle of nowhere."

"They're just landing at random?" Cassie said.

"No," Sierra said. She drew in a sharp intake of breath. "They're headed towards fault lines. They're going to drill into the crust at just the right places to make groundshakes and tidal waves. It's gonna be like when I was sick with the Scourge all over again, but worse. A lot worse." She swallowed. "They're gonna crack me apart. Shatter me into pieces."

"They mean to end us," Siv said. "They ain't holding anything back."

"Then neither can we," Cassie said.

"I believe this attack, combined with the devils' obstinance, makes you morally justified to use lethal force to stop them," Pastor Kolbe said. "I wish I knew how to do that. But God certainly does, and I pray he shows you how. What else can I do?"

"If there's no secret rituals we need to learn, no ultra-effective prayers or anything like that," Cassie said, "then the best thing you can do is gather the entire town here, conduct Lenerstelen services, and pray for us. Get everyone to pray for us and for all of Verde. Pray we figure out what Krulgoth did to kill the Murderer and that we can repeat it on the other two."

"And if you could arrange an exorcism on a planetary scale," Annalie said, "it wouldn't hurt."

Pastor Kolbe pulled a grunblume out of his pocket and handed it to Cassie. "I think you might require one of these. I don't remember how or where, but I thought I heard you say you recently lost yours."

She wrapped the string of beads around her hand and kissed it. "Thank you," she said.

"This may look hopeless, but don't lose faith," Pastor Kolbe said. "Faith the size of the smallest seed can move a mountain."

"So can those ships," Sierra muttered with a wavering voice. She was terrified, and Cassie couldn't blame her. The sky was full of them now, and their drill-like elements weren't slowing as they had when they'd first arrived in Verde's orbit. If anything, they were spinning more rapidly every second.

"Well, everyone," Cassie said. "We ended sickness, ended disease, ended violence and war. But it seems if we want the Revival to continue, we need to do more. How about we end the devils, too?"

"Amen," Siv said. "How?"

"Don't know," Cassie said. "But I know we can. And we will. Because we have to."

Chapter Twenty-Six

Mandolin and Rebel raced one another down the hill from the church with Cassie and Siv on their backs. Sierra flew through the air beside them. They turned onto Main Street and ran past the general store, the saloon, the livery, and onto the road out of Hondo.

A Celestine *Seraphim*-class capital ship hung in the sky ahead. It was unfathomably massive, as tall as the remains of the pre-Blackout scrapes-the-sky buildings up north in Mondorf. Its auger-like blades – pointed straight down towards the surface – spun faster than a tornado. It sounded like a wire scrub brush trying to claw its way through a chalkboard, at a volume louder than thunder and dynamite. It descended quickly and would soon rip into the surface about a quarter-mile from town.

Though all their capital ships looked alike, somehow Cassie knew this was the cathedral ship, the one with the fallen angels themselves aboard. Because of *course* they'd bring their flagship here. They'd made this personal. Daphne had murdered Fritz. Their disease had killed Elise. Nariel had offered to make Cassie a devil, and that offer had been rebuffed. They wanted a front row seat to the destruction of her home. They wanted her to die not in any kind of cataclysm but by their own damned hands.

Cassie was *not* going to let that be part of the plan.

Sierra watched the ship descending towards *her* surface and trembled. She flew close enough for Cassie to reach a hand out and lay it on her shoulder. "You're a healer now," she yelled over the cacophony of thundering hooves and roaring spaceship engines. "You'll be OK."

"Look at that thing," Sierra said. "When that gets deep enough into me, it's gonna hurt like hell. And there's a hundred-and-four others all over the planet. Not sure I'll be able to heal from all that."

"How long until the first ships touch down?" Cassie asked.

"They already have," Sierra said. "The real question is: how long until they geet deep enough to–"

Sierra dropped out of the air, rolled across the ground, howled in pain. Cassie tugged back on Mandolin's reigns, dismounted, and knelt beside her, putting an arm around her shoulders. "Where are they?" she asked.

"Barking everywhere," Sierra grunted between gritted teeth. "First eleven ships are tearing through my crust. Places where it's most thin. They're gonna be to the mantle soon, and *that* is going to–" Her last word sounded like it was going to be "hurt," but it deteriorated into a scream.

"Go," Cassie told her. "Fight them."

"Which one?" Sierra snapped.

"As many as you can," Cassie said with a shrug. "All of them."

"You know I'm piss poor at being in multiple places at once," Sierra said. "Especially when I'm getting *stabbed*–" She screamed again.

"Oh, I'm sorry, is Sierra Monet telling me she *can't* fight back?" Cassie yelled over the din of the cathedral ship's descent. "I'm not watching anyone else die today. You *fight* these devils! *Fight them.* You make them rue the day they came here!"

Cassie pulled her to her feet.

"Did you actually just use the words 'rue the day'?" Sierra asked.

"*Fight them all*, you barking crank!" Cassie hollered.

Sierra steeled herself, closed her eyes, grunted with exertion.

And suddenly, out of wisps of air and dirt, there were *ten* of her, lined up in a row. Some clenched their fists. Wind swirled around others. One made an obscene gesture at the descending cathedral ship. Nine of them disappeared, scattered across Verde, apparently.

"We got this one," Cassie said. "Go."

The last Sierra disappeared, too. Cassie climbed into Mandolin's saddle and resumed her charge towards the cathedral ship. Siv and Rebel joined her.

The cathedral ship had seemed large enough out in the vastness of space. Here in Verde's atmosphere? By the Almighty Hand, was it ever enormous. Siv tapped his earpiece to open a voice-comm. "May can we sent Sierra away too early. How in the world we gonna hit that thing?"

"I'm your huckleberry," Annalie said over the voice-comm. Green laser fire came from behind Cassie and over her head – *way* over her head – and pelted the cathedral ship. The distinctive high-pitched whine of the cannons that fired those shots was instantly recognizable.

Wearing Fritz's chipsuit – *her* chipsuit now – Annalie zoomed past Cassie and Siv in the air above them, trails of fire blazing from her rockets. She blasted the ship some more as she curved through the air around it, then she flew sharply down, continuing to fire as she dove. "Dang," she said, "tough shell on this armadillo."

Cassie squinted to see what she was talking about. Where Annalie's shots hit the main part of the ship, they left behind scorches and dents in the hull. Where they hit the spinning auger blades, they did nothing. As poetic as it would have been for Annalie to take solo revenge on the Celestines using Fritz's chipsuit, it didn't appear to be God's plan. The good news was: it didn't have to be.

"Don't make this harder than it is," Cassie said. "We don't need to stop that ship from drilling into the ground. We don't even need to hurt a single Shakren. This is over worldwide as soon as we reach the Celestines inside and end them. With no Celestines to give them orders, the liberated Shakren will stand down. And while I know it seems like a lifetime ago already, remember we've practiced boarding that ship and getting face-to-face with the devils *sixteen* times."

"I'm comparing what I see in front of me to the schematics from Krulgoth's files," Annalie said. She was still far above them in the sky. "I think I– holy moley!"

Six red laser blasts suddenly burst forth from gun batteries on the cathedral ship; all six fired straight at Annalie. The shots seemed to be as wide as tree trunks, fired from weapons apparently designed to combat other space ships. Annalie dodged left, then down, then she burned hard up into the sky and narrowly missed all of them. "Gratitude, Cassie. I'd have just gotten smoked if not for my new danger sense."

"Just find us the door as fast as you can," Cassie asked. "Where did we plan to board this thing before we decided to ram right into their control center?"

"I got it," Annalie said. "I spotted the airlock. I'll just need to cut into its maintenance hatch, pop the release levers, and we'll be inside."

"Then let's go say howdy," Siv said. He climbed down out of his saddle and drew his sword, the Dragon Slayer, from the scabbard on his back. Both edges of the blade lit up with an outline of glowing green energy. "For Fritz. For Elise. Hell, even for Krulgoth."

Cassie dismounted, too. "We're ready," Cassie said, "whenever you are."

Annalie changed direction in the sky and zoomed towards them. "Figure it's about a thousand feet up at the moment."

"I ain't afraid of heights," Cassie said.

Annalie barely slowed as she came to hover a foot above them. "Giddy up," she said. Then taking them each by the hand, she lifted them into the air. Way, *way* up into the air. Cassie and Siv each secured themselves to Annalie's chipsuit with a grappling hook and a safety line, just in case they weren't able to hold on.

When the cathedral ship fired its lasers again, Annalie dodged and zoomed in close towards the ship, so close Cassie could reach out and touch it. Then Annalie ascended straight up past the ship's spinning auger, past portholes and exhaust ports, and past armored hull and access panels. She came to a stop in front of a round door with a window in the middle.

Cassie and Siv transferred their grappling hooks to rings that seemed too conveniently placed adjacent to the airlock door... until Cassie realized they'd likely been designed for this exact purpose. Just not for use in atmosphere. They were probably meant to be used on spacewalks. Once she and Siv were secured, Annalie let go. Cassie had her boots pressed against the ship, a line tying her to it, and nothing but a thousand feet of air between her and the ground below.

Annalie hovered beside them, her chipsuit rockets keeping her in place. She yanked the casing off the control panel next to the door and fidgeted with wires inside it. A few sparks shot out of the panel, then the round airlock door rolled away into a pocket in the hull. The airlock's inner door opened at the same time. Annalie flew inside, and once her chipsuit's boots had a magnetic lock on the deck beneath her, she reached outside for Cassie's hand.

As Cassie climbed up into the ship, she saw a forest just beyond the airlock's inner door. An artificial environment designed for Shakren training, just like they'd planned for and practiced in. Cassie had two hands and one knee in the airlock when her danger sense barked at her. Annalie's must have, too, because both of them looked up sharply. A squad of Shakren – at least ten, all armed with laser rifles – were running towards them, artificial leaves crunching under their boots.

"The welcome wagon's already here," Cassie shouted to Siv as she untethered her grapple line.

"I'll cover you," Annalie said. She took two steps forward so that she was standing in the airlock's inner doorway. As the Shakren's first shots came in, her chipsuit glowed with blue energy that absorbed and dissipated the lasers. The energy barrier shield wasn't designed to protect anything much beyond herself, but by blocking the doorway, she created as broad a shield and as much cover as possible for Cassie and Siv.

And she didn't just play defense. Laser cannons popped up out of the suit's forearms, and she fired back, but it was her two guns against the Shakren's ten – no, make that thirteen, as more were coming up behind the initial wave. No – fifteen. The already-loud laser shots echoed painfully off the airlock's walls. The air was painted with so many green and red blasts of weaponized light screaming back and forth.

Cassie reached out the airlock towards Siv. He took her hand, and she pulled him inside. While he untethered his grapple line, Cassie nocked an arrow, crouched low, leaned just barely out from behind Annalie's cover, and fired through the gap between Annalie and the door frame. Her arrow stuck into a Shakren's knee and brought him to the ground.

Siv put his back against the wall just beside the inner airlock door. "Your danger sense will tell you when it's OK to shoot," Cassie told him. The firefight was so loud, he probably heard her only over the voice-comm, even though they were within arm's reach. He nodded an acknowledgment, then leaned out the door, fired off a bullet from his shotgun, and darted back to cover.

They kept attacking – Cassie slinging arrows, Siv throwing bullets – as often as they could. All the while, the blue energy aura from Annalie's chipsuit absorbed a *lot* of red Shakren laser blasts. "You holding up, sister?" Cassie said.

"My power meter's at 98%," Annalie said. "I can keep this up a good long spell if we have to. And unfortunately, I reckon we will. When we practiced this, there were a lot more folks on our side. Now it's just us three, but *their* numbers ain't been reduced at all. In fact, there may be more of them out there than we planned for."

"Sounds like a math problem," Cassie said. She fired an arrow that took down a Shakren. "You're good at math."

"Not sure I can solve this one," Annalie said. "At least not before this ship starts drilling into the ground."

She never even had time to sharpen her pencil. The first warning of trouble was a scream from their danger senses. The second was a series of clanging sounds from the ceiling above

371

them. It sounded as if something metal had been dropped on the deck above them or into a ventilation tube.

Then the airlock exploded.

The flames scorched Cassie's clothes and seared her skin, but the flames weren't really the problem. The shockwave was. It pushed the air clean out of her lungs, broke a few of her ribs, stomped on her belly like an angry horse... and shoved her through the outer airlock door. Outside the cathedral ship. And down, down, down towards the ground below.

Chapter Twenty-Seven

Sierra hurt. *Everywhere.*

She was physically present in ten places scattered around the planet. Crouched in a treetop in the Naunhof Forest. Rising out of the waters of the Halcyic Ocean. Ankle-deep in the Midphalia Desert sand. Standing in the snow on a ridge in the Lavare Mountains.

But the Celestines' presence was ten times more vast than her own. One hundred five places all across the planet, a Celestine ship was either drilling into her or about to drill into her. And, once it got deep enough under the surface, she felt every single one. When another three ships began drilling into the planetary crust somewhere she wasn't, all ten of her physical forms felt the new ships like icepicks hammered into her eardrums. The pain nearly made her crumple. Two of her physical forms fell apart, though she quickly regrouped and reformed them. She tried to make an eleventh body, but she felt her mind stretching too thin when she tried, and she backed off.

Then two more ships cut into her fault lines, and fresh hell washed over her like boiling water.

And yet, it was comforting, in a weird way, because Sierra and pain were old friends. They went *way* back. Like the time she found out the reason she was in a foster home was that the parents she never knew had abandoned her. Or when the other kids said she was ugly because of her threadbare, third-hand clothes. Remember when the Mantissa had kicked her out of their shiny tower, leaving her without a family yet again? Oh, good times, good times.

373

Yep, pain was an old enemy, but she knew how to deal with it. When shipped off to yet another new foster home, it was time for disobedience and petty theft. That weeded out who really cared for her and who didn't. Turned out none of them really cared. She always got shipped off to a new home, a new not-her-family.

When the other kids thought her clothes were unattractive, she dyed her hair green. Stuck a piece of metal through every part of her that could be pierced. She took their ugly and wore it as a badge of honor.

When the Mantissa kicked her out, she made it clear that she didn't want to be one of them anyway. She'd fight for Verde her own way, and she wouldn't miss them for a moment. Hey – she was a good liar, too.

The Celestine ships drilling into Verde were causing her the most pain she'd ever felt, but it was going to suck to be them because she knew exactly what came after pain.

Her voice boomed from the sky. "After pain comes *defiance*, you prats!"

In the Naunhof Forest, she dissolved her body but reached into the ground with her presence. She extracted as much dirt as she could without killing all the trees she'd just resurrected a few hours earlier. Then she pulled air underneath the soil and pushed it up into the sky, mixing it with water from the forest's stream. She sucked so much of the water out of the stream, its bed went dry, but right now, that didn't matter much. Her new healing power would repair the stream after this was over. *If* she survived.

The water and the dirt swirled together, mixed, formed mud, and coalesced into a shapeless mass half as tall as the tallest tree in the forest. Sierra reached out and added air into the concoction, mutating it into a solid the same way she could mutate air into her physical body. The trees swayed and rattled as the air she borrowed was all funneled into her mass of dirt and water, significantly expanding its size. It thinned out and elongated, reaching high above the trees.

Five tendrils broke off the central mass and formed fingers and a thumb. The sides smoothed into a palm and the back of a hand. Sierra pulled more dirt out of the planetary crust and manipulated air pressure to push it higher and higher up the enormous hand.

Finally, when the hand had nearly reached the incoming Celestine ship, Sierra mutated it at the molecular level. She gathered all the silicates out of the soil and shoved them to the surface. The dirty brown hand of mud became a white, shiny, harder-than-iron hand coated with quartz.

It had only taken seconds to manipulate her dirt, air, and water into this new shape. The crew aboard the Celestine ship never had a chance to alter course or turn back. Her giant metal hand seized the ship and squeezed its middle.

She had hoped to shatter the ship as if it were made of glass, but it wasn't. It was still a barking huge metallic spacecraft diving towards the planetary surface at incredible speeds. She might as well have seized hot barbed wire being dragged by a team of horses. It hurt like *hell*. And her attack wasn't very effective, either. She'd slowed the ship, a little. But not much.

In the Halcyic Ocean, she had so much water at her disposal, she pulled out enough to make *five* giant hands. Drawing the heat out of them and back down into the ocean, the hands changed form from water to ice. The hands were so hard and strong, she was able to hold the ship that attacked the ocean in place, and she might have even been able to snap it in half, but her mind was stretched too thin. She was also trying to attack them in the desert, in Mondorf, on the plains, on the beach. And even with all that effort, she was only confronting a fraction of the ships. So many others were drilling into her unhindered, and every time another one pierced deep enough down into her surface, every one of her physical bodies felt it. It was like having ten kidneys and being stabbed in all of them simultaneously.

In the Naunhof Forest, she fell apart. So did she in the Halcyic Ocean and in the Midphalia Desert. All ten of her physical forms disintegrated. Being in two places at once – or three, or ten – was a matter of concentration. It was hard enough for people to rub their heads and pat their bellies at the same time. Turned out it was damn near impossible to take in and process the sensory input from – and to coordinate separate independent actions for – ten distinct physical representations of herself at the same time.

The fractured pieces of her mind slammed back together into one, and she took a single form in the Lavare Mountains. The giant hand-shape she'd taken there – mostly limestone, but coated with the hardest metamorphic rock in the area – grabbed the Celestine ship drilling into the mountain by its sharp, rotating blade.

The ship shredded the hand back into the dirt and water from which it had been made.

She reformed herself back into her regular body further downhill, where the mountain's slope leveled off into a wide pass. Without intending to, she formed a body that looked how she felt. She collapsed, splayed out on her back in the snow. Blood spilled out of her nose and stained the bottom half of her face. One leg was bent at an unnatural angle. The skin around both her eyes was swollen and puffy. The healing power Reinhardt had given her had met its match. It wasn't enough to fend off the damage of stabbing attacks from a hundred alien spaceships. All it was doing was prolonging her death.

The Celestine ship at the mountain was several hundred yards uphill, drilling deep into the crust – into *her*. The vibration of the penetrating ship spilled powder and rocks down the hill. And eventually, probably, an avalanche. Which would be ironic. She'd once teamed with the Steelterrors to bury Fritz under an avalanche in these very mountains. He'd repaid her attempted murder with forgiveness and friendship. Told her to just do better next time.

She'd tried. But she was outgunned here. Overpowered. Even her rage at their murder of Fritz couldn't give her the strength she'd need.

She couldn't stop them.

"Bollocks," she said.

The cathedral ship seemed to be racing past Cassie, fast. The wind whipped against her skin that had been burned in the explosion. *That* didn't feel very pleasant. But as she fell towards the ground, her healing power went to work on the injuries. She'd probably be fully healed by the time she landed – and she did intend to *land* on the ground, not collide with it.

Siv fell, too. She heard him over the voice-comm. He didn't say any words, and he didn't scream either, but she could tell by the grunts and gasps he made that he was afraid. "It's OK, hon," she told him. "God's Almighty Hand will catch us."

Up near the top of the ship, there was a flash of green and twin streaks of fire.

"And there it is," Cassie said.

Annalie dove headfirst out of the ship and propelled herself at faster than free-fall speeds down towards them. She swooped over to Siv and grasped his forearm just behind his wrist. Then she veered to her left and grabbed Cassie. Less than ten seconds later, all three of them were standing on the ground with Mandolin and Rebel. The horses had retreated behind some cacti and shrubs. It wouldn't do anything to protect them from the cathedral ship's weapons, but it at least felt better than standing in the middle of the open plain staring the ship down.

Siv put his hands on his knees and leaned forward. Cassie touched his back. "You all right? You gonna hurl?"

He shook his head. "I might, if we had time for it. Gratitude, Red."

Annalie snapped open her helmet's faceplate. "They were waiting for us," she said.

"We practiced that assault sixteen times," Cassie said, "with white demons who are on that ship right now and genetically forced to work with the devils. But we had to try because I don't have any other ideas."

The sound of the descending ship changed. Cassie peered around their cover to get a look. The ship's deadly auger blades still spun fast as lightning, but the ship itself seemed to have slowed. It was so close to the ground, the dirt shook beneath Cassie's boots. Three panels spaced equidistantly around the ship folded forward out of its hull and towards the auger blades at the ship's front. They folded out again, and metal columns extended from the panels down towards the ground, configuring themselves into a tripod shape.

"That must be their landing gear," Annalie said. "Reckon those posts will touch ground first, balancing the rest of the ship as it lowers itself the final bit to the surface and starts drillin'."

Mandolin snorted and kicked at the dirt.

"Steady, girl," Cassie said, stroking her horse's head without turning back to face her.

Mandolin shoved Cassie's hand away, snorted again, and stomped her front left hoof. "Mandy!" Cassie rebuked. "Now's not the–"

Cassie gaped at her horse, then back at the Celestine ship. The landing gear columns – three of them. Spread out in a triangular shape. Mandy thought it was a barrel racing arena, and she was fixing to run. And as an idea formed in Cassie's mind, she was inclined to let her. Cassie pulled herself up into her saddle. "I need to borrow your sword."

Siv squinted at her, but he took off his scabbard and tied it to Cassie's saddle. "Not sure I like the look on your face," he said.

"Mandy wants to race," she said.

"Race what?" Annalie asked. "That ship?"

"In a manner of speaking," Cassie said. She leaned forward and patted Mandy's right shoulder. "Ready, Mandy? *Giddyap!*"

Mandolin bolted towards the nearest leg of the landing gear just as it touched the ground. The ship's enormous auger blade wouldn't be far behind. Cassie squeezed her legs against Mandolin's side, dropped the reins, and nocked a bomb-tipped arrow into her bow. She fired at the landing gear. The explosion left it blackened but intact. She fired another arrow, which caused more cosmetic damage, but nothing else.

"The outside of those landing columns are the ablative armor of their hull," Annalie called over the voice-comm. "It would take all the power in this chipsuit to put a dent in it."

As Mandy got closer, Cassie noticed something. The outside of the landing column was scorched but intact, but the *inside* – the side facing the ship's spinning drill – looked more than just defaced. Was it cracked?

"Then I guess I can't just hit its armored side," Cassie said. "I'll have to hit the inside, too."

"Ain't enough room to hit it from that side!" Siv shouted.

"Oh, there's plenty," Cassie said.

The ship's engines and auger blades were deafening as the drill's tip at last touched dirt. Dust particles flew everywhere, turning the entire landscape into a hazy fog. Cassie lowered her head and urged Mandy to keep charging towards what the horse saw as a barrel. She steered to the left, directing them into the narrow gap between the drill blade and the landing gear. Her danger sense voiced concern. If they got too close, it wouldn't be a five-second penalty for knocking over a barrel. They'd be cut to shreds, well beyond her ability to self-heal.

Cassie drew Siv's sword. She pushed the button in the pommel that made both edges of the blade glow with green laser enhancements. Fritz's work. Siv's sword. Her hand, acting on behalf of God.

Please, she prayed.

As she and Mandy squeezed into the gap, the vibrations of the giant drill rattled her teeth and skull. It was so close, it tickled her cheek. Or maybe that was just the dirt it tore out of the ground and threw up everywhere. Her danger sense screamed in the back of her brain. She swung Siv's sword out to her right and slammed it against the landing gear. Sparks flew as she scraped it through the metal. Even the roar of the engines wasn't enough to drown out the horrible metal-on-metal screech. Gooseflesh surged up her arm. The landing

380

column bent a little, then buckled a lot. For a moment, Cassie thought the whole dang ship was going to come down on her. But ultimately, the landing gear held. Damn!

Mandy emerged out the other side and made a tight turn around the landing column. Cassie slashed the outside – the armored side – too, but Annalie was right. It was tough. The laser-enhanced blade put a scratch in it, but nothing more. Mandy ran away from the landing column because you didn't take a second turn around the same barrel in barrel racing. Cassie turned off the sword's lasers, shoved it into its scabbard, and turned in the saddle to take one last shot. She nocked a bomb-tipped arrow and aimed for the place where the column had already buckled. Pulled the string back. Let go.

Guide it, God! Take it in your hand!

Before the fire of the explosion had even cleared away, the cathedral ship began to tilt towards the broken landing column.

Cassie nearly dropped her bow while seizing Mandy's reins. "*Go! Go! Go!*" she hollered.

Mandy ran like the wind. Annalie whooped over the voice-comm. "Get out of there!" Siv yelled.

The cathedral ship drooped wildly to the side, but it didn't fall in a straight line. Because its auger blade was partially in the ground and still spinning like a tornado, the whole ship whipped around and around in wide circles, though well over Cassie's head. Its engines surged in a desperate attempt to lift the ship out of the ground but to no avail. It finally stopped spinning as it crashed in a heap. Explosions like popping fireworks went off up and down the ship. The land beneath Cassie shook as violently as it had during the groundshakes.

If the ship's drilling had created a dust cloud, its crashing created the most enormous dust storm Cassie had ever imagined. Mandy ran purely on instinct, not sight, because seeing anything but brown was impossible. Cassie squeezed her eyes shut against all the debris in the air and gently coaxed Mandy to a stop before she tripped over an unseen obstacle. "Siv?" she called out. "Annalie?"

"Here," Annalie called back, and not via the voice-comm. It was her real voice, filtered and amplified by her chipsuit. Glowing light emerged from the haze, and then Annalie was there, hovering beside her.

"Where's Siv?" Cassie said.

His coughing came over the voice-comm.

"He's OK," Annalie said. She pointed over yonder. "I see his heat signature on infrared. Stay put. I'll guide him over."

As the dust started to settle, Cassie dismounted and stood in front of Mandolin, who was no longer a white horse. She was dirty beige and brown from head to hoof. Cassie laughed, threw her arms around her neck, and hugged her close. "That was the race of your life, girl," she whispered. "Thank you."

A few minutes later, Cassie heard pounding horse hooves and burning rockets before Annalie, Siv, and Rebel all came into view. "Gonna have to disqualify you, cowgirl," Siv said. "You only circled one barrel."

When the dust settled, they found the Celestine cathedral ship laying cracked and broken across the stony plain. Its engines and its massive drill had stopped. Smoke rose from it in a dozen places. Pieces of wreckage had joined the rocks and stones scattered around the area like detritus. They were lucky a piece hadn't flown through the dust storm and hit one of them in the head.

Cassie handed Siv's sword and scabbard back to him. He strapped it onto his back. "We heading back into it?" Siv said. "Might be a bit easier now."

"Not necessary," Annalie said. Airlock doors – or were they emergency hatches – opened across the ship. Shakren peacekeepers, all of them armed, came charging out. Thousands of them. By bringing down the cathedral ship, they'd kicked over a fire ant mound, and all its residents were torqued off and swarming the surrounding area fixing to bite. There were some white demons among the Shakren, too.

Annalie pointed her forearm-mounted laser cannons, Siv aimed his shotgun, and Cassie nocked an arrow. But before any of the Shakren were close to being within range, plumes of black smoke formed in the air two arms' lengths away from Cassie.

Nariel the Blasphemer and Daphne the Liar emerged from them. Their soul-cleaving blades appeared in their hands.

"Sivrin. Annalie. Cassandra," Nariel said. "That's enough."

Chapter Twenty-Eight

"There's someone out there!"

Sierra was so dazed, she wasn't even sure she'd really heard the voice. But then she tilted her head back and looked upside-down at the area around her. Sunlight reflected off of glass. Horizontally stacked logs peeked out from underneath the snow. Smoke rose from stone chimneys.

"It's a woman. She's hurt!"

Oh *crud*. It was a mountain village, probably full of people who'd made their own civilization ever since the Blackout two centuries earlier. Now that she thought about it, she remembered flying the cure over this place. Any moment now, when the drilling of the Celestine ship uphill triggered an avalanche, it wasn't just going to bury her. It was going to bury a village full of people, too.

"Get out," she mumbled, but where was a whole village going to go?

She felt the footsteps before she heard them or before she saw the man approach. She waved him away, not just to urge him to seek safety, but to tell him to leave her. That she wasn't worth saving, and that he couldn't do anything for her anyway. Before she could, in three places scattered across the planet, three more Celestine ships drilled into her fault lines. She convulsed and vomited blood.

And then the ground beneath her shook. The avalanche she'd feared had begun. The village behind her would–

No. The tremors weren't coming from uphill – at least not these new ones. They came from somewhere closer. From the ground just underneath her, and not nearly deep enough to hurt. The source of the vibration – whatever it was – moved laterally across the mountain.

A few yards in front of her, a trench of snow dropped away, as if the ground underneath it had just suddenly vanished into a chasm. Then something burst forth, and the world disappeared into a white fog of powder. All Sierra knew was she wasn't buried, and the village behind her was safe. For now. But what in the world...?

When the white fog cleared, a mass of steel stood over her, but it wasn't the Celestine ship. It was a giant robot with his own drills – much smaller than the Celestine ships – for hands. A robot she herself had dug out of the ground, back before she'd remembered who she was. When she still thought she was Lady Verde, when she waged war against chipware, she'd controlled this titan of power.

It was a barking Steelterror. The Verdant Warden of Soil.

"Samson?!" she said.

The last time she'd seen Samson was right in these mountains. She'd ordered him to help her unearth the Steelterrors' leader, Gravitas, then she and Gravitas had brought a mountain down on top of Fritz. Samson had been collateral damage. She thought he was dead. Yet here he was, seemingly in perfect condition – minus some of his armor. Samson tilted his head and focused his glowing green eyes on her. "Lady Verde?" he said.

Sierra would have rolled her eyes if she wasn't in such pain. Even as she was about to really, finally die, she still was being called that name. "That's who I told you I was," she said. "It's who I thought I was. But I'm not."

The people – there were more than one now – coming from the village to help her gasped. "It's a Steelterror!" someone shouted.

Samson raised one hand in front of his face and activated his drill.

"No!" Sierra yelled back. "He's a Verdant Warden! He... Can you help us? Can you stop that thing?"

Samson looked up the mountain at the Celestine ship. About a quarter of it was now underground, tearing up the mountain, ripping apart Sierra's insides. "I'm done being a weapon," he said in his deep rumble of a voice, but then his voice... changed. It softened in tone, went much higher in pitch.

Sierra didn't know how, but he spoke in *Fritz's* voice.

"But some things are worth fighting for," he said. "Things like the right to be a farmer."

Samson bounded up the mountain, and when he neared the Celestine ship, he refactored his arms into thick steel drums, pushed off the ground, and leaped. In mid-air, he again refactored his hands back into drills. His jump took him above the auger blade, to the part of the vessel that was just a space ship, and he punched it with both drill-fists. The ship's armor crumpled as Samson embedded himself forearm-deep. Pushing off with his giant metal feet, he allowed gravity to pull him down, and he dug ten-foot-wide gashes as he fell. Something in the ship exploded. Smoke and sparks and fire poured out of it. And by the time Samson leaped away from the auger and landed safely on the ground, the Celestine ship tipped over, broken, still, and not digging any deeper into the soil.

Two people from the village – a man and a woman – had finally reached where Sierra was collapsed in the snow. They took her hands, checked her pulse, and looked very confused when they found she didn't have one, although her eyes were open. They frowned at her legs, which crumbled into dirt past her knees. They looked up the mountain at Samson as he descended through the fog of the Celestine ship's wreckage.

"There's more of them," Samson said. "I'll break as many as I can. You'll have to get the rest of them."

"Do I look like I can get any of them?" Sierra asked.

Samson tilted his metal head. "Yes. I remember what you can do. Though you say you're not, you are Lady Verde."

The people helping Sierra gasped. "Lady Verde?" the woman said, squeezing Sierra's hand.

Sierra huffed. A profanity formed on her lips.

"You're right," Sierra told Samson. "I am Lady Verde. Or at least I can be. And that's exactly what I'm afraid of."

White demons had come to Verde and killed Sierra Monet, and after bleeding out into the dirt, after her power had somehow bonded her with the planet, she'd lost herself. Her individuality. Her identity. For *two hundred* years. She thought she'd become exactly what she always expected to become after dying – nutrients for the soil. Food for new life. Only after she'd been recognized by another Mantissa had she remembered who she was.

If she truly let go of her physical shape and her mental presence – if she let Sierra fade away into just another microscopic part of a colossal world...

Would she be able to find her way back?

Or would Sierra be gone again? Forever?

And if the Celestines butchered the planet, did it matter?

"Screw it," Sierra said. "Hey, Samson? If you don't ever see me again, will you find the others? And tell them..."

Somewhere across the planet, five more ships reached deep enough into her crust to hurt something fierce. She screamed and couldn't hold her shape any longer. Her body crumbled back into dirt. She imagined her mind blowing away like the seeds off a dandelion. She was nothing but a part of the whole.

A part of the whole...

A part of the...

Cassie had seen Nariel's soul-cleaving blade in the shape of a sword once before, the night he'd offered her membership in the Celestines. It looked larger in full sunlight. Scarier, too.

"Enough," Nariel said. "I will not allow this error to continue. This ends. Now."

"I agree," Cassie said. "But it ends *God's* way. Whatever that may be."

Siv swung his sword at Nariel, but it was as if he were cutting through mist. He brought the backswing through Nariel's mid-section. No effect. Annalie fired her laser cannons. Her shots passed harmlessly through Daphne's head and chest.

Cassie nocked an arrow, pulled back her bowstring.

I believe it's your will that we stop them, Cassie prayed. *And I know you'll help me.*

She released her arrow.

It passed through Nariel like smoke.

Nariel sighed in disappointment. "You can't do this, Cassandra," he said. "You can't stop us. So you healed your people and destroyed one of our ships. We have more. We are eternal. We will rip your planet to shreds, and you can't beat us. You can't hurt us. You can't. It's impossible."

Cassie nocked another arrow and aimed for Nariel's chest. "I've seen the vid," she said. "That's the same thing the Murderer said to Krulgoth."

She froze. It *was* same thing the Murderer had said. The exact same words. *You can't.* The words hadn't seemed strange to Cassie when watching the vid of the Murderer's death. They just seemed to be the words of a devil begging for his life. But it was a curious phrase for that situation, now that she thought about it. The Murderer hadn't said *don't* kill me. He said you *can't* kill me. Did the devils just have a peculiar dialect?

And did it really matter? She was out of time. The devils were on Verde, and they going to kill her, her husband, her sister, and their entire planet. This was the moment. She *knew* God would help her, but how? What did it all mean?

Pastor Kolbe and Krulgoth were the only two people she knew who'd ever had any kind of effect on a Celestine. What did they have in common? Pastor Kolbe was human, sane, and a man of God, and he'd been able to exorcise the devils out of his church. On the other hand, Krulgoth was definitely not human. He'd been quite firm in his atheistic beliefs. And by his own admission, when he killed the Murderer, he was insane – irrational with grief.

Their names both began with the same sound, and Nariel said names had power. Was that somehow it? It didn't seem likely. Cassie's name also started with the same sound, and the arrow she'd just fired at Nariel had passed through him like mist. Maybe she was looking for a connection where there wasn't one because clearly, Pastor Kolbe and Krulgoth didn't have anything in common.

At least...

At least not from *her* perspective.

390

But Krulgoth? He would have seen this much differently.

She and Pastor Kolbe were both religious people, but to Krulgoth, faith in God was the height of ignorance. *Wholly irrational*, he'd called it. Irrational. Just like how Krulgoth had been *irrational* the day he killed the Murderer.

Pastor Kolbe *knew*, by way of his ordination and his belief in the Almighty Hand, that he could expel the devils from his church even though he'd never done it before. Krulgoth *knew*, by way of his temporary insanity, that he could touch the untouchable and kill the immortal.

Knowing you're capable of something you've never done before could be called confidence. If that something is nigh impossible, it could be called irrational. Or it could be called *faith*.

Siv once told her Nariel was trying to twist the truth, to fill her head with lies. That's why he said she *can't* kill him. By God, that devil had just one trick, and he was *still* playing it for all it was worth. But it wouldn't work anymore, because at last, Cassie understood. She *finally* knew the Celestines' secret.

Nariel brought up his sword before Siv, preparing to bring it down on his skull. Cassie tilted her bow, aiming her arrow at the hand in which Nariel held his soul-cleaving weapon. She released her arrow.

And with a satisfying *thunk* sound, it pierced Nariel's untouchable hand.

Black smoke seeped out from the wound. Nariel dropped his sword, and it disappeared. Daphne stared at the physical arrow impaled in Nariel's hand. Her eyes went maniacally wide. "*Nariel!*" she screamed.

The Liar wasn't the only one gaping at Cassie. Siv and Annalie did, too.

"It's faith," Cassie explained. And as if to prove it, she pulled an arrow from her quiver, nocked it into her bow, and fired it at Daphne. It pierced her kneecap, and she screamed and doubled over in pain.

"It's *faith!*" Cassie said again. "That's how Pastor Kolbe kicked them out of his church. That's how Krulgoth killed the Murderer. On that day, he *believed* with every fiber of his being that he could kill the Murderer and free his people. That atheist son of a gun had *faith*."

Siv feinted a stab at Nariel, and the Celestine actually flinched. Siv barked out a laugh at the sight of it. "And faith the size of the smallest seed can move the tallest mountain," Siv said.

"Or kill a devil," Cassie said. She nocked another arrow and pointed this one between Nariel's eyes.

Nariel and Daphne shared a desperate glance, then smoke enveloped them.

"No!" Cassie said. "You don't get to leave."

The smoke vanished, and they remained right where they'd been.

The hundreds of Shakren charging towards the scene from the crashed cathedral ship entered rifle range. Laser blasts came at Cassie, Siv, and Annalie, but their danger senses warned them, and they dodged or ducked out of the way.

"Call them off," Cassie told Nariel.

Nariel held up his hand – the one *not* pierced by an arrow and bleeding black smoke. "Stand down," he yelled to the Shakren. And the Shakren he'd forced to obey him did the only thing they could. They stopped, and they watched, but they made no further effort to protect their masters.

"You told me free will was a curse," Cassie said. "Yes, free will *does* make evil possible. But it also makes good *better*. Because when someone with free will does good, they considered both options, and then *they chose* the better path. It wasn't just programmed into them. Unlike you, God doesn't want people *forced* to do his will. He wants them to *choose* it.

"But that's not even the point, is it? The dirty little secret is you don't want to rid the world of sin. You travel world-to-world, taking over everywhere you go, because you want to rid the world of *faith*. Because you know it's the one thing that can harm you. You didn't rebel against God in protest over sin's presence in the world. You rebelled because he gave *us* the ability to defeat *you*."

With supernatural speed, Nariel raised his left arm towards her. He'd summoned his soul-cleaving weapon in the form of a revolver. He fired, and a black bullet sped towards Cassie's chest.

It passed through her harmlessly.

Cassie shook her head. "Now *I'm* the one who can't be touched, you God-damned devils."

Nariel roared, tossing away his gun. It vanished into smoke.

Annalie pushed open her faceplate. "I don't believe this," she said.

"No, Annalie, that's the whole point!" Cassie said. "You *have* to believe it. With every fiber of your being, your heart, and your soul, you have to *know* that you are more powerful than they are." Cassie pointed at Daphne. "Go. Face the devil who killed Fritz. And do *not* be unbelieving, but *believe*."

Annalie took a hesitant step forward. Then another. She gave Daphne a tentative shove in the shoulder. With an arrow already in one of her knees, the devil stumbled and fell flat on

393

her back. That seemed to be enough proof for Annalie. She pinned Daphne down with a knee on her chest, powered up her chipsuit's laser cannons, and pressed the business end of one against Daphne's forehead. Daphne trembled, but so did Annalie. She shook, and she sobbed.

"Do you have any idea what you took from me?" Annalie yelled at Daphne. "Do you even care?"

"Yes," Daphne lied.

Annalie pressed her weapon harder against Daphne's flesh. The cannon's whine grew louder as its power increased.

"You afraid to die?" Annalie asked.

"No," Daphne said.

"Liar," Annalie said.

Daphne pressed her lips into a straight line. Her gray eyelids covered her solid black eyes. Annalie moaned and grunted, but she still held off the trigger.

"She's a devil, Red," Siv said. "It ain't murder. You're doing the whole world a kindness."

Annalie's moans built into a scream. "No!" She pulled away and stood up, releasing the Celestine. "You don't know how much I want to blow your filthy head off. I wish I could do it not just once but a hundred times. But that's not what the man you killed would want me to do. He had dreams you could never understand. Peaceful ones. He was *better* than you. Better than you could ever be. And so am I." She wiped the tears off her face. "You don't get to die. You get to live."

Daphne tentatively sat up. She licked her lips, looking from Annalie to Cassie to Nariel and back.

"I'm not sure that's the best–" Cassie said.

"But," Annalie interrupted, "you sure as sin don't get to live here." She looked up to the sky. "You're gonna live up there. At the center of our sun. You're pure spirit. You can survive under that kind of gravitational pressure. And I know it won't be too hot for you, hell witch. You're gonna live there, where you're guaranteed not to ever encounter another person. You *never* get to leave. You never get to talk. And you will *never* hurt anyone else ever again."

The Celestine's eyes widened. Her expression shifted from horror to rage.

Annalie made a dismissive gesture with her hand. "*Git!*"

Daphne vanished.

Annalie looked away, slamming her eyes closed against more tears. Cassie wanted to reach out to her, and she would. They'd sit together and mourn Fritz together and hold a proper funeral for him very soon.

But first, there was one more devil to deal with.

"Unfortunately for you," Cassie said to Nariel, "I'm not nearly as merciful as my sister-in-law."

"Me neither," Siv said.

Cassie pointed the arrow still nocked in her bow at Nariel's forehead. Siv drew his sword and stood beside her. Nariel took two steps backward. Cassie and Siv took two steps forward.

"You knew I was questioning my faith because of losing the university and because of all the loved ones I'd lost," Cassie said. "And so to fully separate me from God – to kill off my faith that could kill you – you tried to take everyone I've ever loved. My entire species. My planet even. You *killed my brother* just to destroy my faith and save your own hide."

Nariel held his hands up – one still pierced with an arrow – in a placating gesture. "Daphne killed your brother," he said. "Not me."

"You're as much a liar as she is!" Cassie roared. "I get that now. I know you ordered it."

His lips curled into a sneer. "So I did," he said. "But don't forget what *hasn't* happened. God didn't stop us from slaughtering your brother, even though he could have. Even though he can do *anything.* He didn't save your father or any of your loved ones. Not because he couldn't, but because he *wouldn't.*"

Cassie put an arrow into his left shoulder for that one.

Siv raised his sword. Nariel raised his right arm, with Cassie's arrow still implanted in its hand, in a defensive gesture. Siv brought his blade down across Nariel's wrist. His severed hand fell to the ground. The devil howled in pain. Black smoke poured out of his wounds.

"Retrieved your arrow, darlin'," Siv said.

"Gratitude," Cassie said.

"If he's so good," Nariel hollered at Cassie, "why does he keep taking people from you?"

Cassie nocked an arrow and pointed it at Nariel's chest, exactly where his heart would be if he had one. "I don't know. I'll probably be asking that question until the day I meet him face-to-face. I don't understand. But I *trust.*"

"*No!*" he roared, but not at Cassie. "I am seraphim! How *dare* you raise sin-stained creatures saddled in *flesh* above us? How dare you elevate *her* above *me?*"

Cassie pulled back her bowstring.

Nariel glared at her with the most demonic expression she'd seen on him yet, and... something happened.

The ground beneath her feet seemed to tear as if it were a piece of paper being ripped in half. And paper was an appropriate analogy because the tear seemed to be without dimension or depth. It was flat, and it spread quickly. In the blink of an eye, the tear reached Cassie and then went past her, underneath her.

And then everything was gone.

Her bow. The dirt beneath her. The crashed Celestine ship, the Shakren army, the scrub brush, the sky and the sun shining in it – all gone. She was in a complete void, a space empty of everything except herself, Siv, and Annalie. They'd been left with nothing but the clothes on their backs. Even Annalie wore her shirt and jeans; her chipsuit had vanished.

For a moment, Cassie thought they'd been transported into outer space because of the blackness and the floating. But not a single star was in sight. The void was so dark. How was she even able to *see* the others? What little light there was came from behind them. She turned towards it and startled.

The source of the light was Nariel.

For the first time, Cassie saw him in his *true* form.

Chapter Twenty-Nine

Lady Verde awoke.

It felt like she'd been asleep for a season. But she was awake now, in the mountains. In the Naunhof Forest. In the Halcyic Ocean. And in the Midphalia Desert.

In the Elde River. On the prairies and in the plains. In the creeks and the rivers. In the deepest of caves and in the highest of clouds. In her sand and her grass and her water and her sky.

She was the dirt beneath disheveled huts where frightened people huddled together as the world seemed to come to an end around them.

She was the snow underneath the giant robot's steel legs.

She was the air between the three people – somehow familiar – who stood facing the incorporeal invaders.

She was the flowers outside the church where the residents of Hondo had congregated to pray for deliverance.

She was everywhere – an entire magnificent planet – the jewel of her star system.

And she was *rage*.

In the Naunhof Forest, tree limbs stretched and congregated on the metallic invader. When its massive drill chopped the first of her branches into sawdust, more limbs grew and took their place. And more, and more, and more. The entire forest swarmed the invader, seized it, and bound it in bark. When it could no longer move, the trees squeezed harder. They only let go once the ship was a twisted, broken, misshapen hunk of scrap.

In the Midphalia Desert, a tornado of sand stirred up around another metallic invader drilling into her land. The storm consumed the ship. She strengthened the storm, making it taller, faster, thicker. Sand snuck its way through holes and cracks and congregated inside the delicate machinery that powered the invader. Its gears seized. Its engines stopped. It fell over onto its side, and the sandstorm pounced. Moments later, the ship was buried, and the desert lay still.

In the Halcyic Ocean, great waves arose around the drilling invader. The waves battered it – first one at a time, then two and three at a time. While a wave bashed the invader above water, a vicious undertow pulled hard on it from below. It fell over, but the waves continued to smash it, forcing it apart and dragging the wreckage underwater.

Similar scenes played out all over the planet, all over her*self*, but Lady Verde only spent a few minutes in that terrible, wrathful state. That was all she needed. And then her waters were still. Her breezes were gentle.

And the invaders were no more.

Now, what had happened? Not with the invaders. She'd already forgotten about them. What had happened to *her?* For so many billions of years, she'd been sky and rock and water, and that was enough. But then she'd awakened. After being awake for only a very short time – two hundred cycles, perhaps – she had slept for a season. And now she was awake again.

It was curious. What caused this slumber? And more importantly, despite her newfound ability to regenerate far more than she'd ever been able to before, she felt as if something were missing. She felt like rain, though all her skies were clear. She felt like warmth where there should be ice or cold where there should be warm. Like a tree deprived of water.

Was she sad?

But again: why?

A part of the ocean swirled, commanding her attention. Water sprayed into the sky, and the air carried it. The winds were trying to speak to her also. They pushed the waters far up into the sky, and the water became a cloud, and the cloud rained, and the rain returned to the ocean from which it had come.

Then it happened again, in another ocean. And again, and yet again. The sea called to her, it rose into the air, and the cycle repeated. But what was so special about this? The rain always returned home to be part of her rivers and oceans, then evaporated to new heights, then came down again. Sea to air, air to sea. Sea to air and back again–

Sea to air and.

Sea air and.

Sea air a–

Oh!

Sierra, whispered Verde.

When Nariel was disguised as more-or-less human, he was a head taller than Cassie. But in his true form, he was enormous – easily at least triple Cassie's size. His skin was still gray, what little of it there was. His eyes were still black, and his hair was still white, but it was mottled and patchy as if wide swaths of his mane had been ripped from his scalp or permanently burned away. Instead of a neat and meticulously pressed cassock, the black robes he wore here were tattered scraps and rags.

He had wings. Of course. They looked just like they had when he'd shown them to her before, on the day he'd ordered Fritz's death. Charred and chipped bones held together the remains of dead, burnt feathers. But in his true form, his wings were *massive*. They dwarfed the rest of his giant body. He flapped them where he floated in the void, and the motion felt like it would have created groundshakes if there were any ground here.

But what took Cassie's breath away was the fire.

Nariel was ablaze. His entire body immolated. If all of Hondo were burning, the flames would still be smaller than the fires that rose off his arms, back, legs, wings, and even his head – all apparently without doing him harm. Back on Verde, the Celestines and their weapons had appeared and disappeared in clouds of smoke. Now Cassie knew where that smoke came from.

Not that she'd doubted it before, but in this form, it was obvious even to an atheist. Nariel was a devil. But whatever he'd done to them, wherever he'd brought them, Cassie was going to let it be a temporary setback and nothing more.

"Send us back" Cassie ordered Nariel.

But he didn't. He just glared at her, rage radiating off of him just like his fire. Why had she lost her ability to command him? She hadn't lost her faith again. It was stronger than ever.

"You can't do anything for yourself here," he said in a voice that bellowed and echoed across the void. Then he spoke a string of words in a tongue Cassie didn't recognize. Merely hearing them made her feel nauseated. Was he spitting curses in some demonic language?

"Is this hell?" Annalie asked. "Did he drag us down into Torment?"

That was a logical, if terrifying, thought. Since they saw Nariel in his true form, they had to be somewhere native to him – somewhere in the spiritual realm. Surely he wouldn't bring them to heaven. Hell was the logical alternative.

"No," Siv said, and Cassie didn't miss the tremble in her husband's voice. "He can't send us there. Or to heaven. Judgment is reserved for God alone."

A cloud of dust trickled past Cassie. It came from Siv. He held his hands up before him, and his skin was flaking off and floating away in a stream of tiny particles. His muscles and his bones, too – his whole body was floating away as dust, leaving behind a transparent afterimage in its place.

"What's happening to y'all?" Annalie said. Then she gasped as she noticed the ends of her red hair were dusting off as if caught in a breeze, and her hands were disappearing, too.

"Flesh rots," Nariel said. "A fitting end for so corrupt a matter."

Their faith could no longer help them. Their bodies were turning into dust. And Nariel was now visible in his true form. But it wasn't heaven or hell.

"We're in Purgation," Cassie said.

Purgation was where you were cleansed of your attachments to sin – and of your attachments to the physical world – after dying. The souls there – here – needed time to orient their hearts fully towards God and not to the world. As such, they could do nothing to benefit themselves.

By the commands Cassie had given him back on Verde, Nariel couldn't hurt them or run away from them. By the fact that he wasn't God, he couldn't judge the state of their souls and send them to heaven or hell. But the devil had precisely analyzed Cassie's commands and figured out something he *could* do. And so he'd brought them all here – a purely spiritual realm where he didn't even have to kill them. The very nature of Purgation was destroying their bodies for him.

"We died?" Annalie said, her breathing coming faster. "He killed us?"

Siv reached for Cassie, but from his elbows down, he was pure spirit now. "Wish we could've been married longer, but the hour or two I've been your husband have been the best of my whole life. I love you forever, Cass."

"I love you, too," she told him quietly. She looked to Annalie. "And you, too, Annalie. I love you."

Cassie wasn't sure Annalie even heard her. She trembled and mumbled her siblings' names.

"You two keep the revival going," Cassie said, fighting past a lump in her throat. Her arms and legs no longer had any substance to them. Her chest and head would soon lack matter, too. "Keep Fritz's dream alive. Whatever it takes."

Siv frowned. "You two?"

The only thing the souls in Purgation could do was perfect their love for *others*.

"Goodbye," Cassie said, just wanting to get it over with to spare herself more pain. "Nariel, send *them* back."

Nariel clenched his fists and screamed, and his flames flared up. The world was torn open again, just as it had been back on Verde, but in two places this time: beneath Siv and beneath Annalie. Through these rips in the fabric of reality, Cassie saw the plain outside Hondo where they'd brought down the Celestine cathedral ship. A moment later, Siv and Annalie were gone from Purgation and back on Verde. Safe. Alive.

Then those windows to the physical realm closed, and Cassie was alone with the devil himself.

Chapter Thirty

Nariel roared and surged forward until his death-black eyes were right in front of Cassie's face, which was especially alarming since they were also now the *size* of Cassie's face. He wrapped his fiery wings around her – not in contact with her, but surrounding her like a cage. Cassie recoiled from their heat, and she was practically blinded by the brightness of his fire. She understood why they were called the Luminous Ones.

The Blasphemer spewed more hatred towards Cassie in his foreign, demonic tongue, but she remained calm. A week ago – a few *hours* ago – she would have been terrified and furious. But what was there to fear? Annalie had permanently banished the Liar. Maybe Nariel could leave from here, but if he could, he certainly wouldn't return to Verde. He'd forever stay far away from Siv or Annalie or anyone else whom could kill him.

Verde and her people would be fine. Her mom would be fine. Annalie and her siblings would be fine. Her husband would be fine. The revival would continue, and life would go on. Including her life – her afterlife, anyway.

She won. She'd beaten the devils.

Despite being trapped in Purgation and slowly dying, she felt peace radiate through what remained of her chest. She had a plan, and she was carrying it out, and her plan was God's plan – for the first time in her life, it was one-hundred percent *their* plan. There were parts of it – huge parts – that she didn't understand. But she accepted it all. Siv had said that when his mother was dying, she'd been utterly calm because of "complete abandonment." A complete surrender of her will to

God's. Cassie understood that now. There was an amazing freedom in complete subjection to the Almighty.

She couldn't wait to meet Siv's mom once she made it through Purgation.

Making the Sign of God's Hand with her incorporeal, ethereal hands further infuriated Nariel. She brought her clasped hands to her breastbone, the only part of her that was still physical besides her head and shoulders. Then she opened her arms and spread them out wide, her incorporeal fingers almost touching Nariel's hellfire. She closed her eyes.

"Into your hands, I place mine," she prayed. "Forever."

Nariel laughed at her and her prayer... until the sound of a whip *cracked* through Purgation, and Nariel's laughter turned to a howl of frustration.

A cord blazing with white light had wrapped itself around Nariel's right wrist. It went taut, and Nariel's arm was violently stretched out and yanked to the side, away from Cassie. She followed the cord to its other end, off at some distance away from Nariel, and–

The other end of the cord was held by a little girl who had the same not-physical, translucent appearance Cassie now mostly had. Except the girl was clad in a robe that glowed as white and bright as the cord that restrained Nariel's arm.

Cassie immediately recognized her childhood friend, Bernice.

How can I help? she tried to say, but she was too shocked to form words.

Nariel turned towards Bernice, but then there was another whip-crack, and Nariel's left wrist was wrapped in another cord of brightest white. This second cord was pulled taut, yanking Nariel's left arm, as if someone wanted to use Nariel to play tug-of-war with Bernice. Cassie followed this new cord to its end to find...

"Dad!" Her father and Bernice struggled with Nariel the Blasphemer, trying to pull him backward, away from Cassie.

Two more cords appeared, these tied around Nariel's ankles. They were held by Eroica and Sebastian – and Sebastian appeared as the human he'd once been, not in the white demon body he'd had when he sacrificed himself to save Harbrucken. Eroica smiled at Cassie. Sebastian winked. Nariel hollered and thrashed against his restraints. His flames surged from his body and shot out towards Bernice, Dad, Eroica, and Sebastian, but the fire didn't harm any of them.

More cords – and more of Cassie's lost loved ones – appeared. Harlan and Grandma and Grandpa Reinhardt restrained Nariel's right wing. The other was secured by Opa Winkler and Meemaw, who still bore the appearance of a small, fragile old woman, but who tugged on her cord with a godly might.

Helping them was Elise. Instead of white robes like the others, she still wore the skirt and cardigan she'd died wearing.

"Thanks, kiddo," Cassie said.

Her loved ones dragged Nariel away from Cassie, pulling hard on his limbs and wings. Nariel wailed in pain and rage and spat what must have been vile curses in his demonic tongue. He clenched his fist, it flared up with fire, and then he shook away the cords that restrained his arms. Bernice and Cassie's father struggled to get their lines back on his wrists. It seemed Dad almost had Nariel's left wrist secured again when Nariel shook his wings free.

Even with their combined might, they couldn't save her from Nariel. Only Eroica and Sebastian still restrained the devil, and it didn't look like they'd hold him for long. He desperately shook and kicked his legs. Cassie would have wrapped a cord around him herself if she had one.

Maybe there was something else she could do.

"It doesn't have to be like this," Cassie said to Nariel. "Accept his mercy. Please!"

Nariel surged forward through the space between them until his face was back in hers. "I will *never* submit to he who elevates sinful flesh over purest spirit!" He swore again in his demonic tongue. The words made Cassie feel nauseated until–

Until he was silenced by a cord that wrapped around his head, gagging his mouth.

And at the other end of that cord was her brother.

Cassie tried to call out his name, but she couldn't. Fritz was clad in his favorite outfit – shirt, vest, trousers. He pulled on his end of the cord with all his might, standing firm against Nariel as the devil struggled and fought. The distraction was enough to give the others the time they needed to re-secure their cords, and then Nariel was entirely bound by ropes of light.

She'd lost so many loved ones, and each loss had hurt so much. But if even one of them hadn't been here, now, it wouldn't have been enough to protect her.

I have something better planned.

Suddenly there was more brightness. A circle of light had appeared above Nariel, and it seemed to be a gap in reality similar to what had brought her here, because what was on the other side seemed to be a much different place than Purgation. Cassie couldn't even comprehend what she was seeing it was all so radiant, but it all seemed somehow peaceful. Perfect even.

An ethereal hand reached out from that place, beckoning to Nariel. Cassie cried out in elation – pure, instinctual joy. It felt as if her heart would burst. She had to look away, but she found the strength to call out to Nariel. "He wants you to come home. Go to him!"

Nariel screamed, and it felt like fire had shot in through her ears and down into her chest. A second opening appeared, this one underneath Nariel. Cassie couldn't look at that one, either, but for a much different reason. The one glimpse she managed revealed a barren world – more empty even than Purgation. A place without matter... or light... or God. She trembled at the site, willing it out of her mind.

The Blasphemer turned his head downward, and Cassie's loved ones released his light-rope bindings. He sank into the place beneath him, and the gateway to it closed the moment he was through, sealing him inside. In the same moment, the light above Cassie – the window to heaven! – disappeared, too. As did her fallen relatives and friends.

The last two fallen angels were imprisoned. Forever.

Tension drained from Cassie, and she tried to rest her chin against her chest, but only her face and hair were still physical. The rest of her was as translucent and ghost-like as her loved ones had been. That they were gone didn't bother Cassie, not seeing as she was about to join them.

They didn't make her wait long. Fritz reappeared in front of her. Cassie opened up her spirit arms to embrace him – whether she physically could or not.

He fixed her with a sad smile and shook his head.

For a moment, she didn't understand. Then a gap in reality – just like the ones that had sent Siv and Annalie home – opened behind her, and the disappointing truth sank in.

It wasn't her time. She'd be with Fritz again, and with everyone else who had restrained Nariel. But... just not today.

There were so many things she wanted to say, so many feelings flowing through her heart. All she could do was give Fritz a look and hope it said everything. Cassie liked her chances. She and her big brother had spent twenty years writing letters to one another penned only in glances and expressions. One last one – for now – would have to do.

Reality ripped open wider, the molecules of her physical body slammed back into her, and then the void of Purgation was gone. She was back on Verde, kneeling on the plains outside Hondo. The crashed, broken Celestine cathedral ship was off in the distance. When Fritz had died aboard that ship, she'd been so angry that she hadn't been allowed to say goodbye to him.

Yes, but not right now.

She clasped her hands together to say a quick prayer of gratitude, but before she even could, Siv was there, wrapping his arms around her, pulling her to the dirt with him, squeezing, weeping.

"I thought I'd lost you," he said.

Annalie embraced them both – gently, since she was back in her armored chipsuit, with the faceplate opened. Behind her, the air shimmered, and Sierra returned. There was something different about her. She still had her green hair and her half-shaved head and her torn clothes and her pierced face, but she seemed... taller, maybe?

"How we doing against those ships?" Cassie asked.

"They're gone," Sierra said.

"All of 'em?" Siv said.

"All of them," Sierra said.

Annalie gaped at Sierra. "Pardon my cussin'."

"You didn't say anything," Sierra said.

"Not out loud," Annalie said. "But you do not wanna know what I just said in my head."

Cassie didn't want to let go of her husband ever again. But over his shoulder, she saw a group of Shakren, and she remembered they weren't alone. "I hate to spoil the mood," Cassie said, "but we probably ought to say something to the couple thousand Shakren and white demons just staring at us here."

"Oh," Siv said. "Right."

The four of them stepped forward. The Shakren and demons who had served on the Celestines' cathedral ship watched Cassie and her friends expectantly, but they made no move to attack. They were still under orders from Nariel not to.

Cassie recognized Gashg. He cleared his throat, then spoke via the translator he still wore on its neck. "Are they gone?"

She nodded. "They are. Forever." She let that sink in with them for a moment. Then she couldn't help but smile. "You're free."

After several seconds of stunned disbelief, a cheer erupted amongst the Shakren and the demons. Some pumped their fists. Others collapsed to the dirt and put their faces in their hands. Still more took chipware devices from their belts and began relaying messages.

"Freedom!" one called into a comm unit. "Freedom!"

"The Evil Ones are gone!"

"To any Shakren who can hear me – we're free of the Celestines."

"They're gone! The Celestines are gone!"

411

Gashg came forward from the others. The white demon stood on his four back legs and offered Cassie his right hand. She took it in both of her own. He looked like he wanted to speak, but he didn't seem able to form the words.

"Joyful Lenerstelen, Gashg," Cassie said. "Joyful, peaceful, and merry."

Chapter Thirty-One

Waves gently lapped against the beach in a regular rhythm. It was hard to tell where the sky ended and the water began because they were both so blue. The sand beneath Cassie and the sun above her both felt like the same temperature – perfectly warm. Trees poked out above the rocks on the other side of the cove, and they had long, thin, flat leaves unlike anything Cassie was familiar with. Hondo was home, but it didn't have this beach, the ocean, or the divinely delicious fruit that fell off the trees. *This* was the most beautiful place Cassie had ever seen. It was a paradise.

And all Cassie could do was stare down at the blank screen of her mobile.

Out of the corner of her eye, she spotted her husband moseying on over. She shook her head to clear it and tossed her mobile into her bag. "Hi," she said to him.

Careful not to kick sand on her, he sat down. "Now that you're stuck with me forever, I ought to tell you that you ain't the only planner in this marriage."

"That so?" she said.

"That's so. I've had the last day of our honeymoon planned out for a long time now. I'm fixing to show you rough sketches I've drawn of the house we're going to build here. And reveal the exact spot where we'll build. After that, I figured we'd dig the foundation's outline together and maybe even lay down a few ceremonial rocks for it. Then we'd name the house and the settlement we'll build around it. And we'd go home with your favorite thing in the world: a plan."

She smiled. "The plan for our forever home," she said.

"Our forever *beach* home," he corrected.

"Amen to that," she said. She rubbed his bare leg beneath where the old pair of jeans had been cut off. "I'm ready. Show me your sketches."

Siv shook his head.

"Something wrong?" she asked. Was he angered by her distance? She supposed she couldn't blame him. Here they were on their honeymoon, and she was off by herself..

"Nothing's wrong," Siv said. "Everything's right, in fact. I just didn't do any of what I just said, seeing as we're not going to be living here anytime soon."

She tried to contain her surprise, but she knew she'd failed when he tossed back his head and laughed his loud-as-a-gunshot belly laugh. The laugh she'd hated when she'd first met him. The one that was now her favorite sound in the whole world. "You're in deep focus," he said. "You're planning something. And if you were planning the house and settlement you want to build out here, you'd be walking around. Checking things out. Since you're not..." He shrugged.

She rested her head against his shoulder. "You know me well."

"I know you the best," he said.

She looked out at the waves of the ocean and tried to figure out where to begin. "Have you ever been talking to someone, and you feel like you understand them so well you can finish their sentences, but when you do, they say, 'No, that's not at all what I was going to say'?"

Siv frowned. "Umm, can't say that I have."

"I feel like that's what happened between God and me," Cassie said. "When my friend Bernice died, and I took her as

414

my patron saint, I prayed to God that he'd show me what these powers meant. Why I was born with them. And he did."

"He inspired your plan," Siv said. "Become a doctor. Cure–"

"Doctor *by the age of twenty-four*," she corrected.

"By the age of twenty-four, yeah yeah," Siv said. He rolled his eyes. She hit him in the shoulder. "Cure cancer. Make a new village somewhere out in Terrascorcha. Serve as its doctor."

She took a moment to reflect. "Guess I did all right with that, didn't I?" she said. "I skipped over the doctor part, but I cured cancer."

Siv kissed the top of her head. "And everything else."

"Which means it's time to make a new village, here on the coast." She sighed. "The problem is – and please, *please* don't be mad at me – I've come to realize that while everything in my plan was inspired by God, my plan might have been a bit... incomplete. It's like God was explaining his plan for me, and at some point, I got so excited, I stopped listening, and I never heard the whole thing. But on Lenerstelen morning, I saw it all." She picked up a handful of sand and let it fall out of her palm. "What I thought was God's whole plan for me was just a single grain of sand. When all along, it was a whole beach."

"Why would that make me mad?" Siv said.

"Because you adopted my plan as your own," she said. "I know you're looking forward to living out here. And I still want to – someday." She braced herself. "But not right now."

"Darlin'," Siv said, "I don't much care about the destination. I just want to be beside you on the ride."

"That's sweet," she said. "And I love you for it. But maybe you should wait until I've told you what I have in mind."

"That sounds ominous."

She stood up and paced in front of him. Why was it making her so nervous to tell her husband about this? "Before he died, Fritz had visions of a revival, right? He saw a world without hunger, without war, without disease. A world of peace."

"And you made it happen," Siv said. "Everyone's cured of everything now. Fighting's over. The devils themselves are gone."

"Right, right," Cassie said. "And when I first realized I could use Geneditor to accomplish it all, I thought for sure Fritz's revival and my plan were supposed to culminate at the same time. But when Fritz talked about a world-wide revival, what if the world he spoke of wasn't Verde?

"What if it was the entire galaxy?"

She held her breath.

Siv leaned back on his elbows. "Keep talking."

"What if we could do everything we did here on Verde, but other places, too?" she said, bouncing on her heels and gesturing with her hands. "What if we could bring health and peace to other *planets?* What if Verde's revival was just the start?"

"Not sure words exist for how wonderful that would be," Siv said. "But it would take an army. How would we even begin a project on that large of a scale?"

"That's not even a problem. Think about what I'm describing. Does it remind you of anything?" she asked. "Of anyone?"

He *tsked*. "Mrs. McCaig, are you ever going to stop answering my questions with questions of your own?"

"Hey, you're doing that to me now, too," she said. "Seriously. Going planet to planet. Making life better for everyone there. Who does that sound like?"

"Sounds like the Celestines," Siv said. "Like how they imagined themselves anyway."

"Right!" Cassie said. "And the Celestines are gone." She took a deep breath. "But their ships aren't. The Shakren have been able to repair about a third of the ships that attacked us. And there are other ships elsewhere in the galaxy. Bases, too. And millions of Shakren spread all across the galaxy. All looking for a purpose in their newly free life. One might call all that... an army."

"By the stars," he whispered.

She knelt down next to him and took his hand. "Exactly. What if instead of making a new life together here, on this beach, we made one up there? Amongst your stars. What if we brought revival to every world we visited? We could use Geneditor to cure them of their illnesses. You could help them rebuild their infrastructure. Annalie could revive their technology, their food supplies. And we'd have an army of Shakren and white demons to help us."

"The Shakren are free people now," Siv said. "We can't just make them do this."

"Of course not," Cassie said. She reached into her bag, retrieved her mobile, and showed Siv the last message she'd received. "But the surviving white demons and Shakren have been having a lot of long chats with one another ever since Lenerstelen. They've been talking with the Shakren still stationed on planets all across the galaxy, too. They all know they're free. They all know they can choose what they want to do with their lives next. And they took a vote today. Thirty-five percent still don't know what they want to do. But forty-four percent – the biggest group – want something better. Remember what Gashg once told us about how the white

417

demons never did anything with their freedom except defend it? This group wants their freedom to mean something. They want to make the galaxy better. But they have one condition."

Siv raised his eyebrows.

"They want *us* to go with them."

"Us?" Siv repeated.

"Nariel knew exactly how to wrap his poison in sugar to make it more palatable," she said. "Yes, he wanted me to help him conquer worlds, and that's undeniably wrong, but along the way, we'd have ended starvation and conflict and strife. That's why I nearly sold my soul to him. He knew how to make his sin irresistible. And now this opportunity comes along. This offer comes with everything that would have been great about joining the Celestines, but with no strings attached."

"What about the rest of them?" Siv said. "Thirty-five and forty-four don't add up to a hundred."

"The other twenty-one percent of the Shakren still believe in the way the Celestines did things. And now that they have free will, their choice is not to change."

"They can't just–" Siv said.

"We can't just make them do anything," Cassie reminded him of his own words. "A Celestine remnant out there still giving 'blessings' to planets and their people *is* a problem, but one for another day."

Siv reluctantly nodded. She returned her mobile to her bag and sat beside him.

"You have to think this through before you sign on," Cassie said. "We'd be *leaving Verde*. Everything we know. Every*one* we know."

"Yeah," Siv said. "And that'll hurt something fierce."

Waves came up onto the beach almost close enough to touch them, then retreated away. A white bird honked and flew overhead.

"But it's worth it," Siv said. "Ain't it?"

"I want to do this," Cassie said. "I'm sorry if I've seemed distant, but I've been praying about it a lot, and I really feel like this is what God is calling me to do. And the thought of answering that call, no matter where it takes me? It makes me so, so happy. Living here and starting a settlement *would* be a dream come true, but I think God has something better planned. But ultimately, where I most want to be is with you. Wherever that is. So if you don't want to go, then I won't, either."

"I've been looking up at the stars for as far back as I can remember," Siv said. "I never even dreamed of living out there among them. To serve as God's hands not just here, but everywhere, and with you? There's no question about it. I'm with you on this, full chisel."

They held each other. She got sand in her hair, and she didn't care.

After some time, she stood up and offered Siv a hand. "Come on."

"Where we going?"

"I want to see your sketches of our house, and I want to pick the spot where it'll be."

"Could be a mighty long time before we're back here," Siv said. "Sounds like there's a lot of planets out there needing help, and you won't stop until you've helped them all. I know you, Mrs. McCaig."

"All true," she said. Together they looked out at the ocean and the sunny sky. "But someday, it will be time to come

419

home. And when we do" – she stamped her foot on the sand – "it will be here."

Cassie urged Mandolin to charge faster down the road from her house to the village. She pressed her hat tight against her head and tucked her chin to block out the wind. It was a cold day, especially for as far south as Hondo, and Mandolin's gallop made the air even colder. But Cassie didn't care.

"You're fast, girl," Cassie said, rubbing her horse behind her ear. "Fastest ever."

Mandolin whinnied her fierce agreement.

When they reached the village, they blew right through it – careful to avoid people and carriages in the road so as not to hurt anyone, of course. But also fast enough to put on a show. The butcher's young son whooped and whistled as Mandolin raced past. Cassie's grin could have lit the whole sky.

They reached the opposite side of the village before they stopped. Cassie pulled back on Mandy's reins, stroked her mane, and told her what a good girl she was as she turned around and took in the sight of her home town. The chipware lights Fritz had installed were back up. It was morning, so they weren't powered on yet, but they'd been reinstalled. A pair of husky men Cassie didn't recognize were using a hand-driven cart to steer a metal chipware box bigger than either one of them into the saloon. Phil Hersch was going to have the coldest beer in the occupied territories... for now. Others would be getting sparks-powered coolers, too, as quickly as Annalie and her team could provide them.

She prodded Mandolin into a slow walk up the street, back the way they'd come. At a slower pace, it was a lot easier to see what was going on. Andrea Krause sat outside the post office, talking on a mobile. Doc Laubscher used a hand-held scanning device on Mary Engel's hand, and both of them *oooo*ed and *ahh*ed at the real-time image of her bones that appeared on his nearby screen. Two little girls – maybe eight-years-old at most – ran down the wooden sidewalk squealing and chasing after one another.

Cassie had to double-take when she realized one of those girls had green hair. How had she done that? Some leftover pigment from Lenerstelen mixed with hair soap? A natural dye made from leaves or pistachios? However she'd done it, it was obvious who she was trying to emulate.

When she reached Church Street, she didn't turn, but she did pause to look up the hill at the cemetery outside the stone chapel. She said a prayer for all her loved ones, made the Sign of God's Hand, and continued forward before her mind could dwell too much on what had happened in Purgation.

At the end of town, she kept riding and willed herself not to look back.

The trip back home was at a much slower pace. Every sight was so familiar. She knew every tree, every patch of grass, every rut in the road. How different would it all be when she returned? She closed her eyes and took a deep breath to keep herself composed.

Halfway home, the wind stirred beside her, and another horse appeared, this one with a green mane. Cassie *tsk*ed. "I wish you wouldn't do that. It looks creepy."

The horse looked up at Cassie. "Thanks. Creepy is the look I was going for."

"And *talking* while you're in the form of a horse is even worse." Cassie dismounted and walked beside Mandolin. "There. I'm walking now. Can you just be normal, please?"

The horse melted and stretched until Sierra was back in her human shape. Green hair. Black cosmetics thickly outlining her eyes. Ears, lips, and nose pierced. "You trying to insult me? Telling me to be 'normal'?"

"I'm too smart to even suggest you be that," Cassie said. "And also smart enough to know you put on that creepy horse form just to – what's your phrase – take the piss out of me."

Sierra laughed out loud. It wasn't the first time Cassie had seen her do it, but it was still a rare sight. She almost told her to laugh like that more often, but she held back, worrying that if she did, Sierra would stop. Instead, she said nothing and savored the sight of her friend laughing until she got it out of her system.

"What are you going to do with yourself," Cassie asked, "once Siv and I aren't around?"

"The planet's cleaner than it's been in centuries thanks to the healing powers you gave me," Sierra said. "Annalie has the chipware restoration well under control, and she's using renewable energy and moderation to *not* poison me with dynamek particulates, which is a kindness. But I thought I might be able to help her. I plan to bring back the sparks-powered guitar."

"Is that a guitar that plays itself or something?"

"No, it's a guitar that has microphones instead of a hollow body, and you play it through a chipware amplifier. Very loudly. Preferably with an ace distortion pedal."

Cassie blinked. "I'm not a chipware expert, but why would you want to distort the sound of– never mind. You go ahead and do that. Make yourself happy. You deserve it."

The smile fell from Sierra's face. She shrugged. "Not so sure about–"

"Oh, enough with your self-punishment," Cassie said. "But there's something else I think you should do, too. Before the Blackout, Verde had a global government, right?"

"Right," Sierra said. "Bunch of wankers."

"You need to re-form that government," Cassie said. "And lead it."

Sierra stumbled. "Your horse kick you in the head?"

"I am not concussed, no."

"What have I *ever* done that would make you even think I'm a leader? I'm *not* a leader. At all."

"Actually, you're an outstanding leader," Cassie said. "The problem is you've always been surrounded by people who didn't want to hear what you had to say. And who had the power to silence you. And – let's be honest here – you've never been a very diplomatic persuader."

Sierra raised an eyebrow for a moment, then shrugged it off. "Fair."

"But you have *always* had this planet's best interests at heart, and don't even try to argue with me on that."

"So what? No one's gonna listen to me, Reinhardt. You said it yourself that they never have."

Cassie stopped walking and pointed back down the road. "I just saw two little girls in town. They were pretending to be you. One of them even had green hair."

Sierra tried and failed to hide how much that tickled her. "Seriously?"

"I might have been the one who figured out how to stop the Celestines, but the whole world saw their ships try to crack Verde like they were shelling a pecan, and who did they see stop them? You. Lady Verde. You were the one who brought them miraculous curing rains on Lenerstelen morning. *You.*

423

You are their *hero*. Maybe it's for the first time in your centuries-long life, but people *will* listen to you. They already are."

Sierra hunched her shoulders. "I don't know. I... what you're saying..." She shook her head.

"Makes you nervous?" Cassie offered.

"Makes me terrified. I think I'd crap the bed if I had a bed. Or if I crapped."

Well, *that* was a sight she'd never be able to unimagine. Cassie resumed walking and motioned for Sierra to keep up. "If there's one thing this past year has taught me, it's that not everything happens according to our plans. We're sinful and stupid, and we screw things up. But God works with all of that. He takes our best and our worst, he makes adaptations to account for our mistakes, and somehow he makes it all work. Maybe you were born to merge with the planet and live for two hundred years just so you could lead Verde at this moment. Maybe all that was just a happy accident. I don't know. But I do know that leading this world is what you're meant to do."

Sierra hung her head. "Why do you have so much faith in me? We both know I haven't earned it. The good I've done... it doesn't outweigh the bad. It's not even close."

Cassie shrugged. "It's just how I take the piss out of you."

And that made Sierra laugh harder and louder than Cassie had ever before seen.

"Fine," Sierra said. "I'll *think* about it."

"Don't think for too long," Cassie said. "The survivors of the Blackout have done all right scattered around the planet for two hundred years all by their lonesome. But there are global issues now that need to be addressed. The Scourge still needs to be cleaned out of the sky. Seeing as everyone is Mantissa now, most babies will probably inherit those powers, too. But the ones that don't will need to be inoculated with a dose of Geneditor as soon as they're born. With the chipware restoration, there are shared resources and infrastructure that needs to be managed. Regional commerce is going to be a thing, and it will have to be regulated."

"If you're trying to make this sound exciting, you're failing. Miserably."

They came around a bend in the road, and the Reinhardt family farm came into view. A shuttle-sized space ship was parked on the pasture between the house and the barn. Cassie took a deep breath and stopped walking.

"Well. I guess this is good–" Cassie said.

"No," Sierra said. "I don't say that word. Or listen to it."

That sounded like an excellent idea to Cassie. She held her forearm up so Sierra could give it a bump.

Instead, Sierra placed her hands on the sides of Cassie's head and kissed her softly on the forehead.

"I'll be here when you get back," Sierra whispered.

"I don't know when that will be," Cassie said.

"Doesn't matter," Sierra said. "I'll be here. Running the place, apparently. Mercy me."

That made Cassie smile. Then Sierra turned into dust, and the breeze took her away.

Cassie led Mandolin the rest of the way down the road, soaking in every detail. The weathered wooden fence rails and their chipping white paint. The mailbox just outside the gate. The way her boots crunched the gravel of the road leading up to the house. The musty smell wafting out of the barn. She'd grown up here. Even after leaving for the university, this was still home. And based on the ache she felt in her heart, it always would be.

Samson, the giant Steelterror, was using his drill-hands to till her father's fields. Well... *that* was new. At least the fields would be bursting with life again come spring, even if she wouldn't be here to see them.

Siv met her halfway between the gate and the ship, which had its ramp open and pointed towards the house. Further up the gravel drive behind him were her mother, Annalie, Felix, and Duncan. "Take your time," Siv whispered. He took Mandolin's reins from her and led the mare towards the ship. Mandolin wouldn't care *at all* for the shuttle trip up into orbit. But as soon as she could, Cassie was going to put the former cathedral ship's simulated grasslands to good use. She knew Mandy would approve of her new barrel racing arena.

Annalie came to her first, Felix following close behind. Cassie embraced her for a long time, the two of them wordlessly sharing their still-raw grief over Fritz and Elise. Cassie so wished Annalie would come with them, but she understood her desire to keep things stable for Felix. When they let go of each other, Annalie glanced up into the shuttle where Pastor Kolbe was securing his seat belt.

"Sure nice of Pastor to go with you," Annalie said.

"It is," Cassie said. "Church services out in space will be a gift I wasn't expecting."

"I packed y'all a lunch," Annalie said. "It's already on board. It's not much, and I know you'll already have food on the ships, but I just wanted..." She turned away and wiped her eyes. "Just take care of yourself, OK?"

"Celestine interstellar communication is beyond anything we ever had here, even before the Blackout," Cassie said. "You and I will talk all the time."

"Sure," Annalie said. "Needs a different name, though. It ain't Celestine chipware anymore."

"We'll come up with something," Cassie said. "Thank you for staying here with my mom. You really don't have to do that."

"I want to," Annalie said. "We like it here." She put her arm around Felix. "Don't we?"

Felix didn't say anything, but he didn't grunt, either.

Cassie wiped a tear off of Annalie's cheek and brushed her hair out of her face. "I want you to promise me something," Cassie said.

"Sure."

"Promise me you'll love again."

Annalie harrumphed.

"Not today," Cassie said. "Maybe not for a long time. Not until you're ready. But someday, *be* ready. Fritz wouldn't want you to be alone forever. Neither do I."

"I don't know if I can promise that right now," Annalie said. "I still hurt so much. But I promise to try."

"Good enough," Cassie agreed. She looked down at Felix. "Can your sister be my sister, too, Felix?"

Felix nodded, and Cassie was certain he smiled before he turned away.

Then Cassie came to Duncan. He put his arms – his *two* strong arms – around her, lifted her off the ground, and spun her around. "Goodbye, Daddy," she said.

"I'm a lucky man to have you as a daughter-in-law, Cassie," he said. "Go do the Lord's work."

"We will."

And then it was just her and her mother. In the past year, Ruth Reinhardt had lost her husband, her son, and now her daughter was going so far away. Leaving her mom was the one thing that made Cassie reconsider whether or not this was a good idea.

"I'll be fine," Ruth said as if she could read Cassie's mind. Which Cassie guessed she probably could, perhaps through some kind of limited-capability mother-daughter Mantissa reader power. "I'm in great health thanks to you, and you just wait until we send you pictures of the crops. We'll make your dad proud. Or at least Samson will. I'm not sure he'll need any help from us, actually."

"I just don't want to leave you alone," Cassie said, her voice breaking.

"You're not," Ruth said. "Annalie and Felix and Samson will be here with me. You'll call me often. And don't forget the priceless gift you were given."

Cassie frowned at her. Between curing the Scourge and the Celestines' attack, they'd never actually exchanged Lenerstelen presents. What did she mean?

"You got to see your dad and Fritz in Purgation," Ruth said. "They're *alive*, Cassie. They're watching over us. With the two of them up there, how can I ever be alone?" She held Cassie out at arm's length. "I'm so proud of the woman you've become."

Cassie glanced over to where Siv and his father were embracing one another tightly.

"I can do this – *we* can do this – but not by ourselves," Cassie said. "Pray for me?"

Her mother kissed her cheek. "Every day."

Cassie found Siv. They held hands tightly and walked up the shuttle's ramp together. At the top was a man with fair skin and a mop of brown hair. He wore a very Verde-style button-up shirt and jeans, but he was definitely not a native. Now that the Shakren and the white demons were free, they weren't wasting any time making choices for themselves. This one had decided he didn't want to be a Shakren *or* a white demon.

"Gashg," Cassie said, shaking her head. "Hard to believe it's you."

"I think I'll go by Greg now if you don't mind," he said. "It rolls off this human tongue a bit better."

Siv clapped him on the back. "You tried beer yet, Greg?"

"What is beer?" Greg said.

"Proof of the existence of God," Siv said. "Not that we really need that anymore. But we will *always* need beer."

Greg sat down in the pilot's seat and began warming up the shuttle's engines. Cassie and Siv strapped themselves into seats near the door. As the ramp raised up into its closed position, she gave one last wave to her mom, Duncan, Annalie, and Felix.

Then the door closed with a bang and sealed air-tight with a hiss of hydraulics.

"Is this going to be faster than riding in a carriage?" Pastor Kolbe asked. "I don't care for carriages. Too bumpy for my tastes."

"You see that paper bag on the back of my seat, Pastor?" Cassie asked. "You might want to keep it within reach. Your healing power should take care of motion sickness, but just in case..."

Pastor Kolbe groaned, closed his eyes, and counted off silent prayers on his grunblume.

The ship ascended into the sky.

"Next stop, our flagship," Greg said.

"The *Krulgoth*," Cassie said. She gazed out the side viewport at the surface of Verde, which grew smaller and smaller. She spotted the west coast – maybe even the exact spot where her future house would be. "Have you found a good place to start?"

"We have," Greg said. "Mecheb Three – that means the third planet orbiting the star Mecheb."

"One of the stars in the Blooms constellation," Siv said under his breath. Cassie smiled. Her husband was going to be her life navigator in more ways than one.

"About a third of their population is stricken with a disease in childhood," Greg said. "It malforms their spines and legs and makes the rest of their lives difficult and painful. And to make matters worse, they've had famine the past three seasons. Their food supplies are running low. Geneditor can easily cure their health maladies, and we can have hydroponics and other advanced food growing chipware set up in no time. Things are about to get a lot better for them."

The view out the front of the ship had changed from blue skies to black space. A single Celestine ship, one now called the *Krulgoth*, loomed large in front of them. Stars twinkled everywhere else. So many stars, many of those with millions or billions of souls depending upon their life-giving light and heat.

How many of those people could they help?

Every single one that needed it, God willing.

"It'll take about a week to get there," Greg said. "We can leave as soon as we have you all aboard."

Cassie smiled. "Sounds like a plan."

430

Acknowledgments

I began writing the first novel of this trilogy, *Yesterday's Demons*, on August 23, 2013. At that time, I was the father of four children and was working in an unfulfilling day job. As I write these acknowledgments, it's December 2022, I'm the father of seven, and I work in a day job I love. A lot has changed even just since this particular novel was started on December 10, 2018 – four years ago. It hasn't been an easy journey, and there are a lot of people who have helped me get here.

Jesus, Mary, and Joseph, I love you very much. Save souls. St. John of God and my dear friend St. Therese of Lisieux, my writing patron saints, thank you for your prayers. *Ad maiorem Dei gloriam.*

To my beloved wife Rose: you are everything to me. I'd be so lost without you. Your love and support can get me through anything. Likewise, to our seven children – Todd, Joseph, Gianna, Rose, Giovanni, Mary-Elizabeth, and now also Augustine: you are the seven best children a dad could ever ask for. I pray I can always be everything you deserve.

Thank you to all my parents, to my friends, and to my beta readers for being there for me these past four years and for helping me finally get this book complete. Special mention must be made here to Will Munn and JWL.

My personal soundtrack for this book is fairly eclectic. The songs literally run the gamut from heaven to hell. Thank you to the artists who performed them: Evanescence, the White Stripes, Natalie Imbruglia, Green Day, Fugazi, Creed, Rage Against the Machine, Rodney Atkins, the Eyeliners, and the two artists who probably could have covered the entire soundtrack on their own: Alkaline Trio and Matt Maher. Sometime I'll have to wipe the dust off my blog and post an article listing all the songs and their relevance to the story.

Gevalia Columbian coffee... *chef's kiss*

And finally, to you who is reading this right now. Thank you for supporting my work and for allowing me to tell you this story. I don't know whether or not I'll ever again find the time to write another. But even if I don't, that's OK. These three have been a blessing. I've had to learn the same lesson Cassie did. Not my will, but his will be done.

Deus vobiscum.

–Michael Ripplinger

Michael Ripplinger writes both novels and computer software. He is a certified introvert who enjoys breakfast cereal and a variety of indoor activities, but he'd rather be at Disneyland. Michael, his wife Rose, and their seven children make their home in south Texas.

Michael would love to hear from you. Please visit his website at mripplinger.wordpress.com or contact him at michael@ripplinger.us.

Also by Michael Ripplinger:
Yesterday's Demons
Tomorrow's Shepherd

www.ingramcontent.com/pod-product-compliance
Lightning Source LLC
Chambersburg PA
CBHW031943260626
47157CB00017B/2096